FERAL BLOOD

EVA CHASE

BOUND TO THE FAE

BOOK

Feral Blood

Book 2 in the Bound to the Fae series

First Digital Edition, 2021

Copyright © 2021 Eva Chase

Cover design: Yocla Book Cover Design

Ebook ISBN: 978-1-989096-91-8

Paperback ISBN: 978-1-989096-92-5

CHAPTER ONE

Talia

Three men lie sleeping on the red-and-gold rug that stretches the length of the grand entrance room. Their bodies form a loose circle around the spot I recently left. They look totally relaxed now, but vicious claw marks gouge the polished floorboards on either side of them.

I suspect that the floor has seen worse on previous occasions, and that fae magic will heal the wood easily enough. In spite of those signs of violence, the warm midday light beams cheerily down from the windows high above and no sound reaches my ears but the soft, rhythmic rasp of the men's breaths. The scene should give me a sense of peace.

I braved my deepest fears for these men-who-aren't-really-men, the three who freed me from years of cruel captivity and offered me a real home. With a taste of my blood, I brought them out of the curse that turns their wolf forms mindlessly violent under the full moon. I watched them bring the chaos of their wild pack into some kind of order, and then I nestled in the middle of the ring of their bodies to sleep in perfect safety.

But that safety was an illusion. They can't protect me from everything in this strange, savage faerie realm—and I've just seen one of the gravest threats this realm poses lurking in sight of the keep.

I hesitate in the doorway, regret twisting through my chest. I don't want to wake them up to bad news. I'd give anything for a few more hours by their sides, basking in the joy *I* woke up with. But that joy has vanished. However serious this threat turns out to be, Sylas will want to know about it right away.

It turns out I don't even have to wake them. With my first uneven steps, the wooden slats of the brace around my warped foot tap against the floor, and Sylas stirs. He pushes himself into a sitting position and rolls his shoulders, his head turning so he can watch me approach.

The fae lord who rules over this keep and the pack that lives alongside it looks every inch the stalwart commander even in the simple shirt and slacks he wore for last night's transformation. He studies me with one darkly penetrating eye and one gone white with the scar that bisects his tawny skin from eyebrow to cheekbone. The purple-brown waves of his shoulder-length hair part around the high points of the ears that mark him as one of the few "true-blooded" fae, a status that gives him his authority over his cadre and his pack.

Even sitting, his tall, well-muscled frame exudes authority. So do the multitude of arcing black lines supernaturally tattooed on his body, everywhere from his temples to his neck to his forearms and, I know from past experience, the sculpted planes of his chest beneath that shirt. Each one of those marks represents the true name of some plant or animal or material he's learned, that he can bend to his will through his powers.

As recently as a few days ago, I found him intimidating. Now, the warm welcome I can recognize in his gaze and the reserved smile that curves the corners of his lips offset his imposing aura. Sylas was a little frustrated that I ignored his instructions to stay locked in my room to release them out of their wild state, but he also appreciated the dedication I showed with the gesture. The greatest thank you he gave me wasn't those words themselves but when he referred to me to the others as "our lady."

I don't belong to these men, but I belong *with* them, standing beside them. I proved it last night, to all of us.

And now I might be bringing a new threat down on their heads, after everything they've already risked for me.

That last thought must show on my face, because Sylas's smile fades. As I reach the edge of the rug, he stands, looming more than a foot taller than my slim—not long ago half-starved—figure. The movement rouses his cadre. Whitt rolls onto his back with a muffled groan and a stretch of his brawny arms; August swipes his hand over his broad, boyish face and aims a bright if slightly groggy grin at me.

Sylas's attention stays focused on me. "What is it?" No "Good morning" or inquiries about how I slept. How does he see so much with only the one working eye? Sometimes I feel like he looks straight into my head.

I come to a stop a few feet away from him, the news I have to deliver forming a lump in my throat. I force it out. "I think I saw one of the men from Aerik's cadre on the hills past the houses, watching the keep."

Sylas's lips pull back from his gleaming teeth with a restrained snarl. I thought of him as a grizzly when I first met him, and he's never fit that impression better than right now. August leaps to his feet with surprising nimbleness given his strong but stocky frame, his gaze darting to the door, his posture tensed as if ready to lunge straight into a fight. Whitt draws himself up at his typical languid pace, as if he's not particularly concerned despite the others' reactions, but his ocean-blue eyes have turned stormy.

"He left," I add quickly. "A few seconds after I saw him, he took off. He was in his wolf form—I'm not completely sure it was him. But the color of his fur was just like his hair, this blueish white, and the way he moved…"

Just remembering the cock of the wolf's head so like the cruelest of my former captors, I find myself wrapping my arms around my chest. Sylas takes a step toward me and sets a firm hand on my shoulder. Ferocity still smolders in his unscarred eye, but it's *for* me, not at me.

"He will not touch one hair on your body," he says, so emphatically I can hear the vow in the words. "Not him nor his cadre-fellows nor that pissant Aerik." He looks at his cadre. "From her description, it'd be Cole."

Whitt nods, his mouth slanting at a displeased angle. August runs his fingers through the short strands of his dark auburn hair, his golden eyes more unearthly than ever with a protective fury burning in them. His voice, normally buoyant with its enthusiasm, contains the edge of a growl. "He was trespassing on our territory."

Sylas looks at me. "Did he see you?"

I think back to my frozen moment by the upstairs window just minutes ago. "I'm not sure. But he was far enough away that even if he noticed me at the window, I don't think he could have made out much other than the shape of me and the color of my hair."

One of my hands rises to finger the strands that trail over my shoulders. In an offering of kindness when I first arrived here, August used magic and faerie fruit pulp to dye my natural dusky brown a deep pink that wouldn't be *un*natural on a fae woman.

At the time, the change seemed frivolous, a superficial way of moving beyond the abused captive I'd been for the past nine years and reclaiming something of my real self. Now, it's also a line of defense—my former jailors aren't searching for a pink-haired woman.

Cole. I have a real name for the man with the blue-white hair and sharply jointed limbs who took such pleasure in using the pointed edges of his body to draw pain from mine. A memory flickers up of my cheek being mashed into the hard metal floor of my cage, a harsh chuckle in my ears. Fingers digging into my cheek and an elbow ramming against my ribs as Aerik's other cadre-chosen sliced my wrist to steal my blood…

I don't realize I'm shaking until Sylas's grip on my shoulder tightens and I feel myself shudder against his hand. My lungs have clenched up, my throat straining to draw breath into them. I hug myself again, tighter, fighting to get a hold of myself.

It's over now. It's over, and I'm not going back to that filthy cage or the horrible monsters that look like men.

"Not one hair," Sylas repeats, his deep baritone managing to be both fierce and soothing. "I'll tear their throats out if they so much as try."

August steps toward me as if he can shield me from the horrors inside my head, his teeth bared. "If I don't get to them first."

I take gulps of air, focusing on the solid warmth of Sylas's hand, the determined blaze in August's eyes. The tremors subside. My chest still aches, but the panicked tension releases enough that I can inhale fully.

Whitt has stayed where he was, a little apart from our cluster of three. In the past, he's defended me—but he's also accused me of threatening the cohesion between the cadre and their lord. I'm still not totally sure where I stand with him.

As long as Sylas wants me here, Whitt will follow his lord's orders—I'm sure of that. But will this new development change his mind about whether my presence here does them more good than harm?

Even if it does, I wouldn't expect him to show it. Whitt rarely lets much obvious emotion slip from behind his nonchalant front. He rubs his jaw, the storminess in his eyes retreating but not vanishing as his expression turns pensive.

"Whatever he was doing here and however unwelcome his visit, Cole can't have observed anything damning," he says in his dryly melodic voice. "Without the benefit of our mite here, Aerik and his pack will have lost themselves to the wildness of the curse last night as much as every other Seelie. He wouldn't have been in any state to observe that the three of us appeared to have kept our heads."

An idea that chills me rises up in my head. "What if they saved some of their 'tonic' and didn't go wild at all?"

Sylas shakes his head. "It wouldn't have worked. We tried that once, on the rare occasion when Aerik deigned to share portions of the tonic with us. Only some of the pack took it, so they could shepherd the others, and we set aside the rest in anticipation of being skipped over later. The next month, they didn't bother with us, so we took some of the remainder—and it had no effect at all. It appears it's not only necessary to get a taste of your blood but for it to be fresh as well."

I guess that's a small comfort.

Whitt makes a vague motion with his hand. "It is a concern that Cole was snooping on our lands at all. I've gathered that they've been traveling around asking questions all over the realm, but for them to have been here specifically on the night of the full moon doesn't bode well."

August frowns. "Yes. Why us? You don't think Kellan let more slip than we realized…?"

He glances at Sylas in question. Kellan was the third member of Sylas's cadre, but he wasn't satisfied with that honor. From what the others have said, he'd been challenging Sylas's authority and generally making trouble for a long time before I came into their midst. He particularly hated humans, and when he took that animosity to the point of attacking me, Sylas was forced to kill him to save me.

I didn't like the man any more than he liked me, but the thought of him still sends a pang of guilt through my gut, knowing how it wrenched at Sylas to have to go to such extreme measures against one of his own.

Kellan made his unhappiness known to at least a few fae from other packs, but it'd sounded as if he'd been vague about the latest developments in the situation here. If it turns out he mentioned that Sylas had brought a human girl into the keep, one with some sort of special power—it wouldn't take long for Aerik to put the pieces together.

Sylas stays silent for a moment, his thumb running up and down my shoulder in a steadying caress. "It seems unlikely that he could have said enough to alert Aerik without our recent guests also having some idea. Tristan didn't raise any questions that had anything to do with Talia. But we were in and around Aerik's fortress for some time. It's possible we didn't cover our tracks quite as thoroughly as we would have hoped."

"If he had definite proof, he'd challenge you about it," August says. "If they're just skulking around, they might suspect, but they don't know for sure."

"That would be my conclusion as well." Whitt swivels toward me. "What exactly did you see? Every detail from when you first spotted him."

I drag in a breath, letting myself lean into Sylas's touch as I dredge up the images. "Less than half an hour ago, I went to the window upstairs that faces south, wondering how the rest of the pack was doing. Cole—his wolf—was at the top of one of the nearest hills to the east of the forest. I couldn't see *him* all that well either, that far away, but the color of his fur was obvious. When I noticed him, he was just standing there, staring at the keep. It couldn't have been more than a minute. He didn't move except tipping his head like—like I've seen him do as a man. Then he ran off down the far side of the hill, out of view."

Whitt taps his lips, his face still solemn but a glint lighting in his eyes. "I'll speak to the sentries and send a few to make discreet inquiries farther abroad. He was acting boldly, showing himself like that—they may be preparing for some kind of overt move. I'll find out whatever I can so we can be ready for that."

Sylas nods to him. "Good. Let me know as soon as you discover anything at all." He turns me to face him with a gentle squeeze of my shoulder, his gaze catching mine with all that lordly intensity. In spite of my anxiety, my heart skips a beat with the memory of that dark eye smoldering as he touched me in his bed several days ago, of his mouth claiming mine just last night.

Both he and August have become something more than protectors to me. I'm not sure what, or where it'll lead, but the thought makes my pulse thump faster all the same.

"I'm afraid we'll have to delay your introduction to the rest of the pack by at least a couple more days," he says with obvious regret. "We should wait until we have a better idea of what Aerik's next move will be—and it'd be best if no one associated your arrival too closely with the full moon. It's not my wish to keep you trapped in the keep. As soon as we can—"

I set my hand over his much larger one, giving him the bravest smile I have in me. "It's all right. I don't *want* to leave the keep if it might mean Aerik finds me. And I don't want to put you at risk either."

The affection that darkens his gaze sends another flutter of heat through my chest. "Our lady indeed." He raises his hand to stroke it over my hair. "I swore you'd be safe here, Talia, and I mean to make good on that promise —come what may."

CHAPTER TWO

August

The day after a full moon, I'm always ravenous. Even though I was only in the feral state of the curse for a short part of last night, today's no different. So, when my older half-brothers set off to deal with the potential threat of Aerik, a business that Sylas doesn't seem to have any use for me in yet, it's only natural that my first impulse is to head to the kitchen, which is my favorite room in the keep anyway.

No matter what my lord and my cadre-fellow are doing that I can't fully contribute to, they'll always need to eat.

Talia drifts with me toward the hall, her arms crossed loosely over her chest. At least she's not still hugging herself as if that's the only thing keeping her from shaking to bits. Still, the shadow of worry that lingers on her pale, pretty face makes my body itch to let loose fangs and fur and go racing across the realm until I can maul Aerik and his cadre beyond recovery.

It was horrifying enough seeing the state she was in when we came across her in that cage. Imagining her having to endure that treatment for nearly a decade, from when she was little more than a *child*...

I catch my growl before it creeps from my throat. My temper is rising on her behalf, but letting it out in front of her will only make her more anxious. We can't deal with Aerik yet. The best thing I can do for her is offer a way to keep her mind off those worries.

I give her hair a playful rumple, reveling in the softness of it, in the way she brightens at my touch. "We could all use some breakfast—or I suppose lunch at this point. Can I get the help of my favorite kitchen assistant?"

She beams up at me. "Of course. I'm starving. What are we making?"

"I haven't decided yet. Let me take a look in the pantry and see what that inspires."

Before I do that, I spread some butter on a thick slice of bread to address the worst of her hunger—it's no good creating an elaborate meal if she's too famished to enjoy it while she's shoveling it into her mouth. And the last thing I want is to give her any further reminders of her time in captivity. I gulp down a hunk for myself as I peruse our current stash of ingredients.

The lake quails in the cold room won't take too long to bake. I gather several of those, the makings for fresh rolls, and duskapples to poach for dessert.

When I emerge with my haul, Talia's eyes widen where

she's perched on her usual stool. "How many people are you expecting to feed?"

I laugh, the sound startling me but instantly lifting my mood. "We worked hard last night. Now we have the appetites to match."

I toss together the ingredients as quickly as I can and get Talia started kneading the dough for the rolls while I stuff, season, and truss the quails. For several minutes, we work in companionable silence. When I sneak glances at her, she's intent on the movement of her hands in the dimpling mass of dough, a small but definite smile curving her lips.

She likes having something useful to do with herself just as I do. And I was able to give her that when she must have needed it more than ever.

The pride that tickles through me comes with a memory of last night, of the fog clearing from my head when the taste of her blood reached my wolfish maw, of gazing up at her resolute form and understanding what she'd done. Sylas was with her then, but she must have approached him in his slathering beastly state alone. This wisp of a girl, filled out some now that she's getting proper meals but still slim and delicate—yet not remotely fragile.

Somehow the torments Aerik subjected her to forged a soul that's so resilient without hammering the kindness out of her.

She looks up and catches me watching her, and the corners of her mouth lift a little more even as a flush colors her cheeks. A hint of longing seeps into the sap-sweet scent her skin gives off. Suddenly I want to set so much more than my gaze on her.

The serious cast that crosses her face a moment later snuffs out my flare of desire. Her hands pause over the dough. "Most of the summer fae, like you," she says. "The 'Seelie.' They think about humans more like Aerik does than like Sylas, don't they?"

I grapple with my answer, buying myself a little time as I arrange the quails in their roasting dishes. I won't deceive her, but I'd rather not terrify her any more than she already is either. After I've washed the grease and herbs from my fingers, I take the dough from her and begin forming it into balls.

"I think it'd be most accurate to say they're somewhere in between," I said finally. "And it's not simply about attitudes toward humans. Pretty much all fae see mortality as a weakness. They look down on those of us with a lot of human heritage too." I motion toward my ears, their rounded shells resembling my human mother's so much more than my true-blooded father's. "I can't say even the three of us are immune to that kind of thinking completely."

"Kellan definitely wasn't." Talia gives a little shudder.

"Exactly. And he also, like Aerik... Many fae use that sense of superiority as an excuse to become cruel. They enjoy crushing whoever they can with their powers; they deal with boredom by squabbling over lands and possessions. They'll just as happily ruin a fellow true-blooded fae as a human. It's just easier to exert their will over beings with no magical protections."

"You aren't like that at all. Or Sylas and Whitt, from what I've seen. It was only Kellan."

"That was the largest point of conflict between him and Sylas." I set the last of the shaped rolls on a baking tray and turn to face her. "Sylas's main ambition is to provide for the pack as well as he possibly can—to see everyone have everything they could want, including peace. Any glory beyond that would cost our pack-kin pain and possibly even their lives. He'll fight to protect the pack and the Seelie in general, but not out of selfishness. And there are other lords who prefer peace over conquest too."

Talia runs her hands down her thighs to her knees, her shoulders hunching slightly. A ruddy, raised scar caused by tearing fangs pokes from the neckline of her shirt above her collarbone: a stark reminder of just how cruel the lords who *aren't* like Sylas can be. "So, if it comes out that I'm here and what my blood can do, pretty much every fae will think they have more rights than I do, but some of them won't want to outright torture me?"

Those words sum the situation up far more accurately than I like. I can't leave her bearing the burden of that understanding alone.

I move to her, touching her arm, bowing my head over hers. My voice drops low. "It doesn't matter what anyone outside these walls thinks. You're with us now. Sylas meant what he said—we're not letting Aerik—or anyone else— hurt you. If they try, I won't hesitate to make them regret it."

My voice turns fierce with that last promise, my own fangs tingling in my gums, but Talia doesn't flinch at my vehemence. If anything, it appears to restore some of her own confidence. Her shoulders straighten again, her mouth firming but her eyes staying soft as she gazes up at me.

"I know he meant it. I know *you* mean it. That's why I wanted to do everything I could for you last night."

She reaches up to rest her fingers against my jaw, and all my awareness narrows down to the heat stirred by that tentative caress and the memory of what else she did for me last night—of the moment when she turned from Sylas after he kissed her and immediately drew me to her, marking her own sort of claim. Showing that she wanted me just as much as she did him, that she wasn't going to leave me on the sidelines.

I don't know how I got so lucky to have earned that devotion from her when she could have offered it all to my lord, but I don't have it in me to refuse it. I can't even refuse the hunger that surges through me now with her body so close to mine, her scent in my nose, and those tender words in my ears.

I lean in, and she tips her chin up so she can meet my kiss. That simple gesture nearly undoes me. My wolf rears its head, and what I intended as a gentle peck transforms into a scorching melding of our lips.

As I capture Talia's mouth, a needy, breathless sound escapes her, sending a bolt of lust straight to my groin. Her hand slips to my chest, her lips part to welcome me, and it's all I can do not to outright plunder the tart heat within.

It's hard to believe this is only the third time we'd ever kissed. As I tug her closer, every inch of her body feels familiar; every breathy noise falls into harmony with the pounding of my pulse. I've watched her; I've longed for her; I *know* her. And she embraces that yearning with all she is.

I want to hoist her onto the island and bury myself completely in the arousal that's already lacing the air, want to bring her gasping to a climax ten times as ecstatic as the one she found with my guidance in the basement sauna pool. Want to feel her come apart around me, clutching me and arching against me, every fear and worry forgotten.

Skies above, how I want it.

But as I let my tongue delve between her lips, as hers flicks out to tease over it, a tremor runs through her frame. Her fingers grasp at my shirt as if she needs to hold onto something or she'll be swept away. The eagerness doesn't fade from her kiss, but my lust recedes at the reminder of how new this sort of encounter is for her. Two weeks ago, she hardly knew what pleasure she could bring to her body on her own.

If I follow my hunger to its intended end, she might go along with it, caught up in the sensations I'm provoking within her—but will she be happy afterward? How can she know how much *she* wants if she's too overwhelmed to consider that question?

I will not be like— I will not use her. I won't let my wants trample over hers, human as she is. Until she's had more space to decide—until she's sure of what this all means—until *I'm* sure I can be everything she needs—

I brace my hand against the edge of the island behind

her and ease back just a few inches. Talia's pale green eyes glow with desire, her cheeks flushed, her lips darkened by the kiss. I swallow hard, having to master myself all over again.

"I'd love to keep doing this all day, Sweetness," I murmur, brushing the lightest of pecks to her forehead. "But I did promise you a meal."

From her smile, I've managed not to make my retreat feel like a rejection. "Better not to find myself among three starving wolves?" she teases, and glances past me to the counter. "How long will the quails take in the oven?"

"Twenty minutes or so."

"I should probably take the opportunity to get some clean clothes on, then. If I'm going to be 'lady' of the keep, I'd better at least kind of look the part." She tugs at her shirt, which is rumpled from being slept in but doesn't at all detract from her charm. I force myself to step farther back so she can slide off the stool. A very large piece of me is gnashing its teeth in self-reproach for not having taken the opportunity to strip her of those clothes myself.

I watch her slip out of the room, so nimble now despite the faint limp the foot brace Sylas made for her can't quite correct, and then turn to my baking. As I set the trays in the oven, my mind is still on Talia, the heat of our encounter thrumming on through my veins, a more ardent warmth wrapping around my heart.

I've never felt this all-consuming adoration for anyone before. There hasn't been anyone in our diminished pack who roused enough attraction for me to think it was worth courting them and risking the tensions that might follow if my interest dwindled. When I've passed the fringes of the Mists into the human world to blow off more carnal sorts of steam, I've always gone to women who make a job of it, who I can compensate with money with no chance of misunderstandings about the encounter leading to more.

What am I supposed to do with so much feeling? If I offer it all up to Talia in a deluge of emotion, will she welcome *that* or shy away from the implicit hope of receiving just as much in return?

Those questions leave me restless, but I don't know where to find the answers. All I do know is I have to show her she's so much more to me than an object to lust and fight over. There's got to be more I can do than cook for her, kiss her, and unleash my rage when an immediate threat appears.

A vague but forceful sense of resolve grips me. As the scent of roasting quail wafts into the air, I head upstairs to Sylas's study.

"Come in, August," he answers at my knock. Does his deadened eye give him a glimpse of who lies on the other side, or does he know us well enough to differentiate the sound of our knuckles? That seems like an impertinent question to ask.

When I step inside, shutting the door behind me, my lord is at his desk, frowning at a map and a page of notes set across it. He rests his elbows on the corners of the map and looks up at me expectantly. "I assume you're not here simply to summon me to lunch."

His unshakeable aura of measured authority always sends me back to the days when I hadn't yet come of age to join his cadre at all and he oversaw much of my education. Probably because nearly a century later, that level of studied control still eludes me. But I have plenty of other skills to compensate—at least, I'd like to think so.

I square my shoulders to better look the part of cadre-chosen. "I know my main duty has been defending the pack from physical threats as they come up, but I'd like to become more involved—in the planning and strategizing. It might not be my greatest strength, but I'm sure I have enough experience by now to contribute something, and you and Whitt have so much more on your plates now with Kellan gone."

Sylas considers me with a contemplative expression. I suspect he can guess that this proposal has been driven at least partly by my desire to protect Talia in every way I can. I did brawl with him the other day to secure a better fate for her. He seemed to respect the show of commitment even as he rebuked me for the insubordination, though. It might work in my favor more than against it.

"Did you have anything particular in mind?" he asks.

I came up here in such a rush I hadn't taken the time to think that through. "Well, I—I'm not sure what you and Whitt have already discussed or how you'd want to approach the situation with Aerik. But I'm at your disposal. And if I could be included in discussions of those strategies from now on, I'd happily share my views."

"Fair enough. Perhaps I should have brought you into them sooner." Sylas rubs his temple, the subtlest sign of the burden he's carrying as lord. I might have gotten frustrated with him over his plans for Talia before, but I can only imagine how difficult he's found this balancing act, weighing the needs of the pack against her safety. He saw a way through, as difficult as it might make our lives going forward, and that's why I'd throw myself into any fray in front of him.

After another moment's thought, he motions to the wall in the direction of the pack houses. "You *are* my general of sorts. There's a chance this dispute could escalate into a battle. With most of our warriors at the border, we need *every* pack member as prepared to defend what's ours as they can be, regardless of age or physical prowess. Let them know that tomorrow you'll begin training them."

The thought of a battle sends an uneasy prickle through me—most of the pack *isn't* in any state to go to war. But that's exactly why he's giving me this responsibility.

I nod sharply. "I can do that. Thank you for trusting me with the task."

"Of course. I'd have had you do it sooner if I hadn't wanted to spare our people the stress of wondering *why* we're preparing them. But as things look now…" He exhales with a grimace and pauses. "Talia should learn whatever you can teach her too. Work with her here in the keep for the time being, and with the others once she's revealed herself to the pack. She's had to fend off claws and fangs too many times already without the means to give her a fighting chance."

Yes. The image of a wolf lunging at her swims up from my memory, and my muscles tense instinctively. Anything I can to do to teach her how to protect *herself* is twice as good as the protection I can offer.

I dip my head to my lord again, drawing myself up even straighter. "I'll see to both. If it comes to blows, we'll be ready for them."

Whether we'll be ready enough to *win*... That'll come down to how well I do this new job I've demanded.

CHAPTER THREE

Talia

A hand slams my head down, fingers digging into my scalp in five bruising points of pain. The weight of the man's body squashes me into the cold floor so forcefully I can't breathe. My legs flail instinctively—no, *no*—and all at once he wrenches backward.

He snatches my foot, fingernails sharpening into claws. With a violent twist, the bones snap. Pain floods my leg. I shriek, and the stale air clogs my throat with the stench of urine and blood, choking me, suffocating me as the agony blares on and on—

"Talia."

A steady but determined whisper. A hand, much gentler, stroking down my arm. I jerk awake, barely processing those sensations, my heartbeat booming with panic for the few seconds before the bleariness clears from my gaze and I make out Sylas looming over me, sitting on the edge of my bed.

A nightmare. I've had another nightmare about my time in captivity. I've thrashed the covers off down to my waist; the thin fabric of my nightgown sticks to my back with sweat now turning clammy. A sour, acidic flavor laces my mouth. I swallow hard, trying to rein in my racing pulse.

The fae lord's hand stills by my wrist. He peers down at me with his mismatched eyes, and not for the first time I wonder which sees more. "You cried out," he says evenly. "More than once."

Crap. As my terror retreats, embarrassment prickles in to take its place. "I'm sorry I woke you up."

He shakes his head dismissively. "I was still working, but even if you had woken me, it wouldn't be your fault." He pauses, his thumb grazing my forearm in an arcing caress. "You haven't had one that bad in some time."

That's true. During the month I've stayed here, the nightmares never went away, but in the past week or so, they'd lost some of their potency. The sense of Aerik and his cadre stalking me must have riled up those fears all over again.

I'm sure Sylas can connect those dots himself, so I simply say, "I know I don't have to really worry. Here you are saving me from them even when they're only in my head. Thank you for breaking me out of the dream."

It isn't the first time he's called me out of one of those nightmares, and I doubt it'll be the last.

His mouth twists. "I wish defeating our foes in reality were half as simple. But we *will* shield you. Are you all right now?"

My heartbeat has nearly evened out, and the

suffocating sensation has faded from my lungs, but I hesitate at the thought of being alone again. Sylas takes that momentary silence as an answer in itself. Without another word, he stands and scoops me out of the bed, the covers falling away from my legs. His arms tuck me close to his broad chest, the rich earthy, smoky scent of him washing over me with his warmth.

"I'm okay," I feel the need to clarify, even though it's hard to want to be anywhere but nestled in his embrace now that I'm there.

The fae lord gives a low rumble that sounds amused. "But you could be better. You told me before you felt safer in my room than yours."

As he strides out of the room and down the hall, carrying me as if I weigh nothing at all, the warmth condenses into a deeper heat at the thought of the things we did in his room the last time I slept there. The heat pools between my thighs, but I'm too groggy still to sort out whether I'd want to make some kind of move now and if so, what.

Is Sylas expecting something? Other than that night when he caressed me while encouraging me to take myself to a bodily release, we haven't shared more than a few kisses.

When we enter his bedroom, I glance up at him, searching out his expression in the dim moonlight that drifts through his window. He meets my gaze.

"I do want you to sleep," he says, setting to rest those anxious questions. "Sleep here where you know any enemy, real or imagined, will have to get through me to reach you."

"And after I sleep?" I ask tentatively.

The curl of his lips brings out an ache low in my belly, the rumble of his low baritone only intensifying it. "We'll see what tomorrow brings." He brushes those lips to my forehead and lowers me onto the far side of the bed. "I'll make no demands. When you're sure of what you want, I'll be more than happy to oblige."

The heat flares in my cheeks, but as my head settles into the down pillow, sleep is already creeping back over me. Sylas lies down a couple of feet away from me and tugs the covers up over us. I scoot a little closer, not quite touching him but basking in his smoky warmth.

The last thing I'm aware of before exhaustion pulls me back under is the stroke of his fingers easing a few stray locks of my hair back from my face.

———

I wake up to bright sunlight and the impression of body heat fading from the mattress by my arm. As I rub my eyes, Sylas emerges from his private lavatory, his dark hair falling damp across his shoulders from a shower. He finishes securing the ties that close the sharp V neckline of his shirt and lifts his gaze to meet mine, that now-familiar smolder kindling in his unmarked eye.

"Back to work already?" I say, hoping I don't sound too disappointed. I'm not sure if I was hoping for a repeat of the last morning I slept in his bed or even more, but I definitely wouldn't have minded cuddling up to his brawny form while I was alert enough to fully appreciate it.

Sylas's mouth twitches into a smile that holds a hint of apology. "One of the sentries reported evidence of intrusion near the borders. I want to take a look at it myself as soon as possible. Stay here and sleep as long as you like."

He bends over the bed in a motion that's almost a prowl and steals a kiss that's quick but impassioned enough to leave me flushed all over. With the passion it rouses in me, I'm tempted to grab hold of his shirt and pull him right back into the bed, but he's already drawing away with a purposeful air. Nothing will keep the fae lord from an urgent duty—and those duties are partly aimed at protecting me, so I can't really complain.

For several minutes longer, I sprawl in the bed, soaking in Sylas's scent and the last tingles of warmth. But after years of having no more than a cage less than half the size of this bed to roam around in, I'm not one to squander my new freedom by lolling around. I get up and limp to the door, intent on retrieving some clothes and my foot brace from my bedroom and then discovering what August has planned for breakfast.

When I slip out, another strapping figure is just stepping out of his own room on the other side of the hall. Whitt pauses and cocks his head, the tufts of his sunkissed-brown hair typically mussed and his bright blue eyes sparkling, as inscrutably gorgeous as ever. He's left his high-collared shirt unbuttoned partway down his chest, giving a glimpse of the true-name tattoos winding across the tan skin over his sternum. August told me Whitt has nearly as many as Sylas.

"Good morning, mite," he says in that tone that

always seems to skirt the line between teasing and outright mockery. "I'm guessing it was a good night as well."

A fresh blush burns my cheeks. I'm abruptly aware of the thinness of my nightgown and the fact that I have nothing at all on underneath it, although Whitt is keeping his gaze rather studiously on my face. I cross my arms over my chest. "I had a nightmare."

He arches his eyebrows. "Hmm, don't let Sylas hear you talking about your trysts with him that way."

"I wasn't—" I cut myself off at Whitt's smirk and settle for glowering at him. I could tell him that all I did in there was sleep, but he might not believe me anyway—and I *wanted* to do at least a little more than that, so what does it matter if he thinks I accomplished it?

Whitt chuckles, and something in his expression softens just slightly. "I like this new ferocity you've been cultivating. One of these days I may have to promote you from 'mite' to 'mighty'."

"You could call me Talia. That *is* my name."

"But where would be the fun in that?"

He starts down the hall—in the same direction I need to head in, naturally. I could hang back and let the conversation die, but that feels awfully wimpy after he just complimented me on being fierce.

Whitt told me not that long ago that he's glad I'm here, that he wants me to stay. I shouldn't need to be nervous of him, even if something about his temperament always seems to put me off-balance.

"Does having fun matter a lot to you?" I ask, summoning a little more boldness as I follow him. "Is that why you hold all those revels for the pack?"

"I arrange our revels for many reasons, but enjoyment is certainly a significant part of them." He glances at me, the teasing glint in his eyes sparking brighter. "I suspect you'd enjoy them too. You'll have to attend one and find out what all the fuss is about."

"I *can't* attend one right now," I remind him. "I'm not supposed to let the rest of the pack see me still."

"True, true. Just something to keep in mind for future plans. I'll have you know—"

I don't get to find out what he thinks I need to know, because right then he halts in his tracks, his head cocking again as if he's listening intently to something with those lightly pointed fae ears, though my human ones haven't picked up anything unusual. His smile tightens into a more determined shape. "As enjoyable as *this* talk has been, you'll have to excuse me."

He stalks off and vanishes into the room where I've gathered he carries out whatever work exactly it is that he does for Sylas. The room where I overheard him talking to a pack member once—a pack member who somehow vanished from the room without leaving through the door. They were discussing a conflict with the fae from the winter realm, the ones the men of the keep call the Unseelie. Has more news come about that?

What if Sylas ends up having two wars to fight?

That question twines uneasily through my gut. I grab a change of clothes from the assortment the fae men have gathered for me over the month I've stayed here—they must travel into the human world now and then and... steal them? *Could* they even buy them properly if they wanted to play fair?—and duck into the lavatory so I can wash myself as well as get dressed.

Even though Sylas and I *didn't* do anything all that intimate, my skin probably picked up plenty of his scent from sleeping in his bed. August might have agreed to the idea of both he and Sylas pursuing some sort of relationship with me, but smelling the other man on me one time before upset him enough to send him charging off in wolf form. I'd rather not risk provoking any possessive inclinations if I can help it.

I don't really care what Whitt thinks of my nighttime activities, but I don't want August thinking I've devoted myself much more to Sylas than to him after all.

When I've finished, less exposed in my daytime clothes and skin tingling from the scrubbing, I nearly run into Whitt striding down the hall outside with a more purposeful attitude than I'm used to from him.

"Is everything all right?" I ask.

He stops long enough to say, "Yes. Better than we expected, I think, though I'll have to see what Sylas makes of it."

Before he can hurry onward, I make a vague motion toward the stairs. "He's gone out. He said a sentry reported something and he wanted to take a look."

Whitt lets out a faint huff. "Well, then. I suppose this matter is hardly earth-shattering enough to require his immediate attention. No reason I should go chasing after him when I could wait here while indulging in a leisurely breakfast with prettier company." He winks at me.

Even though I know he's teasing, my lips can't help twitching into a smile. I toss my nightgown into my bedroom and have just tapped my way down the stairs when the front door at the other end of the keep thumps. The fae lord comes around the bend looking as collected as always, so whatever he checked out couldn't have been too much of a problem.

Whitt appears at the dining-room doorway in an instant. "A word, my liege?" he says in a sardonic voice.

Sylas comes to a halt by the doorway. "What is it?"

Whitt casts his gaze toward me where I'm approaching them and hesitates. I brace myself for him to draw his lord aside to speak with more privacy, but then he gives a curt nod. "You may as well hear this too."

I wanted to know what was going on, but now that he's implied that his news affects me somehow, my pulse stutters. I join them, shoving my hands in the pockets of my jeans to stop them from clenching into nervous fists.

Whitt focuses back on Sylas. "One of the people I sent to check up on Aerik reported in. From what he gathered and overheard, Aerik's cadre and some others from his pack have been making comments rather publicly about how we've seemed pleased that no one has the tonic now. Trying to raise suspicions about our motivations or what have you."

"That's all?" Sylas says. "Nothing more damning than assumptions about our attitudes?"

"That was it. It might be simply an attempt to displace attention from themselves when the packs who relied on their regular deliveries of the tonic must be upset, but in combination with their interest in our territory... Aerik probably does see us as among the likely culprits in this one's disappearance." He gives my shoulder a swift pat.

"But not the only ones—there's no certainty to it. He's trying to lay the groundwork for a larger case against us in case he needs to make one, yes, but he hasn't got anywhere near enough ammunition to do a thorough job of it. We do make easy scapegoats."

Sylas hums to himself, considering Whitt and then me. "We'll wait until the others give their reports," he said. "But if the rest of the word aligns with that… We can't hide her forever, and it seems to me that showing we have nothing to hide may be a better tactic for dealing with such unsubstantiated concerns."

"What does that mean?" I ask.

"If all's still well tomorrow, we'll introduce you to the pack and get you settled in as a regular fixture in their lives. Once that's done, perhaps it's time we invite Aerik and his cadre for a dinner to show there are no ill-feelings over their frequent neglect of our 'friendship'."

Wait, what?

Whitt grins. "Give him a chance to investigate up close and find nothing, and he won't be able to justify continuing to suspect us. I like it." He aims that grin at me. "With a few careful glamours, you'll slip by right under his nose as a totally different woman."

Sylas regards me with a solemn expression. "If you feel you're ready for that, Talia. We won't rush the matter— and I wouldn't ask you to be around them at all if I didn't think it's our best hope of getting them to back off for a long while afterward."

Face my former captors again. See them here in the keep that's become my sanctuary. An icy shiver ripples over my skin.

It's not just for myself. How much more danger will the men of this keep have to face because of my presence here? Aerik's already being so hostile toward them. They shouldn't have to deal with him at all, let alone invite him into their home where he can attack them up close—an attack that might involve not just words but teeth and claws if the truth comes out.

I'm drawing them here, just like before—just like—

Images of blood splattering grass and leaves in the darkness flash through my head. Snarls and cries, the strained rattle of a last breath. I flinch, holding in my shudder as well as I can. *No!*

But even as panic clangs through my chest, I understand why Sylas is suggesting this strategy. Stealing me away has already set him and his cadre on this path. It doesn't seem like we can avoid Aerik forever. Wouldn't it be better to get the confrontation over with and have him gone from my life than to be constantly on edge waiting for them to spring at us?

At least this way, Sylas can control the circumstances, completely on guard rather than taken by surprise.

I take one breath and then another, thinking of curling up between the three fae men last night, about the warm shelter of their wolfish bodies. When I manage to speak, my voice comes out quiet and a little hoarse but steady. "Are you sure you could disguise me enough that they wouldn't recognize me?"

"You barely look like the little scrap we stole away anymore, even without magic," Sylas says. "The main identifying factors will be your shoulder scars, your wounded foot, and your scent. The first can be covered easily enough with clothing, and we won't reach out to them until I'm sure beyond any doubt that we can mask the other two."

My body balks again all the same, but I force myself to nod. "All right. If this is the best way to make sure they don't keep sneaking around here, we should do it."

"Then tomorrow you make your debut." Whitt claps his hands. "It looks as though you may get to attend one of my revels before much longer after all, mite."

CHAPTER FOUR

Talia

I've only left the keep once before, and that was several evenings ago, in such a hurried mission that I didn't dare look back. I've seen most of the scenery from the windows before, but it's different taking it in at my leisure with the fresh outside air all around me and warmth of the ever-summer breeze licking over my skin. And I haven't gotten a really good look at the keep itself before.

I turn on my heel where I've stopped on the soft grass that tickles my bare feet. Beyond the nearby fields, patches of forest darken the horizon in almost every direction except the low, rolling hills to my left. To my right, spires of pinkish stone jut up from the distant treetops in spindly towers, dotted with lime-green vegetation. And behind me...

Getting a good eyeful of the place I've lived in for the past month, my breath catches. Inside the keep, it's easy to

imagine that while the structure is a bit odd—every wall
and ceiling made of the same polished wood as the floors,
lighting fixtures that look like branches—it's still simply a
very grand house. Outside, it's both one of the most
beautiful and the most alien buildings I've ever seen.

It looks as though several immense trees sprouted up
and fused into one being, only the curves of one bending
into the next showing where they might have begun and
ended. Nothing sprouts from the smoothed bark of the
outer walls, but above the second floor, branches weave
together into an intricate pattern like the finest sort of
lace. Delicate rings spiral out around the arched windows
as if they used to be knots in the wood.

"It doesn't quite live up to Hearthshire, but we built it
under direr circumstances," Sylas says beside me, as if he
thinks I'm underwhelmed rather than overwhelmed by the
sight. He tips his head toward the pack village. "Are you
ready?"

Right. We did come out here for a reason. One I
haven't really forgotten, nervousness making my stomach
jump. I might have been using the view as an excuse to
dawdle. I square my shoulders. "As I'll ever be."

Heading over to meet the larger pack feels weirdly like
showing up in a new classroom halfway through the
school year. The people Sylas is about to introduce me to
have their own friendships and probably rivalries, histories
that stretch back farther than I've even been alive. How
am I going to fit in with all that?

Actually, it's a gazillion times worse than a classroom,
because these "people" aren't even people. They're fae, and

I'm human, and August has already told me that pretty much every fae views humans as something lesser than themselves.

I limp along beside Sylas, his pace slowed in consideration of my own, sucking the wildflower-scented air into my lungs and willing my heart not to hammer straight through my ribs. Several fae are already moving around their houses, which look like much smaller versions of the keep's construction: enormous tree stumps that've been twisted off to form a pointed roof a few feet above their heads.

A woman is tending to a garden full of bright leaves and berries in a cacophony of colors. A couple of men are working together to bend several pieces of wood into some kind of contraption, it appears with magic, while small pearl-gray hens peck at the grass by their feet. A small group is just tramping back into the middle of the village with weapons over their shoulders or at their hips and a large doe carried on a harness between them.

At the sight of their lord, all activity ceases. Sylas's pack leaves off their work to approach us, more emerging from the houses as if his presence alone sets off some sort of signal to alert them.

Sylas and I come to a stop at the edge of the patchier grass on the foot-worn paths between the houses, his hand rising to my shoulder. It's a gesture mainly for their benefit, I suspect—to emphasize that I'm under his protection? That they should treat me with all the respect he'd require?—but his firm grasp helps me stand straight and steady before all these strangers.

And there are a lot. Not compared to most packs, from what the men of the keep have indicated, but to me, when I haven't been around more than four other people at a time in nearly a decade... My gaze darts across them too nervously for me to do a proper count, but I'd guess there are about thirty. And this isn't the full pack. There are others off on sentry duty or fighting in that conflict with the Unseelie too.

I couldn't say all of them are exactly *attractive*, but there's an eye-catching, unearthly quality to their faces and forms, as difficult to look away from as Sylas and his cadre's stunning features. They range from twig-thin to barrel-chested, dressed in simple shirts and slacks or dresses of a thin but tightly woven flowy material. Most of them have favored the earthy tones Sylas and August generally wear, but some, a few of which I recognize as regulars at Whitt's revels, are decked out in vibrant jewel tones closer to his preferences.

They're eyeing me with open curiosity, but that makes sense. Sylas told me he hasn't taken human servants since Kellan joined his cadre because of the other man's intense hostility toward mortal beings, so these fae haven't seen someone like me in their domain in quite a while. Whether they've *ever* seen a human with starkly pink hair is debatable. I'm just glad that I don't pick up any obvious animosity or disdain in their expressions.

"It's good to see you all looking well," Sylas says in his authoritative tone. "I'd like you to meet a newcomer to our pack. This is Talia. She's come from beyond the Mists. My cadre-chosen August has brought her here as a companion—*not* a servant—and she's still becoming accustomed to our ways. I expect you all to help ease that transition and to offer every reasonable kindness."

Heads bob in acknowledgment all through the crowd. I smile at them, hoping my mouth doesn't look as stiff as it feels. How much kindness will the fae consider "reasonable"?

Sylas scans his pack with a smile of his own. "Excellent. Why don't you take leave of your work for a short while and tell me how you find yourself these days? And if you wish to get to know Talia a little better, I'm sure she'd be more than happy to make your acquaintance."

No pressure at all. I shift my weight on my feet, a faint tingle reminding me of the illusion that's hiding my brace and any unevenness to my gait from our spectators. Since bodily magic is one of August's specialities, he contributed to the glamour, instructing me to focus on steadiness over speed. If I lurch around too much, the glamour won't be enough to disguise my old injury.

Sylas glances at me, probably appraising how well I'm coping. Even if my nerves are jittering all through me, I have to show him I can handle this. He's taking on my enemies for me; I'd better at least be able to take care of myself among my allies.

I raise my chin a little higher and take a step forward to meet the fae heading our way. Apparently reassured, Sylas ambles on into the crowd, pausing here and there to speak with his people.

Many of the pack-kin gather around him to wait for his attention, but several drift closer to me. They look me up and down tentatively as if I might prove unexpectedly dangerous, but one woman who doesn't appear to be much older than I am plants herself right in front of me.

Her long, smooth hair gleams such a pale but warm blond you could believe it was made out of sunbeams. She peers at me with close-set blue-grey eyes that are just a tad overlarge, giving her an unsettling insect-like appearance. But her grin is broad and as far as I can tell genuine when she thrusts out her arm at an awkward angle, as if she's been told shaking hands is how humans greet each other but has never actually done so to know what it should look like.

I clasp her hand in return, finding her grip warm and firm, and give it a quick shake, even though I feel a bit silly. "Talia," she says in a silvery voice, lingering over each syllable as if tasting it. "You've come a long way. I'm Harper of Oakmeet—I mean, obviously. I hope you like it here."

"I like what I've seen so far," I say, which is true if we don't count anything outside this domain or Kellan or the fae from other packs who've intruded here.

More fae have drawn up around her. "What part of the human world are you from?" a burly young man asks, his voice gruff but his eyes gleaming with curiosity.

"Um, America." I'm not sure if I should get more specific than that when I can't answer any specific questions about what's been happening there recently.

He hums as if that's good enough anyway, and a knobby middle-aged woman pushes between him and Harper to inspect me. "You're taken with our August, are you?" she asks in a possessive tone, as if evaluating whether I'm worthy.

I guess it's not much surprise that August with his cheerful, kind demeanor and innate protectiveness would have a lot of fans in the pack. A blush tingles across my cheeks at the thought of what they might already assume about our relationship, but with luck that only makes my answer sound more honest. "It's hard not to be."

"You wanted to come, then?" Harper says eagerly. "Did you know where he was bringing you?"

"I—I knew a little, but it's hard to be prepared before you've actually seen the place."

She hums to herself, her gaze going distant. "It must be so exciting."

A pleased exclamation pulls the attention away from me for a moment. Sylas is brushing his hand to the forehead of a willowy woman in what looks like a gesture of benediction, his face glowing with happiness.

"A new member of the pack," he booms with such blatant delight a smile catches my lips that I don't have to force at all. "What a blessing. We'll make his or her arrival a safe and joyful one."

My gaze skims down the woman's body and catches on the slight swell of her belly. Fae are nearly immortal, but the trade-off is that they struggle to have children. How long has it been since this pack last had a child in its midst?

The woman and the man at her side who I assume is her husband—mate?—duck their heads with pleased smiles of their own, but all at once something clenches in my chest. Sylas has so much to defend here, so many people who are depending on him, who couldn't easily fight for themselves if Aerik or some other lord launched an attack. It isn't just the men of the keep I'm putting in danger but all of the pack as well.

He's risked their security for me. He's put it all on the line to give me some kind of freedom. I don't know how I'm ever going to repay him for that.

I don't know how I'll live with myself if Aerik hurts any one of them.

Before those gnawing worries can grip too much of my mind, one of the fae women near me leans in and twists a lock of my hair around her finger. "How is your hair this shade? It can't be natural."

"August dyed it," I say quickly. "He thought it looked nice like that."

She makes a slightly disgruntled sound. From what I understand, only the truest of true-blooded fae with barely any human heritage in the mix would generally have coloring this unusual. Even Sylas only has a purple-ish tint to his coffee-brown hair. Maybe she thinks I'm attempting to rise above my proper place.

A stout man at my other side jabs at my thigh. "What are these pants? It's an unusual material."

I manage not to flinch away from him, but it's a near thing. My pulse skitters at how tightly they're closing in around me now. "They're called jeans. They're very popular in America these days."

More fae nose in on our gathering, volleying another question and another. "Have you been out to the pastures yet?"

"Are you going to stay here forever?"

"Do you know any crafts?"

"Will you be hunting with us?"

"What of your human family?"

I have no time to come up with answers under that bombardment, and the last question gouges straight through my heart. The smack of pain constricts my throat. Before I can manage to regather my smile and my voice, a wiry figure elbows her way through the throng to my side.

The woman who reaches me is the first faerie I've seen who actually looks *old*, so she could have a couple of millennia on me. Her serene forest-green eyes study me from a pale, wizened face framed by tight coils of slate-gray hair. She stands half a head shorter than me but not at all stooped, her posture straight and bearing commanding enough that I doubt she bows to anyone other than Sylas. There's a kindness in her expression, though, that lessens the ache of my loss like a balm.

She spins to frown at the others, who've already backed up a step, whether out of respect for her seniority or her general presence, I can't tell. "Let's not badger the poor thing," she says in a spirited if raspy voice. "I'd imagine she was overwhelmed plenty already before you lot started hailing questions on her head."

"It's all right," I say, not wanting any of the pack members to think I've taken offense, as grateful as I am for her intervention.

She glances at me with a twinkle in her eyes and a wry tone that makes me like her even more. "Very polite of you to say so. Speaks well of your upbringing. Still…" She turns back to the other fae. "Give her some space. August isn't the fickle sort. I expect she'll be here more than long enough for you all to indulge your curiosity bit by bit rather than in a deluge."

The others start to drift away with a few offers that I should seek them out if I'd like to see this one's garden or that one's weaving, leaving only the wizened woman and Harper, who's stayed with an air of impenetrable confidence as if it never occurred to her that the woman's orders might apply to her too. I don't mind. Two is a much easier number to cope with than a dozen.

I lower my voice in the hopes that the other fae won't overhear. "Thank you."

The newcomer pats my arm. "Think nothing of it, my dear. Our days around here tend to be much the same, so it's not surprising they get overeager with the appearance of someone new, but that's no reason you should have to weather a storm of interrogation." She steps away herself. "I'm often out on sentry duty, but if I'm around and you need a helping hand, you can always ask for Astrid."

"Thank you," I say again as she heads off.

Harper tucks the silky fall of her hair behind her ears, as if she's anxious about making a good impression herself. "If there's anything in our territory you might like to see— I don't know what sorts of things you enjoy—I'd be happy to show you around. Without *too* much badgering." Her shy grin suggests she has at least a few more questions she'd like to ask.

Explore the domain—experience more of this world I've spent the past nine years in but have seen so little of. My spirits lift at the idea, but a twinge of fear deflates some of that elation. How safe is it for me to roam farther beyond the keep, especially without Sylas or his cadre ready if the wrong fae crosses paths with us?

"I—I'm not sure," I say, stumbling. I don't want to

dismiss her friendliness. If I'm going to be living here for a while—maybe even forever—I'll probably be happier the more I integrate with the pack. And Harper seems like one of the friendliest of them, with no sign that she's put off by my mortality. "I should talk to August before I make any plans. I think he'd be worried if he came looking for me and found I'd wandered off without telling him."

He probably would be, and Harper doesn't appear to take offense to the excuse. "Well, whenever you want to." She pauses and sidles closer, her voice dropping to a stealthy undertone. "What Astrid meant to say is that living here can be unspeakably *boring*. But I think you just might change that."

She looks like she might say more, but at Sylas's return, she settles for flashing me another grin and meandering off toward the forest. The fae lord sets his hand on my shoulder again, watching her and then glancing down at me with a trace of amusement. "Already making friends, are you, little scrap?"

I'm comfortable enough with him now to wrinkle my nose at his old nickname for me, even though I kind of like it—or at least the tenderness with which he says it. "Maybe. She seemed as if she'd like to be friends."

He nudges me toward the keep, and we stroll across the grass to the main door. In the entrance room, he stops and turns to face me. "It might do both you and Harper good to spend some time together. She's one of the few of the pack who was born in Oakmeet and hasn't had the opportunity to venture beyond this domain... She's dedicated enough to have remained with us when she could have struck out on her own, but I can tell she's restless. As I suppose you must be too after staying cooped up so long."

"I can't complain about the treatment I've gotten here." My gaze travels back to the door. "But it was really nice getting outside. Do you think—she suggested that she could show me more of your territory—would it be safe?" And there's also the matter of my foot. Disguised or not, with the misshapen bones and their perpetual ache, I'm not up to any extended hikes.

Sylas pauses, considering. "Until the most immediate concern of Aerik is dealt with, I'd prefer that you remain within hearing—in the fields around the keep, on this side of the hills, or no more than a few steps into the woods. One of us can reach you quickly at a single shout, and it's unlikely anyone would harass you that close by anyway. Perhaps we could arrange a venture farther afield with appropriate transportation and August accompanying you when the timing seems right."

"Okay," I say. "That makes sense."

He gazes down at me and strokes his fingers over my hair, trailing heat in their wake. "I want you to have as normal a life as I'm capable of offering you here, Talia. I know what it's like to lose a home you loved and to be unable to safely return... Whatever is in my power to make up for that loss, you'll have it."

The intensity of his tone strikes a chord deep inside me. A home he loved—the Hearthshire he still uses in his title, even though he and his pack haven't lived there in ages. That they were driven from after his soul-twined mate was killed over the crimes she committed.

I swallow hard. "You still miss your old domain a lot, don't you?"

He shrugs, but with a weight to his shoulders that stops the gesture from looking remotely casual. "It was the first territory that was truly my own, and we built our home there from the ground up by our own power, with every feature I could have wished for. The thought of it falling, neglected, into disrepair…" A growl creeps into his voice. He dismisses it with a shake of his head. "We will have it again. As many centuries as it takes, I will earn it back for us."

And it may take centuries longer now that he's decided not to use me as a bargaining chip. Emotion swells in my chest for the sacrifices he's made, this powerful and devoted man who's barely known me a month and yet saw something in me worth shielding. I grasp his wrist. "Thank you."

When he meets my gaze again, I bob up on my toes, and he lowers his head to accept my kiss. The ardent press of his lips leaves no doubt that he's satisfied with his decision. When I drop back on my heels, giddiness is tingling through me.

"I didn't mean to pull you away from your new friends for long," he says, his voice a touch rougher after the kiss. "Don't venture far, but explore all you like within those boundaries. This place is yours as much as it is the rest of ours now."

I squeeze his arm and let him go, stepping toward the door. But as I slip out into the sunlight, a question I'm afraid to voice sinks heavy in my stomach.

What *will* become of Sylas and his people if Aerik does

discover their theft of me? Will they lose even this backwater fringe domain they've made their own?

How many more lives will be ruined because of my blood and the monsters who crave it—because I'm too weak to stand against them alone?

CHAPTER FIVE

Sylas

"Y ou wouldn't know it at first glance, but she's got grit
to her." Astrid gazes toward the waning moon from
where we're standing at the edge of the northern woods
before shifting her attention to me. "I suppose she needs it
if she's going to carve out a real place for herself here.
You're expecting her to be around for quite some time, my
lord."

It isn't a question. Astrid has been with me long
enough to recognize these things without asking.

"August has already become quite fond of her—and
she of him," I say, measuring my words. "She has little to
return to." Not after Aerik and his cadre slaughtered her
family. It's pained her too much to share the details, but
from what she has said and her reactions when the subject
comes up, I can picture the scene far too vividly. The
image brings a snarl to the back of my throat.

Perhaps Astrid notices that defensiveness, or perhaps

something in my demeanor when I introduced Talia this morning gave it away. Either way, the smile she offers me holds a grandmotherly amusement along with due respect. "I'm guessing the fondness extends beyond August."

I'll accept that prodding—she is as old as my actual grandmother, after all, and she's been a presence in my life since I was born. I count it as an honor that she left my family's domain to follow me to Hearthshire and then here. That doesn't mean I have to confirm her suspicions, though.

"She is pleasing enough to have around," I say in the same even tone. "But somewhat unsure of herself in such unfamiliar surroundings. I'd prefer that her transition to this life didn't involve any trauma." Any more than the immense amounts it already has. "The rest of the pack has accepted her well enough? There hasn't been any muttering or disparaging?" I kept my ears pricked after Talia returned to the village, but without standing over her shoulder monitoring every interaction, I can't be sure of what might have been muttered or conveyed in a hostile glance.

Astrid shakes her head. "Not that I witnessed. You laid out your expectations clearly—and she hardly made it difficult to follow them. It didn't take half an hour before Brigid had her gamely mixing paints for some new mural her lot has going up in their house, and after that a bunch of them had her going from garden to garden so they could show off their coming harvest. She never gave any sign she was anything but pleased to compliment their work."

Relief sweeps through me, more intense than I'd

expected. She's already fitting in here, establishing bonds —it's not the life she'd have had if Aerik had never rampaged into her childhood, but it's the closest to a normal one I can offer her.

I tip my head to Astrid in thanks for her report. "I'm glad to hear it. If any trouble does come up, even a murmur of it—"

"I'll make sure you're aware of it, my lord. Though I will say, if you'll allow it, that I think the girl could hold her own all right against a sharp remark or two. She'll garner more approval if anyone with doubts sees her stand up for herself rather than having you intervene."

No doubt she's right. I can't help that picturing Talia receiving even a hint of cruelty from my pack makes my hackles rise, though. Bad enough that she had to tolerate Kellan's viciousness behind my back. If he hadn't been kin-of-my-mate…

Well, that is dealt with now, even if I wish it could have happened in a better way, and the fae of my pack are much more of my choosing.

"Your service and your wisdom are as appreciated as always," I tell Astrid.

She sketches some semblance of a bow and slips into the deepening shadows of the evening to take up her sentry duty. I head back to the keep. As my gaze skims over the horizon, my deadened eye conjures a brief wisp of a vision: three hazy figures on horseback cantering toward us, there for a blink and then vanished back into the aether the image arose from.

A hint of our future or a glimpse from our past? It could be either. With no news that suggests Aerik has any real reason to suspect us of wrongdoing, Whitt has sent out an invitation to him and his cadre. I might have gotten a backwards echo of their arrival.

My spymaster has also slunk into Copperweld to spy on their reaction firsthand as well as he can, not trusting anyone else with that job. There's no telling whether Whitt will return later tonight or perhaps not for another day or two, if he becomes concerned and stays to monitor the situation further.

As such, the keep is even quieter than usual. I have to walk the whole length of the hall before my ears pick up the thump and the grunt of activity from the basement gym.

Apparently ingratiating herself with the pack didn't wear Talia out too much. I come to the gym doorway to find her and August circling each other on the mats, the sweat shining on her forehead a testament to how long they've already been sparring. Her slim body is tensed in the T-shirt and sweats my younger brother obtained for her training, her balance impressively steady despite her damaged foot in its brace.

I stay to the side in the shadows, but August picks up on my presence as I'd expect him to. He acknowledges me with a flicker of a glance but otherwise stays focused on his pupil, his teeth gleaming in his eager grin. Talia doesn't appear to notice me at all, her concentration entirely on her opponent.

"Ready?" he says.

The second she nods, he springs, snatching at her waist. Talia ducks and tries to dodge to the side, but he catches her, swinging her back in front of him with a force that sends a ripple of protectiveness through me even though I know he'll be careful with her.

Her sputtered curse makes August chuckle. "You can't always get away. How would you make an attacker let go?"

They must have gone over some of the strategies before, because that's all the prompting Talia needs to ram her elbow toward his nose. When he jerks his head out of the way, she slams her good foot into his knee. Releasing her, August falls back with an *oof* that's only partly feigned, and Talia scrambles around, crouched animal-like on the mats but beaming at her success.

A strange cordial of emotions floods my chest. Fondness, yes—Astrid wasn't wrong about that. But a surge of admiration twines through it, for the strength this scrap of a woman manages to summon from somewhere within that delicate mortal body. It can't be easy for her, practicing these moves against an opponent twice her size while she has a permanent injury holding her back as well, but she's throwing herself into the training whole-heartedly.

Isleen would have laughed at a human imagining they might brawl with fae and come out anything other than beaten to a pulp, but Isleen would never herself have tackled a challenge this great to begin with. My departed mate, Heart keep her soul, bristled with frustration when any task became difficult for her. She had many talents, to be sure, but that led to her expecting *everything* to come easily and to finding fault in anything that didn't rather than seeking to improve her own skills.

I hadn't expected to encounter a disposition that so puts that aspect of hers to shame in a human.

And through the fondness and the awe winds a sensation too clawed to be called protectiveness now. No, that's pure possessive instinct, the drive in me to shove August away from this ever-surprising woman and gather her up where he can't set a single finger on her.

Not because I have any fear he'd hurt her—oh, quite the opposite. There was no mistaking the way his eyes flared as he held her in his arms, no mistaking that the flush in Talia's cheeks now is more than just exertion. A trace of arousal laces the tang of sweat in the air.

I will the barbed urge to claim her down with a tightening of my jaw. She isn't mine. If I tried to force the issue, I've no doubt she wouldn't have a single thing to do with me from that moment onward.

Why *shouldn't* she have August to turn to as well? It isn't as if I can offer her all the attention a devout lover should. I have too many responsibilities pulling me in too many directions… I should be glad she trusts me enough to allow me any intimacy in the times when I can be at her side.

If I truly mean to give her the best possible life here, then sharing her affections is part of that.

Talia straightens up, and I catch August's gaze with the slightest twitch of my eyes for him to stand down. We should find out how our lady reacts when she hasn't been given a chance to prepare for an assault.

In the swiftest of strides, I sweep into the room to whip my arms around Talia's shoulders from behind. Her flinch tells me she clearly hadn't registered my arrival at all in the midst of their tussling.

She yelps, but rather than crumpling, her limbs strike

out, her elbow jabbing my ribs, her heel smacking my shin in the instant before she realizes who holds her and how gently. The blows land hard enough to sting.

"Sylas!" she gasps, jerking in on herself with a deeper flush blooming across her face. "I'm sorry—I didn't—"

I can't pass up the opportunity to nuzzle her hair. "You did well, Talia. Your defensive reflexes are already becoming honed." I give August an approving smile over her shoulder, aware that he may now be experiencing the same jealousy I felt a moment ago and hoping to assuage it. "A credit to both yourself and your teacher."

August's grin comes back easily enough. "She's an avid student."

As I release her, Talia's head dips humbly. She glances from me to August, a hint of pride coming into her expression but worry clouding her light green eyes. "How likely do you think it is that I'll need to use these lessons for real?"

"You've already had a couple of aggressive confrontations," August says. "I think it's better for us to assume the worst, and if you never find yourself under attack again, we'll all celebrate that fact."

Her lips twitch with another smile that doesn't reach her anxious eyes. "But no matter how much you train me, I'm never going to be able to fight off someone who's fae, am I?"

If only I had a better answer to give her. "That's not your fault. No human would have an easy time of it. But every extra second you can buy for yourself, fending off severe wounds or capture, allows us another second to reach you and finish the battle on your behalf."

"It isn't even physical strength, really," August adds. "We can bring magic to bear. Without that, you can't help being at a disadvantage." He chuckles roughly. "If I could teach you *that* part of battle…"

Something in Talia's hesitation after that statement puts me on the alert. She looks down at her hands and swipes one of them across her mouth, her body tensing all over again even though the sparring is over. I'm about to ask her what's wrong when she raises her head, her expression determined.

"I—I think there's something I should tell you. About me and magic."

CHAPTER SIX

Talia

When I finish my account of how I unlocked my cage door using the magical true word for "bronze" and later warped an attacker's dagger the same way, Sylas and August stare at me in stunned silence. A nervous itch runs up my arms.

I've been afraid to tell them about this additional strangeness, adding to the qualities that a typical human who's been dragged into the fae realm wouldn't possess. Will my seeming ability to use magic make me even more a target than when the only inexplicable specialness about me was my curse-curing blood?

But these men have saved my life more than once— Sylas has *killed* for me, a member of his own cadre no less. Keeping the secret from them when the subject has been brought up directly felt too close to lying for comfort. I should be able to trust them with this. I want to show them I trust them.

Not to mention that it sounds like my unexpected talent could be a deciding factor in my surviving another attack.

Sylas recovers first, peering down at me intently. "You're absolutely sure that you produced those effects yourself and using magic? Aerik might have failed to secure the cage properly…" He trails off, obviously unable to think of a reasonable explanation for how the fae woman's blade could have gotten bent out of shape.

"I tried the lock that day," I say. "Several times before I got it right. And I *felt* the word work, like there was some kind of power to it when I said it right."

August gives his lord a perplexed look. "Have you ever heard of a human who could call on true names—not from the legends but in our lifetime?"

Sylas shakes his head. "Not one. Even in the legends— which may have some truth to them—it's always been men and women with at least a little fae heritage in the mix." He frowns as he examines me even more thoroughly, leaning close and inhaling—testing my scent. "In all the tests I conducted before, I've noticed no signs that you're anything but human through and through. But if it were a small enough element, with the other power of your blood as a distracting factor, it might be nearly imperceivable."

I might be a tiny bit fae? A shiver runs through me that's as much anxiety as it is excitement. I don't know if that makes my situation better or worse. "Is it all that common for people in the human world to have a fae ancestor?"

"No. Given our issues with conception and inheritance, we're particularly careful with potential and actual children. But very occasionally one slips by and is a weak enough half-breed to go unnoticed during their mortal lives, continuing to spread that heritage to their children. You would have to be several generations removed from the source to show no physical signs of it, though." Sylas's brow is still furrowed. "I find it hard to believe that with so weak a link, you could have managed to teach yourself not just a little trickery but an entire true name without any outside guidance."

"What else could it be?" August asks.

"Who can say? We don't understand the effect Talia's blood has on our curse either. Perhaps the two factors are intertwined somehow—arising from a common feature we haven't yet discovered." Sylas rubs his jaw. "I don't know of any other way to investigate the cause that we could easily pursue in our current situation. There are resources that might help elsewhere in our world, but that would risk exposing Talia's secrets to our brethren."

I hug myself, the idea of the impenetrable mystery lurking inside me overshadowing any satisfaction I felt in sharing this secret even with these two men. "But even if we're not sure how it happened, it's a good thing, right? You were just saying that the reason I'll never be able to defend myself against fae on my own is magic. If I can learn more true names or other spells…"

Sylas appears to shake himself out of his pensive state. "I don't like dealing with dynamics I'm uncertain of, but it can't be helped. You're right—this should work to your benefit, so long as you continue to keep it secret from everyone other than my cadre and me. If word got out that we'd gotten our hands on a magic-wielding human, we'd face nearly as much scrutiny as if they knew what benefits your blood offers."

A chill ripples down my spine. "Of course." I'm getting more practice at keeping secrets than anything else these men are training me in.

August moves toward the door, his usual cheerful energy coming back. "You'll have to show us what you can do already, and then we can build from there. I have some bronze utensils in the kitchen that it wouldn't be any great loss to see mangled."

As I follow him, my stomach knots. What if I can't manage it? What if I *am* somehow wrong even with the two instances of proof?

It won't matter. I don't actually think Sylas or August will judge me for a lapse like that. I just don't want to let them down now that I've raised their expectations.

Sylas comes with us, his demeanor more reserved. Not because he doubts me, I don't think, but because of his qualms about the consequences this revelation might lead to. But I already had a huge bullseye on me for my blood, so I can't really regret the possibility that a second oddity about me might allow me to fend off the people who'd want to use me for the first.

The smells from our dinner—roast fish in a wine sauce and a bake of mixed berries and leaf vegetables that made a startlingly delicious combination—linger in the kitchen. August goes straight to the drawers beneath the counters and digs around until he produces a slightly battered bronze ladle. He sets it on the larger of the two islands and motions me over. "Give it your best shot."

What exactly am I supposed to do with it? I step up to

the countertop and eye the lone spoon, picturing it bending in the middle like the fae woman's dagger did. It's hard to summon much determination over an act that seems so random. I nibble at my lower lip and mentally sound out the syllables I spent so much time committing to memory. *Fee-doom-ace-own.*

I reach out my hand to grasp the spoon's handle like I clutched the latch on my cage. The cool metal warms against my palm. Focusing all my attention on it, I propel the true name from my throat. "*Fee-doom-ace-own.*"

The two fae men watch, tensed in anticipation, but the spoon just sits there in my grasp looking as spoony as it did before. My heart sinks. I try to gather all the energy inside me and declare the word again. "*Fee-doom-ace-own!*"

Nothing. No tingle on my tongue, no change in the utensil I'm holding. I swallow hard, a ridiculous burning forming behind my eyes.

I know I did it before. It must have taken a thousand tries, but I got there eventually with the lock on the cage. And the woman who attacked me, her dagger—I warped it on my first try.

With panic and anger surging through my nerves. When I finally managed to unlock the cage, it was after that man from Aerik's cadre—icy Cole—suggested they break my other foot and have me crawl around their fortress cleaning the rooms like a slave.

"Talia," Sylas starts, so kindly the tears threaten again, but I shake my head before he can finish whatever he means to say.

"Let me keep trying. I think—I think I need to get

back in the same mindset as when I did it before. Maybe some of the power came from my emotions."

He falls silent, giving me the space I need without any sense of impatience. I reach back through my memories to the terror of the fae woman's attack, but that was a sharp jolt in the face of a sudden threat, hard to stir again when I'm here in one of the few places I feel safe.

My years under Aerik's control—those have stuck with me much more deeply, the horror twined through my spirit to the point that it seeps into my dreams, grips me at just the mention of my family. I hate the gut-wrenching chill that fills me when I think back to my imprisonment, but if I can use it, if it can give me power after everything he stole from me...

My heart thumps faster, the sickly chill expanding through my abdomen, but I force my thoughts to return to the filthy, starved existence of my captivity. To the endless hours where I had nothing but a few harsh words spat at me, a little food and water shoved between the bars, and my imagination offering a far too ephemeral escape. To the days when Aerik and his cadre would come to cut my wrist and drain a vial full of my blood, Cole pinning me beneath his body as painfully as possible, all of them laughing and sneering. To the splintering of pain and the crack of bones fracturing in my foot the one time I dared fight back.

To the wolfish beasts that lunged out of the shadows that night I teased Jamie into chasing me through the woods. Fangs and blood and guttural shrieks.

My legs tremble under me. My lungs have clenched, but I manage to produce the syllables, imagining myself facing those beasts again, preparing to do everything I can to defend myself and my family. I can't save them now, but maybe I can save Sylas and his pack from more violence.

My fingers tighten around the spoon. "*Fee-doom-ace-own. Fee-doom-ace-own!*"

With that second utterance, an almost electric energy quivers over my tongue. The spoon shudders and hitches farther forward, the rounded end jutting and narrowing into a point vicious enough to stab.

August sucks in a startled breath. Sylas traces his fingers over the back of my hand, and I jerk my arm back from the makeshift weapon I shaped using a magic I barely understand. The fae lord picks up the spoon-turned-spike and turns it over, studying it from all angles.

"You really did it," August says, awe glowing in his eyes. A grin leaps to his face. "You called its true name, and it answered. Do you have the mark?"

I glance down at myself as if one of those curving black tattoos might have appeared on my body just now. "I haven't seen it. I checked everywhere I could see on my own and with a mirror after you told me what those are."

Sylas lowers the spoon. "The magic might not leave its stamp on humans the same way it does on fae. Impossible to know when we have no other examples. And regardless, you haven't fully mastered the word. Once you're completely in tune with it, it shouldn't take that much out of you."

"If she was fae," August puts in. "Maybe that's different for humans working magic too."

The thump of footsteps at the doorway draws all our attention away from my handiwork. Whitt stops just over the threshold, his hair windblown and his eyebrows arching. "Humans working what now?"

August points at the spoon-spike. "Talia knows the true word for bronze—she called on it, and it followed her will. That used to be a ladle."

Whitt blinks, some of his usual nonchalance fading behind a flicker of shock. "*What?* You're sure it was her and not—"

"We both watched her do it," Sylas interrupts firmly. "I was certainly skeptical of the idea, but there was no mistaking what I saw. It was a struggle for her, though."

"But she'll improve with practice." August looks as though he's barely holding himself back from jumping with joy. "We can start trying to teach you more words—I guess we should start with the simplest ones—"

"Those that are relatively simple but also useful for self-defense," Sylas says. "No more than one or two to begin with. We don't want to strain her budding abilities."

Will I have to take myself back to the awful moments from my past *every* time I want the magic to work? A shiver shoots through my gut, but there's elation in it too.

I've proven it. There's something magical in me. Whatever I have to do to use that power, it'll be worth it to have a chance of standing up for myself against our enemies.

Whitt stares at me for a second longer before his face snaps back into a more typical unconcerned expression. He clears his throat. "We have another, more pressing matter to discuss. Aerik accepted your invitation, my lord. We can expect him and his cadre for dinner in three days' time."

CHAPTER SEVEN

Whitt

I never enjoy Ralyn's visits from the Unseelie border. They've rarely brought any news worth celebrating—generally the opposite. But this report promises to be even more troubling, when rather than meeting me in my office via the concealed outer entrance, he instead sent a leaf gliding through a window to me on a conjured lick of breeze. Its message asked only that I meet him at the edge of the southwest woods.

Does he have some reason to fear being seen approaching the keep? He could have waited until nightfall when he'd have blended into the darkness. Instead the leaf's urgent patter against my face got me out of bed much earlier than I'd have preferred, especially after spending most of yesterday prowling around Aerik's domain. The mid-morning sunlight glares straight into my weary eyes.

As I reach the forest, my nostrils flare. Amid the

pungent scents of pine and cedar, I pick up a trace of the man's scent from just a little farther south—mingled with the metallic tang of fresh blood.

My pulse quickens, all my senses going on alert. I stalk into the cooler shadows between the trees, and Ralyn's lean form rises from where he was crouched in the underbrush some twenty feet away.

Rises and then sways. I hurry forward and catch his elbow just before he collapses. When I squint, I make out a dark, damp patch that stands out against the deep green fabric of his tunic by his waist.

"What are you doing here?" I demand, checking him over for other wounds and taking in the scrapes on his wrists and knuckles, the splotch of a bruise at the corner of his jaw, the talon-shaped scratches across his temple that look inexpertly sealed. "You should be in one of the healers' tents, not roaming around here. And you'd better not tell me the arch-lords have done away with healers along the front."

Ralyn manages a hoarse chuckle at my disparaging tone. "Saw a healer. He didn't do a good enough job, apparently. Rushing when there were so many— I tried to give it a chance to heal on its own, came when I thought I was good enough to travel, but the cut opened up again while I was heading here. I thought… it wouldn't be good for morale if the pack saw me staggering up to the keep like this."

He's lucky I was there to receive his message. So wretchedly loyal he'd have rather bled out here in the woods than come straight for help. I inhale with an irritated hiss that's mainly directed at whichever Unseelie bastards inflicted his wounds. "Better if we get August to look at it. Patching people up is much more his specialty than mine, especially if the battlefield healers weren't quite up to the job."

The last bits of color drain from Ralyn's already sallow face. "I'm not sure I can even make the walk at this point."

I wave off his concern before he can protest more. "If I can make the trip across the fields, my cadre-fellow can join us here too." I pluck a leaf off an oak—possibly the same tree Ralyn made use of—and murmur my intention to it. It flits toward the keep, where no doubt the whelp is puttering around in the kitchen as he so enjoys.

"What are you doing back here at all?" I ask, guiding Ralyn down until he's sitting. "A regular report could have waited until you'd given yourself more of a chance to recover. Has the tide turned? Do the others need more supplies?"

Ralyn grimaces. "The blasted ravens hit us twice as hard a few days ago—the morning after the full moon. We were still disorganized after the wildness. None of the squadrons were fully prepared. We—we lost Filip and Ashim. The pricks tore them to pieces. A couple of the others took bad blows, worse than mine." His voice has become even more ragged. "Reinforcements from farther south came in time to push the feather-brains back, but I don't think there are more than three or four of us from Oakmeet out there who can give our all going forward, and that's hardly enough to hold our own. None of the other squadrons will have our backs."

My jaw works. Of course not. They can't forget about maintaining appearances in the hierarchy of the packs even when our mutual enemies are slaughtering us wholesale. Maggots eat all those mangy bastards.

"They attacked *after*, not during the full moon?" I have to clarify. If the stinking ravens have discovered that weakness—

But to my relief, Ralyn nods. "I'd hate to think what would have happened if they'd been bold enough to strike during the night and found us in the grips of the curse. The usual glamours and the rest must have convinced them we were standing strong then." He pauses. "I thought you should know as soon as possible. The moment this wound is sealed again—"

I cut him off again. "You're not going back until *you* can give it your all. Stay and rest at least a few more days once August has patched you up. And consider that an order."

The man doesn't look happy about it, but he holds his tongue on that subject. "I don't know how we can gain an advantage if they keep at us that fiercely. There always seem to be more of the ravens, and they're only ramping up their efforts. When we're barely holding our own..."

"Don't fret over it. That's for me to think on."

With a pounding of paws, August dashes over to us as a wolf. He straightens up into his regular form, his expression already worried. "What's happened?"

I explain Ralyn's situation in as few words as necessary. My younger half-brother is already kneeling next to him before I've gotten out the second sentence. He grunts disapprovingly at the sight of the re-opened wound.

"See that his innards will stay securely in his belly and that he makes it to his house for some much-needed recuperation," I instruct August when I'm done, and glance at Ralyn. "I'll come check on you tonight."

As I cross the fields to return to the keep, my gaze slides over the cluster of houses our pack-kin call home, instinctively taking a tally of who remains and how fit they might be to join the battle against the Unseelie. My gut twists at how sparse the pickings are.

We have a few good fighters left and a handful of decent ones among those who keep up the sentry duty, but they're barely a large enough force to hope to push back someone like Aerik if he decides to storm our domain. I've already allowed our resources to be stretched so much thinner than I'd like. If I send even more of them to the border, we'll be nearly defenseless.

But without a cure for the curse to get us back in the arch-lords' good graces, bringing about any kind of noticeable triumph on the battlefield is our best chance at re-earning their favor and leaving this fringe backwater behind. I might not have the same sense of ownership that Sylas does when it comes to Hearthshire, but I miss the stronger pulse of the Heart's energies, the greater ease with which any act of magic came when we lived so much closer to its light.

And if we regain Hearthshire, perhaps we can find real peace there, at least for a time. After several decades, this constant holding pattern while living in disgrace starts to wear at the nerves.

I can't offer Sylas that gift yet. I may never be able to offer it if we continue to falter in the conflict with the Unseelie. I'm the brains of his cadre, the schemer—I should be able to deliver this one thing to him.

And now we're several steps farther from achieving that goal. Two pack members lost to dust, others badly injured—I can already picture how the news will pain him.

Before I deliver *that* dire admission, I want to conjure some inspiration that'll give at least a little more cause for optimism to go alongside it. A revised strategy for our presence at the border. Some other approach to proving ourselves to the arch-lords. There could be scraps of information in all my notes and records that I haven't quite connected before.

Inside the keep, I head to my office rather than seeking out Sylas. I'll give myself an hour to unearth that inspiration, and then there'll be nothing for it. If he realizes I've delayed reporting to him, he won't be pleased.

I stride around the corner in the upstairs hall—and find our human interloper poised outside my office door. She's a few feet away but eyeing it with obvious interest, her head cocked and a few waves of that absurdly pink hair drifting across her cheek.

At my arrival, Talia startles, drawing back a step with a guilty expression. A few weeks ago, I might have taken that to mean she'd been up to no good. Now, with everything I've seen of and heard from her... I have to admit the most likely reason for her anxiety is that she *does* still feel like an intruder despite the official welcome into the pack she's gotten, as if she has no right to so much as look at the entrance to a room she hasn't been granted access to.

I did come down on her harshly enough to give her a

panic attack the last time I caught her out here, eavesdropping.

The pinch of guilt that comes with the memory dispels any rancor I'd feel now. How can I blame her for being curious? Most of the secrets we fae have kept from her have been to her detriment. If anything, I've got to admire her tenacity.

"Even Sylas couldn't unlock a door simply by staring at it," I say with a playful lilt. "Getting awfully ambitious with those unexpected powers of yours."

The mite blushes, but she squares her shoulders at the same time, no longer half as intimidated by my light-hearted heckling as she used to be. Maybe she shouldn't be, given that we've now discovered her specialness extends to supernatural talents I'd believed only fae could possess. *That* memory, of walking in on Sylas, August, and her in the midst of their little experiment last night, sends a renewed twinge of uneasiness through my chest, but I ignore the sensation.

Sylas has decided she's staying with us, and while that's the case, the more ways she can defend herself, the better off we'll all be. Even if it's yet another inexplicable variable surrounding her that I can't account for in my plans.

"I wasn't trying to break in," she says. "I only stopped for a moment. I just… wondered what you do in there."

She overheard me talking with Ralyn in the office before. I suppose Sylas hasn't spelled out to her what my responsibilities to him and the pack are.

I tip my head toward the other end of the hall. "Our glorious leader has a workspace. Why shouldn't I have one too?"

"August doesn't have a study, or whatever." She pauses. "At least, he's never mentioned it."

I can't help smirking at that. "You could say August's office is that gym downstairs where he's been beating your fighting skills into shape. Preparing to lead the charge should we need to do battle doesn't require much paperwork."

"*You* were talking about some kind of war the other day with… one of the pack members?"

"My area is more logistics than dealing out the blows, although I'll bring out the claws should I need to. Believe me, August would be more than pleased to be out there tackling the Unseelie if Sylas didn't want him here in case the rest of the pack comes under threat."

As I reach for the doorknob, the spell on it keyed to my touch, Talia adjusts her weight on her feet. "Why is *anyone* having to fight the Unseelie? What are they attacking you for… or are the Seelie attacking them?"

"So many questions," I tease, but the truth is that her desire to understand everything she can about this place strikes a chord in me. She's found herself here through no will of her own, been mistreated or outright savaged at nearly every turn, and nevertheless she's determined to learn enough to hold her own. I've met plenty of fae with less drive than that.

I roll the question around in my mind before releasing it. "Do you want to come in?"

Her eyes widen slightly, but with an eager glint that lights up those grass-green irises to something as brilliant as polished jade. It's enough to elevate her from fairly pleasing to dazzling, enough that a different sort of sensation reverberates through me: a twang of desire that settles low in my gut.

For a second, I regret my offer, but it's already out there. I'll have to make the best of it.

I push the door open wide and stalk inside, assuming Talia will follow without further invitation. She eases over the threshold. Her momentary return to timidity subsides as she takes in the desks and the bookshelf, the drawer units built into—or perhaps more accurately, grown from —the wooden walls, and the map of the Mists stretched out above them.

Not surprisingly, it's the last of those that draws her first close inspection. She walks up to it, her hand rising as if to trace the lines of our world with its erratic borders.

She points to the mark like a sunburst in the center of the uneven circle. "That's the Heart of the Mists. This is all Summer realm on the west side? And the Unseelie live on the east… Is it always winter there?"

"Milder or harsher depending on their proximity to the Heart, but yes. I'm told they like it that way. But given our present conflict, I may have been misled."

She glances back at me. "They're trying to steal parts of the Summer realm?"

I nod. "As far as we can tell. They haven't made any actual demands. They simply began storming domains along the edges of the border and attempting to claim those lands for themselves. They took the first couple of domains they tried, but once our arch-lords caught wind of what was going on, they summoned enough of a force to push them back. But it's been a constant clash since then, them vying for more ground and us aiming to hold ours."

"How long has that been going on?"

My gaze drops to my desk, to the stack of leather-bound notebooks at one side, the sheaves of old reports at the other. I'll have the exact date of the first incursion written down somewhere, but it's not something I've spent much time mulling over recently.

"Not quite three decades," I say. "Longer than you've been alive. There've been lulls now and then, but in the past few years they've started to press particularly viciously."

"Has anyone tried *asking* them why?"

I give her a baleful look. "I'm sure our arch-lords have reached out to their Unseelie equivalents to some extent. The content and outcomes of those attempts wouldn't be shared with a fringe-banished pack like us. But there've often been tensions between the two realms—it's in our natures to clash—and I wouldn't be surprised if they haven't been inclined to share much. They'd rather simply take what they want than negotiate."

"Even if it means thirty years of fighting?"

"Thirty years is barely a blink for fae, mite."

Talia makes a face at the indirect reference to her human mortality and turns to face me where I'm standing behind my desk, my arms resting on the top of my chair. "And there are people from this pack out there helping fight the Unseelie. I wouldn't have thought Sylas would want to risk *anyone* when he's said the pack is already a lot smaller than it was before… before you ended up here."

"Ah, well, we're hoping that with a little well-placed

assistance, we might win over the arch-lords again and reverse that whole 'ending up here' situation. That's where I come in." I motion to the mess on the desk. "I work out how we can best contribute with the warriors we can spare —and how many of them we *can* reasonably spare, given the likelihood of other trouble coming our way. I have other contacts stationed in or making the rounds through various other domains, passing on information to help me judge those odds."

I can't deny that it's a delight seeing comprehension dawn on her face as she puts more of the pieces together. "That's how you found out how Aerik's been talking about Oakmeet—those contacts."

I offer a modest shrug. "Any lord worth his while wants to keep tabs on what his brethren are doing. Even among the Seelie, we squabble plenty over territory and whatever else we take a mind to wanting."

Now that she's been in the room for a short while without that bringing any catastrophe down on us, I feel comfortable enough to sink into my chair. Leaning back in it, I rest my hands on the arm rests and give her an appraising once-over. "Do you think you're ready for Aerik's visit? I know you must have… reservations about seeing him and his cadre again."

I'm being polite with my phrasing. What I really mean is she's undoubtedly terrified—a terror that stiffens her posture and tightens her lips the moment I say his name. Spirited as this woman is proving herself to be, I've seen her spiral into panic at even a reminder of her former captors. Confronting them in the flesh won't be easier on her nerves.

"If seeing them in a couple of days means I won't ever have to be around them or worry about them coming for me again, I'll make it through," she says, managing an air of defiance even though her breathing has gone shallow. She swallows audibly and adds, "I'm getting better at coping. I faced the three of you as wolves in the full moon wildness, didn't I?"

She did. I wouldn't have expected that—couldn't have been more startled to emerge from the brutal haze to find her standing with my half-brothers, the flavor of her blood in my mouth. She deserves full credit for that.

As I continue to size her up, a kernel of a possible scheme sparks in the back of my mind and tickles its way to the fore of my thoughts. The moment I've latched onto it, I know it's perfect, but part of me balks.

I'm going to be asking her to endure so much more anguish than I'd imagine she's been preparing herself for. How does she deserve *that*?

But she wants to be a full member of this pack, and I should at least give her the choice. It'll benefit her in the long run too. This is my job, and right now I can do it well, however the proposal might sound to her.

"What if you had to see them for longer than a quick passing-by?" I ask.

Talia frowns. "Why? Do you think they'd insist—"

"No, not at all. But I'm thinking the best way to remove any suspicion from their minds about a human in our midst is for us to show off that human rather than giving any hint of trying to hide you. You're supposed to be August's recently acquired lover. Him insisting on you joining us for the dinner would support that story."

Her arms come up, stopping just shy of hugging herself. The fear that flashes across her face provokes a sharper pang of guilt. But she draws herself up straighter. "I'd have to sit with them through the whole meal?"

"Yes. At the same table. We can tell them you're shy to give you an excuse not to talk or even look at them much. And you'd be with *us*—we could seat you between Sylas and August. You'd have both of them right beside you through the whole thing."

I'm not going to delude myself that she'd take any comfort from my presence, even if my fangs itch in my gums both at the fact that she wouldn't and the fact that she'd take so much reassurance from my brothers'.

That isn't my part to play. Why should it be? I can keep my paws off what isn't mine.

Talia worries at her lower lip, which tugs my attention to that lovely rose-pink mouth of hers. She appears to gather herself. "All right. I'll practice coping with the panic —I think I'll be ready. I'll just focus on August. And if—if I feel like I won't be able to handle it after all, we'll stick to the original plan?"

"Absolutely." And there definitely isn't an ache closing around my heart with the knowledge of just how much I'm asking this gentle soul to handle.

"Okay. Okay." She drags in a breath and gives me a tense smile. "I'm sorry—I should let you get on with your work. I didn't mean to badger you with questions."

"Badger whenever you like," I say breezily, half-hoping despite myself that she'll take me up on the offer right now. Any conversation with her sounds exceedingly more enjoyable than the one I need to have with Sylas.

But the mite slips away, leaving me alone in the office with all the scribblings and reports that, if I'm honest with myself, I already know won't give me any brilliant solutions to offer to my lord. I sit there staring at the piles on my desk for a few minutes longer, and then I heave myself out of my chair with a sigh to go in search of him. No point in putting off the inevitable any longer.

CHAPTER EIGHT

Talia

The basement gym feels larger in the darkness, as if the walls might have fallen back with the thickening of the shadows. I crouch on the moss mat, its surface spongy beneath my feet, and fix my gaze on my hand, which is little more than a silhouette even though it's only inches from my face.

"*Sole-un-straw,*" I murmur at my fingers, attempting to propel some kind of power into my voice. "*Sole-un-straw.*"

Behind me, August shifts his weight with a rustle of his clothes. "A little more emphasis on the last syllable."

I try again. "*Sole-un-STRAW!*"

Nothing sparks. From August's tone when he speaks next, he's swallowing amusement. "Not *quite* that emphatic."

I grimace in his general direction and exhale raggedly. It took me years to get bronze right. Maybe there isn't any point in attempting to master more true names. By the time I get this one, all our battles might be over with—in victory or in failure.

But I said I'd learn—I *want* to learn—so I have to give it a proper shot. Anything that'll make me feel a little more powerful before I have to face Aerik and his cadre again is a good thing.

At least this time I have a teacher instead of going it alone.

"*Sole-un-straw*," I say, with just a little extra force at the end. The air around my hand stays dark.

August steps closer and grazes his fingers over my hair. "That sounded pretty much perfect to me. You'll get there. Have you tried using your emotions like you needed to before?"

I think back to Aerik's fortress, to the cage, but the distress that quivers through me doesn't quite fit my intentions. I'm attempting to produce light, and that terrible room was always already lit up when he and his cadre visited me. If anything, I'd have wished for more darkness during those times to escape their disdainful gazes.

How can I magic up some light if I'm picturing a place that's already bright?

My grimace softening into a frown, I give it a go anyway. If I could have summoned a full-out blaze, cast it right into Aerik's or Cole's face...

The idea stirs a little satisfaction, but no light sparks with my next few recitations. Sighing, I sit back on my ass, resting my hands on the mat. "Didn't you say this is one of the easy spells?"

With a gesture from August I feel more than see, the

globes that normally illuminate the room flicker on. "It's one of the first most fae children learn," he says. "But it still usually takes them weeks or even months to master."

"When they're kids."

"When they're *fae* and it comes naturally to them. Don't forget it's practically a miracle that you can work any magic at all." He hunkers down next to me, cupping his hand over mine. "You're not going to get there in a couple of days—none of us would expect you to."

But the longer it takes before I can pick this up, the more time we'll all sit with the uncertainty of whether I'm just a one-hit-wonder. I press my fingertips into the mat as if I can dig the power I need out of the thick layer of moss.

"We should take a break from that now," August says. "Getting frustrated only makes it harder to connect to your goal. What do you say to burning off some of that frustration with a little more physical training?"

I raise my eyebrows at him. "That's what you'd rather be doing anyway, isn't it?"

His grin is sheepish. "Hey, I've never denied that hand-to-hand combat is my area of expertise. If you think you'd do better practicing the magic side with Sylas or Whitt—"

"No," I say quickly. "You're good at teaching that too." The tattoos etched across his arms and neck—and more beneath his clothes—prove that he's mastered plenty of magic even if it isn't his go-to solution. The last thing I want is to put another responsibility on Sylas's shoulders, and Whitt…

Would that unpredictable man even agree to teach me? Maybe if Sylas ordered him to, but having a reluctant teacher, especially one known for snarky remarks, doesn't sound like much fun.

I push myself to my feet and stretch out my arms and shoulders in preparation for the sparring. My gaze travels to the far wall, picturing the landscape outside, the houses of the village. "When do you think I'll be able to start joining the rest of the pack while you're training them? It'd save you time not having to give me separate lessons for the actual fighting techniques."

"Time spent with you is never a waste, Sweetness," August says, his grin turning cheekier. He tugs on a lock of my hair, his golden eyes so brightly eager that a giddy flutter passes through my chest. "Unless you're getting sick of having so much of my attention."

"No, not at all." The words spill out so quickly that a blush flares in my cheeks, but the way August beams at my enthusiasm takes the edge off my embarrassment. "But if I'm going to be a real part of the pack—if they're going to get used to me and accept me even though I'm human... I thought it might be good for them to see I'm working at this stuff too."

"They will see," August promises. "I just—I want to be sure *they're* ready to train with you. None of them have any recent experience working around humans... They have to know what they're doing well enough to adjust to your differences."

"My weaknesses, you mean." I say it matter-of-factly—I know the fae are naturally stronger. I don't really want any of them coming at me as if I'm one of their own either. Although I guess that's the end goal: fending off the supernatural beings despite my frailer human body.

August winces. "It might turn out you have an advantage or two. I want to be careful about it; that's all."

"I do appreciate that," I say honestly. But I'd still feel better knowing I stand some kind of a chance if Aerik turns on us during his visit. Of course, I can do plenty of work toward that goal with just August.

I roll my neck and raise my hands the way he's shown me, poised to block a strike or deliver one depending on my opponent's moves. "What should we start with?"

August cocks his head, considering. "We've gone over a lot of the strategies for when you have room to punch or kick. Why don't we cover grappling today?"

"Grappling?"

His grin returns. Before I have a chance to react, he's sprung at me. In one swift movement, he knocks me off my feet and tackles me to the floor, his arms braced against me to make sure I don't hit the mat too hard. He's so gentle about it that only the faintest flicker of panic darts through me, extinguished with one glance into his fond eyes.

"When you end up tussling wolf-style on the ground," he says, close enough that his warm breath tickles my face. "You don't have to worry about balance, so your injured foot won't hold you back, but you've got much less room to maneuver. How do you think you could get me to back off, at least long enough so you'd have a chance to get free?"

An actual attacker wouldn't be this polite about the whole thing, body held a respectful distance above my own. I know that from prior experience. Thinking about more likely scenarios if I were knocked to the ground...

"Claw at your eyes?" I suggested. That was a technique we'd already gone over for being grabbed while upright, but my assailant's face might be even easier to reach in a situation like this. "And a knee to the, er, groin if I can manage that."

August laughs. "Right for the tender spots. Good. Another option that's surprisingly effective: if someone goes for *your* face, grab their fingers and twist as hard as you can. Those joints are easy to dislocate, and put your attacker in a lot of pain while making it harder to grab you. A fist to the nose can be awfully distracting too if you can't quite get at their eyes. Try all that out to get a feel for the motions."

I rake my curled fingers in the vicinity of his eyes, aim my knuckles at his nose, and raise my knee—*very* careful to not actually land that particular blow. When August makes a mock swipe at my hair, I catch his index finger and give it a light jerk to the side, evaluating how much more strength I'd have to put into the move to really break something.

Having him looming over me while I'm lying here like this brings an uncomfortable possibility to mind. "What if my attacker pounces on me as a wolf?"

August pauses, a trace of his own discomfort with the idea showing in his expression. "It's not likely anyone who simply wanted to capture or subdue you would use that tactic against a human who can't match them. We can control ourselves in wolf form, of course, but it's harder to moderate a bite or a slash of claws than it is to pull a punch, and a wolf can't pick you up and cart you off... If a fae comes at you like that, they're probably aiming to kill you."

My throat tightens. "Good to know. How do I make sure they *don't*?"

"The eyes and the nose will still be vulnerable areas. And the throat, if you can get in a solid strike." He eases back on his knees, rubbing his jaw. "We'll get you a small dagger to carry with you too—I'll teach you the best spots to hit with that."

I can read what he's not saying from his hesitation. No matter what he teaches me, he doesn't believe I'd survive an attack if a fae came at me in full wolf mode, not unless I got extraordinarily lucky. But then, is that really so surprising? I'm not sure there's any way I could fend off a regular wolf that was determined to savage me, let alone a fae one capable of complex strategy.

"Okay," I say, suppressing a shiver. No need to dwell on that right now. "Let's focus on the human-shaped attacker tactics for now."

His stance relaxes. "Get ready then."

August gives me a few seconds and then lunges at me. He deflects my first jab at his face with a smack of his hand against my forearm, but I manage to bump a fist just below his nose. He pulls back with a nod. "That's a good start. See if you can manage to land that first strike."

We run through that scenario several more times until I'm anticipating his movements well enough to have a decent shot at his eyes. Then we try more intensive setups where I have to start defending myself while he's tackling me.

By the twentieth or so run-through, sweat has broken over my skin and my breath is coming short. After I've lashed out with my hands and knees in the ways we've been practicing, I sink into the mat with a huff of exhalation.

August chuckles. "You're doing great. Go ahead and take a breather."

He leans in to nuzzle my cheek. The affectionate gesture wakes up a whole lot more of my body. The exhilaration of the exercise deepens into a headier sort of thrill, desire tingling low in my belly. Down by where I'm abruptly twice as aware of his leg poised between mine, of his arm braced next to my chest, his wrist brushing the side of my breast.

August inhales with a rough sound, and I can tell before he speaks that he's picked up on my reaction. "Talia," he murmurs, and then, as if drawn by a magnet, lowers his head to press his lips to the side of my neck.

My breath catches, a sharper wave of heat rushing through me. Longing twists through my torso from my sternum down to that now-blazing spot between my legs. August's tongue darts out to lick the sheen of sweat along the crook of my jaw, and an eager whimper tumbles from my mouth.

There's so much I've wanted to do with this man, to discover about how his body can feel against mine, from even before I totally understood what I was longing for. I have a better idea now. The clear indications that he's longing for it just as much only electrify me more.

My hands rise of their own accord to grip his close-cropped hair. August lets out a pleased rumble. He teases his kisses along my jaw with nips that send shivers of giddiness over my skin. My hips lift toward him instinctively, the most sensitive part of me grazing his thigh, and I can't restrain a gasp at the flare of pleasure.

With a groan, August's mouth crashes into mine. I melt into him, lost in his musky scent, floating on the swell of passion that feels as though it might carry me all the way to the bright sky above the keep. Our breath mingles, hot and shaky with need, and all I want in that moment is to give myself over completely, to finally satisfy the ache for bodily connection that's never quite been answered by him or Sylas.

There isn't anything to stop us here and now, is there? No responsibilities August needs to attend to, no breakfast at risk of burning or likely interruptions, no worries that he's somehow betraying his lord by following his desire.

A trace of nervousness flickers through my chest. What if it hurts? What if I can't please him in the same way as the women he's been with before, women who must have known what they were doing at least a little better than I do?

Then August shifts his weight on his arms so he can stroke one hand over my breast, and the fresh wave of heated giddiness, the possessive growl that works from his throat as he kisses me even more deeply, wash my worries away. This man who isn't exactly a man won't let any harm come to me, not while he's in charge, and he's showing nothing but delight in what I have to offer.

August tugs up my shirt so he can caress me skin to skin, his fingertips circling the tip of my breast. They flick over my nipple and massage it to a stiffer peak until I'm whimpering for release.

My body squirms beneath his, not entirely sure how to move. For a moment, he pauses his teasing exploration of my chest to run that hand down the side of my body to my hips, urging my core more solidly against his thigh. My sex pushes against his leg, setting off a flood of bliss. My fingers trail down his back to cling on to the flexing muscles there.

When August pulls away from my mouth, I almost cry out in protest, but the next second his lips have closed around my pebbled nipple. A very different cry escapes me. My back arches up, and he sucks harder with a lap of his tongue that leaves me quivering like a stretched bowstring. I want, I want, I *want*—so much it's almost frightening.

My hand slides up under his shirt, tracing the scorching planes of his back. August drops his head lower, slicking his tongue down the center of my chest toward my stomach—and stops just above my belly button. His whole body stills where he's poised over me.

His voice comes out strained. "We can't—we can't do this."

He may as well have dumped a bucket of icy water over me. My back stiffens against the mat.

"Why?" I ask, the question coming out in the timid whisper I thought I was done with among these men. Is there something wrong with me—did he realize he doesn't actually want to be that intimate with someone so—?

Before the worries can even finish forming in my whirling mind, August looks up to meet my gaze, his expression fraught but the warmth unmistakeable in his golden eyes. "It isn't anything you've done, Talia. By the

Heart, I want to take you in every way. But I can tell—there's a difference in scent—you're fertile right now. Children don't come easily even between a faded fae and a human, but there's still a chance. I don't want to risk it."

The chill recedes, and I relax enough to tug at him so he eases back up alongside my body. The thought of getting pregnant—with *August's* child—sends a weird, wobbly sensation through my stomach. There's a tiny thrill to it, but mostly the awareness of how unprepared I feel for even the idea of motherhood.

"So fae don't have some magical kind of birth control?" A ridiculous image of a glowing condom pops into my head—not that I've ever seen a regular one used other than on a banana in health class.

"No. It's so difficult for us to conceive at all that attempting to prevent that while enjoying the act is considered basically sacrilegious. In defiance of the Heart."

Okay, then. I reconsider his refusal along with the fact that he didn't ask me for my thoughts on kids and can't help asking, "Do you not want children at all?"

August brushes a kiss to my temple with a tenderness that rouses my desire all over again. "Someday, I'm sure. But not—it would bind you completely to this place. To me and the rest of the pack. We've just given you back a small bit of choice over your fate; I'm not going to steal that away."

An emotion that's much more than longing rises up so swiftly that it takes my breath away. It winds around my heart until my whole chest aches with it.

I care about this man so much. Admire him so much.

I might be bound to him already in ways that he can't control. I think—I think this must be what love feels like.

My pulse hiccups with the thought. Would I be willing to leave August now even if staying here put my whole life in danger? Even if what I'd face by his side would be so much more torment than otherwise? I'm really not sure. A significant portion of me already balks at the idea of being apart from him even for a day.

I don't know what to do with all that feeling. Saying it aloud, making it that much more real, unnerves me even more. So I swallow the ache down and trail my fingers over his dark auburn hair. *He* still looks unsettled, even though I haven't argued with his decision.

"Some humans end up wanting to stay, to have kids and—" I hesitate, realizing I don't actually know whether fae ever take humans officially as mates. August's mother obviously had a relationship with his father, but that father is also Sylas's and Whitt's, by two other women. Only Sylas was the child of his soul-twined mate.

"It's generally not quite a choice." August sinks down on his back beside me, our shoulders touching. "If they want to, it's because the glamours have convinced them to —or the fae who keep them never bother to check whether they do or not. That's not the fate I'd want for you."

That was why he hesitated to get involved with me at all. He told me weeks ago that he'd seen how badly things often turn out for humans who became lovers of the fae. The fervour in his voice stirs a suspicion I can't shake—the best reason I can think of that would explain how vehemently he's defended me from the moment I came into this keep.

"Is that how it was for your mother?"

He's silent for long enough that I start to worry I've overstepped somehow, pried more than I should. "I'm sorry," I say. "I—"

August takes my hand and tucks it close to his cheek. "No, don't apologize. It's a good question. I'm just deciding the best way to answer. It's not something I've ever really talked about. Even Sylas doesn't know all the details."

The ache around my heart sharpens at the anguish already bleeding into his voice. "You don't have to talk to me about it either."

"Maybe I should, though, so you can understand. I just—I'm so ashamed I didn't stop it…"

He closes his eyes and then opens them again, gazing up at the ceiling. "When I was not quite old enough to be considered out of childhood, my mother made some comment or minor mistake with her chores—no one ever bothered to tell me what it was, it mattered so little. But my father was in a particularly dark mood, and he decided he'd had enough of her hanging around the palace. I was with her when he stormed in with three of his warriors. He ordered me to sit and watch while they—while they transformed into wolves and tore her to pieces."

My stomach lurches. August's hand has clenched tight around mine, and I squeeze it back with all the sympathy I have in me. "That's horrible. Why would he be so cruel—and not just to her but you too?"

August shrugs, his shoulders as rigid as his jaw. "He

didn't go out of his way to torment the human staff, but he didn't see their lives as meaning much more than a mouse's either. He never had any real affection for her. She was a convenient vessel to satisfy his carnal urges with when he no longer had his mate, and then she was a convenient vessel for him to act out violent urges as well.

"As for me—he thought it would help harden me up. That I needed to understand how expendable every life, but particularly mortal lives, could be. He believed that the best way to rule was to have all your subjects aware that at any moment, if they made the slightest misstep, you wouldn't hesitate to dispatch them."

I shudder. "That's awful."

"And I just sat there…"

"If you were just a kid, against the four of them—you *couldn't* have stopped it."

"I don't know. I did jump up when they first attacked her, and my father enchanted the chair to hold me in place. But maybe if I'd tried harder, I could have broken that spell, I could have done *something*…" His voice has gone so ragged it's painful to hear. "I was frightened of him, of going against him, of what he'd do to *me* if I provoked too much of his anger."

I let go of his hand to wrap my arm right across his chest, nestling my head against his shoulder. "That sounds totally understandable to me. *He* was the one who gave the orders—you can't blame anyone but him."

August lets out a breath that's equally ragged. "He treated me well more often than not, you know. Even though I wasn't his true-blooded son. He paid for good tutors and had me sit with him at official meals like a real part of the family—in his good moods sometimes he'd come around and invite me on a hunt or coach me in my training himself. It'd be easier to look back and simply hate him if he'd been equally horrible all the time. Sometimes I think I have so much trouble restraining my anger because I used up all my self-control not aiming it at him the whole time I lived under his rule."

"*I've* only seen your anger come out when it was deserved." I push myself up on my elbow so I can look him in the eyes. The love I thought I felt a few minutes ago has somehow grown even larger with his confession. "And I know you'd never treat me *anything* like he treated your mother. I'm not the tiniest bit afraid that you'd ever hurt me. So you shouldn't be afraid of that either. Okay?"

August stares at me for a long moment, anguish still plain on his face but retreating behind a light that looks more like hope. All at once, he lets out a strangled sound and rolls toward me, hugging me to him as his lips seek out mine.

Somehow these kisses are more tender but also more urgent than the ones before, as if he'll die if he can't show me just how much he cherishes me. The flames of passion that had dwindled during our talk blaze up. I kiss him back as hard as I can, over and over, until every part of my body is clanging with need.

"August," I murmur against his cheek in a brief space for breath. "I—I don't want to be getting pregnant right now anyway—but there are other things we could do that would feel almost as good without taking that chance, aren't there? Together?" Not just me finding my pleasure alone, as he and Sylas have guided me through before. I want to do this *with* him.

"Yes," he mutters around a shaky exhalation. "By the Heart, yes."

He eases his hand down my body and cups it between my legs, where he taught me to touch myself to such blissful effect. Feeling his fingers there now, rocking against me, lights me up twice as bright. A moan slips from my lips.

It's not enough, though. This can't be all about me. I reach for the bulge pressed against my hip through his pants, reveling at the shockingly hard length of it as my hand curls around it.

August groans and kisses me fiercely. As our mouths collide again and again, I buck with the motion of his fingers and stroke him as skillfully as I can manage. When I'm starting to tremble, August tugs my workout pants down and tucks his fingers right inside my panties. They skim over the slickness of my arousal in a caress that has us both groaning.

"You feel so good," August says, his voice low but so heated I practically catch fire. "Both touching you and the way you touch me. You're perfect, Talia."

The words send a giddy quiver through my chest. I pull myself tighter against him, hooking one of my legs over his instinctively.

As our bodies lock together, August plunges a finger right inside me. Oh, God. I hadn't thought anything could feel better than when I got myself off this way, but knowing it's him, that he's filling me the way he wishes he could with the erection I'm still fondling, sends me spiraling up on a wave of sensation like nothing I've ever experienced.

My hips sway to meet his careful thrusts, matching him and urging him on until he adds another finger, faster. His breath spills hot and shaky against my lips. His thumb swivels over the sensitive nub just above my opening.

It's so much, so good. Before I can catch myself, try to bring him all the way with me, I've already careened over the edge, my vision whiting out with the surge of bliss. My hand clamps around his hardness, and August presses into my touch as he nuzzles me in my return to earth.

My limbs sag, wanting to slump boneless into the mat, but the ecstasy he just brought me to only makes me more determined to offer the same to him. I fumble with the waist of his pants and work my hand beneath the fabric until I encounter the surprisingly soft skin that encompasses his rigid length.

"Talia," August whispers as I close my fingers around him. I'm afraid he'll try to tell me I don't need to, even stop me, but after a moment's pause he tugs me to him instead. His mouth scorches mine with kiss after fervid kiss as his hips drive into my grasp. Moisture beads on the tip of his erection and slides with my fingers down his length.

I don't know what I'm doing, not really, but my unpracticed attempt has him twitching against my palm, grunting when I stroke him firmly from base to the thickness of the head. There's no mistaking how genuine his responses are. With the simple grip of my hand, I'm conjuring the deepest of pleasure in this powerful man.

The man I love.

Maybe I'm not ready to say those words out loud, but I can show how much I adore him with connection between our bodies. Following his reactions, I clutch him harder, jerk my hand faster. His chest heaves, his muscles clench, and then he's shuddering against me with a spurt of wet heat over my wrist.

"Oh, my Sweetness," he says, gathering me in his arms. He hugs me so close I feel I could meld right into him.

Joy blooms through the ache of love around my heart, shining and fluttery. It comes with a tingle that sends a sudden jolt of certainty through me.

I draw back just enough to speak clearly and lift my hand between our chests. "*Sole-un-straw.*"

The tingle dances over my tongue, and a spark shimmers between my fingers. Only a faint one, and only for a second before it snuffs out, but clear enough that August goes still, watching. Then he beams at me, his expression so full of pride and adoration that any fear inside over the depth of my feelings for him is swept away.

CHAPTER NINE

Talia

I t's strange seeing people other than August working in the kitchen. A few of the pack members have taken over the space, bustling to and fro with their final preparations for tonight's dinner, because it wouldn't do for someone from Sylas's cadre to be cooking for or serving the guests. Even with my stomach twisted into a tight little ball at the thought of those guests, the savory scents of roasted boar and seared root vegetables make my mouth water.

August comes up behind me, tucking his hand around my waist and pressing a kiss to the top of my head. He peers past me into the room, his muscles flexing as if he's holding himself back from striding in there and taking over. His scent, like fresh-baked cookies with a musky undertone, is delectable in itself.

I let myself lean into his chest, taking comfort in that smell and his arm wrapped around me. Since getting so intimate in the gym the other day, I've found it even easier to relax around him, knowing how much of my affection he returns, how much he treasures the connection between us. If anyone can get me through this confrontation, it's him.

August hugs me tighter as if to shield me from what he's about to say. "We've gotten word from a sentry that Aerik's people should be here in the next ten minutes." He glances down at me, a worry line forming on his brow. "Are you sure you want to go through with this? We can still—"

I set my hand over his. "I'm sure. It's better to do it now when I'm ready for it than some surprise attack if they decide that's justified."

I will get through this dinner without falling apart. I just *will*.

Turning in August's embrace, I tip my head back and hold out my arms. "Am I ready for my role?"

He eases back to look me over with unusually pensive consideration. He and Sylas worked together to weave the subtle glamours that should make my eyes appear more brown than green and that adjust the planes of my nose and cheeks, as well as the one disguising the misshapen ridge of bone on the top of my right foot.

They adjusted the notes of my natural scent as well, although how much Aerik will remember of that after leaving me in filth most of the time I'm not sure. As long as I'm not openly bleeding, he won't be able to smell the aspect of me that mattered most to him.

Whitt confirmed that he couldn't sense the magic clinging to me unless he came within a few inches of those spots, which Sylas has no intention of letting Aerik or his men do. They'd be insulting their hosts if they nosed in on a woman August has claimed like that. By all expectations, I should be safe from discovery.

I'm dressed much more for the part of a lover tonight. This afternoon, August brought me a calf-length dress of the same thin, flowy material most of the pack members wear, narrow enough in the neckline and with enough of a sleeve to completely cover the scars on my shoulder. It's a sky blue that looks striking with my deep pink hair, and the fabric must be made out of some substance we don't have in the human world, because I've never felt anything so soft and airy. I spent the first several minutes after I put it on swiveling this way and that just to feel it lick across my calves.

I wish the men of the keep were the only ones who'd get to appreciate it on me, the way I can tell August is from the heat that's tinted his golden eyes. I feel more like a lady in it compared to my usual jeans and T-shirts, but also more exposed, even though technically the dress covers nearly as much skin. My legs are bare beneath it all the way to my feet, where I'm not even wearing my brace. It was easier to shape the illusion closely over just the limb rather than adding the wooden frame to the mix. We're planning on avoiding having me do any real walking in front of our guests.

"You're spectacular," August says, his eyes glowing as they meet mine again. "Any man, fae or otherwise, would be honored to have you at his side. And the glamours appear to be holding steady."

His flattery sends a flush from my collarbone up my

neck. August strokes a finger along that path as if charting it, and the heat of it deepens. He's dressed more formally too—in a finely woven V-neck tunic like those Sylas often wears and fitted slacks that show off the muscles beneath. The outfit definitely suits him.

I grope for my words. "Good. Then everything's in place. Except me. I'm supposed to wait in the dining room, right?"

August nods and walks with me down the hall. "I'll have to be with Sylas and Whitt greeting the visitors as they come in, but we'll be back here quickly. I'll make sure I come into the room before they do, so you'll have me with you the whole time. If you start to get overwhelmed, just give my hand a few quick squeezes in a row, and I'll find a way to get you out of there."

"Right." I inhale and exhale, willing myself to become as steady as the magic disguising me.

The dining room is decked out more elegantly than I'm used to. A sapphire-blue cloth drapes the table, embroidered with silver thread that shimmers as if it's made of stardust. The usual amber globes that dangle from branch-like fixtures on the ceiling are tinted a matching moonlight shade. Silver plates, goblets, and utensils with intricate floral patterning already sit at each seat we expect to be filled.

Behind me, August chuckles at my awed hesitation. "It was even fancier for Tristan's visit. After what Sylas pulled out for an arch-lord's cousin, I have trouble imagining how we'd top it for an actual arch-lord. Aerik doesn't command half as much respect."

I slip into the room, walking slowly to offset my limp. "But you all still want to impress him."

"Not so much impress as show him the respect *he* believes he's due so he can believe we have no bones to pick with him." August's smile turns grim. "He can keep believing that until we have a chance to cut the bunch of them down like the curs they've proven themselves to be."

Whitt sweeps by, tapping August's shoulder as he does. "They're arriving. Time to look sharp, Auggie." He spares me a quick glance and a lip-twitch of acknowledgment.

"We'll get through this," August tells me, and steps away.

I haven't even heard the sound of the front door, but my pulse stutters. As I circle the table, my heart keeps on beating at a nervous tempo.

The plan is that I'll wait here standing by the corner of the table, next to my chair. Aerik and his cadre will get to see me standing solidly and then taking my seat without my having to do much actual walking before their eyes.

Of course, that depends on me keeping my head through my growing panic. I thought I was prepared for this moment, but now that it's actually happening, my skin has turned clammy and the knot of my stomach is churning with queasiness.

Voices carry from the other end of the keep. The front door thuds shut. My spine goes rigid, and I have to take several breaths to relax it.

Why did I agree to do this? Why did I let myself believe I could handle seeing my former tormenters again? What if they take one look at me and see right through the magical disguise?

I close my eyes, willing down my bubbling panic. Sylas wouldn't have agreed to this plan if he wasn't sure he could keep me safe. As long as I don't collapse in a trembling mess at the sight of them, it'll all go smoothly.

If only that didn't feel like such a tall order right now.

The voices travel down the hall, getting louder with their approach. I try to concentrate on Sylas's measured baritone and Whitt's jaunty interjections, but I can't tune out the flat rasp that belongs to the man I now know as Aerik, the one who watched his cadre torment me with constant disdain, or the sharply nasal tenor of the equally sharp-limbed one with the blue-white hair.

Cole. Just the thought of his name turns my stomach all over again.

A bead of sweat trickles down the back of my neck. My fingers curl around the edge of the table until I force them to release it. August promised he'd come in before them. I'll see August—I can focus on him and pretend the others aren't even here.

Yeah, right.

It's actually Sylas who strides into the dining room first, looking downright regal in his embroidered vest over a stiff-collared dress shirt. He stops just inside the doorway to conduct the others in, the confidence in his bearing reinforcing my own. Then August hustles past him. He flashes me a smile and comes around to stand beside me just as the visitors enter.

I can't stop my gaze from jerking straight to Aerik's face, topped with that daffodil yellow hair. A hint of a sneer is already playing with his lips, and it hardens at the sight of me.

My heart thumps even faster, a wave of dizziness surging through me from gut to forehead. Everything blanks from my mind but the memory of him looming over me while I crouched, aching and grimy, in his horrible cage—

Strong fingers close around my hand where it's fisted beneath the level of the table, holding me tight. August's arm rests against mine from wrist to shoulder. My thoughts tilt and scramble, and I grip his hand just as tightly, yanking my awareness back to the present. Back to the men who've sworn to defend me, who I know would enjoy nothing more than to rip the throats from the villains they've admitted into their home if they could get away with that retribution now.

Sylas's voice reaches my ears as if from much farther away than the other side of the room. "This is Talia, a recent... acquisition of August's. He's rather attached to her at the moment. I assure you she won't disturb our conversation."

My former captors never asked my name or used it, so as far as we know they can't connect it to the girl they stole. I stare at August's muscular chest in its fine shirt for long enough to get a grip on my nerves and then dare another glance toward our enemies.

All three of them have entered now. Cole and the portly fae man who always did the cutting and collecting when they took my blood flank their lord. I manage to keep all of my attention on Aerik, to avoid the even more vicious jolts of terror I suspect the others' faces would provoke. His nose has wrinkled, his sneer still in place, as if I'm a dog turd someone has left on the dining table.

For all his apparent disgust, I catch no sign of recognition in his expression. With a shiver of relief, I force my mouth into the briefest of smiles and then look to August again.

My lover slings his arm around my shoulders just for a second, with a broad grin I know is as forced as my smile was. "She's a shy thing. Wouldn't speak to anyone but me for the first week. I don't like to leave her alone for very long."

Aerik lets out a huff as if this kind of deviance is only to be expected from a cadre like Sylas's and moves at the other lord's gesture to his spot across from August. "I'm sure we'll find her of no significance."

From the corner of my eye, I think I see Cole's piercing gaze trained on me. Thankfully, Sylas directs him around the table to sit beside August, where he can't study me very easily. He still gets in a snarky remark: "Doing her hair up like that won't make her any closer to fae."

August gives a laugh that only sounds a little stiff, still gripping my hand. "Oh, I wasn't the one who chose this color. She had her own ideas of fashion well before I found her."

The fae avoid lying as much as they can—Sylas explained to me that it damages their connection to the Heart of the Mists, which gives them their magical power —but August is purposefully making it sound as if I'd already dyed my hair when he met me without saying anything untrue. If Aerik believes August really did grab me from the human world just a little while ago, he'll be even less inclined to connect me to his missing blood dispenser.

August tugs me gently to sit down as he does, and it's only as I sink into my chair that I recognize how wobbly my legs are, how rigidly I've been tensing the muscles in my calves to keep myself from visibly swaying. The second my ass hits the wooden seat, those muscles turn to jelly. I stare down at my blurred reflection in the silver plate, wondering how I'm going to manage to swallow any of the lovely food the pack has prepared.

Even as I think that, the kitchen helpers glide into the room carrying platters with the first course of appetizers. Aerik views them with only slightly less disdain than he showed me, and some small part of me that isn't frozen with fear bristles on behalf of Sylas's—of *my*—pack-kin.

"I haven't scented any other humans around," he says to Sylas. "I heard you preferred to keep your domain clear of them."

"Not due to any aversion," Sylas says. "My other cadre-chosen, Kellan, has a particular animosity toward them that it's been best for all of us not to provoke."

"But you're changing your tune for the young one? Where *is* Kellan?"

Another treacherous subject the men of the keep will need to tread lightly around. Sylas can't easily explain why he had to end Kellan's life. I stare at the fried dumpling and fresh-picked salad that August sets to my plate rather than risk watching the conversation play out. My heart is pounding so loudly it's a wonder it isn't deafening me.

Sylas spears a few sprigs of greens with casual ease. "He departed a few weeks ago by my decision. He had many concerns about how we've been handling our affairs and wanted to investigate other options. I don't expect to see him back any time soon, and on such a return, if the girl is still with us, at least she'll have had a chance to settle in."

If we count his death as a metaphorical departure, it's all true. Kellan did have concerns; if he did somehow return, I'm quite settled in now. The smoothness with which the fae lord disarms his enemy's curiosity soothes my nerves enough that I bring the dumpling to my mouth. If I don't eat at all, they'll wonder why.

The other lord appears to buy the story, but he isn't done prodding. "She's still the only human you're keeping here, then?"

At least he doesn't seem to think *I'm* the specific human he's searching for.

Sylas nods. "For the time being. I promised August a trial run after he made his case. If that goes well, we could consider bringing over a few servants to help with the running of the keep."

Cutter grunts. "It does seem as though your pack is stretched thin enough, sparse as it's become."

Sylas doesn't let the mild jab affect his poise—or even acknowledge the words. He keeps his gaze on Aerik. "Are you looking for more humans to add to your own staff?" he asks in a slightly wry tone that implies he finds it odd that the other lord is so fixated on his dealings with mortals.

Aerik's shrug doesn't look remotely casual. "I have no issue with quantity of manpower," he says, which feels to me like another subtle sneer at Oakmeet's pack. But then, to my immense relief, he drops the subject of humankind completely, as if he's already convinced he was barking up the wrong tree by suspecting Sylas.

"The Unseelie bastards have stooped to new lows, haven't they?" he says in a tone that suggests the outcome of those battles affect him very little anyway, and the men all fall into a discussion of the ongoing conflict.

I want to pay attention to the threads of that discussion, to better understand the tensions Whitt sketched out for me, but it's hard to keep my thoughts in order. Every minute or two, one of my former captives snaps out a comment, makes some gesture, or rasps out a laugh that yanks me back weeks ago to the bone-white room where they set up my cage. The spurts of panic hit without warning, blanking my mind and clamping around my lungs, over and over.

So I look at my plate or at August, still gripping his fingers without any complaint from him even though he wouldn't normally eat left-handed, and pick at my dinner bit by bit. By the time the kitchen staff takes away our plates in preparation for dessert, not even the honeyed notes drifting through the air can soothe my frayed spirits. I'm so exhausted I'd lay my head down on the table if these guests weren't here.

August brushes a reassuring caress over my knuckles. All I had to do to claim victory was survive this meal, and I've just about managed that. To achieve anything else was probably asking too much of my shaken nerves, stripped raw all over again in the presence of these monstrous men.

Aerik leans his elbows onto the table and considers Sylas with a more penetrating expression than before. "I've appreciated the food and the talk, but let's not beat around the bush any longer. You must have had some particular reason for inviting me to enjoy your pack's hospitality."

My pulse hiccups, but Sylas offers a reserved smile, as if he expected that question. Well, he probably did.

"Tensions have been high throughout the summer lands in recent weeks," he says. "I'd rather mend bridges than burn them down. It was important to me to show you that we hold no animosity over past... oversights."

Snubbing them when distributing the tonic, he means, as Aerik can obviously tell from the distasteful curling of his lips. "We had to make our choices as we saw fit," he says, as if they couldn't have stolen a tiny bit more of my blood each full moon to produce a slightly larger batch of tonic. "And I did have to consider how any favoritism toward your domain might look to the arch-lords, after they consigned you to this distant spot."

Whitt leans back in his chair. "After all these years, I'd imagine the arch-lords have seen they have no reason for concern when it comes to our loyalties."

Cole lets out a harsh guffaw that raises the hairs on the back of my neck. "Arch-Lord Ambrose and Lord Tristan don't exactly speak highly of the bunch of you still."

Aerik's gaze flicks to Whitt for only a moment before returning to Sylas. "When you make a misstep that grave, it's a wonder anyone bothers to remember you're here at all, unless they happened to take a mind to wipe the realm of your pack completely."

He speaks with an odd lightness, as if he means the cruel words as some kind of joke, but I can taste the acid underneath. His disparaging tone takes me from cringing to bristling on Sylas's behalf.

"If the arch-lords felt our crimes were severe enough to warrant that level of sanction, I'm sure they would have carried it out in the beginning," Sylas says evenly, with just a hint of a growl as the softest of warnings.

"No doubt it's convenient to view circumstances as you do when one is out to scrape up whatever favor they can from crumbs dropped for them," Whitt adds.

Aerik glowers at him for longer than his previous glance before cutting his gaze to Sylas once more. "I trust no one in your pack resents our making use of what resources we had at our disposal to raise our standing. It would have been ridiculous not to share that boon and reap the benefits."

The boon of my blood. "Reap the benefits," he says—how much prestige did these monsters gain from *using* me, tormenting me, while Sylas's pack languishes so far from their real home? And this jerk thinks that's something to be proud of, something he *earned*, when it was nothing more than a bit of horrible luck that he stumbled on me?

Real anger stirs somewhere in between the tightness in my chest and the knot of my stomach. The thought that any part of me helped these awful fae win glory makes me want to vomit—and to punch that smug expression right off Aerik's face.

He's nowhere near the leader Sylas is. If anyone should have been banished, it's him and his people. But no, here they are expecting some kind of red carpet to be rolled out for them while they mock my pack's hardships.

My free hand balls into a fist where it's resting by my thigh. I bite my tongue. There's nothing I could say even if I dared to open my mouth that wouldn't make things worse for the men I care about.

"Certainly I wouldn't have expected anything different

of you," Sylas says to Aerik in an inscrutable voice, and then the kitchen workers arrive with glistening pastries topped with dollops of peach-colored cream, and the men all have something other than talking to do with their mouths for a little while.

As I pick at the dessert, my anger simmers inside me, gaining vigor by the second. By the time I've choked down as much as I'm capable of, delicious as the treat is, the furious energy thrums through me so strongly that I almost believe I could walk without a single hitch the whole length of the keep if I needed to.

And maybe I will need to, because the careful way Aerik is eyeing the kitchen helpers suggests his suspicions aren't entirely put to rest. He licks the last of the cream off his fork and says offhandedly, "You built this place from the ground up, didn't you? I wouldn't mind having a look around."

Not even asking for a tour, just expecting Sylas to leap to offer one. More indignation sparks inside me—and then Cole leans his knobby elbows on the table, his slim form tipping unavoidably into my view. His mouth curves into the vicious smirk that always came before he'd ram me into the cage floor.

"Yes, let's see what you've made of *your* crumbs," he says, and thumps one elbow on the table hard enough to rattle his plate.

Like the rattle of the bars as he'd clamber into the cage after me. The smack of his elbow as he'd pin me down. The sound reverberates through my back with an ache between my ribs as if he's bruised me there all over again, and a silent wail of horror snuffs out the power of my anger in an instant.

A tremor runs through my limbs before I can stiffen against it. August's hand clamps firmly around mine. I drag air through thinly parted lips, grappling desperately to fill my terror-clenched lungs without outright hyperventilating so the visitors won't notice my reaction, but the dinner has worn me out so much, the control I've been holding onto has unraveled—

August stands, offering a respectful bob of his head to the guests even as he scoops me out of my chair. My body settles against his solid chest, his warmth washes over me, and his scent floods my lungs. With my face tipped out of sight against his shirt, I gulp just enough breath to keep from suffocating.

"I'll join you for that tour once I've tucked this one away where she belongs," he says, putting on a cheerful front. "It'll be easier without her underfoot."

He must give a convincing enough performance, because the only response I hear is Aerik's chuckle followed by, "Yes, and I'm sure you'll want her well-rested for later."

"Don't be long," Sylas tells him with an impression of exasperation, as if to say this is all youthful folly, and then August is marching out of the room with me in his arms, leaving my former tormenters behind.

He ducks his head close to mine the moment we reach the hall, and the tension gripping my muscles starts to unwind. I'm abruptly aware of my bare feet dangling beyond his arm—they'd have been in plain view of all three of those monstrous fae men—but maybe that's a good thing. They didn't spring up with accusations of theft, so the glamour must have fooled them. August provided them with one more reason to believe I'm just a regular, random human girl.

We're halfway up the stairs before he risks speaking, in the quietest of undertones. "You were amazing, Sweetness. I can't imagine how hard that must have been. Be proud of yourself."

Unexpected tears prickle my eyes, driven by a swell of affection that chokes me up. I curl my fingers into his shirt and nestle even more closely into his embrace, utterly protected. But at the same time, the jeering words of our enemies flit back through my head. The anger they stoked flares again, spreading with a steady burning through my abdomen.

No one will ever use me like Aerik did again. I get to decide who I'm a "boon" to from here on. And I'll do everything in my power to see that Sylas, his cadre, and the rest of the pack return to the home they deserve with their reputations restored so well the fae like Aerik won't dare insult them ever again.

CHAPTER TEN

Sylas

As I walk into the kitchen, I'm struck again by the shift in energy between August and our shared lover. There's a synchronicity to their stances, their expressions, as they exchange smiles and remarks over the lunch preparations. When I first noticed it a few days ago, I caught a whiff of their mingled scents as well, undeniably intertwined. Something happened between them that day other than training and sparring.

They pause in their conversation at the sight of me, and an image swims up from my deadened eye: hands tangled in each other's hair, mouths locked passionately together. It's a mere flicker, but my wolf stirs in an instant.

I come to a stop and smile at them, hoping I've summoned enough genuine warmth to hide the itching of my fangs in my gums behind that smile. I meant to launch into my purpose here immediately, but it takes me a moment to yank back the wolfish possessiveness lunging up inside me.

I will not claim her. She'll slip away from me completely if I go back on my word and start picking fights over who's gotten how close to her when.

But skies above, the urge is nearly overwhelming—to sweep her up now like August did at the dinner table yesterday and carry her straight to my bedroom so I can demonstrate every intimate pleasure *I* could inspire in her.

There'll be time for that later. And I'm more lord than animal, thank the Heart. I clamp down on the defiant howl within and turn to the business at hand.

"You wanted to be included on more of our strategy discussions," I say to August. "I'd like to consult with you on a few matters. But if you're already occupied, it can wait until after we eat." It's early for lunch yet, but my cadre-chosen does sometimes get rather ambitious in his meal-planning.

August's eyes gleam eagerly at the opportunity, even without any idea what I'm looking for from him. He really has been craving this kind of recognition far beyond what I realized, hasn't he? Maybe it was Kellan's presence, that constant thorn in all our sides, that stopped me from noticing before how capable the youngest member of my cadre has become. All I can do to make up for that oversight is honor his loyalty and determination in every way I can now.

He brushes flour from his hands and glances at the loaf he was shaping. "It's nothing too elaborate. Just needed to get started now to leave time for the baking.

Give me five minutes, and we can talk while the oven's doing the rest of the work."

"Excellent. I'll be waiting in my study." I tip my head in greeting to Talia, about to turn on my heel and leave, but she slides off her stool onto her feet with a flash of her own determination.

"Can I—would it be all right if I came too?" She hesitates, her shoulders drawing up in a hint of the defensive pose I saw so often during her early days here and wish I never needed to see again. She's still a little uncertain of her place here, still nervous about asking for anything beyond what she's already been offered. "I mean, I'd like to know about what's going on. Even if there's nothing I can do to help, it's scarier not knowing what problems you're dealing with."

How could I deny the request framed like that, even if I wanted to? I'd rather she didn't need to worry about the conflicts we face beyond this domain, that she could simply roam the village and relax among the pack, but she's seen too much of our world to believe in the appearance of peace whole-heartedly. If being included in our discussions will give her more of that peace, then I won't stand in her way.

I give her a deeper nod of acknowledgment. "Fair enough. I have no plans I intended to keep secret from you. I'll only ask that you hold any questions until we've worked out what we need to."

"Of course. I won't get in the way." She beams at me, the fearfulness melting away, and it's hard to imagine *not* wanting her at my side, wherever I am and whatever I happen to be doing. I can't resist giving her cheek a brief caress before I depart.

This little scrap of a human woman has worked her way so much deeper into my regard than I would have thought possible a month ago.

As I head to my study, I knock on Whitt's bedroom door to let him know the meeting I already warned him about is proceeding. He came to me around dawn with a report from one of our few warriors remaining at the border, and as far as I can tell he promptly went back to bed—if he'd even gone to bed before that in the first place.

Despite the late hours he's kept, he saunters into the study just a few steps ahead of August and Talia, his eyes perhaps a little weary but his stance alert enough. Knowing he's mainly there to witness my conversation with August and offer his opinions if need be, he drops into the armchair in the corner and steeples his hands over his chest. His eyebrows arch at Talia's entrance, but he makes no remark.

August comes to a stop right in front of my desk, his head high and his shoulders rigid as if he's doing his best to give every impression of dedication to whatever purpose I might have for him. Talia lingers near the doorway, her head swiveling as she takes in the room she's never seen before. After a moment, she relaxes enough to lean against a nearby cabinet, her slim arms folding loosely over her chest.

I focus on August. "You know our contributions in the conflict with the Unseelie have... not been proceeding well."

He grimaces. "Yes. It's looked like Ralyn is recovering

from his injuries fairly quickly, at least. This morning he even joined part of the training exercises I organized for the pack—moving at his own pace, of course."

"I've been glad to see him pulling through. He's given a lot for the pack—he deserves a chance to get some rest." I inhale deeply. "But between that and the losses we suffered in that last battle, we have barely enough people in our already small squadron to have an impact in the conflict. There's no point in leaving *any* of our people in harm's way if what they're doing won't help us win back our home."

August rubs his mouth, clearly thinking over the problem. His gaze is uncertain but steady when he meets my eyes again. "Where do you think I can help? Did you just want to know if I had any ideas for proving our worth against the Unseelie?"

"I'm definitely open to ideas in general," I say. "But in particular, since you've been working with our pack-kin here, I wondered if you've noticed any of them showing particular aptitude and enthusiasm for combat that they might not have previously—if we might have enough between them and our existing sentries and other warriors to send a few more to the border."

I don't ask with a great deal of hope. Plenty of fae aren't cut out for battle, especially the sort of sustained conflict we've faced with the Unseelie. We'd already sent every capable pack member Whitt and I felt we could spare. But attitudes and proficiencies can shift and develop —and it's possible August has seen things from his differing perspective that we haven't.

August rocks on his heels with a more pensive

expression than he usually shows, but the eagerness in his eyes hasn't faded. "I could answer that more easily with a better understanding of what our warriors are facing out there. What sort of tactics have the Unseelie been using lately?"

A reasonable question. I glance at Whitt, who's been getting most of the direct reports. He leans forward in the chair, his expression intent but his voice in its typical dry drawl.

"The stinking ravens like to keep us on our toes. From what I've gathered, there's been no clear pattern to when they strike. The forces assembled along the border might have to defend the lands there every night for a week or spend a month or two simply waiting, on guard. Anytime they *have* let down their guard, thinking maybe the bastards had given up, they've regretted it. The bastards have tried both swarming and picking us off one-by-one at a distance, flying overhead to avoid the patrols completely, taking hostages of vulnerable pack members…" His lips curl with distaste. "There's little they won't stoop to. As best as anyone can determine, they'll do whatever they can, whatever looks like a reasonable approach in the moment."

"Then we'd want people with a good amount of experience, who can adapt quickly to changing offenses." August frowns. "I don't think any of the pack members not already part of our defensive force would be prepared for that. We'd be sending them to be slaughtered. I'm sorry."

The regret in his voice, as if he's letting me down somehow by saying what he knows to be true, sends a sharp twinge through my chest. "I appreciate your candor, August. Then, if you were making the decision… Would you withdraw the few warriors we're already contributing?"

"They haven't been able to count on any of the other squadrons cooperating with them," Whitt adds, his tone darkening. "With their numbers diminished, they're easy pickings for a slaughter themselves."

Talia has been so quiet I'd stopped paying her any mind, but now she lets out a disgruntled sound that's almost a wolf-worthy growl. "The other fae would really leave your people to *die* rather than work with them so they can fight off the Unseelie together?"

Her vehemence provokes a tight smile. "Our politics are… complex. But at the core of it, the other packs don't wish to be tainted by our misfortune—to risk any victories they win being dismissed because of our warriors' involvement or any losses to be blamed on their associating with us. Until we can prove on our own that we have just as much honor as we always did, any action we're a part of will be seen as suspect."

"It isn't fair," she mutters, but softly enough that it's obvious she realizes fairness hardly comes into it. She's experienced plenty of evidence that many of the fae value their own interests far above anyone else's wellbeing.

While the rest of us have talked, August has been mulling over my last question. He shifts his weight from one foot to the other. Then he exhales in a rush. "There is someone you can send who might be able to turn our part in the battle into something good."

Whitt's eyebrows shoot up higher than before. I can

barely prevent my own surprise from showing. "Who?" I ask.

"Me." August holds up his hand before I can even think about responding. "I know you haven't wanted me to leave the domain—but if it's that or give up on this chance completely, I think we have to take the risk. Kellan isn't around anymore to stir up trouble. Aerik seems to have backed off. We don't face any immediate threats, other than the threat of losing the chance to win back the respect we deserve."

My instinctive reaction is to deny him, but I can't refute the points he's made. I bite back the arguments I'd like to make and motion to him. "I'm not convinced yet, but you can continue making your case."

"I have plenty of training—you know I had the best possible teachers—and I've made it through enough skirmishes over the years to know my way around a battle. I'll just go out and speak with our squadron myself, plan out the best approach when I can see exactly what we're dealing with—or tell them to come back with me if that seems like the best we can do. If there's an attack while I'm out there, so much the better. Maybe I'll win us a few allies by showing that our cadre is willing to join the fight."

He might be able to spin the situation around from a total disaster into something closer to victory. And as long as no one launches a full-out assault on us while August is gone, we should manage without him.

The older brother in me doesn't want to say yes, but the lord knows I should. I catch Whitt's gaze again, and while he doesn't look any more pleased than I feel, he inclines his head in the slightest of nods.

I return my gaze to August, forcing myself to see the man, the proven warrior and cadre-chosen, not the boy whose progress I guided so many decades ago.

He can handle this. The fact that he kept his cool around Aerik despite all the animosity he holds over Talia's torment is all the proof I could ask for of the control he's gained over his fiery temper. And a little fire might be just what they need out there on the endless front.

"All right," I say. "You'll take a short time longer to increase the defensive skills of the rest of the pack, and when Ralyn is ready to return, you'll join him. I'll give you ten days, but if you feel you may as well bring them all back, of course you may return sooner. I want you back with us well before the full moon."

August gives me a brief bow, looking both proud and relieved that I saw him as worthy, and I hope with all my heart that I'm not making a mistake.

CHAPTER ELEVEN

Talia

I n theory, I've already said my goodbyes. Then August turns before stepping onto the conjured carriage that's going to whisk him away to the battlefield and gives the assembled pack one last wave. I can't help dashing to him as quickly as my foot allows to wrap him in one last hug.

Everyone knows we're lovers. It shouldn't look strange. But still my face heats a little at the public show of affection even as his arms come around me in return.

"It's only ten days," he murmurs close by my ear. "I promise I'll come back to you, and in one piece, Sweetness."

I know it's not that long. I waited almost ten *years* to get out of Aerik's prison—ten days is nothing.

At the same time, it feels like forever. I've seen this man every day since our lives collided. I'll have no idea what's happening to him out there at the border where other members of the pack have already died at Unseelie hands.

I understand why he's doing this, though, and if he finds a way to impress the arch-lords, it'll be more than worth it. The last thing I want is to make him feel guilty about going. So I force myself to step back with the best smile I can summon for him. "I'll hold you to that promise," I say, relieved that my voice doesn't waver.

As he gets into the floating wooden carriage next to the man named Ralyn, Sylas comes up behind me with a steadying hand at the small of my back. I exhale, letting him take just a little of my weight. He must be worried for August too, and he's managed not to show anything but confidence in his younger half-brother. If both he and Whitt think this was a reasonable plan, August can't be in *too* much danger, right?

I'm not sure I actually want the answer to that question.

The carriage glides off, and the pack members drift toward their houses, other than the couple of fae who are taking over cooking duty in the keep while our usual chef is away. My relationship with Sylas *isn't* public knowledge, so he ruffles my hair where otherwise he might have offered a kiss. His voice comes out low and gentle. "Do you have enough to occupy yourself with, Talia?"

I don't, but I know I need to find something to do, or the anxious questions will take over my brain. "I'll get my exercises in—August gave me some moves that I can practice on my own." Maybe imagining I'm kicking our enemies' butts will take me from feeling helpless to formidable.

Working out in the basement gym does distract me for a little while, but when I sink down on the mat, sweaty and panting, after putting myself through the paces, memories of my interlude with August here rise up in my head. A lump forms in my throat. I shove myself to my feet and limp to my bedroom to change out of my damp clothes.

The sun shines warmly through my bedroom window. I bask in its glow for a minute before reminding myself that I can go right out into it for as long as I'd like now. I still feel a little shy intruding on the pack's village, even though everyone has been uninterested at worst and friendly at best, but Harper did encourage me to drop in on her whenever I wanted to. Maybe her cheerful curiosity will give me a longer diversion.

Harper pointed her family's house out to me when I last spent time with the larger pack. Though they all look very similar in their immense twisted-off tree-trunk forms, the smaller details make them easy to distinguish. She shares her home with her parents and one set of grandparents, and true to her name, there's clearly a musical inclination in the family. Someone has carved an elegant image of a flute embraced by a fiddle on the door.

Her father is crouched outside the house tending to the garden. As I approach, I'm embarrassed to realize I've forgotten his name. "Hi," I say tentatively. "Is—is Harper around?"

He bobs his head with a soft smile and motions me toward the house. "Deep in her work, but I expect she won't mind you interrupting."

Because she doesn't mind interruptions in general or because she wouldn't want to turn me away? I haven't quite figured out what Harper finds so fascinating about me, other than from what I've gathered she's never gotten to talk to any human at all before. I guess that's a reasonable explanation right there. Maybe it's also that I look like a newcomer who's about the same age, even though I know her youthful appearance is deceptive. She might be just out of adolescence, but in fae terms that means she's still several decades old.

I venture into the house cautiously, met with an odd hissing sound from behind the door to my left and a disgruntled muttering. I hesitate and then knock. "Harper? It's Talia."

"Oh! Come in."

I nudge open the door to find her grappling with a sheet of satiny lavender-purple fabric draped across a table. She gives it one last tug, snatches up her scissors, and shoots me a bright smile. "Sorry. Sometimes spider-weave just won't behave."

A wooden dummy stands on the other side of the table, a few pieces of fabric already pinned around it to form a bodice and the start of a waistline. It's a more elaborate construction than the simple dress Harper's wearing right now—the kind most of our pack-kin appear to prefer. Maybe there's a celebration of some type approaching.

"You're making a special outfit?" I ask. "What's the occasion?"

"Oh, no occasion." She pops the head of a pin into her

mouth, snips a chunk of fabric off—that hissing sound I heard from outside was the scissors, I realize—and fixes it against the dummy with a shallow fold. "This is just… practice. I figure the more proof I have of my skills—and the more I can improve them—the better off I'll be when I really want to use them. I've already got a pretty good collection."

She waves me farther into the room so I can see the rack by the far wall. The rack holds at least a dozen dresses in every color from bright ruby red to deep earthy brown, all in a formal evening-gown style with long skirts and fitted bodices adorned with sashes, gauzy panels, or delicate flowers and leaves sculpted out of fabric. Stepping closer, I run my fingers over a vine that looks almost like an actual plant winding around a skirt and find it silky soft.

"These are amazing," I say.

Harper sets down her scissors and breezes over to join me. "You should try one on! I don't get many willing models around here—the only ones who think dressing up is fun would probably end up spilling wine all over them. Here, I think this would fit you."

After giving me a glance up and down, she plucks a gown with panels of alternating grass- and spruce-green that make it look like a landscape of distant treetops, caught here and there by golden glints of embroidery like sunlight. "And it'll go perfectly with your eyes."

My heart stutters at the thought of putting on something this beautiful—and valuable. But it's not as if I have anything around that I could spill on it, and Harper only looks eager at the prospect.

"Are you sure?" I ask anyway.

She gives me a little shove toward a curtained area in the corner that can serve as a changing room. "Go on, go on. It'll help me see if there are any little flaws I missed. It's hard to tell for sure on the dummy or myself."

Well, if it'll *help* her ... I bundle the delicate fabric in my arms and duck behind the curtain. I'm so careful ensuring I don't rip it that it takes me a few minutes to ease the dress onto me and adjust it against my chest and hips, especially wary of the fluttery sleeves against the ridges of scar on my shoulder. The glamour stops Harper from seeing them, but it won't stop the fabric from catching on them.

"Are you planning on making a business selling these or something like that?" I ask as I settle the fabric against my skin.

"That's the gist of it." Harper pauses, and for a moment there's nothing but the hiss of her shears through the spider-weave. Her next words tumble out in a rush. "I don't want to sound ungrateful to Sylas and everything he's done for us here. I know how hard he's worked to keep the pack safe and give us a good home in spite of everything. But—I never got to live anywhere other than here. And here is kind of... boring. None of the other packs want to visit us. Heart knows they never invite *us* to visit them. I want to see more, do more."

The longing in her voice resonates with something deep inside me. My position in the world of the fae is too precarious right now for me to want any more excitement than I've already got, but I remember the pangs I felt as a kid before, thinking of all the incredible cities and landscapes I hadn't gotten a chance to experience, pasting printed-out photographs into my travel scrapbook as if having a concrete representation of those dreams would help make them real.

At that time, I was way too young to travel on my own anyway. I might have made those dreams come true if Aerik hadn't torn my life apart. Harper has been stuck in the same place for ages longer than I've even been alive. I don't think Sylas would blame her for her restlessness.

"And the dresses will help you get out more?" I say.

"I hope so. The ladies of the more prestigious domains —they're all having balls and banquets and things like that. Wanting to show off that they've got clothes nicer than anyone else. At least, that's what I've heard from how the older folks tell it." She gives a little laugh. "If they're right, then I figure the offer of a dress could be my ticket into getting a warm welcome other places, if it's spectacular enough."

"They are pretty spectacular." I edge out from behind the curtain, still checking that I'm not about to snag one of the panels anywhere. The fabric shifts with my steps like the softest of breaths rippling over my limbs. I can't tell how it looks on me, but when I glance up at Harper, she has her hands clasped over her chest, her eyes shining.

"It's even better than I pictured. Oh, so lovely. Hmm, but I think a couple of the bits here need a few extra stitches."

She dives in with needle and gold thread at the ready, sewing a portion by my waist. I keep my arms raised so I don't bump her head. "It feels nice—wearing it," I say. "I wouldn't have expected clothes this pretty to be comfortable."

"That's the best thing about spider-weave. It holds its shape so well but stays so soft at the same time." She leans back, cocks her head, and pinches another spot closer to the back. "Almost perfect. Do you think…" She glances up at me. "Do you think humans would like this sort of thing too? I mean, most of them. I'm glad that you do."

I don't have much sense of adult fashion tastes, especially in the current decade, but I can't tell her that. What I do know: "I'm sure there'd be some people who'd *adore* dresses like these just because they're so unique. We don't have spider-weave or whatever back in my world. And anyone would be able to tell these are gorgeous."

"Oh, good." She giggles again, a hint of a blush coloring her cheeks. "I've thought about forgetting all the snobby Seelie who live closer to the Heart and going in the other direction, to see the mortal world… But I know a lot less about how to impress them. Maybe, if you ever take a trip back there, I could come with you and you could teach me a few things?"

She says that last bit so bashfully that any lingering shyness in me falls away. That's why she's been so friendly —because she's honestly intrigued by all the things I've experienced that she hasn't, as mundane as my former home feels to me compared to this place.

The thought of returning, of having to navigate everything that's changed alone, unnerved me before. It might not be so bad with an enthusiastic tourist along for the ride, turning it into an adventure.

"I don't know when I'd be going there or if I will at all," I say. "But if I do, I don't see why I couldn't show you around. The place I lived wasn't all that amazing, though."

"It'll all be new to me! And very different from here. But, no pressure, no pressure. You just got here. You should enjoy yourself. I'm sure it's much more interesting when you're not used to it."

Interesting is definitely a word for it. My mouth twitches with a bittersweet smile—and then I freeze as an unexpected but familiar figure ambles through the doorway.

Whitt's stride is casual, but I've been around him enough by now to see the tension in his jaw. He halts at the sight of me, blinking with a slight widening of his eyes that makes my cheeks heat. That startled—and maybe even appreciative?—expression vanishes a second later, his gaze snapping down not to check out any provocative part of me but to my feet, just barely visible beneath the hem of the dress.

Is he worried that Harper might have noticed the brace beneath the illusion while she's been standing so close? Should *I* have been worried about it? She hasn't touched my feet or ankles. At Whitt's entrance, she's leapt to her feet and dipped her head.

Before I can panic over the possibility that I've blown my cover, Whitt flicks his hand toward us. "Talia, we have need of you in the keep. Finish up whatever exactly you're doing here, and come speak to Sylas as soon as you're able."

He strides out as quickly as he arrived. Harper stares

after him and then glances at me. "What do you think that was about?"

"I don't know." That's true, but I have more of an inkling of the various possibilities than she would, since she has no idea that I'm anything more than August's lover. I grip the skirt of the dress. "I guess I'd better get this off and go find out as quickly as possible."

When I emerge from behind the curtain in my regular clothes and offer the green gown to Harper, she shakes her head. "You should keep it," she says with a sly little smile. "I've got plenty. Surprise August with it. I'll think of it as a gift to both of you."

My face outright burns then. I stumble over my words. "Are you sure? It's so lovely—I wouldn't have asked—"

"You didn't ask. I probably owe you at this point for all my questions. Go on, before our lord or his cadre come to round you up again."

I hustle back to the keep with the dress clutched to my chest. The thought of welcoming August home in this treasure of a gown is giddying enough to push back my apprehension until I've tucked the garment into my bedroom wardrobe and am heading down the hall to Sylas's study. What could have made not just him but also Whitt concerned enough to call me back from my visit with Harper?

Probably hearing my footsteps approaching, Sylas opens the study door before I've quite reached it and ushers me in. Whitt is standing to one side of the desk, his posture unusually tense. Knowing that whatever this is about is enough to rattle even his careless air, my skin prickles with twice as much uneasiness as before.

"What's going on?" I ask, glancing between them as Sylas crouches down by my legs. He inspects my foot and its brace like Whitt did.

"I agree, the glamour appears to be holding well," the fae lord says to Whitt, and moves to his chair, focusing his attention on me. "Whitt has made a small but disconcerting observation this afternoon."

The other man's mouth twists. "That's one way of putting it. I've personally been conducting an extra patrol since Aerik's visit. It hasn't turned up anything before, but today I caught a whiff of magic along the southeast border of our domain that had a distinctive scent to it. I'd be willing to place a sizeable bet that Cole cast whatever spell left that trace—and within the past day."

A shiver I can't suppress runs through my body. "He's still sneaking around here?"

"It appears that way," Sylas says. "It could be that Aerik simply sent him to quickly check up on us once the dust of the visit had settled, and since there wouldn't have been anything shocking for him to notice then either, that's the last we'll hear of them."

Whitt makes an even sourer face. "Or he could be making a continuing habit out of it."

"None of which matters as long as he sees nothing to raise the suspicions we hoped we'd put to rest." Sylas offers me a small, tight smile. "They *can't* know you're their missing prisoner."

I rub my arms, chilled despite the summer warmth in the air. "But you expected them to leave us alone after that dinner. They mustn't be convinced after all." *What is it going to take for those monsters to give me some peace?*

"Unfortunately, that's the only conclusion I can draw, although we can still hope it was only a brief and temporary re-flaring of their interest."

"I'll increase my patrols even more," Whitt says. "And tell the sentries to attack any unknown fae in our grounds matching Aerik or his cadre-chosen's descriptions without hesitation. If we can catch them intruding, we'll have the high ground."

"Or perhaps you'll find that there are no further intrusions." Sylas sighs. "But if there are—it's poor timing with August having just left."

A jolt I didn't anticipate rattles my nerves. "You're not going to call him back, are you? He'll have only just gotten to the border!"

Sylas's eyebrows rise at my vehemence. "Wouldn't *you* rather he was here? If Aerik escalated to an actual attack, we'd do everything possible to defend you, but our pack against his... As much as I hate to admit it, it'd be a difficult victory even with August alongside us."

Which means if I asked Sylas to call him back... I could simply be summoning him to be slaughtered.

Flashes of memory waver up—the searing pain in my shoulder, the branches seeming to wheel over my head, my brother's choked off wail. My voice tearing up my throat with a sob. *Mom! Dad! Help!* The thudding of their footsteps, snarls and rustling of monstrous furry bodies spinning around—

My stomach lurches. I hug myself, shoving those fragments of the past away with all the force I can manage.

Focusing on the solid wood of the floor beneath my feet. On my arms pressed tight to my chest. The images recede, but the nausea that came with them remains.

"Talia?" Sylas says gently.

I shake myself and look up at him. The resolve that prompted my protest only grips me harder, for so many reasons, at least some of which I can find it in me to say out loud. "No. He went to oversee the war against the Unseelie for good reasons. I—I don't want you jeopardizing that over some small risk to me. It *is* a small risk, right? That Aerik would launch some kind of assault on your domain out of the blue?"

I've already inadvertently contributed to the villain's increase in prestige. No way am I going to be the reason Sylas and his pack lose their chance at restoring their proper place in their society.

Whitt eyes me, a bemused expression playing across his face. I can't tell how much of that emotion is aimed at me.

"I'd say it's quite small," he says. "But not impossible. Less so if I manage to restrain myself from doing what I'd like to if I get my claws into that mangy prick from his cadre." He bares his teeth in the fiercest of grins.

Sylas rests his elbows on his desk. "You're the one most threatened by his interest in our pack, Talia. I swore you'd be safe here. Regardless of the circumstances, if you'd feel more secure—"

I shake my head emphatically, ignoring the ache of my heart at the knowledge that I'm giving up the chance to see August again so much sooner than planned—and safe from the Unseelie's weapons and talons. The only reason

I'd really need him here is if I'd be dragging him into even more danger.

"I'll be fine. Do whatever you'd do if I wasn't here and you didn't have to take me into account. That's what would make me happiest."

And if I come to regret that decision later, the only one who'll be suffering for it is me.

CHAPTER TWELVE

Talia

I thought playing August's video games might be soothing, giving me the impression of him being here with me, but really it's the opposite. How can I get absorbed in the game when something as simple as the digitized music makes me sharply aware of the empty space beside me? He would have given me a teasing nudge with his elbow, bantered about who was winning, and then nuzzled my hair in consolation any time he took the lead.

After just a few minutes, I turn off the game and flop down on the recreation room sofa. I've already watched a movie. After dinner, Sylas and Whitt went off to discuss some new plans with their sentries. They haven't found any more signs of Cole lurking around in the past few days, but he could just have gotten sneakier. I'm glad they're not taking any chances, even though my stomach knots at the idea of what might happen to the pack if Aerik figures out who I am after all.

An amused baritone carries from the doorway. "Becoming a lay-about, are you?"

I push myself upright to see Sylas standing on the threshold, his expression weary but a small smile curving his lips. He's tired from staying on top of all the steps he's taking to protect *me*. The knots in my stomach pull tighter.

"If there's something I can do to help the pack—"

He makes a dismissive sound and walks over to give my head a fond caress. "You do plenty already. Ivy's told me how much you're contributing in the kitchen. I'll remind you again that you're not a servant here."

"I know. I kind of got to like it after helping August so much. And it keeps me busy." But working in the kitchen doesn't feel like enough, not when I know Ivy and the fae man who pitches in too could handle the meals on their own easily enough. "You've been working on training some of the pack like August was. He was thinking I might be able to join in with them soon."

Sylas shakes his head. "If Aerik is still keeping an eye on our activities here, having my cadre-chosen's supposed lover learning combat skills would raise concerns even if he has no idea who you really are." When I start to make a face, he taps my chin. "But I was thinking we shouldn't neglect another area of your training. How have you been coming along with your magic?"

"I think I'm getting better at quickly bringing up the emotions I need to command bronze." I've been practicing several times a day, and picturing enemies charging at

August on the battlefield stirs up my fear and anger in an instant. "I just keep making that spoon twist into different shapes, since I don't think August would appreciate me going through all the bronze equipment in the kitchen."

Sylas chuckles. "No, I expect not. He was attempting to teach you the true word for light as well, wasn't he?"

"Yes." I look down at my hands, remembering the brief spark I conjured while filled with joy and love in August's arms. While he's been gone, I haven't been able to summon *that* feeling again, not strongly enough to bring another flash of light with it. Every happy memory of him is tainted by the knowledge that he's beyond my reach where those enemies could stop him from ever returning. "I haven't had as much success with that. But he did say it usually takes even fae a while to learn new true names, especially when they're just getting started learning magic."

"It does." Sylas lowers himself onto the sofa next to me, stretching out his impressive legs. "Why don't you give it a try now, and I'll see if I notice any areas you could work on?"

Doubt fills my gut, but he asked me to try, so I will. He's the most adept magic user out of the men of the keep, from what August has said. Maybe there is something I've missed that would make the process come easier to me, without needing quite so much, er, inspiration.

I sound out the syllables in my mind before rolling them off my tongue with all the energy I can channel into them. "*Sole-un-straw.*"

I can tell even as I speak that no magic is reverberating through me. I pause to gather myself and think back to the one moment it worked before, to the afterglow of pleasure shimmering through my body and the adoration in August's voice as I brought him to his own peak. Will we get to be that close again—or closer?

A flutter runs through my chest, but it's joined by a pang of worry. "*Sole-un-straw*," I say, willing the word to call light out of the air, but nothing flickers around my splayed fingers.

Sylas rubs his jaw, studying my hands and then my face. "You've gotten the sound of it right to my ears. I'm surprised you're not seeing at least a small effect. I assume you're drawing on your emotions as works when it comes to bronze. Have you managed to produce any light at all during previous practice, or is this how it typically goes?"

Heat creeps up my neck. "Well, I—I managed to conjure a tiny bit once. It seems like the light might rely on different emotions from bronze."

"Interesting. What sort of emotions?"

"Well, happier ones. I don't know if it would *have* to be exactly like this, but—" The heat tickles across my face. "When I managed it before, it was after August and I had —we'd been making out." That would be the right word for it, wouldn't it? Even if what we did together felt nearly as intimate as I imagine actual sex would.

An answering heat glows in Sylas's unscarred eye. For a second, I'm afraid he'll let some hint of aggression slip out at the thought of August and me together, but to my relief, all that crosses his face is a broader, knowing smile. He rests his arm against the back of the sofa and strokes his thumb down the side of my cheek, taking the skin there from hot to searing. "I see. And you've tried drawing on *those* memories to no effect?"

"It hasn't worked so far. I mean, it's hard to know when any time I think about him, I can't help remembering where he's gone and getting anxious…" I duck my head. "And obviously it won't be very useful if I can only speak to light if I've just been intimate with someone."

"No, but you've progressed in how you can work with bronze, getting better at calling on the power you need even if you're not in literal danger. I'd imagine you could do the same with light." Sylas pauses. "Would you be open to seeing if you could stir up some of that power with me?"

His voice has dropped so low it sends an eager quiver right through my body. I glance up again, meeting his intense, mismatched gaze, recalling so vividly how good his capable hands felt traveling over my curves, his mouth branding my skin. The breathless answer slips up my throat without a second's hesitation. "Yes."

The fae lord gives an approving rumble and traces his fingers along my jaw to draw me into a kiss.

The way his mouth meets mine is every bit as thrilling as when I'm with August, but at the same time as different as the two men's dispositions. Sylas's kiss is all controlled power, capturing my lips with the giddying impression that he's moderating the full force of his passion, keeping fiercer impulses that might crush or bruise in check. As my mouth moves against his, parting with the commanding probe of his tongue, he makes a hungry sound that's almost a growl. But I don't for one instant fear he'd mark me in any form I haven't made clear I want.

His other arm comes around me, tucking me closer— trailing over my hip to shift my legs across his lap, then circling my knee. I never thought of my lower legs as being all that sensitive, but they wake up with a tingling rush that shoots straight between my thighs.

My fingers curl into his shirt, grazing the taut muscles of his chest. Sylas pulls back just an inch, his breath still mingling with mine.

"You deserve better than a hasty tryst on a worn sofa," he says roughly. "Come with me?"

The moment I nod, he scoops me up in his arms, much like August did taking me from our dinner with Aerik what feels like years ago. I lean against Sylas's even brawnier frame, his smoky, earthy smell filling my lungs, and am struck by the urge to melt right into him, as if I could.

The lights in the first-floor hall have dimmed. The kitchen staff have returned to their homes for the night. As Sylas strides on up the staircase to the bedrooms, a warm ache forms in my chest amid the heat blazing between our bodies.

This man has offered so much to and given so much for me. He's valued my safety above the security of his pack; he's awarded me with every ounce of freedom he can at the expense of recovering the honor he lost so unfairly and has spent decades striving to recover. I've seen how deeply he cares about the pack—I know it hasn't been easy for him. I know he'd fight to the death for any of us.

I told him I didn't belong to him, but nevertheless he's made me his own.

I don't know how I could possibly deserve all the compassion and generosity he's shown me, but I can't help reveling in it, beaming from the inside out with the awareness of it. And burning at the same time to give just as much back to him, as if there's any way I could.

How can I feel this much for him when I only just recognized that I'd fallen in love with August? But the pang can't be denied. It isn't just desire coursing through my veins but that bone-deep affection that brings a nervous shiver with it.

I told *both* of them I didn't belong to them, and yet my heart already does. Where will that leave me in the long run? For all they care about and desire *me*, I'm still only a human girl, and a damaged one at that.

How long can this last? How much could they possibly feel for me beyond the affection they've already shown?

What a horrible irony it would be if it isn't Aerik's torments but my saviors' kindness that breaks me in the end.

As Sylas shoulders past his bedroom door, I try to push all those worries aside. He lays me out on the bed, both his eyes gleaming with their disparate lights, and so much wanting swells between my legs and behind my sternum that I practically yank him to me, raising my head to meet his kiss. For a short while, between his dizzying kisses and the scorching caresses that remove my blouse, I lose myself in the bliss of the moment just as I did before.

But when Sylas's mouth closes over my nipple, stoking the pleasure that's already inflamed me, my head arches back into the pillow with a gasp. The fresh woodsy scent of the linens hits my nose more sharply than before—and I remember cuddling next to him here, sheltering from my nightmares.

I tangle my fingers in the thick waves of his hair, but I can't shake the conflicting emotions—the sense of careening toward uncertainty contrasting with the comfort I took from him here before, the fire of my hunger for him and the ache of my love for him, and the fear that wrenches through it all.

I could lose myself with this man, and then what will become of me?

I must tense up without realizing it. Sylas stops, raising his head to gaze down into my eyes. My mouth is tender, my breath shaky with need, but he sees more than that, maybe with that ghostly eye of his.

"Is it too much?" he asks. "You only ever have to say the word, Talia. I'll never force anything on you."

Out of nowhere, a lump rises in my throat. How can I feel like crying just like that? "I know," I say, fighting to keep the rasp from my voice. "I *want* this. I just—It doesn't make sense."

He hums. "It's my experience that 'making sense' is rarely a quality that can be ascribed to one's feelings." Lowering his head, he brushes a softer kiss to my cheek. "If you're willing to try to tell me about it, I'll listen."

How can I deny him when he asks so sweetly? The words clamor to spill out, but there's too much—I can't say it all. How ridiculous would he think I am if I start making proclamations of love out of the blue when he clearly isn't offering any kind of forever?

I focus on the parts that don't make me want to outright squirm away inside my skin. "It's—it's a little scary, feeling like I depend on you so much. You keep me safe and take care of me, and I also want so much more with you than I've ever had with anyone." I find myself staring at the dark scruff along his jaw instead of meeting his gaze, worried that I might inadvertently offend him with the admission. "It's not your fault. So much of this is new to me."

"Little scrap." Sylas says the old nickname with nothing but affection, tipping my chin up. "I told you before that your situation here doesn't depend on what you do with me in this bed—or anywhere else in the keep, for that matter. That will hold true as long as you're with us. I won't inflict my desire on you like another sort of cage. You spent too long in the last one as it is. Heart knows I want you, but only as long as it truly is making you happy, in every way."

I inhale shakily, relief smoothing some if not all of the jitters from my nerves. "Okay. It will. I'm not sure—I just have to get my head on straight."

He nods. "Take all the time you need. You decide how far we go, what you're ready for. And if there are things you're never ready for…" His mouth curves into an uncharacteristically teasing grin. "I can't say I won't feel at all disappointed, but I'll be glad you drew whatever lines you needed to."

And just like that, I love him even more. I smile

through the ache that's squeezing my heart. "Thank you. For everything."

"Believe me, I enjoy every bit of it—protecting you… and the rest." He gives me another tender kiss on the lips and sinks down on his side next to me, apparently having decided it's time to put a stop to our intimate activities today. As much as the hungry part of me still throbs low in my belly, I can't say he's wrong to hold off for now. My emotions are still too churned up.

I can't imagine asking him if he thinks he could ever love me or if it would even be possible for us to have any sort of official relationship. But I can't help wondering about the one woman he did have a bond with already. His soul-twined mate, fated for him, their entire spirits aligned. Just how far out of my reach is that kind of connection?

"What did it feel like, having a soul-twined mate?" I ask tentatively. "How do fae—the true-blooded ones who get one—know when they've met theirs?"

Sylas slides his muscular arm around my waist, collecting me closer against him. It takes a while before he answers.

"The connection doesn't solidify until you've both reached adulthood," he says. "You might meet them before then and never know. But the first time you see each other once the bond is fully formed—the first time your eyes meet or your bodies touch—it hits you like a lightning bolt straight down the center of you. Like being suddenly burned through by a blast of energy, and that hollow is immediately filled with impressions and thoughts that belong to your mate. From that moment on, you're not only yourself anymore. They're part of you, and you're part of them."

Having a stranger blast their way right into the core of your being sounds more unsettling than romantic to me, but I guess it wouldn't be so horrifying to someone who hadn't spent years stripped of every bit of privacy and freedom except what went on inside their head. Still… "It must be hard to adjust."

"Well, we anticipate it. All true-blooded fae know it's bound to happen eventually—and earlier is better so you can build your lives together."

"So, you just always know what the other person is thinking and feeling? There's no separation at all?"

"There is some. Unless you're purposefully sending thoughts to one another, what you pick up is fairly vague sensations and flashes of ideas. And you can tune even those out to some extent if you need to."

Sylas pauses, his thumb stroking up and down my naked side, but the rest of him has gone so still that the caress doesn't reignite my desire. When he speaks again, it's in a tone so measured I can tell he's being extremely careful with his words.

"That's one of the reasons I can't fault the arch-lords for placing some of the responsibility—and the penalty— for my mate's actions on me. I *should* have picked up on the fact that she was planning something that treasonous before she had a chance to try to carry it out, but we'd been arguing for some time and she acted in a way she knew would wound me in retaliation for my refusal to support her. It did wound me, enough that I withdrew so that I didn't need to have any more knowledge of it than

I'd already been forced into. But that meant I missed other knowledge too."

I frown, tucking my arm over Sylas's with a sudden flare of protectiveness—as if *I* could defend *him* from any threat. "What did she do?"

Another long silence. I'm about to take back the question when Sylas drags in a breath. "It's often expected that fae lords will dally outside their marriages. When children are so rare in a true-blooded coupling, it's the typical way of ensuring any heirs will have close blood to choose for their cadre, although we can draw from outside the family if we need to."

"That's how you have Whitt and August." I restrain a shudder at the memory of the story August told me about their shared father.

"Well, not exactly. Our father has more than his share of faults, but he was utterly devoted to my mother while he had her. Whitt came about before they found each other, and August... after she left. I subscribed to the same attitude, especially because true-blooded *ladies* are expected to remain completely faithful to their mates, since any outside pregnancy could obstruct the one that should be most wanted. When I married Isleen, I swore to her that she would have all my affections as I would have hers."

That matches the just and devoted lord I've gotten to know. But he still hasn't answered my question. "That seems fair," I venture.

"Yes, we agreed it was. She knew how seriously I took my vow and how much our loyalty to each other meant to me as a foundation to hold our relationship steady even when we disagreed. And then she shattered it all in the course of an hour." His arm tenses against me. "She sought out another lover. I felt her pleasure at their coupling—and her *glee* at knowing I would feel it—and I was afraid if I let in any more of it, if I caught wind of who she'd broken her vows with, I'd ruin our partnership even more than she had." A ragged laugh escapes him. "Of course, in the grand scheme of things, it turned out I couldn't possibly cause more ruin than she'd planned."

My arm tightens around his. To think of someone hurting this noble, passionate man so horribly—not just anyone, but the person in all the world who should have had his back the *most*—makes me want to punch someone. Preferably her, if she wasn't long dead.

Then a jolt of cold shoots through my chest. My voice quavers. "Is that why—you were upset that I'd done something with August, before—"

"Hey, no, *you* didn't do anything wrong." Sylas hugs me close and kisses my temple. "I had no claim over you. You'd made no promises to me. Sharing doesn't come naturally to me, but under these circumstances, I'm satisfied with the choice I've made."

"Okay." I nestle my head against his shoulder. "Why would you *want* to stay with her after all the arguing and then her betraying you like that? Is it impossible to leave a soul-twined mate?"

"No. It happens from time to time. But the bond withers with distance and often it turns into something rotten. I told you my mother left my father. He was devoted to her but cruel in so many other ways that after a time she couldn't bear to continue supporting him. So she left to join another pack in a distant domain—and that's when he became truly cold-hearted."

"She left you behind?"

"Oh, I was fully grown by then. I could take care of myself. And she needed to take care of herself, so I can't blame her for going. But after seeing how it broke something in my father... I was afraid of what would happen to Isleen if I abandoned her." He grimaces. "In essence, I took the coward's way, and it's for that my pack and I were punished."

With everything I've heard about soul-twined mates so far, I'm starting to think it's a good thing that "faded" fae like Whitt and August won't have to deal with one. I press a kiss of my own to Sylas's shoulder. "I don't think you were a coward. It was an awful position to be in. Anyone would have had trouble finding the right thing to do."

"But most wouldn't have had so many who paid the price with them. I appreciate your affirmation, though."

Fae live such a long time. If looks are anything to go by, I don't think Sylas is even middle-aged yet. I'd have put him in his late thirties at most. "Could you ever take another mate? Not soul-twined, I know, but a regular one, like you said Whitt or August could? Or are fae only allowed to marry once?"

"There are no limitations in that regard," Sylas says. "Of course, I haven't exactly been in a hurry to fill the position that was vacated so violently."

Why would he? As I soak in his warmth and his powerfully gentle embrace, it occurs to me that in a weird way I should be grateful to Isleen. If she hadn't been a traitor, she might still be around, and they'd still be living in Hearthshire. Sylas would never have come looking for Aerik's cure and found me. And if she hadn't been so vindictive in her resentment, he might have already offered his affections to another fae woman, and there'd have been none left for a damaged human girl like me.

What I get might not come close to the wrenching bond he shared with her, but I'll take every bit of it without complaint.

CHAPTER THIRTEEN

Talia

E verything is dark. Metal groans.

The cage—the cage is collapsing in on me.

A bar slams across my belly. I can barely see it, only feel the battering of metal against my body, the pain welling in my gut.

I flail and twist, trying to shield myself, but my arms are leaden, my back glued to the hard ground—

And then I wake up. It's still dark, the room lit with the faintest of starlight from beyond the window, but I've got a mattress beneath me rather than the rigid floor of my former cage. Only soft sheets are wrapped around me—tangled after my nightmare-induced squirming, damp from my sweat.

Everything is safe. Everything is as it should be... except a prickling pain that sears through my belly again.

I tense beneath the covers. The sharp ache digs in for a

moment and then fades to a duller twinge, but it doesn't go away.

My hand slips down under the covers to touch my stomach, but the skin there is smooth and uninjured. The pain radiates from somewhere deeper inside.

Is it just my anxiety? Has so much of the horror seeped out of my nightmare into reality that I can't completely shake it?

I shift my weight on the bed and freeze, my posture stiffening even more than before. The linens beneath me aren't just sweat-damp. They're *wet*, with a slickness that creeps across my legs. And even as I notice that, a sour scent reaches my nose, far too close to the raw, sickly scent of the animal carcasses that I've watched August carve into roasts.

Panic bubbles at the base of my throat. I shove myself toward the headboard and jerk my hand at the lantern orb fixed to the wall over my reading chair. After a few desperate waves, the amber light washes the room. I wrench back the sheets, and a strangled cry escapes my throat.

Blood. There's blood streaked all across my thighs, blood soaking through the pale fabric of the sheets.

The smell of it thickens, and my stomach lurches. So much blood—I must be *dying*—oh God—

The bedroom door flies open, Whitt barging past it. His face is flushed, his eyes gleaming with an odd erratic light as he takes in me hunched on the bed. He stops just over the threshold, abruptly uncertain.

"Are you all right?" he asks. "I was coming up the stairs—I heard a yelp."

He can't see the blood from where he's standing. I have the absurd impulse to shoo him away, to claim everything's fine, to not have to admit that I've somehow mortally wounded myself while *sleeping* as if the embarrassment of it is worse than bleeding out.

Even if I would have attempted that tactic, Whitt has his wolfish senses. Before I can form any words at all, he inhales sharply and strides straight to the side of the bed. But when he comes up next to me, the concern that tensed his features relaxes. He looks at the mess and then at me.

"I—I don't know how—" I stammer, and it occurs to me that I feel reasonably okay for someone on the verge of bleeding to death, no pain anywhere except that dull knot in my gut.

Whitt blinks and then chuckles softly, stroking his hand over my hair to rest on my shoulder. "It's your monthly bleed. Have you never had it before? I had the impression it was common knowledge in the human world."

Oh. A rush of embarrassment twice as scorching washes away the chill of my fear. Of course. Of course. The cramps, the blood in that specific spot…

I drop my flaming face into my hands. "It's been so long since I had one—I forgot." And waking up to it out of a nightmare, I guess I wasn't thinking all that clearly. I had a few periods back home before Aerik took me. But never one after he tossed me into that cage. I'd remember the shame of trying to deal with it if there'd been even one.

Whitt makes a rough sound that's almost a growl. "It

doesn't come to a body that's been starved or put through too much trauma. All those years…" His hand drops back to his side, his teeth baring as if he'd rip Aerik to pieces out right now if the man were standing in front of him. With visible effort, he reins in his anger. "Having it come now is a good sign—that you're healing. Everything's working as it's meant to."

That is a relief in some way, but still, my stomach flips when I look at the sheets again. "I made such a mess."

"Easily dealt with," Whitt says briskly, back to his usual blasé self. "I believe human servants—well, the females—are given cloths with approximately the same enchantment we use on bandages to absorb the blood. I should be able to manage that. And magic will clean your sheets just fine as well. Hold on a moment."

He sweeps out of the room and returns a minute later with a folded cloth he must have grabbed from the kitchen, apparently already enchanted, because he hands it straight to me. "I assume you can determine where to put this."

I scramble out of the bed, wobbling when I put too much weight on my warped foot. "I—yes." I glance toward the wardrobe, unsure about fiddling with my undergarments right in front of him.

He motions to the door. "I'd imagine you'll want to get cleaned up. You can bring your things to the lavatory while I handle the bed."

He's going to—? But then, would I rather he woke up the others or called in someone from the pack to clean up after me? It isn't as if I've got any magic that could take care of it myself. Whitt must have a fair amount of experience with other sorts of blood, so maybe it's not that uncomfortable for him.

I've limped to the wardrobe and retrieved a new nightgown and a pair of panties when a strange sort of inspiration strikes. I spin around.

"Could the blood from this—if I'm going to bleed every month *anyway*—"

Whitt can clearly follow my thinking even though I'm having trouble getting the full idea out. He cocks his head and leans closer to the bed. His mouth twists. "I'm afraid the answer isn't likely to be that simple, mite. Even if we could line up the timing, this sort of bleeding isn't pure blood like from the vein. The scent is altered. I suspect we'd see the same result as when we tried to hoard some of the tonic to use after it'd gotten old."

A pang of disappointment hits me, but I hadn't had time to get all that hopeful about it anyway. It's not as if I even mind the thought of letting these men take my blood from my arm as long as I'm treated like I have the right to decide whether I do. Getting it this way might have sat easier on Sylas's conscience, though.

I scurry down the hall to the lavatory and wipe myself off as well as I can, cringing at the reddish streaks flowing from the sponge down the tub's drain. The folded cloth fits into my panties without any trouble. I pull them on and my fresh nightgown, then rinse the ruddy streaks from the nightie I was wearing as well as I can.

When I return to my bedroom, Whitt appears to have finished whatever magic he worked. The sour tang has left the air. My sheets lie neatly on the bed without a hint of a stain. When I set my hand in the area it was worst, they're not even slightly damp.

"Hurray for magic," I say with a laugh that comes out a bit shaky.

Whitt grins, taking his striking face from handsome to breathtaking. "It does make a great many things a great deal easier."

"Thank you." I tear my eyes away from him and climb back into the bed. Sitting there, I tug the sheet to my waist, feeling abruptly shy. The fae man might be hard to read at the best of times, but he's been patient with me, *kind* even, in between his wry remarks. Not just now but throughout the past couple of weeks, even when I intruded on his work—answering my questions, taking my ignorance and uncertainties in stride.

I wish I could express how much I appreciate that, but I'm not sure how, at least not in any way that wouldn't come across as awkward. I settle for focusing on the moment at hand. "Thank you—for checking on me and everything else. I didn't mean to interrupt whatever you were doing. I should have realized what was going on instead of panicking."

Whitt dismisses my attempt at an apology with a flick of his hand. "I was merely turning in for the night after our revel. It'd probably have taken me at least this long to clear my head for sleep anyway. This way I was able to use that time productively." He pauses, and his expression gentles again. "Will *you* be able to get back to sleep now?"

The image darts into my mind of him sweeping me out of the bed and carting me off to his own like Sylas has after other nightmares. A weird thrill shoots through me, as much unnerved as excited by the thought. Maybe some small part of me wonders what it'd feel like to be caught in this inscrutable man's embrace, but that's definitely a bit of curiosity I'm not looking to indulge.

I exhale slowly, releasing as much of my lingering tension as I can. "I think so." And yet I don't feel quite ready to return to the darkness and the dreams that might emerge from it. I fidget with the edge of the sheet. I could at least show a little more friendliness. "Was it a good revel?"

"I'd say it was. Much love made and very little war. Spirits were high; complaints were few."

His tone is so carefree that the final prickles of uneasiness leave me. How could anything be all that wrong when he's that at ease? I find myself unexpectedly smiling back at him.

A sly twinkle lights in Whitt's eyes. "A few of my pack-kin inquired about you. I told them you were busy pining for August."

I glower half-heartedly at him, and he chuckles. "Don't worry. I'm sure the whelp will be home where he belongs soon." Whitt turns to go, with a final remark tossed over his shoulder. "There's no shame in leaving a lantern on. Sometimes the best way to fend off darkness is to keep it at bay in the most literal sense."

He steps out with a light click of the door, leaving me wondering what darkness *he's* had to fend off that he could say that so confidently.

CHAPTER FOURTEEN

August

A damp breeze greets me when I clamber out of the carriage, the grass dewy beneath my boots. I drag in the cool air of the dawn, tasting daisies and clover, and let it settle against my skin for a moment before I head toward the keep.

Oh, how glad I am to be home. And oh, how I wish I was bringing better news with me.

Unsurprisingly, no one in the keep is up yet. I hesitate at the base of the staircase, debating whether to wake Sylas to deliver my report immediately, but the bad news isn't *urgent*, at least. I'd rather pass it on to him when he's fully rested.

I haven't gotten a whole lot of sleep myself over the past week and only managed a couple of hours during the carriage journey. Tired as that's left me, there's too much uneasy energy thrumming through me for me to think I'll be able to doze off any time soon. I head into the kitchen to reacquaint myself with the part of the keep that falls the most under my domain.

The pack members who took over cooking duty have left it clean and tidy—almost too much so. A little mess would have given me something to focus on, would have made me feel missed. Well, I'll just have to remind my family how good the cooking is when I *am* here. A decadent breakfast might help my report go down smoother. I can always hope so, anyway.

I fall into the familiar rhythm of measuring flour and cracking eggs, the motions grounding me. Out by the border, even without any attacks, the meal situation was pretty dire. We generally ended up eating whatever the warriors could hunt down or scavenge in their brief treks away from the line of defense, charred over an open fire. When I had the chance, I managed to scrounge up a few savory herbs to add some flavor. With all the sacrifices my pack-kin out there are making for us, the least I could do was ensure they got a few good dinners into them.

I'm just shoving the first batch of pancakes into the warmer to keep them hot when Sylas appears in the doorway. "I thought I heard something unusual going on down here. Although given that it's you, I suppose this isn't unusual behavior. Welcome home, August."

His smile is typically reserved, but there's no mistaking the happiness—and maybe a little relief—in his tone. "Glad to be back," I say. "I take it no one starved without me around."

He chuckles. "We managed, but that's not to say we won't appreciate your culinary talents now that you've returned. Have you been up to see Talia yet?"

My heart leaps and pangs at the same time, picturing my lover's sweet face, how she'll feel in my arms when I get to embrace her again. "I didn't want to wake her."

"She worried about you. Somehow I don't think she'd mind the intrusion."

I imagine walking upstairs and climbing right into her bed next to her, tucking her into my arms and inhaling her sweet scent. Yes, I'll do that—but I have my duty to my lord to fulfill first. I can't let my desires distract from that.

"I assume you'll want my report too," I say.

He walks in and leans against the island across from me. "Naturally. Although it'd appear the situation isn't incredibly dire, since you returned alone rather than escorting the rest of our warriors with you."

I take a moment to flip the next batch of pancakes, gathering myself and taking comfort in the ease with which the spatula moves to my will. Then I look at Sylas again. "It wasn't bad enough to call the whole effort off, but—it wasn't good either. All around, not just for our pack."

Sylas's smile fades. "Go on."

"What Whitt has heard about our situation is true. The nine warriors we have out there are essentially shunned by the packs stationed nearby. I saw no Unseelie attacks while I was with them, but it's clear they're on their own when one occurs, and that if the enemy broke through the area they're protecting, they'd be blamed for failing, not the others for refusing to support them."

"Unfortunate but unsurprising. Was there something else?"

I think he already knows there is. I balk instinctively. My nature demands loyalty to the arch-lords—the fae who rule over *all* the packs, above even my own lord. But I don't obscure the truth for them, not to the man I directly serve.

I turn to check the frying pan. "The arch-lords came out to check on the squadrons along the northern stretch while I was there. Their leadership… was not as I'd have hoped."

Sylas hums to himself. "In what way?"

In every way? I restrain a grimace. "They seemed very tense, to the point that they couldn't hide it, which made the squadron leaders restless too. I didn't speak to them directly—none of them were particularly interested in our small group—but I followed the proceedings as well as I could, to try to find out more, and I overheard a few squabbles between them over the best way to proceed, within hearing of many others as well. I would have expected them to present a united front at least in public."

When I glance over my shoulder at Sylas, he's outright frowning. "As would I. That doesn't bode well. What did they argue about?"

"It wasn't totally clear. They didn't give any details, and parts of the conversations they kept hushed. All I gathered was that they feel some urgency about coming up with a new strategy soon. Maybe they've gotten wind of some new development they don't want to share widely yet. In any case, after they finished their inspection, they each left one of their cadre-chosen to continue patrolling that whole stretch at the far north, overseeing the squadrons' operations."

Sylas's eyebrows rise. "They spared cadre-chosen on a permanent post away from their domains? Whitt hasn't mentioned hearing of that sort of presence before."

"It hasn't happened before. Our warriors said this was the first time in years that the arch-lords themselves have come so far along the border, and the first time they've *ever* left anyone that high ranking posted there." I toss the pancakes onto a new tray and reach for the bowl with the remaining batter. "I didn't like it."

"No, I can't blame you. It definitely sounds as though they're anticipating some new, larger offensive. Did you leave our squadron as they were, then, or did you come up with some advice to improve their situation?"

The hiss of the batter hitting the hot pan gives me a moment's reprieve before I have to answer. "I made a pretty major adjustment to their approach, one you may not be completely pleased with... I didn't think we were likely to make much of an impact or, honestly, become anything other than corpses and scapegoats by acting as though we could hold an entire section of the border. So I had our warriors pull back behind some of the other squadrons where they can take a supportive role. The other packs may not want to come to *our* aid, but they're unlikely to shun help from us in the middle of an attack."

I shoot Sylas a quick grin. "I did tell them to be especially alert to any opportunities to shield one of the arch-lords' cadre-chosen. That could win us some points."

He rumbles in apparent agreement, but his expression stays gloomy. As I get started on the next batch of pancakes, my stomach clenches. "If you don't think that was the right call—"

"No, it sounds like a wise decision. Possibly even wiser than I'd have expected of you, so clearly I haven't been giving you enough credit." Sylas's smile comes back, but only for a moment. "I'm just considering how we proceed from here… and I'm not liking any of the options."

The portent in his voice casts a shadow over the pride I took in his compliment. "Do you think we *need* to do something else right away?"

"Soon, in any case. If the arch-lords are becoming that invested, we may be on the cusp of a major shift in this war—it might be coming up on the point where we have to throw ourselves all in not only to regain our good names but to protect the entire summer realm."

Uneasiness ripples through me at his words. Could the Unseelie really take over enough of our lands to make a difference? What would they do with us—slaughter us? Enslave us?

It's difficult to wrap my head around the idea. I've barely even seen any of the raven-shifting winter fae across my lifetime. For them to suddenly become an unavoidable part of our lives seems impossible, but Sylas clearly believes there's a chance they could take things that far.

Before I can ask him what he means by throwing ourselves all in, a faint tapping on the stairs reaches my ears. My head snaps around with a joyful skip of my heart. I'd know the patter of Talia's feet anywhere.

I drop the bowl on the counter and hurry past Sylas into the hall. My sweet woman is just reaching the bottom of the stairs. The moment she sees me, her face lights up so bright it's almost magic.

"You're back!" she says, and anything she might have

added is lost when I sweep her up into my arms. She hugs me back with a strength in those slim arms that still surprises me, her face burrowing into my shoulder, and lets out a quavering sigh that tells me everything I need to know about how relieved she is. A strangely delighted ache fills my chest, pained at the thought of how she must have worried but undeniably pleased that she cared so much about my safe return.

How can it be that less than two months ago I didn't even know this woman existed, and now I can't imagine my life without her?

"And I'm perfectly fine, as promised," I tell her. "I didn't even see an Unseelie warrior the whole time I was out there."

Her arms tighten around me, and then she loosens her grasp so I can return her to her feet. As she gazes up at me, her mouth slants downward. "All the pack members still out there will have to fight them again, though. How much longer is this war going to go on? I still don't understand why the Unseelie won't just *talk* to all of you about what they want."

Whitt's lazy voice carries from behind her. "Probably because whatever they've gotten their feathers in a twist over, they realize we'd never give it to them willingly." My oldest brother comes to a stop on the lowest step and props himself against the railing. "It seems you all decided to have a party down here without inviting me. I'm very offended."

"We know how much you value sleeping in," I reply, rolling my eyes at him. "Good to see you too."

Whitt smirks at me. "Oh, don't worry, you were very

missed, Auggie." He sniffs the air. "And so were your epic breakfasts. There are a *few* things I'm occasionally willing to peel myself out of bed at this hour for, and fallowroot pancakes is one of them."

I'm home, surrounded by the three people I care about most in the world, and just for a moment, that knowledge melts away any apprehension inside me. I grin back at him. "I guess I'd better start serving, then."

Talia's already heading to the kitchen. "I'll get the plates!"

"How has your practice been going?" I ask her as I follow her in. "The physical exercises and the magical ones?"

She hops onto her knees on a stool to reach the plates stacked on a shelf over the counter. "I think I'm pretty solid with most of the moves you wanted me to focus on. You'll have to try me with some sparring to make sure my form is good enough for you." She aims a sly glance at me that heats me up far more than the stove I've just leaned over. "And the magic—I still haven't made much progress with light, but I can bend bronze pretty easily now."

"I'd like to see that." I rummage in one of the drawers, searching for another bronze utensil old enough that I don't make much use of it anymore, and hand her a slightly singed skewer. "You made a spoon into a spike. Think you can make that into a spoon?"

I'm mostly joking about the spoon part, but Talia turns her gaze on the skewer in full seriousness without protest. Last time I watched her work her inexplicable magic, it took her a few minutes to gather the power inside her. Now, it can't have been more than ten seconds, her jaw clenching and her eyes narrowing in a way that takes her from pretty to fiercely gorgeous, before she spits out the true name like a command. "*Fee-doom-ace-own!*"

The upper half of the skewer shudders and flattens into a wider, circular shape. It's not *exactly* a spoon, really more like a narrow trowel, but I'm not sure I could have fashioned a much better spoon out of the thing myself. Talia looks up at me, hesitant in her pride, and I can't resist leaning in for a kiss.

"That was wonderful. You've really gotten control over it."

"Not enough," she says, though my kiss has left her flushed and smiling. "If I needed to work something bronze quickly and I wasn't already scared or angry, I might not manage it in time. But I'm definitely getting better!"

"So you are," Whitt says, watching from the doorway with his arms crossed loosely over his chest. "You know, with all that skill, you might even be ready to hold your own at the next revel I host. You can be reasonably sure you won't need to skewer anyone there."

Talia smiles at him too, more shyly. "I'd like that."

A sharper sensation prickles up from my gut at the look they exchange, familiar and almost fond. But then, why shouldn't they be becoming fonder of each other the longer they've been living together? I should want them to be.

And I do. I just can't completely tune out the murmur inside me that wonders how much room there'll be for me if she has both of my older brothers' affections to enjoy as well.

CHAPTER FIFTEEN

Talia

The sunset stains the distant clouds purple and gold. The colors ripple down over the spires of pale stone that rise above the western forest. It's a beautiful image, like the world has turned into a watercolor painting, but I can't help thinking about all the uncertainties that lie beyond this scene. I came outside after dinner to breathe in the fresh air, but the soft warble of the breeze isn't settling my nerves the way I'd hoped.

Astrid wanders over from the village and comes to a stop beside me, following my gaze. When I turn to her, I think I see sadness in her wizened face.

"The battles are a long way off," she says. "Unlikely they'll touch any of us while we're here. If that's what's making you look so serious now that your man is back."

August is back, but whatever he saw at the border still haunts him. A shadow has been hanging over his normally cheerful demeanor all day. But then, he hasn't faced a conflict like this before, has he?

How many wars before this one has Astrid seen in all the centuries she's been alive? Is this one really the worst so far?

I can't quite bring myself to ask that, so I let a simpler question slip out instead. "Have you ever needed to fight against the Unseelie?"

Her thin lips draw back with the slightest baring of her teeth. "Once or twice, when a few of them needed to be put in their place. But they *used* to generally know well enough to stick to their own territory and leave us to ours. It's the Murk that's caused most of the trouble if we don't stamp their little insurgencies out quickly enough."

"The Murk?" I repeat, trying to remember if the men of the keep have mentioned that.

Astrid takes on a creaky singsong tone.

"Wolves of summer, winter ravens
Where they dwell find no safe haven.
But most beware the rats of Murk
Sowing spite wherever they lurk."

A shiver runs through me at the lilting words. When she's finished, Astrid glances at me. "I suppose the young ones don't sing that rhyme in the human world anymore. When *I* was young, enough of them knew what to watch out for. But anything tied to the Mists fades from mortal minds quickly."

I shake my head. "I've never heard it. Where's the Murk? Is it part of the Mists?"

She makes a rough sound in her throat. "The fae of the Murk live nowhere and everywhere. They gather in the grimy shadows of the human world and along the fringes of ours, wherever they can steal a little space and spread their rot. They're rats, after all." She shows her teeth again, this time in a thin grin. "No match for a wolf's jaws, much to their dismay. They mostly trouble humans, not us."

"So, they don't have their own realm like you have summer and the Unseelie have winter."

"No. They've always been the dregs, the fae that didn't quite fit anyplace. And they resent that we do." Astrid lets out a huff. "But don't worry yourself about them. This once, it is the ravens causing the strife. I expect we'll sort them out soon enough."

I hold myself back from pointing out that the war has already been going on for decades. From Astrid's aged perspective, a century would probably be "soon."

The elderly but sprightly fae gives me a light pat on the arm. "Really, you shouldn't worry yourself about *any* of this. I can tell you with the wisdom of much experience that nothing ever truly ends; it only changes."

With that declaration, she walks off again, across the field toward the hills. She must have sentry duty tonight.

Her remark isn't exactly comforting—there are plenty of things I'd rather not see even change—but I slip back into the keep more at peace than when I stepped out, which was my goal, after all.

Sylas and his cadre are standing in the hall outside the dining room in intense discussion. As I approach, Sylas sighs and makes a gesture as if waving the subject away. "I have more thinking to do. But I value both of your perspectives."

He turns toward me, his somberness falling away with

a quiet smile. "Talia, there you are. There's something I wanted to show you. And you should come as well, August."

As the fae lord ushers the two of us toward the staircase, Whitt eases back. When I glance his way, he's disappearing into the basement, already too deep in the shadows for me to make out his expression. It feels strange, splitting their group up with the three of us together and him on his own.

I've tried so hard not to come between Sylas and August. Have I severed the cadre in a totally different way instead?

But then, Whitt has always seemed to enjoy his independence, and he definitely hasn't shown any interest in becoming part of our carefully negotiated arrangement. If he took issue with where he stands with his half-brothers, I'm sure he wouldn't hesitate to tell them.

"What's this about?" I ask Sylas, curiosity nibbling at me.

"Patience, lady of the keep," he says lightly. "I've conducted a minor... renovation, you could say. It's best explained when you can see it."

August gives me a shrug that seems to say he has no idea what Sylas has in mind either. At the top of the stairs, the fae lord leads us down the hall to the area where the men's bedrooms are. He stops at a door I don't remember noticing before, just beyond his and August's rooms, and rests his hand on the knob as he turns to me.

"I was thinking about the things you said the other day, Talia, and about how entwined you've already become in our lives... How difficult it might be for you to draw boundaries when you're relying on us for so much. So I think this might help make those boundaries easier for us all to navigate."

He nudges the door open to reveal a small but cozy room. A large skylight in the high ceiling shows the stars starting to twinkle in the darkening heavens. Amber orbs at the edges of the ceiling flood the space with a broader, warmer light, glowing over the four-poster bed that takes up most of the floor. The silver and blue duvet draped over the bed looks so fluffy just looking at it makes me want to dive right into it. A small vanity and a dressing screen stand in one corner.

"I tried to think of an appropriate name for this spot, and the best I came up with was 'the tryst room'," Sylas says, one side of his mouth quirking up into a crooked smile. "Your bedroom can remain your own place of refuge, and if you need to come to either of us in our own bedrooms for security in the night, you shouldn't have to worry about whether there'll be expectations beyond that. I think we can manage to keep our paws to ourselves unless you invite us in here."

He glances at August with a mildly questioning expression, and the younger man laughs. "I can agree to that. Anything that makes it easier for Talia to fend for herself amongst us beasts is good with me."

"You're not *beasts*," I protest automatically, still staring into the room. The sight of it and Sylas's explanation fill me with a glow as warm and bright as the lanterns beaming over the bed.

This is exactly what I needed, this clarifying of expectations and knowing I wasn't offering more than I realized or disappointing anyone by not making the offer. Sylas figured it out without my even being able to fully express it to myself.

I bring my gaze back to him, reaching for his hand. "Thank you. It's perfect. I didn't expect—you've already given me one whole room—"

"Well, this one is for all three of us, after all." He squeezes my hand gently and then moves as if to drop it.

Something inside me pangs in sharp objection. I grip his fingers before they can completely release mine. The words stick in my throat for a second before I can propel them out, my cheeks flaring at the same time. "Maybe... we should give it a trial run?"

Between the looming threat of the Unseelie and the uncertain truce with Aerik, I don't know what's going to become of us in the days ahead. But right now, standing between these two men with this show of devotion... I can't imagine feeling safer or more cherished.

What does it matter if they'll never see me as quite as valid a mate as someone of their own kind? I can still love them with all my heart and make the most of what they're offering me—which is already more than I would have dreamed. They've made me a part of their world in so many ways, and I—I want to experience everything that can come with that. Before one or both of them has to leave again and might never come back.

Heat sparks in Sylas's dark eye. He runs his thumb over the back of my hand in a tingling caress. "I suppose you can make whatever invitations you'd like as you'd like to, Talia. I have nothing urgent to otherwise occupy me."

At my other side, August starts to pull back with a dip

of his head. No. That's not—I want something more, something that doesn't exclude either of them.

I don't know if they'll accept that, I don't know what it will even look like, but my gaze jerks to the other man and the question tumbles out with only a slight stammer. "What if—what if I want to invite both of you? At the same time?"

The moment I've said it, my entire body flushes, embarrassment at my awkwardness burning beneath my skin. But neither of them laughs or scoffs. Sylas hesitates for a second and meets August's eyes. There's a subtle flexing of muscles and shifting of stances between them, as if in some silent conversation. Maybe even a debate.

With each other? With themselves? Have I asked for more than I should have?

August drops his gaze first to look at me instead. Something fierce and hungry shimmers in his golden irises. "If it would please you, I'd happily see what we could do for you together."

Sylas chuckles, and some of the tension I'd barely noticed building in his posture relaxes. "Yes. A collaboration for our lady. Perhaps that would be good for all of us." He sweeps his arm toward the bed. "Lead the way."

My momentary elation at my victory falters in my limping trek to the bed. The tapping of my foot brace sounds so loud in the stillness of the room. Wanting to do away with that reminder of my human fragility, I sit on the edge of the mattress—where the duvet really is soft and puffy as a cloud—and reach to remove the contraption.

The men follow, Sylas shutting the door and uttering a quiet word I assume will lock it so we're not interrupted. My pulse kicks up a notch in anticipation. My mouth has gone a little dry. I set down the brace against the side of the bed and look up at my lovers, abruptly shy despite the bold request I just made.

"I'm not really sure what to do now," I admit.

August sinks down on the bed next to me and kisses my cheek. "Why don't we take it slow and just see how it goes?" He glances at Sylas, and again I get the impression of a silent negotiation, although this one only lasts a moment.

Sylas nods, sitting at my right. "Show us when you want us to continue—or tell us if we should stop. We'll only go as far as you enjoy."

Nestled between their bodies, my nerves settle. "Okay. That sounds good."

August eases across the bed to the far side, giving me a gentle tug to follow. He sprawls out with his head by the pillows, and as I lie back next to him, Sylas follows suit at my other side.

When I look toward August, he teases his fingers up my jaw and brings his mouth to mine. At the same time, Sylas kisses the top of my head, his hand coming to rest on my waist. I'm contained between them, heat sparking everywhere they touch.

It's a good thing we're taking this slow, because these first sensations are already overwhelming me with giddiness.

As August's lips brand mine, Sylas's thumb traces an arcing line just below my ribs. Then August drops his head to kiss my neck and my shoulder, and I turn my head, instinctively seeking out the other man. Sylas is right there, his head ducking so he can meet my lips. The brush of his mouth sears right through me. I grasp his hair, pulling him deeper into the kiss.

Just this is so good. I thought it was some kind of paradise being cherished by just one of these men's hands and mouth, but both of them—I don't have the words for it. However seriously they take this arrangement, I mean enough to them that their desire to please me matters more than the instinctive possessiveness I've seen in them before. What's happening between us no longer feels like two separate relationships but something we're building together.

For several blissful minutes, we lie like that, the two men restrained in their caresses, one claiming my lips and then the other. As I adjust to the rush of stimulation, a growing need thrums through my veins. When August strokes his hand right over my breast for the first time, I'm so ready for his touch that my back arches up in encouragement.

"Hmm," Sylas murmurs by my ear, his breath deliciously hot as it spills down my neck. "I think our lady needs more attention than we've been offering."

His hand rises to cup my other breast, the flick of his thumb over the peak sending a jolt of pleasure through my chest. I gasp and make an encouraging sound in my throat, in case there's any doubt at all that I'm *very* much enjoying how this "tryst" is proceeding.

August claims my mouth again, the slide of his tongue over mine echoing the movement of his fingers over my curves. I kiss him back hard, and then turn to Sylas again, more and more heat flooding me with every skillful touch. With each swivel of their fingers over the tips of my breasts, my nipples stiffen with headier tingles.

The pleasure quivers down through my belly to pool between my legs. I'm unspeakably grateful that my first period after my long starvation only lasted a few days, and I was able to do away with the enchanted cloth Whitt gave me this morning. No need to worry about bloodying *these* sheets, whether my lovers would actually mind or not.

Sylas slips his hand up under my shirt, and I break our kiss to push myself farther upright. He takes my cue to ease the loose blouse right off me, August helping from his side. The room is warm enough that no chill touches my bared skin, but looking at the two men still fully dressed doesn't feel quite right.

"You too," I say with a tentative tug at Sylas's shirt. I glance at August to make it clear my request also applies to him. With a grin, he sheds his typical T-shirt, revealing all the muscular, tattooed planes of his chest. As I trace my fingers over the curving lines of the true names etched on his pale skin, Sylas undoes the lacing at the V-neck of his more formal shirt and sheds it.

His brawn is equally impressive, with even more of the interlaced lines dappling his darker skin. Taking it in, I have the sudden urge to taste those solid ridges of muscle.

When I lean closer, the fae lord's rich earthy scent with its hint of woodsmoke fills my nose. A low, hungry growl escapes him at the cautious graze of my lips. He tastes even smokier than he smells, like a midnight campfire in the depths of a dense forest.

I test Sylas's skin with the tip of my tongue, and a rumble sounds from lower in his chest. His fingers tangle in my hair, trailing across my scalp in a way that makes my own skin shiver eagerly. August kisses a scorching line from the nape of my neck to partway down my spine, fondling my breast with his warm, broad hand, and certainty swells through the twist of longing inside me.

This is where I'm meant to be. This is who I'm meant to be with. It may have taken the most horrific of paths to get me here, but I can't imagine feeling any happier than I am right now, doused in affection from these two different but equally awe-inspiring men.

I raise my head so I can kiss Sylas on the mouth, melting into him skin to naked skin. The throbbing between my legs intensifies. I roll over, their hands tracing lines of pleasure across my body with the movement, and reach for August. His mouth collides with mine just as passionately, drawing a needy whimper out of me.

Our breaths mingle and part, back and forth. I drink in both of them until my head spins. Every inch of my skin that brushes theirs lights up with a sharper flame of pleasure.

August ducks down to suck the peak of my breast into his mouth, and when my head arches back with a breathless moan, Sylas is there to meet me, his mouth blazing against my jaw, my neck. I slip my arm back in a partial embrace, hugging him to me, and stroke my other hand down August's bulging arm. My hips sway between them, driven by more desire than I can hold in.

I don't want slow anymore. I've waited weeks to see all

this desire through to its natural finale, and my body is so ready my blood sings with it.

But first I want them to know just how much this means to me.

August swipes his tongue over my nipple once more and releases me. I slide my fingers along his jaw so he raises his gaze to catch mine. All the emotion in me bubbles over.

"I love you," I say, quiet but steady, and twist so I can meet Sylas's mismatched eyes. "And I love you. Both of you. So much."

August's voice comes out hoarse, maybe even shocked. "Talia…"

Sylas cups my face, his dark eye as intent as I've ever seen it. "You are a treasure, and I will treasure you as you deserve."

It isn't exactly the same sentiment I expressed, but it's more than I expected. I lean into him as he captures my mouth, grasping August's hand when he wraps his arm around my waist, not so much lost between the two of them as so very deeply *found*.

August rains kisses across my shoulder blades. His hand glides down my belly to the fly of my jeans. My breath spills shaky against Sylas's mouth, and I squeeze August's forearm to urge him on.

As he tugs the zipper open and peels the jeans off me, I flip over and kiss him hard. Sylas's hands smooth over my hips and join August's in freeing my legs. I reach for August's trousers with a jerk of the waist, and he growls against my lips as he kicks out of them. Then he turns me back toward Sylas, his mouth burning where he nips my earlobe, his hardness unmistakeable against my thigh.

I keep one hand on August's shoulder, clutching tightly, and run the other down Sylas's chest, watching his expression. The smolder in his unscarred eye deepens as he rids himself of his own slacks. He grazes my lips with a teasing kiss that travels down my throat to my collarbone and then devours the tip of my breast.

August dips his fingers between my legs over my panties, sparking a bolt of electricity. I buck into his touch, the pressure of his fingers showing me just how wet I already am.

More pleasure pulses from his caress, tingling through my limbs and lungs. He keeps stroking me there as Sylas works over my breasts with devout attention, until I'm squirming between them, caught in the currents of heated desire.

"Please," I mumble. "I want—I want everything." The core of me aches with emptiness. Every particle in me demands to know how it feels to be truly filled.

August exhales in a shudder against my back. He yanks my panties down and tucks his fingers right against my slick folds. His touch inflames me.

At my whimper, he groans. Then he raises his head to look over my shoulder as he slides his hand along my leg to open my thighs.

"I believe she's ready for you, my lord," he says. He doesn't sound disappointed at the thought of offering me up to Sylas—not with that rasp of eagerness in his voice.

Sylas releases my breast, taking in August's expression

and then mine. His fingers trace a gentle line down my cheek. "Do you agree, Talia?"

"Yes," I gasp out. I let my hand drop to the fae lord's silky boxers, almost gasping again at the corded length pressing so solidly against the fabric. I want all of him.

Sylas kisses me fiercely, stroking my belly and then my sex as I trail my fingers up and down his rigid erection. August teases my inner thigh a little longer before taking over fondling my breasts. Somewhere in the midst of that whirlwind of sensation, Sylas tugs his boxers off. I wrap my fingers around his length, shivering with delight at his groan, guiding him toward me.

He clasps my hip and rubs the head of his erection from my most sensitive spot to my opening and back until I'm throbbing twice as urgently as before. Easing my leg over his thigh, he pushes ever so carefully inside me.

That first moment of penetration comes with a burn that's both pain and pleasure. A sigh stutters out of me, and Sylas stops completely. He stays there, no more than an inch inside me, circling his thumb over the sensitive nub above, kissing me gently. August squeezes my nipple and nibbles along my shoulder with little flicks of his tongue.

The burning eases back into a headier heat. I flex my hips just slightly, and Sylas groans. He presses a little farther in, and a little more, until the stretch is nothing but a blissful ache. I clutch at him. "It's good. It's good."

I can feel the control wound through the fae lord's muscles as he pulls back and plunges in, again and again, each time a little deeper than before. The bursts of pleasure make me cry out. I rock into him, our careful pace gathering momentum.

Some distant, wild part of me calls out for him to unleash every bit of his passion, but I'm not sure I'm ready for that yet. This is so much on its own.

He's treasuring me with every movement of his body, just as he promised he would. The expanding fullness inside is like nothing I've ever experienced before, as if he's splitting me in two but in a way that's inexplicably satisfying, like I've been waiting all my life to be cleaved apart.

Sylas's mouth melds with mine and pulls away again, his breath erratic. August keeps up his dizzying caresses of my chest. He lifts his head to kiss my jaw, and I manage to turn enough to meet his lips. His tongue twines with mine as his lord drives into me.

We're all one being, one act, moving and burning together. The glow I felt looking into this room sears through me to light up my skin.

Somehow my need is growing again, even though I couldn't be more filled. I push into Sylas's thrusts, trying to find that final horizon. He rocks harder to meet me, but it's not quite—not quite—

Just as the pressure inside me skirts the edge of painful again, Sylas's voice tumbles out hoarsely. "Let's both bring our lady to the finish she deserves."

"Yes, my lord." Without hesitation, August drops his hand from my breasts to my sex, to the spot that throbs the most just above where Sylas and I are joined. He teases over that spot and presses harder, and something in me crackles right apart.

I shudder and moan, my fingernails digging so deep into August's arm and Sylas's shoulder that I must leave marks. The surge of my release crashes through me from the deepest part of my being to my curling toes and my quaking scalp.

Sylas pulls me even tighter against him with a few last bucks of his hips. His muscles go taut beneath my fingers, and his head bows next to mine with a searing exhalation.

After a few moments, he eases out of me as gently as he first entered, running his fingers along the side of my face, over my arm, and then stealing a peck from my lips. His eye searches mine, brightening when I beam at him. I'm spent and riding on a ripple of the pleasure still echoing through me. Not just thanks to him.

I shift over to tug August into a proper kiss. He returns it so enthusiastically that it steals my breath all over again. After, still nestled against Sylas's chest, I peek up at him. "You—I should do something for you."

I can't offer him everything I just did with Sylas. A faint burn lingers inside me, like muscles on the verge of strain after an intense workout—unused to this intimate act, for now. But I could still—

August shakes his head and brushes his lips to my temple. "You've given me plenty. All I want is this."

He tilts my head on the pillow so it's tucked against his chin. Sylas ducks his own face close enough that his warm, slowing breath ruffles my hair, his arm hooking around my waist. My adoration of these two men swells inside me and tingles onto my tongue. I can give them one more thing.

I hold up my hand toward the starry sprawl beyond

the skylight and murmur with all the joy inside me, "*Sole-un-straw.*"

It's more than a spark this time. A flicker like a flame wavers from my palm, a visible manifestation of my love. It's there and then gone, but clear enough to bring delight into the faces on either side of me.

"Beautiful," Sylas says, kissing my temple. August hums in agreement and nestles even closer to me.

As I relax into the bed, I wonder why anyone has to be so cruel as to try to tear a happiness like this apart.

CHAPTER SIXTEEN

Talia

Brilliant sunlight streams over my closed eyelids, but not from the angle I'm used to. I yawn and blink at the odd glow—coming from above me rather than beside my bed.

Because I'm not in my bed in the bedroom that's only mine. The sunlight is beaming from a skylight overhead in the room Sylas made—through magic?—for those times when I want to do something in a bed *other* than sleep. Apparently I was content and cozy enough after last night's tryst that I drifted off accidentally.

The fluffy duvet has been drawn up over me to my shoulders, but I'm not the only one warming the space beneath. My arm rests against August's bare chest. As I stir in my waking, he wraps his arm around me and nuzzles my hair. "Good morning, Sweetness."

It is good. I've never slept next to August before, and he's definitely an excellent morning companion. I snuggle closer to him before registering that it's just the two of us in the bed.

As I glance toward the other end of the mattress, my pulse stutters. It isn't totally unexpected that Sylas might have gone—he seems to be an early riser, based on the times I've slept in *his* bed—but after the intimacy we shared last night…

Before my doubts can fully form into words, August rolls me toward him so his golden eyes can seek out mine. "Sylas wanted me to apologize to you for him. It was urgent that he check with the night sentries as soon as they came in from their shift." A smile crosses his lips, lit with unmistakeable pride. "He said he's glad our arrangement means you nonetheless have someone worthy you can wake up to."

I can almost hear Sylas's voice saying those words, and they send a thrill through me as bright as August's face. So far, the two men—especially Sylas—have treated my refusal to let one or the other of them claim me solely for himself as a challenging situation they're only tentatively accepting. For him to suggest that sharing my affections might be a *better* situation is a big deal, and he included a compliment that obviously pleased August as well.

I can't resist meeting August's smile with a quick peck. "He said that's why cadres sometimes share mates—isn't it? Because you're all so busy with your duties you can't devote as much time to a partner as a regular fae could?"

August chuckles. "Yes, but lords generally aren't expected to be so generous with their lovers. The honor of being chosen is supposed to make up for the limited attention, I guess. You get the best of both worlds." A sparkle dances in his eyes.

"Yes, I do," I say, meaning it with every particle of my being, and cuddle up to him again.

August tucks his arm right around me and rests his chin against my forehead. "You're still feeling good about everything that happened last night, then?"

"No regrets," I assure him, remembering the worries about fae-human relations he admitted to before.

"It must have been different from how you'd have imagined your first time would be."

I shrug and breathe in his musky sweet scent, like manly fresh-baked cookies. Yum. "I didn't have much of a chance to imagine it before. It felt exactly right for what my life is and who I'm with right now."

"Good."

We lie there for a bit just enjoying each other's warmth. I skim my fingers over August's shoulder and chest, tracing the lines of his true-word tattoos. The one that circles the right edge of his collarbone looks like a teardrop that's grown claws. Curiosity nibbles at me. "What's this one for?"

August cranes his neck to see which one I'm touching. "Slink salmon. Makes an excellent dinner. There were a lot of them in the main river that cuts through Hearthshire, so it made sense to pick up that one at the time."

Of course he'd focus at least some of his magic on meal preparation. I tap one partway down his sternum next, an angular spindly shape. "And this one?"

"Skin. Which helped me fix this lovely color to your hair, since it's nearly the same material." He teases his fingers over the pink waves and then points to the other marks in a column down his chest from neck to belly. "All the bodily ones formed in a line. Bone, eyes, blood, skin, muscle, heart, stomach, teeth, liver, lungs. I've been working on brain for nearly a decade now, haven't quite mastered it to get the mark. That's the most difficult one. Many never fully conquer it."

"I bet you will. I guess no one is teaching you like you're teaching me light."

He nods. "The simple ones—air, light, water, earth, and fire, basic metals, common plants and animals—get passed on in our early training. Anything more specialized, those who've mastered them guard the knowledge more closely. When I have time to spare, I meditate with the idea, I speak to the tissue in the animals I've hunted, that sort of thing. It's hard to explain. The sound of the word slowly forms in your mind as you get closer to it."

I'm pretty sure I'm never going to meditate my way into that kind of magic, considering how much trouble I have with total guidance. I'm about to ask what the mark for light looks like when my stomach gurgles loud enough that August laughs. "Sounds like I'd better magic up some breakfast."

He presses one last kiss to my forehead and moves to get up. I push out from under the duvet after him. "I'll help. Um, I just need to get some clean clothes."

Since I'd rather not streak down the hall, I grab yesterday's blouse and jeans from where they've fallen onto the floor and shimmy into them, not bothering with my foot brace when I'd just have to take it off again while I change. August tugs on only his shirt, but then, everyone else living in this building are his siblings, and he only has to walk one door down. He waits for me to finish and holds the door open for me all gentlemanly.

As he crosses the hall to his room, I set off for mine, buoyed by a vaguely floaty feeling, as if my happiness has grown wings. I've only made it to the branch that leads to the staircase when unexpected footsteps thump across the floor behind me.

Before I can turn more than halfway, August has caught me in his arms. He hugs me close and then kisses me with an urgency that leaves me giddy, as if he thought he might have lost me just by letting me out of his sight for a few seconds. His voice spills out low and rough, his head still bowed next to mine.

"I love you too. I should have said it last night when you did, but I hadn't thought about it quite so—I didn't realize—and then I thought I'd wait until it was the perfect time. But I want you to know now. I love you. You are the sweetest, kindest, bravest woman that I've ever met, fae or human, and you *should* know that."

An odd trembling spreads through my body. In that moment, I have the impression I'd float right up to the ceiling if he wasn't holding me. I hug him back so tightly my shoulders ache, but not as much as the ache of joy that's condensed around my heart.

"Thank you," I say, not knowing how else to answer. That he could feel so much for me, that I could matter that much to him… It leaves me speechless.

But the sweetest and kindest man *I've* ever met doesn't appear to need more than that answer. He kisses me again, more lingeringly, and forces himself to draw back to smile down at me. "I do still need to get some breakfast into you. I'll meet you in the kitchen?"

Sudden inspiration sparks in my head. I squeeze his arm. "Meet me outside my bedroom after you've changed. I want to show you something first."

As I hustle to my bedroom, even my warped foot barely seems to touch the ground. I throw open my wardrobe and grab the dress Harper gave me. She said I should show it off to August—and what better time could there be?

I slip it on, a little less nervous now that I've worn it before without doing any damage to it. The delicate material hugs my slender frame just as smoothly as I remember. Looking down at it, I feel as if I've become one with the forest outside. As if I could be almost as fae as the beings around me.

At the sound of steps beyond my door, I limp over and peek out. August comes to a stop just outside, his head tipped to the side, an eager gleam in his eyes. "What's the secret, Talia?"

"I think I've made a friend in the pack. And she gave this to me." I pull the door farther open and step into view.

I'm not sure any sight has ever been quite as gratifying as the widening of August's eyes as he takes me in. When he meets my gaze again, so much fondness shines through his expression that I couldn't possibly doubt what he told me earlier.

"I forgot gorgeous," he says. "Definitely the most gorgeous woman I've ever met too."

My face flushes, both pleased and embarrassed. I

doubt *that's* true, having seen just what kinds of otherworldly beauty the fae can possess, but I'll take the compliment anyway. I turn a little from side to side, letting the intricate skirt rustle around my legs like so many leaves. "I just thought you'd like to see it. I should save it for some kind of special occasion. If I wear it to breakfast, I might end up making a mess of it."

"Oh, I can ensure that doesn't happen. You've seen how enthusiastically the fae can party from watching Whitt, haven't you? I'd bet a spell to protect clothes from stains was one of the first pieces of fae magic ever invented." He grins at me and then pauses. "If you'd like me to work that on your dress, that is."

I beam back at him. "Please." It feels like a day for a dress like this. A day to look the part of lady of the keep.

My happiness keeps tickling up inside me like fizz in champagne while August casts the spell with a couple of syllables and a gesture of his hands, while I wash berries next to him in the kitchen, and while we lay out the table for breakfast together. It's spread so deeply through me that I can hardly believe I could ever be unsettled again— until Sylas walks into the dining room with an expression so serious it stops my heart.

Whatever's weighing on him, it can't have anything to do with me. The moment his whole eye catches on me, the shadows retreat for an instant, an approving smile curving his lips. He makes a detour on his way to the head of the table to steal a quick kiss. "Looking every bit the lady," he says, his hand lingering by my cheek. "You slept well?"

I get the impression he's asking not just about my

sleep but how I felt when I woke up. "Very," I say, and wrap my arms around his torso in a hug that I hope says everything else I'd want to.

Sylas returns the embrace with a pleased rumble. But after I let him go and he's settled into his seat, his somberness has returned.

Watching him, I debate whether it's my place to ask what's wrong. Before I come to a decision, August does it for me. "Did you get concerning news from the sentries?"

Sylas shakes his head. "I have something important to discuss with all of you—but that includes Whitt. I did indicate to him that he should make an appearance in a reasonably timely fashion..."

Whitt's jaunty voice carries from down the hall. "And your wish is my command, oh glorious leader." He ambles into the room, his high-collared shirt as rumpled as his hair as if he's just rolled out of bed with both, and drops into his usual chair, already reaching for the egg-glazed pastries. "What announcement is so important that it couldn't wait until a more respectable hour of the morning?"

Sylas gives his strategist a baleful look. "It's closer to noon than dawn. And I expect we'll want the rest of the day for preparations."

As I watch him, my fingers tighten around my fork. "Preparations for what?"

The fae lord's solemn gaze lingers on me long enough for my stomach to plummet all the way to my feet. Then he glances around at the others. "I believe we should travel to the front. The three of us."

Whitt's jaw halts in mid-chew, his eyebrows leaping

up. He swallows. "All of us? A couple of weeks ago, you were hesitant to send even August."

"That was before I heard his report. With the observations he made on top of what we've heard from our warriors previously, I'm convinced that the arch-lords are aware of some imminent escalation in the attacks. Something they feel is a large enough threat that they needed to become directly involved. Something that could change the entire course of our world's future."

August is studying him. "And if we're there to play a decisive role in that battle, it could be all we need to redeem ourselves to the arch-lords."

"Exactly." Sylas nods to him and turns back to Whitt. "I don't make the decision lightly—and as always I'll consult with you on our best approach. But if we're going to make a major show of loyalty and strength, we have to do so decisively, and this may be the only chance we get. I don't want to risk the opportunity slipping through our fingers or our pack being slaughtered in the fray. I have to be there, and I want my cadre with me."

"Fair enough," Whitt says. "As long as you two do most of the battling and I get to call out advice from afar." He smirks, but the humor fades from his expression as his gaze slides to me. August's follows it.

I swallow thickly. "What about me?"

Sylas meets my eyes steadily. "What I've heard from our sentries is that there's been no sign at all of intrusion —from Aerik's people or anyone else—since that first trace Whitt encountered many days ago. By all appearances, they've given up their suspicion of us. We would lay down magic around the keep before we leave, and I'd assign

Astrid—whom you seem to have gotten along with—to stay here with you for direct protection, as well as others from the pack if you wished. What warriors we still have in our domain would watch over the keep from the outside. I think it's highly unlikely you'd face any trouble, or I wouldn't be considering this at all, but if you did, they could hold off most until we got word and could return."

His evaluation of the risks is probably correct—he knows so much more about this world than I do—but my body balks all the same. "How long would you be gone?"

"Unfortunately, I can't know for certain. Once we're out there, we'd gather whatever information we can on the expected threat. If it appears to be less pressing than we assumed, we'll return straight away. Otherwise, we'll wait it out. The first stretch will only be a matter of days. It's only a week until the next full moon, and we won't leave you to fend for yourself during that, obviously."

Then I'd be going nearly a week without seeing *any* of them—and after that, for who knows how long, they'd only return for brief visits? The rest of the time, they'll be out at the border fighting enemies who've *killed* other Seelie, all so that they can reclaim their honor that way rather than risking my safety.

And meanwhile, what am I going to be doing? Puttering around the keep uselessly? Watching movies and reading books and worrying three times as much as when it was just August in the line of fire?

Every part of me resists that imagined future. My throat constricts, but I force out the question. "What if I want to come with you?"

Sylas blinks in a rare show of confusion. "It would

hardly be safe for you by the border, Talia. The sort of fighting we'd be engaging in—I wouldn't put you in danger like that."

I gather more determination into my voice. "I don't mean I want to fight. I—I know I'm not in a position to take on a bunch of fae warriors. But you'll have some kind of camp set up while you're waiting for the next battle, won't you? A place to live. I could stay there—I could get food ready for you and the other pack members, maybe help with whatever equipment you need. *I'll* feel safer if I know you're close by… and then none of you would have to worry about what's happening to me back here." I spare a glance at August, hoping he might argue on my behalf.

Whitt chuckles, staring at me in bemusement. "So eager to leap straight into the fire after everything the fae have already put you through, mite?"

A shiver runs through me, but it doesn't shake my resolve. That glimmer of fear only reminds me of why this matters so much.

"It doesn't feel that way to me," I tell Whitt, and focus on Sylas again, since the decision will be his. "I spent more than nine years shut away from everything important that was going on around me, knowing barely anything about the world beyond that room… I don't want this keep to feel like that too. I promise I won't get in the way and I'll help every way I can. I'll follow whatever rules you give me. I just… I want to be a part of this, not the kind of treasure that gets locked away for safe-keeping."

Have I gone too far, throwing his term of affection from last night back at him? I can't read the fae lord's expression. He considers me for a long moment. August reaches for my hand beneath the table and twines his fingers with mine. He draws in a breath as if to speak up for me, but Sylas lifts his voice first.

"I suppose you are in fact in more danger from Aerik than from any Unseelie. We could construct our living quarters well away from where any fighting should reach. And I did promise you as much freedom as I could give you. If this is what you really want, Talia, I can give it."

Relief swells inside me, shot through with another quiver of nerves. "Yes. I want to go."

I'll brave whatever waits out there a thousand times before I'd ever consign myself to another kind of cage.

CHAPTER SEVENTEEN

Talia

"Are you sure you won't come with me?" I ask August with a playful tug on his arm.

He laughs and gives me a quick kiss by the keep's front door. The glowing orbs lining the entrance room reflect off his golden eyes, making them shine even brighter. "It's better for the pack if we all keep to our areas of expertise. They don't want to *think* about their lord or the cadre-chosen who's supposed to be prepared to defend them at the drop of a hat getting high on faerie wine, let alone see it. You don't have to worry. No one ever gets *too* wild, and Whitt will look after you."

The other man did promise as much when he extended the invitation, pointing out that it might be my last chance to enjoy one of his revels in a while—and that I was already dressed for one. I think he's holding this one specifically to raise the pack's spirits before their leaders depart for some unknown length of time. Still, an anxious quiver runs through my stomach as I step toward the door.

"You don't have to join in if you're uncomfortable," August reminds me.

I shake off my nerves as well as I can. "No, I'll be fine. I've been curious about these parties for a while."

That's true, but it's not just curiosity compelling me out into the thickening dusk. Sylas may have accepted my arguments for why I should come with him and his cadre, and August seems happy that he'll be nearby to defend me if need be, but I got the impression that Whitt was still skeptical. How can I expect him to believe I can handle being on the fringes of a war zone if I won't even brave a revel with the pack I now call mine?

When I step outside, my gaze flits first over the shadowy fields to the southeast, the direction we'll be traveling tomorrow morning to head to the border camps. Our fate there feels as murky and uncertain as the darkness before me. I turn away from it, toward the rollicking music drifting from around the other side of the keep.

As I circle the towering wooden building, the warm summer breeze licks at the hem of my dress. In the nearby field just beyond the village houses, bordered by the orchard on one side, several lantern orbs float in midair. Their orangey glow lights up the blankets and pillows laid out here and there, the fae men and women sprawled on those and others wandering between them, and the two musicians perched on seats that look like bent saplings, one with an instrument like a clarinet and the other with a fiddle.

With each swipe of her bow across the strings, the woman with the fiddle sways, the smooth fall of her flaxen hair slipping across her shoulder. Even with her eyes narrowed in concentration, I can tell they're just a little too large and close-set to look totally human. Harper's mother passed a lot of her looks on to her daughter.

But not her interest in music, apparently, as deft as Harper's fingers are with a needle and thread. The younger woman isn't joining her now.

I spot Harper lounging on a velvet cushion at the other end of the revel area, watching her pack-kin alone. The other fae are dressed up more than the pack typically is during the day, the magical glow catching off silver embroidery and tiny gems woven into their clothes, but Harper's dress outshines them all. It must be one of her own creations, the filmy gold fabric billowing around the skirt and bodice like dawn clouds drifting over a turquoise sky.

When she sees me, she scrambles up and skips over to me with a warm, wide grin that offsets the alienness of her features. "I heard you were joining us tonight, so I had to come," she says, and glances around. "I don't usually bother."

I smile back at her. "You'd rather be making your dresses?"

"Most of the time." She drops her voice, as if anyone is paying all that much attention to us. "The revels are for people who want to *pretend* they're somewhere else for a little while. I'd rather be getting to work making it really happen. If I can."

"Well, I'm glad you do that work, because I love this

dress even more now that I've gotten to wear it for more than a few minutes." I skim my hands down the intricately patterned sides. "August likes it too, by the way."

Harper gives a pleased little clap. "Perfect, perfect. Maybe someday he'll take you to one of those balls or banquets in some other domain, and if the other ladies like it, if they ask where you got it—"

I laugh at her eagerness. "I'll tell them all about you, I promise."

"It's a good thing we fae live so long, because you may have to wait a while yet on August attending any festivities abroad, Harper," Whitt remarks from behind me, resting his folded arms lightly on the back of my shoulders and tipping his head past mine. His bare forearms conjure more warmth in my skin, and I'm abruptly aware of all of him just inches behind me, of the corner of his jaw grazing my hair. "I'll add 'procure ball invites' to my to-do list, but I'm not sure anyone we'll meet where we're going will have dancing on the mind."

Harper ducks her head bashfully. "I wouldn't expect— I mean, I'm sure you have more important things to do anyway. I wasn't trying to imply I'm not happy with everything we're provided with here."

I feel more than see Whitt's smirk. "Don't worry, I'm not going to report you to Sylas for treason. You're allowed to get restless." He straightens up, giving a lock of my hair a playful tug. "Have you introduced our first-timer to the refreshments yet?"

"Oh! No—I should have—" Harper beckons to me, hurrying off between the blankets. "There's lots to eat and drink, whatever you'd like."

As we follow her over to a low wooden table set up beneath a couple of the glowing orbs, I glance over my shoulder at Whitt. "Are you trying to give her a heart attack, thinking she's not being hospitable enough?"

He's still smirking. "Oh, if I *wanted* to give someone a heart attack, I could do a much more efficient job of it. I enjoy giving the pack their entertainments, but I can't have them getting too complacent either. A little anxiety is for her own good."

I jab my elbow at his chest, but he dodges the half-hearted blow with a chuckle. "Clearly I need to make sure I don't get too complacent around *you* after all these combat lessons with August."

"Don't harass my friends, and we're good," I tell him.

I think his grin softens a little around the edges. "I'm glad you're settling in with the pack enough to consider some of them friends."

I'm not sure it's so much "some" as "one"—or maybe two, if I can count Astrid, although I don't know that she enjoys my company particularly rather than simply watching out for me on behalf of her lord. The other fae of the pack have been welcoming enough if they've bothered to pay attention to me, but they treat me like more of a novelty than any sort of equal. Like right now, watching me cross the revel area with apparent interest but only speaking to each other.

Well, I guess seeing me as a full member of the pack will take time. Hopefully joining in their revel will help with that too.

Harper gestures toward the table, where silver platters are heaped with jewel-like fruits, brownie-like squares, and more fae delicacies, as well as several tall bottles next to a few remaining empty goblets. "You can eat whatever you'd like—the mirrornuts are particularly good at this time of year. Some of the wine is my father's brew."

I hesitate, my fingers curling into my palm. A nearby woman draped across her partner's lap is breathing out a stream of glittering smoke from a spindly cigarette. Beyond her, a cluster of fae are giggling madly between sips from their goblets.

I've experienced what effects some of Whitt's preferred "refreshments" can have on a person's mind as well as their stomach before. I can't imagine he'd have anything here that would muddle my head and twist my gut quite as horribly as the pulp Cole forced down my throat more than once when Aerik wanted me incoherent, but the memory rises up anyway with a shiver through my belly.

It's probably better to keep as much of my good sense as I can during this party anyway. If I turn all goofy again, won't he be even more convinced that I *shouldn't* be coming to the border?

Then again, I also don't want to look like a coward.

I glance at him where he's come up beside me, his hands slung casually in the pockets of his elegant slacks. "What's normal food, and what has… special effects?"

He quirks an eyebrow at me. "Not looking for the full revel experience? You seemed to enjoy letting loose before."

Before I hadn't realized what I was getting into—and I made some embarrassing remarks, like about how beautiful that admittedly stunning face of his is. I wrinkle my nose at him. "Maybe another time."

He hums to himself as if disappointed but points to the nuts Harper mentioned, little spheres so bright and polished they reflect the shapes around them as if they really are mirrors, and a bright blue fruit that looks jellied within its brittle husk. "You'll be safe with those. The tumblemeld will give you a slight lift to your spirits but nothing that'll addle your thoughts. You may need to avoid the beverages entirely."

"Thank you." I pick up a handful of the mirrornuts and pop one into my mouth. It crackles apart with a delicate flavor that reminds me of the tea my mother used to make for me when I wanted to join her in her morning ritual on the back porch—mine always decaf and mixed with a large helping of sugar.

A mix of fond nostalgia and homesickness squeezes my throat. I chew the next one more slowly and nod to Harper. "Those are really good."

She snatches up a few for herself and then sighs when her father calls her name. "Enjoy yourself," she tells me, and marches off to see what he wants.

Whitt is still watching me. Wondering whether I trust him enough to take both of his recommendations? Maybe I should show that I do if I want *him* to trust me.

I pick up one of the husked fruits he called tumblemeld and nibble at the jelly-like lump. The flesh dissolves on my tongue with the consistency of caramel, but tart almost to the point of sourness rather than sweet. When I swallow, a flicker of warmth kindles in my chest in its wake. Okay, that's not so bad.

"You appear to have survived," Whitt teases.

A fae couple drifts by, their dreamy smiles suggesting

they've been consuming more potent stuff than I have. "Aren't you going to dance, human girl?" the woman asks. "I thought mortals loved to frolic with the faeries."

"I'll take her for a spin-around," the man offers, dipping in a bow and extending an arm in a sweep so extravagant he nearly loses his balance in the process. The woman titters.

I'm not sure how to answer, but Whitt saves me from figuring it out. He grasps my hand and tugs me away from the table. "She's already promised me all tonight's dances, I'm afraid."

Drawing me into the center of the gathering, he raises my arm to turn me in a circle slow enough that it doesn't challenge my brace-bound foot. When I'm facing him again, he sets his other hand on my shoulder. We sway and swivel together with the music like the other fae around us, although many of them are more tightly intertwined.

"This doesn't seem to be a very complicated dance," I say. "I don't think I'm going to need your guidance the whole night."

"Perhaps not, but I think it's best you stick with me for anything handsy."

"They know I'm with August. What do you think they're going to do?"

Whitt shrugs, his voice dipping secretively. "Intoxicated fae don't always make the wisest decisions. And you do look awfully charming in that dress."

I make a face at him. "Are you sure I don't need to worry about *you* then?" I haven't seen him drinking yet, but he never seems to go anywhere without his flask, and his breath carries a faint tang of alcohol.

"Definitely not. For one thing, I'm never half as drunk as I seem."

"I guess that's reassuring."

"It should be." He turns me again but only halfway, stopping me when my back is to him with a clasp of my waist and lowering my arm so it falls across my torso. "What do you think of your first revel, then, mite?"

I look at our fellow dancers and the fae sprawled around us, taking in their laughter and the lilt of the music, the sweet and tart flavors still mingling in my throat. More tension than I realized I was holding in unravels with my next inhalation. Seeing everyone enjoying themselves so free of concern makes it easier to shed my own worries. "It's nice. I'd like to do it again. Although it'd be nic*er* if the pack wouldn't think it was strange for August and Sylas to join in."

"Am I not enough protection for you?"

"That's not what I meant." I twist my neck to glance up at Whitt. "And is that what you're doing—protecting me?"

He leans in close enough that his lips graze my ear, his voice so low now that no one other than me could possibly hear it. "Every expression, every comment, is useful information. Just by having you out here with us for a short while, I know much more than I did before about who looks the most benevolently on you and who I wouldn't count on to dose you in water if you were on fire, who I should be sure to *never* let dance with you and who would probably be safe as long as they've gone easy on the absinthe. If you're going to stay with us as long as it appears, I may need to bring every bit of that information to bear."

I hadn't realized he was paying that much attention to everyone around us—or that so much of his attention was centered on their reactions to me and what that could mean for my safety or simply my comfort. I hadn't realized my safety and comfort mattered enough to Whitt that he'd focus that much thought on it. Of course, he's probably doing it for his brothers' benefit more than mine.

I turn myself in his grasp, trying to suppress the tingle that races over my skin at the slide of his fingers along my waist, so I can look at him without straining my neck. "Is that what these parties are about for you? Just gathering information?" When I watched him from the keep's windows before, I thought he was basking in the festive energy.

His blue eyes glitter. "I get plenty of fun out of them too, and it's always a pleasure to bring some delight into my pack-kin's lives. Although nothing I pull together out here compares to the grand revels I could put on back at Hearthshire, closer to the Heart's power and with so many more to join in. Oh, we did have a time or two then…"

A hint of melancholy crosses his face, suggesting he misses their old home just as Sylas does. It vanishes quickly, though, leaving him with the same sly expression. "But a spymaster's work is never truly put aside for the night. I wouldn't be much of one otherwise."

He says those words flippantly, but something about that breeziness, maybe because of the commitment he just made to my protection, sends a pang through my gut.

"You must be able to relax *sometimes*. You don't have to

be on guard like that when it's just Sylas and August around."

He guffaws. "I'd argue that being aware of my lord's and my cadre-fellow's concerns is even more vital than any other's."

Is that really how he feels about them? Like they're part of his job more than family? "But—you need someone in your life you can just *be* with, without having to think about all that."

"Do I? I seem to be getting by just fine as I am."

Getting by, sure, but what about being happy? What about having the space to just be *himself*, not a spymaster or whatever?

I know what it's like to stay constantly wary, evaluating everyone around you for warning signs, never having a chance to fully relax. It wore me down even when I was living here in the keep with proper food and shelter. To just accept that as a permanent state of being...

I'm probably reading too much into it and Whitt doesn't mean it the way I'm taking it. Still, I can't help wondering what that handsome face of his would look like lit with the kind of open, unfettered joy I saw on August's this morning when he told me he loved me. I think I'd like to see that.

An odd flutter passes through my chest, and I yank my gaze away, abruptly aware that I've been staring. "I guess you've been gathering information on me too? Making sure I'm up to tomorrow's trip?"

Whitt adjusts his hand against my side, his fingers barely touching me now. "As far as I can tell, your participation in our 'trip' has already been decided."

"But you're not convinced it's a good idea."

"Did I say that?"

I can't help raising my eyes again. "You didn't have to."

He tsks at me with a slanted smile. "You made a perfectly convincing argument. As many distractions as you might create at the border, I'd imagine certain parties would find it even more distracting contemplating what might be happening to you back here beyond their reach."

"So you think I'm going to distract them if I'm with you. I said I'd stay out of the way—"

"Talia," Whitt says firmly, cutting me off. He bows his head next to mine again. "You don't have to prove anything to me. I made my decision that night in the woods, and I'll defend your right to be with us—wherever we go—with claws and teeth if it comes to that. Of all the things you have to worry about, you can rest easy when it comes to my good will."

He sounds serious when he so rarely ever does. The night he must mean is the one when he practically ordered me to flee to the human world so my presence wouldn't provoke any more conflict between Sylas and August. When they caught up with me, fighting off another fae who'd attacked me, Whitt told me he'd changed his mind, that I was good for them. He asked me to stay.

I didn't know how much I could trust that unexpected flip, but apparently he meant it even more than I'd have imagined.

A lump rises in my throat. I want to reach out to him somehow, which doesn't make any sense because I'm already less than a foot away from him, one hand enclosed in his.

Whitt turns us with a lift in the music and falls back into his usual breezy tone. "We've been talking far too much about my predilections. This obviously isn't where you could have pictured you'd be at this point in your life, back before Aerik rampaged into it. If you'd never left the human world, what do you suppose you'd have been up to by now?"

My earlier homesickness hits me with a fresh twinge. "I guess I'd have gone to college. I was going to study something like environmental science—ecosystems and climate patterns and all that." If I'd even stuck with that by the time I had to choose. I hadn't researched it a whole lot, only snagged onto an idea that might give me the chance to explore the world and get paid for it at the same time.

"Hmm, so practical. What would you have been doing for *fun*?"

My mind drifts back to my scrapbook, to the hours spend reading up on exotic locales across the continents. "If I'd gotten together enough money, traveling. There were all kinds of places I wanted to visit. It seemed like there was so much out there that was so much more interesting than our little town, so many *different* things…"

Whitt laughs, with a note that sounds almost sad. "You couldn't have come much farther than you have now, could you, my mighty mite?"

I manage to smile, even though my throat is outright aching now. "I guess not." I pause. "You know, I wouldn't have complained about coming to this place if I'd had more choice in how I came. To the Mists in general, I mean. It's not exactly the kind of adventure I imagined going on, but now that I have more say in how I live here… there are definitely a lot of good things along with the bad."

Whitt is silent for a long moment as we sway together and the music winds around us. Then he inhales sharply and raises his hand to my cheek in the briefest of caresses. "And tomorrow we'll manage to take you even farther."

"Yes." Another shiver travels through my body, but this one is almost giddy, and not just because of the heat his touch woke in my skin.

"And you're not a fraction as frightened as you probably should be." He tsks at me teasingly again.

I meet his eyes steadily. "I don't think it can be worse than what I've already been through."

"No, perhaps not. I'll give you that."

Whitt rotates me in one more slow spin, my misshapen foot only just starting to twinge at how long I've been putting my weight on it, and then lets me go. "Have a little more tumbleweld, mite. We won't have treats like that out at the border."

Harper has returned from her chat with her father, and I settle onto a cushion next to her with another husked fruit to nibble on. The ache inside me fades with the blooming warmth the stuff sends through me. We trade more stories, my memories of human life in exchange for her limited but still fantastical rambles around this part of the fae realm, and then lie back to peer up at the stars, Harper pointing out the constellations the fae have legends about.

Every now and then I peek Whitt's way, watching him circulate through the other revelers, bringing a smile to each face with his passing remarks. This might be work for him, but I think he does like it too.

When my eyelids are starting to droop and the cushion is feeling so comfortable I'm not sure I want to bother getting up, the music dwindles. A few pack members sprawl out on the blankets to sleep beneath the stars. Others gather the now-empty dishes from the table. As Harper sits up with a stretch of her arms, Whitt comes for me.

"Up you go," he says, lightly but briskly. "I have something else to end off your night."

I peel myself off the cushion drowsily but with an itch of curiosity and follow him to the keep. The lantern orbs waver on to meet us.

Whitt leads me up to his office and simply points to a silver box about the size of a textbook on his desk. He stays standing off to the side as if he doesn't want to come too close to it.

Opening the box, I find a velvet bag that sags across my entire hand with a shifting weight. As I tug it open, a mineral smell reaches my nose.

It's full of salt crystals—maybe ten times the small portion August secreted to me weeks ago so I had some small protection against Kellan. The salt I used to break the magic locking the keep's doors. The salt Sylas chided August for giving to me.

When I stare at Whitt, his smirk comes back, though it looks a bit tired now. "August's job might not be cleverness, but that doesn't mean he never has any good ideas. Salt will work just as well against the winter fae as those of summer—and I can't promise every Seelie you might run into by the border will be friendly besides. We couldn't have you coming completely unarmed, could we?"

I do also have the small dagger Sylas presented me with this afternoon that August taught me a few basic techniques with, but that would only make for a last-ditch defense. Salt is one rare thing I can wield that none of the fae can match.

Whitt managed to get this from the human realm, however much discomfort being near it would have caused him. He must have gotten it *today*, since they didn't know I'd be coming with them until then.

Just how much is going on behind those ocean-blue eyes, feelings and intentions that he hides with his smirks and mockery?

My fingers curl into the thick fabric of the bag. "Thank you. Does—does Sylas know?"

"You don't need to hide it from him. He seemed pleased enough when I suggested it. I wouldn't go flashing it at any fae beyond the three of us unless you mean to use it right then, though."

"Of course not." I have the urge to hug him or to figure out some other gesture to show I recognize how much he's offering, but I'm not sure how he'd react. He seems to want to treat it as if it's no big deal.

I'll never scoff at the idea that he intends to protect me again, I can say that much.

Whitt gives me a gentle nudge toward the door. "You'd better get your rest. We have a long trip ahead of us tomorrow."

CHAPTER EIGHTEEN

Whitt

I always forget how much I hate dealing with arch-lords and their cadres until I'm faced with the pompous bastards again. Of course, given the way the three cadre-chosen representatives are eyeing me, I'm lucky they agreed to meet with me at all.

"What's so urgent that Sylas of Oakmeet felt the need to come all the way out here himself?" asks Cashel—the one who belongs to Ambrose, so naturally the most obnoxious—folding his arms over his chest. We're meeting in one of the temporary war camp buildings near his post, and the sunlight seeping through the massive woven blades of grass that make up the walls turn his ruddy skin sickly greenish. "If he had a matter to bring before the arch-lords, I'd imagine he hasn't forgotten how to make a standard petition."

Sylas would be here himself standing up to these pricks if it wouldn't have been an act of humiliation for a lord to negotiate with another lord's cadre, as if he didn't trust his own cadre to do the job. I doubt they'd offer him much more respect than they're giving me regardless.

"My lord isn't here to *ask* for help," I say, smoothing as much of the edge out of my voice as I can manage. "We're here to offer it, as I believe I already mentioned."

Maeve, the hawk-nosed woman from Celia's cadre, snorts. "And why would any of the arch-lords require 'help' from Oakmeet? Your pack hasn't exactly contributed any stunning victories so far, and I'm not sure I want to hear any ridiculous schemes you've come up with, 'Wild' Whitt."

My reputation, carefully cultivated as it is, does occasionally have its downsides. Never mind that I'm truly ridiculous even less often than I'm fully drunk. Never mind that the warriors we can spare are no more than half what any other pack would be able to send out—or that not even the arch-lords have won any truly decisive victories with their far greater numbers. If they had, we wouldn't be standing around in a stuffy hut having this damned conversation.

"They've contributed enough that we're aware of shifts in the tide," I say, glancing from her to Donovan's man, Hollis, and back to Cashel. "You're anticipating a strike beyond anything the Unseelie have pulled off yet, aren't you? How many of the other lords have put together the pieces—and bothered to make an appearance to show their support?"

None of them bothers to answer that. Hollis adjusts his weight on his feet, his narrow face tight with apparent discomfort. Out of the three arch-lords, his tends to be the most lenient. But even Donovan didn't argue all that hard against our banishment to the fringes, so I can't expect much cooperation from that quarter.

Like any fae, they're not inclined to lie, but that doesn't stop them from talking around the truth. Cashel raises his head at a haughty angle. "We have no news to report. Perhaps you've come here on a misguided errand."

Perhaps, not *definitely*. And they have no news they want to report to *me*. If the fact that they reacted with defiance rather than confusion hadn't already convinced me that Sylas's theory was correct, that response would have done the trick.

I restrain myself from rolling my eyes. "All three of you know that our pack's current standing can be blamed on the unfortunate ambitions of my lord's deceased mate—which he did not share or act in favor of—not any deficiencies in strength or wits. Whatever's coming, we'll push it back however we can, but we'll be a much more effective tool in the arch-lords' arsenal if you share what you've learned about the Unseelie's plans."

Maeve tosses back her tawny hair. "Even if we did have some foreknowledge, anyone with *wits* would be able to figure out it'd hardly be sensible to share it with a pack that's been associated with treachery against our arch-lords once before."

Cashel nods in agreement. "Yes. Tell Lord Sylas that he may as well go home. We have no scraps to offer you poor beggars."

The two of them stride out without another word. Hollis shoots me a grimace that might be slightly apologetic and follows, equally silent. I glower at their retreating backs and draw in a breath to settle my temper.

I hadn't really expected them to say much. Getting confirmation that some scheme is afoot was enough. Judging by their attitudes, I feel confident in telling Sylas that they don't know exactly what to expect from the Unseelie themselves. They know *something* bad is coming, but not enough to want to toss some sort of "scrap" our way to let us take the brunt of the attack.

Stepping out into the thin early-morning sunlight, I roll my shoulders and then stretch out into my wolfish form to lope back to our own camp.

The meeting tent of sorts stands about a mile back from the border, near enough that I can see no raven warriors are piercing the haze there at this particular moment. Beyond the scattered buildings constructed based on their inhabitants' magical affinities for plant-life or stone or metal, the ephemeral wall that separates the summer half of our world from winter rises all the way up to tint the stark blue sky gray. Minor eddies whirl through the haze's glinting surface, which combines the shimmer of heat rising off a scorched earth with the clotted fog of a cold damp night.

If I were to lope *that* way, within a few steps of heading through the haze I'd find myself treading on icy ground in frigid air—for however few seconds it'd take before the Unseelie warriors descended on me and bashed my brains out.

The Seelie camp buildings stand in clusters for each squadron, spaced apart across the flat terrain here. Most of the tall, hissing grasses that cover the fields have baked beneath the sun so long the blades now shine like brass. Here and there, one squadron or another have cut the grass down to make room for scruffy gardens.

Warriors don't enjoy playing farmer, but they must also tire of hunting and foraging. Some of them, like many of our own, have been stationed out here for years on end.

A few distant wolfish figures prowl along the base of the hazy border, reassuring me that our fellow packs are at least organized enough to be keeping up their patrols even though there hasn't been a full-out attack since the one that sent Ralyn back to us weeks ago. I turn away from them and speed up my strides, weaving through the grass and skirting the beehive-like hillocks that rise from it farther afield.

I'm just coming around one of those pocked protrusions when an unpleasantly familiar form stalks into view—the skinny, pale-haired man from Aerik's cadre: Cole. The one who's been spying on our domain for reasons still not entirely clear. And now he's lurking near our current settlement?

I veer toward him, and he stops at the sight of me, cocking his head. I can't tell whether he recognizes my wolf, but the moment I shift to stand upright in front of him, my skin prickling with the abrupt transformation, his lips curl with an equally familiar sneer. He must have learned it from his lord.

"What brings you all the way out here?" I ask in a conversational tone that may be slightly undermined by the fact that I haven't bothered with so much as a greeting.

Cole's eyes narrow, but he makes a careless gesture as if unperturbed by the question. "The same thing as you, I'd imagine. Hard to keep the squadron's spirits up if they start to feel abandoned by their leaders. Especially so in your case, given the history, I'd imagine."

I ignore the barely concealed barb in that remark and glance around. "And where exactly is this squadron of yours? Awfully far from home all the way out here, aren't they?" Sylas would never have picked this spot if he'd thought we'd be near neighbors with Aerik's warriors. Last I'd gathered, they were farther south along the border, closer to the Heart and to Aerik's domain.

"We decided a change in scenery was in order. As it seems your lord has too." Cole's grin is so sharp it can barely be called a smile. "Has Sylas nothing better to do than dawdle around waiting for a battle to come to him? Or perhaps he doesn't trust his cadre to handle things without his direct supervision."

I bristle inwardly but keep my expression mild. He's given away more than he might realize. Aerik isn't here, only Cole. And I have a strong suspicion this interest in seeing another portion of the border was driven by curiosity after hearing that Sylas had arrived here himself. Cole is chasing glory and guessing there's no reason Sylas would have come if an opportunity wasn't imminent.

"You'll have to ask him yourself, if you're so concerned," I say, baring a few teeth of my own, and spring forward as a wolf again.

I glance back once to check which direction Cole heads in, and then set off at a full run. Within a few minutes, I reach the stream where the current sings like harp strings, bound across the swaying reed bridge, and skirt the edges of the village built on its far bank.

No one likes to live both this far from the Heart and this close to the winter lands, especially now that the Unseelie have made themselves a continuing, concrete threat. The fortress that rises beyond the cluster of houses is a lopsided affair grown of brambles, looking like little more than a massive thicket. I hate to think what the walls and floors within must offer.

I may be biased, but I have to say that the building August and I helped Sylas call up yesterday evening, about a half a mile farther west, looks a damn sight more appealing for all its flimsiness. We're a little closer to the Heart here than right out on the fringes in Oakmeet, but not enough to change the fact that we were attempting to conjure an entire multi-bedroom home in the space of a few hours. It's certainly not as elegant as the Oakmeet keep, let alone the castle in Hearthshire, and a bad windstorm could knock down those thin oak walls, but it'll do for the few weeks we're staying here.

Heart help us, let it be no more than a few weeks.

My own heart is thudding in my chest at a pace I can't entirely blame on my swift journey. It hitches faster when I spot a head of deep pink hair off to the side of our new building, which looks like the polished stump of a mountainous tree. Talia is crouched in the hasty garden Sylas and August coaxed into growing, pulling berries off of the plants there.

If Cole slunk by here recently, he'll have seen her.

It shouldn't worry me so much when I know Sylas bolstered the glamours around her just before we arrived yesterday and no doubt checked on them again this morning. I shouldn't worry about her at all when she has her two paramours doting on her at every turn.

It *definitely* shouldn't send an icy twinge through my chest when her eyes widen with terror at the first sight of my wolfish form—or warm me quite so dizzyingly when that fear flees in the wake of one of her shy but brilliant smiles as she recognizes me.

She isn't mine, I remind myself as I have so often in the past few weeks. She isn't mine, and she won't be. But the way she gazed at me the other night during the revel, so concerned about my happiness of all things—the way she looked when she talked about finding her own happiness in our world—

I shake those thoughts away and shed my fur at the edge of the garden.

As she takes in my expression, Talia's smile falters. "Is everything okay? Did they get angry with you?"

More concerned for me than for herself yet again. I jerk my head toward the arched door of our new abode. "The people I went to speak to were exactly as much pricks as I expected. But I had a less expected conversation we should discuss."

She grabs her basket and heads inside without argument—trusting me. In the open-concept space of the first floor, a couple of our warriors are sprawled asleep on the cushions in the living area, having come from the main camp area to wait on their lord. Talia sets the berries on the short span of kitchen counter, and I motion her up the stairs to the four cramped bedrooms.

Hers is the farthest back from the narrow staircase, I suspect because Sylas wanted any intruder to have to get

by all of us before reaching her. No sign of Sylas or August
—August mentioned meaning to hunt, and Sylas wanted
to speak to a few of the other squadrons, as much as they
might tell him.

Talia limps straight to her roughly-hewn bed and stops
there, waiting until I've closed the door behind us. We
need the privacy, but I'm abruptly aware with a quiver
over my skin of how little space lies between us.

"Is it safe to talk now?" the mite asks, canny enough to
understand why I'd have brought her away from everyone.

"We set down all the magical protections we could
around these rooms," I say. "It'd better be." Then I
hesitate, because I don't actually want to tell her what I
need to. But I do need to. "I don't think you should be
pitching in outside the fortress anymore."

Talia blinks at me. "Why not? If I did something
wrong—"

I wave off any question of that. "It's not you. Aerik's
squadron has moved nearby. Cole is already sneaking
around. I'd imagine he's wondering what brought Sylas
and the rest of us out here just now. That bunch are always
looking to improve their advantages any way they can. I
think it's best if we give them as little opportunity to study
you as possible."

She has already tensed up, her back stiffening. "With
the glamour—he shouldn't have been able to recognize
anything about me, right? He didn't come close enough
that I saw him."

"You should be fine for now. We simply don't want to
push our luck. Let me check the glamours, just in case."

I can see already that the one across her shoulder, to

hide any trace of her scars that might peek past her shirt, is solid as ever. I motion for Talia to sit. She sinks down on the edge of the bed, and I kneel to examine her malformed foot.

Close up, I can squint through the illusion and make out the awkward jut of the bones, the curves of the wooden slats that form her brace. But when I set my fingers against her ankle, the glamour obscures even them. Cole would have to be mere inches away to see through Sylas's magic.

That doesn't mean he couldn't notice something odd about her gait if he watches her walking around outside, though. I hate telling her she should stay confined—but she doesn't want another encounter with that bastard any more than the rest of us do. Less so, presumably.

"Is it okay?" Talia asks, and I realize I'm still crouched there before her, holding her ankle. Stroking my thumb across her skin to tease out its warmth, without even thinking about it.

I drop my hand as gracefully as haste allows and look up at her. Her vivid green eyes pin me in place.

"Yes," I say. "Nothing to worry about."

"For now."

"Exactly." I pause, considering. Her words from the other morning, when she said she didn't want to stay locked away, ring through my memory. "If you didn't venture far from the building, and you kept particular care with how you walked when outside—you shouldn't have to stay completely cooped up in here."

Her bittersweet smile could slay me. "This was the risk I took when I insisted on coming out to the border. I'll manage. The house is still a lot bigger than Aerik's cage. I'll just focus on the cooking and other tasks I can do indoors."

"So stoic, oh mighty one," I can't resist teasing.

As my reward, her smile brightens for a moment. She gives my arm a playful kick. "It isn't easy for you either, is it?"

I raise my eyebrows. "What do you mean?"

"Well, you must have to be even more on your guard all the time out here. The other packs' warriors are all over the place. None of this territory is actually ours. Even if you're always on alert around other people back home, you at least have the space to get away from everyone if you need to."

I'm not sure what makes my heart twinge harder—the fact that she just referred to Oakmeet as "home" as easily as if she's always lived there, or how clearly and matter-of-factly she's extrapolated about my wellbeing from the few admissions I made the other night. Maybe it's neither but the fact that she cares enough about my wellbeing to consider it that far.

I give her calf one last gentle pat through her jeans. "Save your worries for yourself, mite. I have plenty of practice at tolerating discomfort as need be."

She shrugs. "So do I."

Who could deny that?

I don't know how long I'd have stayed there, kneeling at her feet and basking in her attention if Sylas's voice didn't carry from downstairs just then. "You've returned, Whitt?"

I stand, torn between gratitude and regret at the

interruption. I might have enjoyed lingering longer, but that doesn't mean it'd have been good for me.

"I'll explain the situation to Sylas," I tell Talia. "And maybe we'll all get lucky and the wretched Unseelie will peck Cole's head off before we have to deal with him again."

CHAPTER NINETEEN

Talia

It doesn't make sense, not really. We just came to the border, and now I'm standing in the field outside the keep with the lights and music of a revel all around me.

The initial burst of doubt slips away with the whirling of the dancing figures surrounding me. I turn, the lanterns seeming to spin above me, and Whitt is there. He takes my hand to spin me around like he did at my first revel, and his eyes hold mine with a heat that washes through me from head to toe. His mouth curves into a sly grin.

He looks fierce and somehow free as I've never seen him, as if there isn't a single thought in his mind except me and what he'd like to do with me. A thrill races after the rush of heat.

I twirl before him as if my feet are steady. The dancers around us fade away. The music keeps playing from some distant source. When I come to a stop facing Whitt again, he's dropped to his knees in front of me like he did when checking my foot this morning.

His fingers glide over my bare skin, skimming my ankle and up my calf, raising the hem of my dress until it reaches my knees. As my pulse thumps, he leans in and kisses the inner side of that knee. Then a little higher, and a little higher, his hands easing the dress farther up with each movement of his lips.

A sharper tingling shoots to the meeting of my thighs with every kiss. He's teasing me and worshipping me at the same time. His fingers slide upward until they're nearly grazing the place now throbbing with need, his mouth rising after them, and I want—I want—

A creak shatters the spell. I snap awake amid the coarser sheets of the bed in my temporary new room, my body flushed and my heart still pounding, though in a much more eager way than past moments when I've jolted out of sleep.

In the darkness, I just barely make out the silhouette of a brawny figure in the doorway, lit by the faintest of glows from the hall. The fall of wavy hair and the gleam of one pale eye reveal him as Sylas, not the man I was dreaming about.

The memory of that dream sends a renewed flush over my skin just as Sylas steps inside. He tips his head questioningly. As I sit up, my eyes adjusting to the dimness, I catch the quirk of the corner of his mouth.

"I heard you gasp and thought you were caught in a nightmare," he says, the rumble of his voice low but warm with amusement. "Now I'm thinking it wasn't a bad dream after all."

How well can his wolfish senses pick up my bodily reactions? I wet my lips, willing away the thrum of arousal still coursing through my veins. "It wasn't. I'm all right. I'm sorry if I disturbed you."

He makes a dismissive sound. "I was turning in for the night. There was nothing to interrupt." His voice dips even lower, with no less amusement. "Although now I'm curious exactly where that dream of yours was taking you."

My drowsy mind slips back to the moments before I woke, to the gleam of Whitt's sun-kissed hair below me and his lips hot against my inner thigh. More heat spikes from low in my belly, but at the same time my stomach twists uncomfortably.

Why would I dream that? Whitt and I *haven't* done anything. Even if I've felt flickers of attraction now and then, I already have not one but two men I've promised my heart to. How can I even *think* of anyone other than them?

How would Sylas react if I told him? My tongue turns leaden, my mouth going dry, remembering the flares of possessive aggression when he first found out about me and August. And that was before I'd made any sort of commitment to him. After what his former mate did to him… The thought of him thinking I've betrayed him, that I lied when I told him I loved him, makes something deep inside me shrivel in dismay.

"Talia." When I glance up at Sylas again, his expression has turned so serious that I can see the concern in it even in the faint light. Whatever he's seen in me—with his good eye or the ghostly scarred one—it brings him to the side of my bed. He perches with surprising deftness on the very edge of the thin mattress so he isn't crowding me and takes my hand where it's clenched on top of the covers.

"You don't have to tell me anything," he says, his voice somber as well as quiet now. "Your dreams are your own. I would never make a demand like that—and if it was a dream of August that stirred your body that way, I wouldn't be angry with you. How I reacted in the past was not a reflection on you, only my own urges to deal with."

His determined reassurances loosen the tension in my stomach. I still balk at revealing exactly what my mind conjured up.

But maybe he *should* know. What if my body gives away some hint of desire at a time when I'm awake, when he can see who's provoked it?

"What if it wasn't August?" I say tentatively.

Sylas lets go of my hand to stroke his fingers over my cheek. "I'm certainly not going to take issue with you dreaming about *me*."

My head ducks at his touch. "What if it wasn't either of you?"

He pauses. "Then I'd remind both myself and you that we don't choose our dreams, and be glad this one brought you pleasure rather than terror."

That's true. How could anyone blame me for something I only dreamed of doing? It isn't as if I want to find myself back in Aerik's cage, but how many times has my mind conjured *that* scene up?

I relax enough to lean toward the fae lord, and he tucks one arm around me, nestling me against him. My initial fear seems absurd now. This man has been nothing but patient with me, despite his natural inclinations. That's part of *why* I love him. So maybe that's why the confession tumbles out in the faintest of whispers. "I dreamed about Whitt."

Sylas lets out a soft chuckle. "Well, I suppose you wouldn't be the first lady to do so. Does it bother you to have imagined him that way?"

I consider that question. Now that Sylas has reacted so calmly, my uneasiness has fled completely. "Only if it bothered you. It's never happened before—nothing like that has happened with him in real life. I wasn't expecting it."

"Sometimes dreams reveal desires we hadn't known we were harboring, just as they can reveal buried fears. There's no shame in it. Especially with him. If I didn't think he was among the best of our kind, he wouldn't be in my cadre." He's silent for a moment, his fingers grazing my shoulder with a light caress. "Do you care for him, then?"

"Not—not like you and August. I don't really know him all that well." My mind drifts back to the waking moments I've shared with Whitt—the way he rushed to keep me safe from Cole this morning, the way he spoke about protecting me during the revel, the bag of salt he gave me that's hidden beneath my pillow right now, just in case.

The warmth of his embrace while he apologized for sending me away, weeks ago. The playful remarks that can startle a smile out of me or banish my anxieties when I need it most. The devotion to his brothers I've seen in every move he makes on their behalf, despite how much he heckles them.

"I like him," I add as I sort through those impressions and the emotions they stir up. "I think I'd like to know him better. And I—there's definitely some attraction there. For me. But it doesn't really matter. I'm already happy having you and August. And it's not as if Whitt would be interested in anything... romantic, or whatever, with me anyway."

"Has he said that?"

I frown. "No, but—he's never said he *would*. He's never acted as if he wants something like that to happen. It always feels like there's at least a little distance he's keeping when we're talking." Like he's holding himself slightly apart from me, even when he's literally holding me. All the times when I've seen something like fondness light in his eyes and then fade away as if he's shuttered them, shutting me out.

Sylas hums to himself. "Whitt is capable in many ways, but close relationships of any sort aren't exactly his forte. I'm not sure there's anyone in his life he'd even call a true friend other than myself and August, and even there, he tends to act as a colleague first. If he's doing more than tolerating someone's presence, that's a high mark of approval in itself."

Having seen Whitt in action, I can believe that. But... "It doesn't make any difference, does it? However he feels, I'm with you and August. I know it was already difficult for both of you to share even that much. I'm not going to pursue anyone else."

"Not even if you had our blessing?"

My gaze jerks up so I can stare at Sylas. "What do you mean?"

His face doesn't show any sign of jealousy. "You know that the precedent for an arrangement like ours comes from cadres sharing a lover. Typically in those cases, the lover in question is involved with all of the members of that cadre, not just so that their needs are being met amid the cadre's responsibilities, but also to avoid tensions rising if one or another isn't so favored. It's a difficult balance—one that's already been on my mind as we navigate this unforeseen territory."

I remember the moment back at the keep when the three of us left Whitt behind, the pang I felt at excluding him. "That does make sense. But this isn't a typical situation, is it?"

"No. Typically Whitt would have more claim to join in than I do." Sylas presses a kiss to the crook of my jaw. "I have no intention of giving you up. But I've made my peace with what we have... and in some ways I'm coming to enjoy knowing how well you're taken care of, even though it can't always be by me. If you wanted to explore whatever you do feel for Whitt, and he's developed some affection for you as well, it might serve us all to see how that plays out."

My pulse flutters as I consider it. "I don't know—How would I even start?"

"Hmm. Maybe leave that to me. Perhaps when we have returned to the keep, an ideal opportunity will arise to put the matter to him. Although if you see an opening before then—you do have my blessing."

The love that's a constant pulse behind my ribs swells to the base of my throat. I twine my fingers in Sylas's hair and pull his mouth to mine. The force of his kiss leaves no doubt that this conversation hasn't cooled his desire for me one bit.

"Thank you," I murmur against his lips.

He smiles. "It's the least the lady of our keep deserves. And now that lady had better get some sleep, before I get too tempted to turn this into the new tryst room."

"You forgot to make one of those," I point out as I lie back down.

He stands, a light laugh spilling out of him. "If we find ourselves here for very long, you can be sure I'll rectify that oversight."

———

The late-night conversation leaves me settled enough to drift back to sleep, but when I limp downstairs in the morning, the sight of August already puttering around in the kitchen area reawakens a twinge of anxiety.

Sylas has given me his blessing to indulge my tentative feelings for Whitt. August doesn't even know I've considered it. Even though I haven't done anything yet, a sense of betrayal pinches at my gut.

This wonderful fae man loves me. By some miracle, he loves *me*. How can I even suggest that what we have isn't enough?

But then, maybe he'd feel better including Whitt in whatever exactly this strange relationship is rather than leaving him out. If even Sylas could see it that way, it isn't hard to believe August might.

Either way, I can't keep it from him.

This isn't the time to bring up the subject, though.

Two of the pack warriors, including the one who came back to Oakmeet injured a couple of weeks ago—Ralyn—are hunkered down in the living area. Ralyn is fletching arrows and his companion sharpening a dagger. From the number of balls of dough August is tossing onto his baking sheet, he's preparing a breakfast for the entire squadron I know is stationed a short distance nearby.

"What can I do to help?" I ask, glancing from him to the warriors. Yesterday, along with cooking, I learned the art of sword sharpening and mended a couple of armored vests. If anyone regrets my coming out to the border, it won't be because I failed to carry my weight in every way possible.

August motions me over. Since we arrived here, he's been wearing more formal clothes like the ones he put on for Aerik's visit, not his usual human-style tees. Today's V-neck tunic is a rich pine-green that brings out both the ruddy tones in his dark auburn hair and the golden gleam of his eyes.

I slip past him into the warmth that wavers through the kitchen area from the stove, which is little more than a clay box around a smoldering fire. No time for the complex magics that went into his kitchen equipment back at the keep.

"Slice up the rest of the cheese," he suggests, motioning to the crumbly orange block on the counter. "It won't last much longer."

"You're going to make us all homesick for the foods we can't usually get here," Ralyn remarks. "The cheese they make in this domain isn't any match for Elliot's. All they've got is goats."

"I'll be sure to tell Elliot how much you miss him and his sheep," August replies with a grin.

By the time I've chopped all of the block of cheese into fairly equal portions, August has fried a few panfuls of thinly sliced meat that gives off an appealingly buttery scent and is starting on another. Together, we assemble a couple of large baskets with cheese, apples from the bushel someone picked yesterday, fresh-baked rolls, and most of the fried meat. As the warriors heft the baskets and see us off with a wave, August lays out the rest of the meal on plates for the four of us living here.

Neither Sylas nor Whitt have made an appearance downstairs yet. I nibble on a stray chunk of cheese and debate whether I should try talking to August now. It's not as if there's any rush while we're here in a battle zone... but the subject is going to nag at me as long as I'm keeping it secret.

I open my mouth—and chicken out. "So far, there haven't been any signs of another attack coming, have there?" I ask instead.

"None at all. The ravens are lying low for the time being. Most of the activity around here has been building up our usual magical defenses to scare them off if they try to attack during the full moon. So far we've been able to stop them from realizing how vulnerable our forces are then."

I glance down at my arm. My blood could mean none of the warriors here need to succumb to the wildness... but giving it to them would automatically expose me to Aerik. Even without knowing where I am, he's stopping me from having full freedom.

"Will our squadron be okay when we head back to Oakmeet?" I ask.

"They have been for many moons before. We always make it look as if the border is particularly heavily guarded then, with glamours and the rest. Although with the spats the arch-lords' cadre-chosen keep having about where the squadrons should be directing their energies, it's lucky we're getting that much done." August lets out an exasperated huff.

I grimace in sympathy. "I wish they'd tell you what they think is going to happen."

"So do I. But we're here, so eventually we should see for ourselves. I'm staying ready for just about anything." He slings his arm around me and tugs me closer to give me a peck on my head. "Are you worrying about that, Sweetness? You look like something's on your mind."

I guess I don't have much of a poker face. I swipe at my mouth and decide I might as well just spit it out.

"It's—it's not about the war or anything like that."

"That's fine. I could use a break from patrols and battle plans."

I draw up the courage to push onward, measuring out my words. "You've been okay with me also being with Sylas. What if—what if it was Whitt too?"

August's arm tenses against my shoulders, and my pulse stutters. "Nothing's happened," I blurt out quickly. "I don't even know if he'd want it to. Nothing *will* happen if you aren't okay with it. I'm happy with the way things are. I just—I wondered—and Sylas said it might even be better if we weren't leaving him out—*if* he'd even want to—"

August cuts off my babbling by pulling me right into a hug. "It's all right. It's a reasonable question." He gives a short bark of a laugh. "If *Sylas* is already on board, who am I to argue?"

I peek up at him. "I don't want you to go along with it just because I mentioned it." My arms slip around his broad chest, hugging him back. "I love you. I wouldn't do anything I knew would hurt you."

"You're the last person I'd ever be afraid of coming to harm from, Talia," August says gently. He tips my face up so he can kiss me, long and tender, until I'm tingling all the way to my toes. Then he stays there with his head bent close to mine, his nose grazing my forehead. "And because *I* love *you*, I want you to have all the happiness you can. I'm guessing you wouldn't be asking if you didn't think getting closer with Whitt would make you even happier."

"If he even would want to," I say again.

August makes a dismissive sound. "I don't think that's much of a question. It has felt a little odd the past few weeks, having something so separate from our connection through the cadre." He runs his hand over my hair. "And this way we can hope that at any given time, there'd always be someone there for you, no matter what we face."

I hug him tighter, and he matches my embrace. When I ease back, he's smiling so easily that the nervous pinch in my stomach melts away. "You're sure it doesn't bother you?"

"I promise it's fine. No more worrying. Now sit and let's get some breakfast into you."

Despite his order, I insist on grabbing a couple of plates and carrying them over to the small wooden table between the kitchen and the living area, then coming back for the goblets to go with the sparkling juice August brought from home. As I duck back into the kitchen on one final trip to scoop up a few apples, the stairs creak.

Sylas emerges from upstairs, running his fingers through his dark hair before rubbing his hands together in anticipation of the meal. "Even with as little as you have to work with out here, you manage to impress, August. If the Unseelie knew you're as good with a sword as you are with a carving knife, they'd never cross that border again."

August beams at the praise. "I could skewer plenty of ravens with a carving knife too. We have to make the best of what we've got here, don't we?" He veers toward the kitchen. "Here, I have one more portion of—"

The front door bangs open. Without a word, several armed fae march into the house, weapons drawn.

CHAPTER TWENTY

Talia

At the intruders' entrance, Sylas stiffens and strides toward them. August steps forward too, placing himself closer to his lord—and between me and the unfamiliar fae with their armor and weaponry.

Are these Unseelie? I tense up, but my men aren't acting as if they see these warriors as an immediate threat. And as I peer past August, standing rigid with an armful of apples braced against my chest, I realize the fae who've barged into our house aren't all strangers to me. The five of them standing most closely together I've never seen before, but off to the side, in a bronze vest a little more dinged up than what most of the others are wearing, stands Cole, the icy-sharp spikes of his hair unmistakable. He elbows the woman next to him, who appears to be a colleague of his rather than of the others.

My heart lurches. I curl my fingers around one of the apples as if I can use it as some kind of weapon of my own. Somehow I don't think throwing it at these fae would accomplish anything other than making them very pissed off at me. Maybe I should reach for the little dagger in its sheath at my left hip or the bag of salt I've been tying to a belt-loop at my right, but I suspect a show of overt aggression from a human wouldn't improve their moods either.

I set the apples down on the counter just in case I need to anyway.

"What's the meaning of this?" Sylas demands, planting himself in front of the fae man at the front of the main bunch. "I'd have thought Ambrose's pack was civilized enough to understand the concept of knocking."

Ambrose's pack? Ambrose is one of the arch-lords— the one who blames Sylas for how his former mate and her family attempted some kind of rebellion.

Why have the warriors of his squadron come in here so forcefully? You'd think *we* were the Unseelie they're meant to be fighting, the way they're posturing.

"If you have nothing to hide, you shouldn't mind us paying you a visit, Lord Sylas," the leader says with only the slightest tip of his head in recognition of Sylas's title. His gaze roves through the airy room.

Sylas folds his arms over his chest. "And why would we have come all the way out here in order to hide something?"

"Why have you come all the way out here at all is the real question. We thought we'd best make a real stab at answering it."

"I believe one of my cadre-chosen spoke with one of

your lord's yesterday about that very matter. We haven't made any secret of our intentions."

The other man takes a step to the side to get a better view of the living area. "Forgive us for not being willing to take you entirely at your word. We serve only Ambrose, and we'll ensure no treachery comes from our side of the border."

Do they really think Sylas would have traveled to the border to carry out some scheme against the arch-lords? The idea seems ridiculous to me, but the solemn expressions on all of the warriors' faces suggest they find it totally plausible, the jerks. I have the urge to pelt them with the apples after all.

Cole, of course, is simply smirking, like this is all great entertainment. Sylas shifts his weight, the muscles in his arms flexing, obviously wanting to chuck the lot of them out of the building but wary of the repercussions. These aren't lords, but they're an arch-lord's pack-kin. My stomach knots, watching.

"If there is anything else you want to know, you need simply have asked," Sylas says tautly. "But I'm sure you can see there's nothing startling within these walls. I've only ever wanted what's best for all Seelie kind, as plenty of our brethren can attest to."

"Hmm. And yet *one* of your cadre-chosen isn't among you. What could Kellan be up to?"

"You wouldn't expect me to leave my domain completely undefended, would you?" Sylas asks, as if it's Kellan back there doing the defending, not a handful of sentries.

The leader of Ambrose's squadron—or whatever part

of his squadron this is, since I'm sure the arch-lord has more than five warriors at the border—makes a skeptical sound, but he doesn't push that line of questioning any further. He marches through the living area and parks himself behind one of the chairs at the dining table, his narrowed gaze sweeping into the kitchen. When it comes to an abrupt halt on me, my stance stiffens twice as much.

The fae man's nostrils flare. His eyes flash, a sheen of magic taking them from a deep indigo to crystalline sapphire in an instant. "You've brought a *human* with you. What could have possessed you to haul a wretched dung-body all this way? Are your pack-kin so inept you don't trust them to wait on you?"

Sylas's lips curl back over his teeth, his sharp canines glinting where they've protruded just a fraction into fangs. "She isn't a servant. She's my cadre-chosen's companion."

The squadron leader glances at August, whose shoulders twitch, the muscles coiled all through his body. I can tell it's taking all his self-control to hold himself in place.

The other man's eyes flick back to Sylas. "You brought a dust-destined *whore* then. Somehow I question whether you truly are taking this fight as seriously as you claim."

August starts forward with a growl low in his throat, but he only makes it one step before the jerk of Sylas's hand stops him. Sylas's mismatched gaze stays fixed on the squadron leader. Somehow he manages to draw his already substantial frame even taller. He's got to have at least fifty pounds of brawn on the other man.

There are five of them—seven if we count Cole and his lackey—and only three fae in this house on our side, one of whom is upstairs still sleeping. And how quickly will they call Sylas a traitor if he lays so much as a hand on them?

"If we didn't take it seriously, we wouldn't be here," he says, a growl laced through his own steady voice. "You've had a good look. *I've* had enough of your insults and insinuations. Let me show you out."

"You're not in your own domain, you forget, Lord Sylas," the squadron leader replies. He ambles around the table toward the kitchen. "And technically all domains fall under our arch-lords' rule. I say this runt is an unnecessary distraction. How much can one frail human girl be worth? Consider how easily she could be removed."

A chill washes over my skin. The threat is barely implicit—he's talking about how easily he could kill me. My hand drops to the pouch of salt, fingers looping through the string so I can jerk it open in an instant. He's only pointing out my fragility, but that doesn't mean he won't decide to act on the threat.

"You keep your paws off her," August snaps.

Sylas moves to form a barricade with him. "We're well aware of the mortal nature of humans. I'm sure you wouldn't make an unnecessary demonstration that destroys a being under my care."

The squadron leader lets out a cold laugh. "If I wanted to, would you challenge the authority of—"

He's cut off by a cheerily melodic voice that carries from the stairs with the thumping of careless feet. "Why, look at this! A whole horde of guests. My lord, you should have told me we'd have company."

Whitt saunters into the room with a feral grin and a

wild glint in his eyes. My pulse hiccups at the thought of how one of his insults might take this from a standoff into a full-out brawl. But Sylas's spymaster takes in the crowded room and the plates on the table with a chuckle, as if we're all in on some joke together.

"Heard about my cadre-fellow's excellent cooking, did you, lads?" he says, clapping August on the back. "It looks like we don't have quite enough for you. Next time you'll have to make an advance order."

The squadron leader blinks at him, completely diverted from his previous goal, whatever exactly that was. With his eyes off me, I shrink back against the counter, my hand lingering on the pouch of salt.

"What are you talking about?" the intruder asks.

Whitt tsks at him. "I suppose if you're so desperate for breakfast, we might make an exception. But it would come at a price. We wouldn't ask you to sing for your supper, but perhaps a little dance would allow you to dine."

The squadron leader simply stares, all of his followers wearing matching expressions of confusion. Cole's mouth has twisted at a sour angle, apparently disappointed that the potential for violence has faded.

Whitt sighs in mild exasperation. "I'm sure you must know how to dance, with all the balls the arch-lords host. Just give it a little whirl, and we'll see what we can do to fill your bellies." As if he thinks they need an illustration, he makes a few graceful steps to some internal rhythm, with a flourish of his arm and a spin to finish.

As he turns, his gaze catches mine, and he shoots me a swift wink. Despite the fear churning inside me, a giggle tickles up my throat. All these fearsome warriors with their blades and their posturing, and he's disarmed them with a few wry remarks.

Whitt looks at the squadron leader expectantly, his eyes gleaming with restrained amusement, utterly in his element. I can't tear my gaze away from him. A different sensation is fizzing through my chest now, one as heady as faerie wine.

That dream last night didn't come out of nowhere. I'm falling for him too. I don't know how long I have been or how far I'll fall, but I recognize this feeling.

How could anyone *not* find themselves overwhelmed with affection, watching him turn this hostile situation around so brilliantly?

The woman with Cole lets out a rough laugh, and that sound shatters whatever remains of the tension. The squadron leader shakes his head, looking a touch embarrassed but not aggressive anymore.

"Have your breakfast," he says, waving his hand toward the table. "We've got plenty of our own. Just make sure your attention is on defending our people, not the dung-body, when the next attack comes."

His ego apparently satisfied, he turns on his heel and stalks out, the other warriors hustling after him. Cole slinks out behind them with one more disdainful glance our way.

As soon as the door has closed behind them, Sylas gives Whitt a baleful look, but his lips have twitched into a smile. "You do choose your moments, don't you?"

"It seemed like the right time to make an entrance," Whitt says breezily, so unconcerned that most of the anxiety melts out of me. He drops into his chair at the table. "I just hope those pissants haven't soured the food."

"I'm sure it's still edible," August replies, his shoulders coming down. He gives himself a little shake as if shedding the defensive energy the intruders provoked and gives me a onceover to confirm I'm okay. When I manage a smile, he returns it and holds out his hands for the apples I'd gathered. I offer them up, gratified to see my arms don't even tremble.

Ambrose's warriors were only throwing their weight around, but I'm awfully glad it didn't have to come to a fight after all, with whatever fallout would have resulted.

Sylas touches my arm, studying me for a longer span than August did. He's relaxed some too, but his face is grim. "I'm sorry. I hadn't thought—clearly I overestimated how well we could shelter you from that kind of aggression here. I don't believe he intended to truly harm you, but you shouldn't have had to hear any of that."

"It's okay," I say. "I mean—it's not okay that they came and talked like that, but I know it's not your fault." I hesitate. "Do you think they'll keep badgering us?"

"I wouldn't expect so now that they've had their look around and come up with no reason to accuse us of anything, but we can't be sure. I'll create an enchantment you can use to signal me if you need help while I'm away —I should have done that to begin with."

I exhale slowly. "Thank you. I'd appreciate that." My gaze slides past him to where Whitt is tossing the apple August passed him in the air with a flick of his wrist, and my smile comes back. "At least this time it ended without any disasters."

"It did." Sylas follows my glance, and his expression lightens just a little. His voice drops. "Perhaps I could see about giving you something that might make your day more pleasant sooner than we discussed... if you'd like?"

A current of warmth ripples over my skin, merging with the pang that echoes through my chest. There's nothing I want more right now than to feel secure in the embrace of my protectors—all three of them, if the third will have me too. Especially when that third is the one who did the most to protect me just now, if not in a traditional way.

My answer slips out in barely a whisper. "I would."

Sylas considers the scene for a moment and then ushers me over to the table by August's chair. "I think our lady might enjoy some special attention after that unsettling encounter," he says to the younger man, lightly and steadily. "Remind her how devoted we are to her wellbeing... among other things."

August looks at both of us, his gaze uncertain and then sparking with interest. He glances across the table at Whitt, who's paused with his fork in midair, and then back at me. At my nod, he eases his chair back and opens his arms to welcome me onto his lap.

I sink onto his thighs, instinctively tucking myself against his chest and soaking up his warmth. My heart thumps faster, but this time with eager anticipation rather than nerves.

Yes, I did need this. To wipe away the awful things the other fae said. To ground myself in August's love.

And to discover whether the man on the other side of the table takes any interest in me like this at all.

"What would you like, Sweetness?" August murmurs into my hair.

I tip my head against his shoulder, offering him my neck. With a pleased hum, he lowers his mouth to kiss me there. Heat floods my skin with the press of his lips and the stroke of his fingers across my torso, just below my breasts.

Right now, I want that heat everywhere. I want to burn so fiercely I can believe I'd sear right through any enemies who ever threaten me again.

Chair legs rasp against the floor, and my eyelids flutter open. Whitt stands up, holding his plate. His voice comes out as flippant as always but with a note of strain. "Well, *I'm* clearly not needed here. I suppose I'll dine upstairs."

My chest hitches at the thought that I've made him feel even more an outsider from his family than before, but Sylas must have observed more than I can. He rests his hand on the table and tilts his head toward August and me. "Or you could take part. That's what you'd like to do, isn't it?"

Whitt goes completely still, looking as taken aback as the squadron leader did faced with his antics not that long ago. His jaw tightens. "I'm perfectly capable of controlling my—"

"But we're not asking you to rein in your desires," Sylas interrupts in the same measured tone. "It was never our intention to exclude you. We simply didn't realize— but I should have been more aware, and I apologize for that. I think August and I have already shown we're capable of sharing."

Whitt looks at me then, for the first time since he got

up. There's a wildness in his eyes again, but much stormier than his earlier playfulness. It's desire, yes, but anger and confusion too, and a starker yearning that shines through all the rest, so raw it makes my heart ache.

"Shouldn't Talia be the one who makes that decision?" he says tartly, but his voice has thickened. I don't know where the anger and confusion are coming from or who they're aimed at, but in that moment, I can feel that yearning for me all the way down to my bones.

Even as a flush creeps over my cheeks, I hold his gaze. My words come out soft but clear. "I have."

Whitt doesn't look relieved by the admission. If anything, his stance goes more rigid, the muscles of his face twitching in shock.

Sylas teases his fingers over my hair with a fond smile. "Talia's been the one calling the shots in this arrangement from the start. If cadres of four or five can form a balanced relationship around one lover, I'm sure we'll—"

Whitt smacks his plate down on the table with a clatter of the silverware. "Did you ever think that maybe *I* wouldn't want to share with *you*?" he snaps, and spins on his heel. He stalks across the room and out of the front door so quickly and resolutely it leaves no doubt that he means to be gone for quite a while.

I stare after him, my throat constricting. How did this go so wrong?

Sylas frowns, but he gives my shoulder a gentle squeeze. "I don't know what's gotten into him, but given space, he'll sort himself out. At least now you have your answer about his interest, whether he decides he's going to act on it or not."

I do. Whitt wants me, with a greater force of feeling than I'd ever have guessed. Only he doesn't seem at all happy about that fact.

I thought reaching out to him would be a chance to bring the three men who've watched over me back into harmony, but what if I've wrenched them apart instead?

CHAPTER TWENTY-ONE

Talia

"F*ee-doom-ace-own*," I murmur, channeling all the protective energy that rises in me at the thought of Sylas or August meeting a bunch of attackers' blades. As I center all my concentration on it, the bronze chink in the battered chainmail vest closes in a loop to connect it to the one above.

For once, I'm using my smidgeon of magical power to defend someone other than myself. Better that I use my copious amounts of spare time to mend armor damaged in past battles than any of the actual fae waste their own when they have so many other responsibilities outside this house.

A rustle carries through the open window next to me. I pause where I'm perched on one of the living room cushions, a slightly lumpy construction that seems to be made out of overgrown leaves melded together and stuffed with I'm not sure what. When I'm alone in the house, I can't help freezing at every sound from outside.

Three days after we arrived, the Unseelie still haven't launched an attack, but that only means that with each passing hour it feels more imminent. I can't even see the border from here other than a vague shimmering haze August pointed out to me far in the distance, but even if *I'm* safe here, Sylas and his cadre won't be.

For a few seconds, all I hear is the whisper of the breeze passing through the tall grass, its crisp, hay-like scent drifting in to me. I've just resumed my work when more rustling reaches my ears. It solidifies into the more definite sound of footsteps.

The steps could simply be someone from Oakmeet returning or dropping in. Of course, if it's anyone other than Sylas or August, I won't feel that much more at ease. I've exchanged a little conversation with the warriors stationed here, but they don't linger for very long unless it's to sleep. They're still essentially strangers to me. I definitely can't continue this work in front of them. And Whitt…

Whitt hasn't said more than the briefest of polite greetings to me since that awkward breakfast yesterday morning. He's barely been around to. Somehow he's always coming or going when we end up in the common areas together, and most of the time he manages to avoid that altogether.

He hasn't been cold or cruel about it, but every time I sit down to a meal without him or watch his retreating back vanish through a doorway, my stomach knots tighter.

Maybe he really is busy—but he wasn't quite that busy

before we pushed him to admit he felt some attraction toward me. For whatever reason, Sylas's suggestion about joining our arrangement upset him, even with my clear approval. I don't know how to mend the bridge between us, especially while so many other tensions are running high by the border.

I have to figure out something. Even if he doesn't want anything more with me than we already have, I miss his smirks and his wry remarks and the cheerful gleam in his fathomless eyes.

I set my hands in my lap, my ears pricked to the sounds from outside. The rustling footsteps become louder, moving toward and then past the window—away from the front door rather than toward it. Just someone passing by?

Then a voice that sends a spear of ice down my spine breaks the quiet. "I told you they were all occupied elsewhere."

It's Cole—I'd know that sharply sneering tone anywhere.

The voice that answers I don't recognize at all, but it might be the woman I saw with him the other morning. "What are we trying to accomplish here?"

A third voice, gruff and male but equally unfamiliar, speaks up. "The mutts of the Oakmeet pack are a bunch of treacherous bastards. Now Sylas comes out here and acts like he's better than every other lord because he turned up personally? He deserves to be put in his place."

Cole chuckles. "Exactly. I'm glad *someone* understands. Now are we going to get on with this, or are you disobeying orders from cadre?"

"No, no, I'm on board," the woman mutters.

I don't like the sound of their conversation at all. Skin prickling, I set down the vest as quietly as I can and ease toward the kitchen. After the intrusion yesterday, Sylas shaped a little wooden bird for me and showed me how to work the markings he etched in it to activate its magic. It's sitting on the counter.

No other sound except the occasional murmuring travels through the window as I cross the room. Reaching the sculpted bird, I hesitate.

Sylas looked so somber when he left after our hasty lunch a couple of hours ago. He said he was going to demand an audience with the arch-lords' cadres and make whatever case he could appealing to them directly. There was some specific strategy he planned to propose. That meeting might already be over, but if it isn't—if I interrupt him at a moment that could make a difference in them finally accepting his offer of help...

A harsh snicker filters through the wall. My pulse stutters. I hold still and silent. Cole's command is just loud enough to carry to me. "Shatter it all, every bit of it."

If he breaks something important to our cause, that could be worse than any interruption. I balk for a second longer, wishing I could drive away the monsters outside myself, but my little dagger and my salt will only get me so far against three fae. From what I understand, the salt's toxic effect will only ward off the fae for a minute or two, and I have no idea when any of the pack-kin will return. These weapons are meant as a last line of defense, not for me to start a fight.

Steeling myself, I grasp the sculpted bird and run my

thumb over its belly. Sylas's instructions run through my mind. Trace the deepest groove here, press the bump there, swipe back and forth over the shallower line in between—

The sculpture's wooden wings flutter against my hands. I pull back my fingers, and the enchanted bird flits away, veering out the nearest window.

Sylas said its magic should send it straight to him. The moment he sees it, he'll know there's trouble here, that he needs to come back. Now I just have to hope he's close enough to make it back before Cole carries out whatever damage he's attempting to cause.

Listening carefully, I dart back to the living room. The hushed voices outside are intoning words I don't recognize. True names? Some other sort of magic? My skin crawls all over again.

I reach to the pouch of salt and loosen the opening, just in case. With careful steps, I slip up the stairs to the second floor and go to my bedroom window. I can peek outside from there without worrying that Cole will spot me right away.

I can't see him from this angle anyway, but the woman from before wanders into view, her eyes fixed on the house and her hands weaving through the air in time with her indecipherable mumbling. When her gaze flicks upward, I jerk to the side with a lurch of my pulse. She doesn't give any indication that she saw me.

Maybe they wouldn't care even if they knew I was inside. Cole must have been monitoring Sylas and his cadre and maybe the rest of the warriors, so he'd have to at least suspect August's human companion is still in the building. Given the way he treated me even when he thought I was valuable and his amusement at the thought of Ambrose's squadron leader "removing" me, I don't think he's sparing much thought to how his plans will affect me. In his mind, hurting me—possibly killing me—might even be a bonus.

I still have no idea what exactly the three of them are up to. I lurk upstairs for a few minutes longer, watching in quick peeks and straining my ears, but the tight space of the small room starts to niggle at me. At least downstairs I have more room to maneuver if they decide to break in.

I hurry down the narrow hall. Just as I'm reaching the top of the stairs, a shudder runs through the floor beneath my feet.

"Almost," Cole says in a tone so triumphant it chills me straight through. "Let's get those final protections down…"

A quavering rush of magical energy flows around me in a wave. My nerves scatter. As I clutch the banister, the entire house shudders again.

Fighting the impression that I'm about to be tossed from the stairs, I scramble down them before the house shakes so hard that I actually will be. The tremors rippling through it grow with every lurching step. I stumble at the bottom, one of the slats of my foot brace catching on a rough spot in the floor and throwing me forward. As I hit the floor with a painful smack of my palms and knees, the walls fracture around me.

I spin around so I'm sitting with my hands steadying me from behind. In every direction, the wooden growths Sylas and his cadre summoned into the house are cracking and crumbling. I jerk my arms up over my head an instant before the floor above crashes on me in a shower of splinters. As the bits rain down, both those shards and the floor beneath me disintegrate into dusty mulch.

When I dare to lower my hands, crumbs of destroyed wood tumble off my arms and trickle through my hair. I'm crouched in the midst of a total ruin. Nothing remains of the house except scattered heaps of that pale mulch, sprinkled with scraps of leaves, wisps of seed fluff that must have filled the pillows and mattresses, and lumps of metal and stone.

My stomach heaves in horror. After all the magic my men put into constructing this house and its contents, Cole and his lackeys smashed it to pieces in a matter of minutes. I'm lucky they didn't smash through me too.

Of course, I'm not safe from that yet. Cole steps forward from where he was standing at the edge of the destruction, the sunlight glancing off his blue-white hair and his teeth bared in a vicious grin. "Look what we have here. Just think of all the fun we can have with you now."

The sight of his cruel face and the familiar menacing pose right in front of me are enough to make my chest clench up. My ribs seem to close around my lungs, squeezing away my breath while my heart hammers against them in vain. As I gasp for air, my head spins.

No. *No.* I can't let the panic take over, can't let myself become helpless the way I was before. I'm not in a cage. I have ways of fighting back.

How *dare* he think he's going to torment another girl the way he did with me.

The flare of anger steadies me. I draw in enough

oxygen to clear my head, one hand dropping back to the ground for balance and the other leaping to my pouch of salt.

My pulse is pounding so hard my body shakes with it, but I've practiced with August enough to move into a low fighting stance without needing to think. My fingers close around a handful of salt crystals. I shift my weight forward.

All I have to do is fend him off for long enough for Sylas to get here. I can't focus on anything but making it to that moment.

Cole strolls closer, his lackeys hanging back to watch. His fitted boots crunch through the dry shreds of wood. His gaze skims over me. "Look at you. Just what do you think you're going to—"

He comes to a halt with a jerk, staring at the ground. No, staring at my *feet*—at the foot I've just slid forward in my defensive pose.

The foot he broke nearly nine years ago, now encased in Sylas's brace.

Oh, God. He can see it. He can see *me*.

Panic hits me in a frigid blast. Whatever spells Cole and his pack-kin cast to crumble the magic that built this house, they crumbled the glamours on me too.

Cole's attention snaps back to my face. To my eyes, which must now be the same color they always were, my features more fleshed out but otherwise a match for his former prisoner. What little color was left in his face drains away. Then his eyes spark with a light that's twice as brutal as before.

"Oh," he growls, "Lord Sylas is in so much more

trouble than I even thought."

The last word has barely left his mouth when he springs at me. A yelp breaks from my throat, but my horror hasn't knocked those weeks of training from my mind. My hand yanks back automatically and flings toward Cole, hurling all the salt I could hold straight into his face.

As they strike his skin, the crystals burst apart. With a pained snarl, Cole reels backward, swiping at his eyes, his mouth.

My flicker of triumph snuffs out as quickly as it appeared. His lackeys who were standing by bewildered a moment ago leap to their boss's aid.

"I'm fine," Cole barks, jabbing a finger toward me. "Get the wretched girl."

I shove my hand into the pouch, every muscle tensing. Panicked dizziness sweeps through me again. The crystals pinch my skin. I can only throw at one of my attackers at once. Who do I have a better chance against: the man or the woman? They both look ready to tear my throat out.

I ready myself, fighting the trembling of my body, and a roar echoes across the fields. Three massive wolves race into view—wolves I know so well a sob of relief jolts out of me.

The one in the lead with the white scarred eye slams into the fae man who's just about to lunge at me. From right behind him, the ruddy-furred one springs at the woman, knocking the sword she's drawn from her hand and sinking his fangs into her forearm. And the sandy-colored one whose ocean-blue gaze stands out starkly in his wolfish face charges straight at Cole.

The lackeys are no match for a lord and his cadre. The man starts to shift, and Sylas clamps his jaws around his neck, halting him. The woman doesn't even try, glowering up at August with lips pressed tight against the pain of her gouged arm.

Cole might be stronger, but he's still distracted by my salt attack. Before he can do much more than swing a couple of fists at Whitt, the wolf has him pinned, claws poised against the underside of his chin.

"I yield," the male lackey cries out.

Sylas shifts into his usual form, gripping the man's throat with his hand instead. "You will leave here and do us and the human woman no more harm."

"Agreed!"

As Sylas frees him, the woman makes a similar promise to August. The two lackeys scramble to the sidelines, the woman clutching her arm to her side. Whitt stays in wolf form, glaring down at Cole, who has recovered from the salt enough to glower back at him.

Sylas strides over to them. "Are you going to yield, Aerik's cadre-chosen, or shall I bury you in the ruin you made of my camp?"

Somehow, even on the brink of death, Cole finds it in him to sneer at the fae lord. "I invoke the right to seek justice served."

Sylas hesitates. Even Whitt's muscles tense up where he's restraining Cole against the ground. The fae lord's head jerks around, his mismatched gaze finding me— hunched, shivering, and glamourless.

August growls out a curse.

"You've stolen my lord's property, Lord Sylas," Cole

says with a vicious grin, looking far too satisfied for a man with a wolf's claws only a smidge from dealing a fatal wound. "Such a crime cannot go unaddressed."

Sylas's lips curl back from his teeth, his fangs out, but he slices his hand through the air in a gesture to Whitt. The wolf recoils, launching himself off Cole but staying in animal form, his snarl daring Cole to give him an excuse to lash out again.

The gangly fae picks himself off the ground and makes a show of brushing off his tunic and slacks. He backs up a few steps to where his lackeys are standing, but his head stays high.

"Lord Sylas of Oakmeet, you have twenty-four hours to make right how you've wronged Lord Aerik of Copperweld," he announces with a ring of power in the words. Then he lowers his voice. "I'll tell my lord he can expect his property returned to him by this time tomorrow, or the whole Seelie realm will know that you're just as much a criminal as your departed mate."

The threat wrenches at me. I wish desperately for Sylas to tell him off, to tear him down after all, but I can already tell my saviors are bound by some tenet of fae law.

My fingers dig into the crumbling wood. Everything they'd spent so long working for could be ruined. Their chances of ever returning to Hearthshire, their standing with the other lords—shattered as completely as this wrecked house. All because of me.

"Let us not see you or your pack-kin before then," Sylas says. As Cole motions to his lackeys to shift and they lope off toward the river, all he and his cadre can do is stand there.

CHAPTER TWENTY-TWO

Sylas

The carriage hitches with a gust of the breeze, swaying beneath our feet. Normally I'd have constructed a steadier vehicle, but in my haste and fury, I may not have given this conjuring the focus it deserved.

It doesn't help that I've urged it to the fastest pace I feel is safe. The landscape of clustered trees and rough knobs of beige stone seems to whip past us beneath the glare of the mid-day sun. At least moving this swiftly, we should make it back to Oakmeet within a few hours.

I'd hoped to spend most of those hours determining our plan of action, but I think we all needed time to settle ourselves in the aftermath of Cole's threat and our leaving. My memory of the events after he dashed off blur together —checking over Talia for injuries, fragmented discussions with my cadre about what to do, my hurried cajoling of the juniper tree into our enchanted ride while Whitt sped off to inform our squadron of our unexpected departure.

My older brother has stationed himself at the prow where it juts out from beneath the arched beams shading most of the carriage. The jostling of the ride must be getting to him, because in the full sunlight his face looks slightly green, his knuckles pale where he's gripping the low wall beside him. He peers out at the passing landscape intently, as if searching for an antidote to a churning stomach.

I can't help noting that he picked that position after Talia tucked herself into the small, padded seat at the stern, where a few sunbeams streak across her vibrant hair. As far away from her as he can get. He didn't hesitate to spring to her defense when it mattered, so I can't chide him for failing her. All my observation leaves me with is a dull ache in my own stomach at the sense that I've stepped wrong with him in a way I don't fully comprehend.

He cares for the woman—I know him well enough to pick out the indications, the remarks and gestures that wouldn't mean a great deal from someone as open as August but from my spymaster are tantamount to doting. His desire for her was clear on his face when he watched her in August's arms. He's never been particularly finicky about monogamy in the past— certainly he's never offered it of himself to any woman I'm aware of, let alone required it from his lovers—but it isn't as if I've demanded a full accounting of his personal affairs.

I've missed something, something that seems to have outright wounded him. It might simply be a misunderstanding, phrasing I used that gave the wrong impression of my meaning, but I can't clarify that without broaching the subject again, and I can tell he wouldn't let me get very far if I tried.

I may be his lord, but I'm not going to command him to share his personal concerns with me. There will be a time; I will make it right.

But first I have to rearrange this much more urgent catastrophe into a shape that's at least vaguely acceptable.

The carriage shudders again, and I decide I'm best off sitting rather than standing. I sink onto the bench along the left side, across from the matching seat August took after Talia asked for space while she gathered herself. My younger brother is leaning forward with his elbows braced on his thighs and his hands fisted together in front of his chin, his golden eyes darkened to a muddy hue. I'm not sure I've ever seen him so troubled, even when he challenged me on Talia's behalf weeks ago.

I tip my head to him. "I don't suppose all that deep thinking has produced any brilliant stratagems?"

August shakes himself and straightens up with a grimace. "I've been wracking my brain for a way I could have prevented us from getting into this situation at all— but that's a waste of time when there's no way to undo it now."

Talia eases her legs down from her huddled pose and glances from me to August and back. Her shoulders remain rigid, as if braced for the worst. "What will happen if you don't give me back to Aerik in twenty-four hours?"

I drag the crisply warm air into my lungs. "Cole couldn't speak for his lord with full authority, but his terms were standard for a claim for justice. I'd expect if we resist they'll either attack our pack at Oakmeet or turn the matter over to the arch-lords." Neither of which would have an outcome in our favor.

"Whichever Aerik thinks will undermine *his* position the least," Whitt says from the front of the carriage, still staring out over the passing landscape. "Cole could have said they'd be taking the matter to the arch-lords immediately. That would have been the simplest solution with their cadre-chosen already stationed right there. But I don't think Aerik and his cadre want to bring the arch-lords into it if they can help it."

Watching him, Talia hesitates for a second before venturing, "Why wouldn't they? The arch-lords could force Sylas to hand me over, couldn't they?"

Whitt shrugs. "Aerik knows that as soon as it becomes clear that the source of his cure is so easily moved around, the arch-lords are likely to insist on taking over the process of making it. He'd lose his bargaining chip and the glory that came with it." He allows himself to glance toward Talia for the first time since we climbed onto the carriage. "But he'd rather the arch-lords end up with you than see us keep you—you can be sure of that."

I wish I could argue against any point he's made, but I agree with his assessment entirely. "It does buy us a short amount of time to come up with a solution."

Whitt's gaze returns to me, alert despite his apparent queasiness. "Do you think the arch-lords' cadre-chosen will be suspicious of our abrupt departure so soon after you spoke to them?"

I grimace. "More likely they'll see it as running off with our tails between our legs, considering they tossed my proposal aside so easily."

Not that I could blame them for their reasoning, which was sound enough. I offered to send a small foray of two or three warriors into the Unseelie realm to pounce on however many ravens it took to uncover more information about their plans. They rightly pointed out that if they approved such a foray and the Unseelie discovered it, the ravens would use that violation to justify further attacks. The arch-lords prefer to keep the high ground of merely defending what's already ours.

But they dismissed the offer so brusquely—showed so little appreciation for the fact that I'd made it—it rankles me that I lowered myself to appealing to them when at least two of them extended no respect at all to me in turn.

"I don't think it should affect how we approach the situation with Aerik," I add.

Talia looks down at her hands, clasped on her lap. "What *can* you do? They know who I am now and that I'm with you. They're going to keep trying one thing or another until they've gotten me back or at least ripped me away from you, aren't they?"

My hands ball at the hopelessness in her voice. If I could wallop Aerik out of existence and all our problems with him, I'd do it in an instant, just to bring the light back into her.

"The only way we could get them to back down is if we forced a yield," August says into our momentary, dire silence. "From everything we know, it doesn't seem Aerik has told anyone other than his cadre about Talia. Too much chance of word getting back to the arch-lords, probably. So if we could get the three of them in a position where their lives hang on the balance and insist they swear to leave her alone…"

He trails off, swiping his hand over his face, no doubt as aware as I am of how unlikely we are to orchestrate that kind of coup, especially within the next not-quite-a-day.

Talia knits her brow. "You tried to get Cole to yield, but he used that 'right to justice' thing to get out of it. Wouldn't they just do that again anyway?"

I shake my head. "The right to justice served can only be invoked once for any given crime. Cole claimed it for anyone concerned with your 'ownership' and had his chance to set the terms. But I can't see any of them putting themselves in a position where we could get the upper hand, let alone all three of them."

"If they don't want to involve the rest of their pack, it'll be just the three of them at any hand-off we arrange." Whitt rubs his jaw, the sickly pallor fading from his skin as he focuses on the conundrum. "That would be our best chance."

"They'll ask for an accord against hostilities," I point out.

"Hmph. We can negotiate that down to first strike. They can hardly expect us to agree to show up utterly incapable of defending ourselves if *they* launch an attack."

August lets out an irritable sigh. "So, your plan is that we provoke them into attacking us and then somehow turn the tables on them? While also keeping Talia out of danger that whole time? They won't engage with us in the first place if we're not at least acting as if we're handing her over."

Whitt throws his hands in the air. "At least I'm *trying*

to think of some way out of this disaster. If you've got a better idea, feel free to contribute."

The two of them glower at each other for a moment until Talia breaks in. "What's first strike?"

I turn to her. "We'd give our magical bond that we wouldn't initiate an attack. Essentially it guarantees their safety as long as they don't lash out at us. It's a typical request for a scenario like this."

She nods slowly, sucking her lower lip under her teeth to worry at it. Her gaze goes briefly distant. Then she aims her attention at me again. "Would you specifically say that you'd only fight if *they* start it, or only that the three of you won't start anything?"

"Usually the wording would be more along the lines of the latter, but I expect they'll also request that we come alone. The most we could hope to agree on is the three of us to match the three of them."

"But… I'll be there too. They won't ask you to swear anything about *me* fighting them, will they?"

Oh, my precious lady. It's hard to imagine I once thought of her as a little scrap, slight though she is, when she lets that inner fierceness show.

A pang runs through my heart that I have to say, "You wouldn't stand a chance against them, Talia. Even if we could arm you for the hand-off, which we can't. The instant you showed them any aggression, they'd hurt you worse than they already have."

Her gaze holding mine doesn't waver. "But there are things I can do that they won't expect. They don't know I have any magic. That's a kind of weapon. And I wouldn't have to beat them—I'd only have to get in the 'first strike' so that you'll have fulfilled your end of the deal, right?"

In the startled silence that follows, Whitt lets out a rough laugh. "She isn't wrong. That's our loophole right there. Find a way to position her so that once she makes her move, we'll have the advantage, and they'll never see it coming."

Everything in me balks at the idea. I promised to keep this woman safe. How can I now toss her to the front lines —to face off against the villains who tormented her for so long, who still feature in nightmares that wake her in a trembling panic?

"She'd be too vulnerable. They're not going to allow us to surround them or be poised right over them. By the time we get to them—"

"They kept her in a cage, didn't they?" Whitt interrupts. "Bars can keep a creature out as well as in. If she's using magic, she doesn't even need to be touching them."

Shove her back into a *cage*? My fangs itch at my gums just thinking of it. I swore to *myself* I'd give her some semblance of a normal life here, a chance at happiness.

But Talia is nodding. "The only true word I can really get to work is bronze, so maybe there could be something about the cage I could use… I don't know if I'd manage to injure them much, but if I could restrain them even for a few seconds, that should help you overpower them."

A grin has stretched across Whitt's face. I can practically see the schemes spinning behind those bright eyes. Even August has perked up, as if this plan is totally reasonable.

And perhaps it is.

Even as I recoil from the possibility, I can't deny it. The strategy isn't solid yet, but it holds up to every challenge I've made.

Every challenge except the one resounding from deep in my soul.

I hold out my arm to Talia, and she comes to me, lowering herself onto the bench next to me. I bring my hand to her cheek, studying her expression. "Are you sure about this? We have more time to discuss—there might be another way. I would never ask you—"

"I know," she says quietly. "I don't expect it to be fun. But given the alternatives... I'm not going to give up without some kind of fight. And I'm not going to let them tear apart your pack to get to me. No one else should have to get hurt when it's me they want."

A tremor runs through her voice with those last few words, but she keeps her chin defiantly high. A rush of affection courses through me. This beautiful human woman, more concerned about the fate my pack might meet than the danger she's throwing herself into.

It's an honor to have earned her love. Right now, I wish I could offer her my own. This deep, unwavering desire to bring her every possible joy doesn't have much in common with the whirlwind of emotions I felt for Isleen, even the positive ones, and I loved my soul-twined mate for all her flaws. I'm not sure I want to place Talia in the same category as her—and not because it would diminish Isleen any.

But exactly what to call my ever-growing fondness doesn't matter. What matters is that the woman who's given me her heart and her trust is asking me to trust her now, to believe that she's capable in taking part in this battle in her own way. To accept that taking on those risks might even be what's best for her.

If I made my old promises for her benefit and not my own, it shouldn't matter how much giving her this opportunity pains me. How can I deny her?

"All right," I say. "Then you will be the bait and the trap in one. Let us work out as many of the details as we can before we reach Oakmeet. I want every particle of this idea so solid there's no chance of it ruining us instead."

CHAPTER TWENTY-THREE

Talia

I pause in the keep's upper hallway, torn between knocking on the door in front of me or simply easing it open and slipping inside. It's past dawn, thin light just starting to streak through the window at the far end of the hall, the birds outside picking up their twittering. The faint clink of dishes that carries from downstairs tells me August is already up preparing breakfast.

We all turned in for the night fairly early after our long hours of planning—Sylas insisted on it so we'd be fresh and alert for our final preparations this morning—but I suspect the man on the other side of this door is still asleep. These aren't the sort of hours he normally keeps.

Would it be better to startle him awake with a rap on the door or to take a gentler approach?

In a few hours, I'm going to be confronting my most vicious enemies. I shouldn't be this afraid of facing one of my allies.

My gut twists. I dawdle a moment longer and then turn the knob.

The door glides open without a sound, none of the creaks and rasps of our house by the border. I didn't appreciate how finely crafted this building is until I had a much less polished construction to compare it to. How long did Sylas and his cadre spend coaxing the wood from the ground into the massive form around me?

Stepping into the room, I nudge the door shut. At the click of the latch, the figure in the bed stirs beneath the thick covers. That damned wolf hearing. I freeze, my pulse stuttering.

Whitt rolls over with a swipe of his eyes and peers toward me, his gaze still bleary. At the sight of me, he sits up with a start. The covers fall across his well-muscled frame to his lap, revealing the full expanse of his tattooed chest. With a tingle that ripples straight to my core, I wonder if he sleeps totally naked.

"Mite," he says, his voice airy but his hands clenching on top of the rumpled fabric. "Clearly I need to start locking that door. If you've come to seduce me, let me save you the trouble and pre-emptively decline."

His wry tone melts most of the nerves that had been prickling inside my stomach. Whatever's happened in the past few days, he's still *Whitt*. I've heard how he speaks to and about people he dislikes. There's no acid in the words he just directed at me. I might even have heard a little genuine amusement.

That realization generates enough confidence for me to roll my eyes. I limp over to the side of the bed, glancing down at my T-shirt and jeans before meeting his wary gaze again. "If I was trying to seduce you, I'd have come in the middle of the night in my nightgown, not first thing in the morning fully dressed."

He chuckles. "Spoken like one who's done it before." When my cheeks flush, he raises his eyebrows. "Ah. Well. You have gotten up to all sorts of adventures since you've arrived here, haven't you."

"I'm not here to talk about that either," I insist, willing the heat from my face.

"Do tell what you've come sneaking into my bedroom for at this wretchedly early hour, then." He folds his arms over his chest, but he draws his legs up under the covers at the same time as if giving me more room. I perch carefully on the edge of the bed by the footboard.

Now that I'm here and he's listening, the words I rehearsed in my head jumble together, every arrangement sounding cringingly awkward. I drag in a breath and force myself to look at him again. "You've been avoiding me since that morning when—when Sylas suggested... I've barely seen you. It's okay if you'd rather not have anything to do with me *that* way. I won't bring it up again. I still liked what we already had—being friendly, or whatever you'd call it."

A lump fills in my throat, and I have to lower my gaze and gather myself before I can go on. "I just wanted to see if we could talk it out."

Whitt is quiet for a moment. Then he says, in a voice gone rough despite its light tone, "And you thought now was an ideal time for that?"

I swallow hard. "I think now's the *only* time for that if

I want to be sure we actually get to talk about it. We don't know what's going to happen with Aerik today."

"Talia." He says my name like a command, and when I glance up at him, his eyes are so fierce my pulse hiccups in the second before he speaks again, just as vehemently. "We are *not* going to let that mangy bastard or his stinking cadre get one claw into you. However things work out with our plans, they won't walk away with you."

I wish I could believe the situation was that simple or sure. "Still, I'd feel better going to the meeting knowing everything's okay—or as okay as it can be—between us."

This time it's Whitt who looks away. His arms loosen, but his jaw stays tense, his eyes stormy. His chest rises and falls with a sigh. Then he turns back to me.

"You haven't done anything wrong. It isn't even exactly about you. And it's not that I'm not interested. It's a complicated situation."

With Sylas and August being involved too, he means? I duck my head, the lump in my throat expanding. "If I've ended up messing up your bonds in the cadre after all—"

Whitt is shaking his head before I can finish the sentence. "No. There are factors that developed well before you were ever in the picture. I promise you, you're not to blame for any of this."

"And because of those factors, you're not comfortable with anything happening between us."

"That's the gist of it." He rubs his hand over his face. "I didn't mean to make you feel shut out. I assumed it would be easier for everyone if we all had some space, but maybe I was mainly thinking of myself."

I make a vague gesture, not sure what to say. "That's all

right. And if you still need space, you shouldn't have to—I mean, just because I—"

Whitt cuts off my fumbling by leaning forward and slipping his hand around mine where I'd rested it on the covers. At his touch, I fall silent, waiting. Trying not to let the feel of his warm, strong fingers provoke too much giddiness. He contemplates our joined hands and lets out a sigh with a hint of bittersweet laughter to it. "Oh, mite. I don't know whether I'm more afraid I'll ruin you or you'll ruin me."

I blink at him, my spine stiffening. "I wouldn't hurt any of you. Not purposefully."

He meets my eyes, his a clearer blue now but no less vast. "I know that. But sometimes events spiral beyond our intentions, faster than we can catch them."

The remark cuts straight through me in a way he couldn't have intended, slicing through blood and bone down to the hollow that formed in the pit of my stomach the moment Cole threatened Sylas. The anxious tension coiled there swells into a vicious ache.

I open my mouth to take a breath, and a sob slips out instead. Tears flood my eyes so abruptly the salt stings them.

I fight to draw them back, to get a hold of myself, but my body starts trembling despite my best efforts. Dropping Whitt's hand, I pull my knees up to my chest and hug them tightly. "I don't want to hurt *anyone* else."

"Of course you don't. I wasn't implying—" The bedspread rustles, and Whitt's arm comes around me tentatively, his fingers stroking over my hair. "It's all right.

I can look after myself, and Sylas and August aren't any slouches either."

Somehow his reassurance makes the tears spill out faster. The ache spreads all through my abdomen. "It's not all right," I mumble against my jeans. "It's never going to be all right." Blood splashed red across patches of shadowed green. The shriek, the gurgles, the sounds of tearing flesh. I squeeze my eyes shut, but they overflow anyway.

I'm never going to be able to undo what's already happened.

Whitt hesitates, and then he's tugging me closer, leaning me against his solid frame. His summery, sun-baked smell trickles into my lungs. That and the circle of warmth of his arms around me should comfort me, but I can't seem to tamp down on the searing inside. I've been stopping up this feeling, this *guilt*, for so long, and now the seal has cracked too wide for me to stuff it all back in.

Whitt's voice manages to be wry and gentle at the same time. "I'm guessing you're upset about a little more than anything that's happened just now. You can tell me about it if you'd like. Or you can simply drench me in snot and tears. Your choice."

In spite of everything, a laugh hitches out of me. I tuck my face against my raised arm so that I'm not actually getting either of those substances on him, but he's broken the worst of the emotional onslaught. I inhale raggedly and exhale in a rush, sniffling and dabbing at my eyes.

Part of me wants to brush it off, to laugh and pretend my lapse was nothing, like Whitt himself might do. But I still ache from sternum to gut, and tears keep burning behind my eyes, ready to tumble free at the slightest provocation.

And maybe someone *should* know—what I did, how I failed.

"I already ruined my whole family," I say in a rasp.

"As much as I loathe giving Aerik credit for anything, I believe he deserves it in that particular case."

"You don't know. I—" I close my eyes again when they prickle hotter. "We wouldn't have been in the woods where he found us at all if I hadn't been teasing Jamie. My little brother. I dared him to chase me away from the road —I knew he was scared of the dark, that if I called him a couple of names, he'd try to prove he wasn't. If I'd just left him alone— If I'd kept quiet when they had me instead of screaming for my parents—" I press my face tighter against my sleeve. "They came running to help us, but there was nothing they could do." And then the wolves ripped them apart too.

Whitt lets out a dismissive huff. "Skies above, Talia, how old were you? Twelve? How in the world could you have known what might be lurking in the woods right then? You had no idea monsters like us even existed. And I've yet to see a child that wouldn't cry for their parents when they were frightened out of their wits. It would have been ridiculous for you to act any differently."

"I still could have. I was—I was selfish, and I got them all killed."

"Aerik and his mangy cadre got them killed. Unless you sprouted fangs and claws, you can't possibly be anywhere near as responsible as they are."

I suck in another breath and raise my head. Whitt eases back, giving me room but staying close. I stare at the wall, my eyes stinging when I blink. "I still wish I'd done things differently."

Whitt chuckles low and raw. "Then you're in fine and extensive company, mite. But I can at least assure you that my own worries have nothing to do with failings on your part. And it is possible I'm being overly cautious even so. We lost an awful lot over a woman before, but she had nothing to do with you, and you're certainly not a speck like her."

I peek over my shoulder at him. "You mean Isleen."

His mouth flattens. "The less of anyone's attention she claims now that she's gone, the better."

"I *could* ruin you all, though. Even get you killed. If I can't pull off the magic I need to today—"

"No one could have expected you to pull off any magic at all. I certainly won't blame you if it goes sideways on you."

"I know. But I'm scared. I was too weak when Aerik caught me, and it took me nine years to find the strength to unlock that cage, and now I'm going back into one like I'm giving up all over again. Even if I'm not *really* giving up, I could freeze up or start stammering—and it'll be the pack who pays for it if you can't overpower Aerik right away." More blood, splattered across the fields outside. My stomach lurches at the thought.

There *is* one way I could make sure that doesn't happen: I could give myself up to Aerik. But every time my mind strays in that direction, every inch of me recoils in horror.

Sylas would probably start a war to get me back if I tried to turn myself over, but that's not the main reason I balk. As selfish as it might be… I'd rather die than end up back in Aerik's prison. And killing myself won't help anyone—even if I was willing to go that far, he'd blame Sylas for the lost "property" anyway.

So what can I do except fight as well as I can?

Watching me, Whitt moves as if to get up. "If you want to talk to Sylas and August about adjusting the plan—"

I rub my forehead. "No. It's not actually a bad plan, is it? You're the strategist."

The corner of his mouth quirks upward. "It's a good enough plan that I'm ashamed I didn't come up with it entirely by myself. I think it's the best possible plan we could have pulled together given the time we had."

"Then we should still do it. If I tell Sylas and August I'm scared, they might decide we can't go through with it no matter what else I say."

"And who's to say I won't make the same call?"

"You won't," I say simply, with total confidence in that one fact. "Because when I say I think we should do it even though I'm scared, you trust me to make that call. Even when you didn't like me, even when you wanted me to leave, you've never *forced* me to do anything. You always let me decide."

Whitt considers me for a long moment, as if he's not sure what to say. Then a hint of his usual smirk crosses his face. "I'm not sure that's entirely true. To begin with, I always liked you, even when I didn't want to. But no, I won't go tattling to Sylas about your qualms."

He pauses before continuing, more quietly than before. "You know, there's a lot of power in pretending to be powerless. Playing into your vulnerability. Most of the time, I learn more when the folk around me believe I'm stumbling drunk than when I try to pry information out of them directly. I don't always love the reputation that comes with it, but—you learn to appreciate the benefits enough not to care. As long as *you* know you're not really that fragile, that's all that matters."

His take sends a quiver of rightness through me. I lift my head, trying out the words. "I'm *not* fragile." That feels right too.

Whitt's subtle smirk stretches into a full grin. "No, you're not, my mighty one. Not in the slightest. And I think Aerik is going to regret ever asking for you back."

I find myself smiling back at him with the same fierceness he showed when he spoke about Aerik earlier. "I hope he gives you all the excuse you need to tear out his throat instead of taking a yield."

An appreciative gleam has come into Whitt's eyes. "Oh, so do I—so very much."

The heat in his gaze washes through me. Not letting myself think, just following instinct, I shift onto my knees.

"Thank you," I say, meaning the whole conversation, and tip forward to brush a kiss to his cheek like I did that last full-moon night.

Like before, Whitt tenses, but I know better than to think it's with revulsion now. As I draw back a few inches, he swallows audibly. His hand moves to my side, only resting there, not pushing me away or pulling me to him.

My heart thumping, I risk leaning in again. My lips graze closer to his jaw.

Whitt closes his eyes. His voice comes out strained. "Talia, it's best that you go now."

Right then, I sense that if I ignored that remark, if I crossed the last short distance to bring my mouth to his, that's all it would take. Whatever dam he's built against his emotions would fracture, and he'd unleash all the passion simmering beneath his artfully composed exterior.

But I don't want him like that if he's going to regret it afterward. Even thinking about it brings the ache back into my gut.

Ignoring the desire clanging through my veins, I shove myself farther backward and then off the bed entirely.

When I reach the doorway, I let myself glance back. To my surprise, Whitt's expression looks startled for an instant before he recovers his typical unruffled self. "I'll come down to breakfast in a bit, mite. Since you've apparently missed my beautiful face so much."

A smile springs to my lips, the teasing rousing only a tiny shred of embarrassment now. "Good. I have missed it."

I head downstairs feeling if not exactly secure in today's plan, then absolutely determined to give it everything I have. For myself, and for these men who've taken me in as their own.

CHAPTER TWENTY-FOUR

Talia

The cage isn't completely the same as the one Aerik held me in for all those years. It's a little bigger, because Sylas wanted me to have enough room to dodge if anyone slashes at me through the bars, and the door has a latch I can easily flip open if I feel it'll be safer for me to make a run for it once the fighting starts than to rely on this structure for protection.

Aerik's cage never had several thin chains dangling from the base either.

But despite the differences, the looming bronze bars and the hard metal surface beneath me bring back all sorts of memories I'd rather leave behind. As Sylas and his cadre lower the cage in the middle of the large, grassy clearing where they've arranged to meet Aerik and his men, my pulse rattles through my limbs. My ribs seem to be digging right into my lungs.

I close my eyes and focus as well as I can on the parts

of this scenario that remind me that I'm loved and cared for, and that the fae men around me are nothing like the ones who tormented me. The soft fabric of my blouse and jeans hugs my skin, a far cry from the rough texture of the filthy blanket that was all the covering I had before. My stomach might be knotted with nerves, but no pangs of hunger resonate from my belly. Muscles flex through my arms where they're braced against the cage floor, toned from the training I've been given.

And a word that shimmers with magic hovers in the back of my throat, ready to be launched like a weapon.

The clearing itself is a far cry from the chilly, windowless room with its bone-white walls where Aerik kept my former cage. Sunlight beams down from the blue sky dotted with a few puffy wisps of cloud. Summer heat drifts through the bars to kiss my skin, bringing a sweet clover scent with it. A squirrel is chattering from the branches of one of the nearby trees. It would be a lovely spot for a picnic if I wasn't shut up behind these bars.

With the cage now set on solid ground, I adjust my pose, trying to find the most comfortable stance to wait in. I might be sitting in here for a while yet. I don't want my muscles cramping up if I need to move quickly later.

We've come early—early enough to hope that Aerik won't have anyone watching this spot yet—although we're taking precautions just in case to make sure he won't become too suspicious. Like having me in the cage for the whole trek from the carriage that's parked about a ten-minute walk back in the forest.

Now, Sylas and August move around the cage as if checking it over, surreptitiously stretching the bronze chains across the ground to nestle hidden in the long grass. Whitt steps back, scanning the clearing and the stretch of forest on the other side. The more normal-looking trees are interspersed with narrow cone-shaped ones that jut with their fluttering blue streamers of leaves several feet above the others.

The spymaster inhales deeply, speaks a few quiet words that I assume hold magic, and then offers a grim smile. "No sign of their arrival yet."

"Nothing to do but wait then." August hunkers down on the grass near the cage and glances at me. Seeing me trapped like that, even knowing our plan, turns his expression pained.

I want to reach through the bars to clasp his hand, both for my comfort and his, but we agreed we wouldn't act or speak as if we're anything but captors and prisoner once we arrived at the clearing.

While Whitt paces the edge of the glade, Sylas stays on his feet too, still and watchful. When he rests his hand on the roof of the cage, I look up at him. Our gazes meet for just a second; I see an echo of the question he asked me during the carriage ride in his.

Are you sure you're up to this?

Yes, I said then, and I'd say it again now if he could voice his concern. Of course, now that we're here, there isn't any turning back. I'm committed.

My heart keeps thudding on at twice its usual pace. I lean against the frame of the door, which is behind me when I'm facing the way Aerik should approach from. My escape route. The thought of flinging open that door and dashing toward the trees only makes my pulse race faster.

I close my eyes again and let my thoughts drift into the escape I took so often when I was truly locked up— the only sort of escape I had, into the landscapes from my scrapbook of travel dreams. My imagination works just as well as it always did. I picture myself floating in a warm pool of turquoise water, gazing up at craggy white rock forming a ring around the sky above. Scrambling up those rocky walls to gaze out over lush jungle surging toward the expanse of the ocean.

There's so much more of *this* world, with all its mystery and magic, that I haven't gotten to experience yet. Maybe if this plan works, if we no longer have to worry about Aerik tracking me down, I'll be able to discover all the epic sights the faerie world has to offer. I should at least be able to trek around Sylas's domain more freely. Harper will be happy about that.

Despite the situation, my lips twitch with a smile at the thought of the fae woman's likely response if I tell her she can play tour guide. I might even be able to show her some of the human world. That could be enough adventure to cure her restlessness for a while.

As long as we have the freedom to roam around like that, that is. Aerik isn't even the largest threat Sylas and his pack face, as frightening as he is to me.

What if the Unseelie break through the defenses at the border and start a real invasion? What if the arch-lords come up with some new reason to accuse Sylas of treason and punish him even more? The way Ambrose's squadron leader spoke to us the other day…

As I shudder at the memory, the rasp of footsteps over

the forest floor jerks me back to the present. The men around me have gone still.

Whitt cocks his head and nods to Sylas, moving into position by the cage. August stands up. I push myself into a crouch, my weight on my feet now, balanced so I won't strain the injured one too much. I'm going without my brace, since that kindness would look extravagant for a prisoner.

Aerik and his two cadre-chosen slink out of the forest. At the sight of all three of the men who orchestrated my years of torture, viewing them through bars the way I did back then and knowing they're here to reclaim me, I have to clench my teeth against the urge to vomit. My heartbeat stutters in its now-frantic rhythm. I press my hands against the solid floor and will back the dizziness sweeping through me.

"You arrived early," Aerik says without any greeting. He, Cole, and the stout man I think of as Cutter come to a stop about ten feet from where my men are poised around the cage.

"So have you," Sylas points out, his low baritone impeccably calm. He motions to me. "As you can see, we've brought her, already restrained. I assume you have a vehicle nearby. We can carry her to it."

He and the others move as if to heft up the cage—immediately, but slowly enough to give Aerik time to protest. That's part of the plan, to make him think they're eager to get access to his carriage.

Exactly as we hoped, Aerik steps forward with a jerk of his arm. "Leave it. We can manage. Just consider yourselves lucky I'm not dragging you before the arch-lords for the theft. If you breathe one word of *my* prize to them, I'll see they get a full accounting of how you and your cadre violated my domain."

Sylas raises his hands and eases back. He and his cadre have to take several paces backward before Aerik and his approach. I tense, unable to shake the sensation of being abandoned.

They haven't left me, not really, but now there's nothing between me and my former tormenters except these awful bars. And in this final move in our scheme, I truly am on my own. The three men behind me gave their vows. They can't harm Aerik unless someone else makes the first attack.

It all relies on me.

As Aerik, Cole, and Cutter inspect me and the cage, still from a short distance, the fae lord's mouth curls into a typical sneer. Watching him, the churning inside me starts to burn into something hotter and fiercer. Currents of anger sear through my fear.

These men—these *monsters*—savaged me for nearly half my life. They slaughtered my family, starved and broke my body, stole my literal life's blood from my wrist over and over, and laughed at my distress.

Why shouldn't this moment come down to me? They deserve every bit of fury I can aim at them. Let them know that when they fall here, it's because of *me*, the 'dung-body' they dismissed as helpless and weak so many times.

I roll the syllables silently over my tongue. Having found no reason for complaint, my former jailors step right up to the bars. The cage is big enough that it'll take all three of them to lift it. They bend down to grasp it from the bottom.

Now's the time. *Now*—but my voice catches at the back of my mouth.

My throat constricts, the fear that I'll mess up the one chance I have nearly stealing the chance from me altogether. Then Cole shoots me a vicious, triumphant smile, and all the rage in me rushes back to the surface.

My lungs unlock. I hurl the word at them like a spear, calling the chains disguised in the grass to do my bidding. "*Fee-doom-ace-own!*"

My voice rings out, so powerful and clear I can hardly believe it's mine. Magic surges through it, and three of the chains whip up and around the men's wrists, melting into place like a larger version of the chinks I wove into that chainmail vest, so tight I can almost taste how they bite the skin.

All three of them jerk back, but the chains stop them from going far. Aerik sputters in surprise, Cole rasps a curse, and before any of them can process what's going on well enough to free themselves, my allies have pounced in full wolf form.

August tackles Cutter, knocking him onto his back on the ground. Whitt launches himself at Cole, his fangs bared in an expression that looks downright eager for a rematch. With a roar, Sylas springs right over his cadre-chosen to land on Aerik, sending the other lord sprawling just as Aerik spits out the true name to loosen the bronze bond.

I've scrambled against the back of the cage, my hand by the latch on the door, my veins thrumming now with a mix of terror and excitement. I did it—but this isn't over yet.

As they struggle, our enemies shift into their own wolfish forms, snarling and snapping. Whitt and Cole roll across the grass, scrabbling at each other with their claws until Whitt manages to shove the white-furred wolf down more firmly with his jaws at the beast's throat. Cole keeps flailing against him.

Across the clearing, Cutter slams a massive paw into the side of August's head. My hands clench with a jolt of horror, but the ruddy wolf just shakes himself and rams his opponent harder into the grass. He slashes Cutter's jaw and rakes his claws down the underside of his chin, just shy of gouging straight through.

Between them, Sylas's dark wolf and Aerik's beige one grapple with each other, Sylas still braced over the other creature but battered by swinging limbs. Snarling, he snatches one of those vicious paws between his teeth and yanks so hard the crack of bone echoes through my ears. Blood spurts across the grass, but this time I don't mind the sight.

Heaving himself into a better position, Sylas swats Aerik's muzzle hard enough that the other wolf lets out a pained huff. My rescuer jams his claws against the most vulnerable part of his enemy's throat. Planting the rest of his body to pin down Aerik's legs at the thighs, he clamps his other front paw against the other lord's unbroken wrist. Then he barks in a sound not quite a word but that even I can understand. *Yield.*

Aerik squirms against him in vain. His eyes roll in their sockets, searching out his cadre—and finding them equally subdued. A wrathful noise hisses out of him, but he must be able to see he's beaten. He sags against the ground, falling into the shape of a man at the same time.

Sylas transforms too, keeping his claws out, jutting from his broad fingers. He glares down at Aerik. "Do you yield?"

Aerik scowls back at him, his daffodil-yellow hair strewn like straw amid the grass, his right arm lying limp at an unnatural angle. "Are you really going to kill me if I don't? There'll be an awful lot of questions about how exactly this confrontation went down."

A harsh grin curls Sylas's lips. "We followed every letter of our agreement. My cadre and I swore not to make the first strike, and we didn't. Ours was the second."

"You can't really expect me to believe that the *dung-body* worked that true name herself."

"I do, because that's what happened. We *couldn't* have gone against a vow so sworn—do you really doubt your ability to judge what magic has been cast? But if you're willing to risk it all on the idea that I somehow deceived you with our oath, I'll be happy to rip your head from your body and show anyone who asks that your soulstone shines true."

Aerik's gaze slides to me where I'm still crouched in the cage. At his cold stare, a shiver runs through me, but I manage to give him a tight little smile. "I don't belong to anyone but *me*."

To emphasize the declaration, I reach back and unlatch the cage door. A sense of lightness rushes through me as I clamber out into the open air.

"But—"

Sylas grasps Aerik's jaw and yanks his face away from me. "Don't you worry about her. In fact, that's the main condition of your yield. I will let you leave here with your miserable life, and you will make no further attempt to gain control over that human woman, nor will you so much as *hint* through word or action that anyone else should take any particular notice of her. You won't mention any special qualities she possesses or of this skirmish here today. And you'll spare me and my pack any further hostilities as well. Considering the years of torment you put her through, I'd say you're getting off incredibly easy. So please, give me an excuse to drench this glade with your blood instead."

The fae lord's voice is even as ever but brutal in its force. As Aerik meets his stare, the color leaches from his face. From this angle, I can't see what rage Sylas's expression holds, but I doubt I'd want it directed my way. He means every word of that threat.

"If you really think this is going to be enough to buy your way back to prominence," Aerik begins, but his voice is too thready for the disdain in it to have any impact. He can't even manage a real sneer now.

"I tire of waiting for your answer," Sylas rumbles. "How many more seconds do you suppose it is before I can reasonably count your delay as a direct refusal? You won't have any prominence at all in your family's mausoleum."

"Fine," Aerik snarls. A magical thrum enters his voice. "I accept your conditions and yield. I'll leave the girl, you, and your pack alone. Now get your mangy paws off me."

Sylas retracts his claws but keeps his hand braced

against the other man's collarbone, holding him down. "Hmm. Not quite yet. Tell your cadre they'd better take the same bargain, or you'll find yourself a little short on supporters."

Aerik tips his head to call to the others. "You heard him. Yield. We did plenty well without that cringing thing; we don't need her."

My hands ball into fists at the way he's describing me, but he doesn't so much as glance my way. It's better for all of us if they yield and Sylas doesn't find his actions under the scrutiny outright killing them would provoke. All the same, in that moment, I wish he would make one wrong move to ensure his murder.

The other men have shifted while Sylas and Aerik debated. Cole grimaces and offers his yield in a sharply snarky tone. Cutter gives his dully, his nose dribbling blood. Then my three men shove off my former captors, drawing back to surround me.

He may not be dead, but it's still incredibly gratifying to watch Aerik stagger to his feet, favoring a knee that seems to have been knocked off-kilter during the skirmish, holding his broken arm carefully against his abdomen. Dirt smudges his lordly face; his yellow hair doesn't gleam quite so bright. He raises his chin, but he can't quite overcome the doleful slump of his shoulders.

"Come on," he snaps at his cadre. "We have no more business with these cast-offs."

They turn their backs on us and shuffle away into the forest. As their forms disappear amid the shadows, sweet relief wells up inside me. For the second time today, tears prickle at my eyes, but these ones barely sting.

It's over. I'm free of them. They might haunt my dreams for who knows how much longer to come, but they can't do one more bit of real harm to me.

Sylas squeezes my shoulder. "You were perfect, Talia. I know how hard that must have been for you, but you showed them what you're really made of. Let's get you home."

Yes. Home. The home Aerik can now never steal me from.

Sylas speaks the true name to melt the cage's materials back into the earth, since we have no more need for it. As we turn toward our own vehicle, I slip my hand around his on one side and August's on the other.

An ache of determination rises up through my joy. These men showed just how far *they're* willing to go on my behalf. I won't really deserve to share their home until I find some way to fight just as hard for them.

CHAPTER TWENTY-FIVE

August

The carriage is just passing into our domain when Talia raises her head. She's spent most of the journey nestled between Sylas and me in grateful silence. Holding her close, reminding myself and her that we made it through the confrontation with Aerik with all our skins intact, felt much more important than anything I could have said.

But there are other important matters we haven't dealt with yet, and somehow Talia is already thinking beyond the freedom she just won for herself.

"Are we going back to the border now?" she asks, glancing up at Sylas. "I guess you'd have to rebuild the house, but at least we wouldn't need to worry about having the glamour on me or what Aerik might do."

Sylas frowns, and my spirits sink. Both of us know we accomplished a lot less than we were hoping for out there.

"I'll have to think on that," my lord says. "The other lords—and arch-lords' representatives—weren't exactly open to our offers of assistance. I'm not sure we were achieving anything more than looking incompetent because we *couldn't* make ourselves more useful."

Whitt swivels on the bench where he's been poised watching the forestlands fly by. "The full moon is only three nights from now. We shouldn't plan to be on the move in the midst of that."

Sylas nods. "We can't leave the pack in Oakmeet completely unguided, but we do have more flexibility with less to hide."

Talia straightens up. "We can give them my blood. The pack-kin in Oakmeet, our squadron at the border —*all* the packs. Make some kind of tonic like Aerik did so we can spread it out without having to take too much from me. No one should have to keep suffering from the curse, not while I can prevent that."

She makes the offer so easily my heart lights up like it does so often in her presence. Of course that would be her first thought at the reminder of the full moon. Of course she'd want to solve this problem as only she can, giving of her own body. That generosity and compassion is what makes her Talia.

The softening of Sylas's expression tells me he's touched too, but he shakes his head. "I don't think we're in a position to make that leap yet. I'm not even sure it's the right leap to make."

"But if Aerik can't come after me again, then we don't have to keep it a secret, do we?" she says. "That was why we couldn't risk helping even our pack before."

"Yes, but— We also have to consider the same possibilities that led Aerik to keep you secret. If I suddenly present myself as the provider of the tonic, there'll be a lot of questions. The arch-lords will demand an explanation, and when they find out where it comes from, it's likely they'll want to take you for themselves. We can't fend them off as easily as we could Aerik."

I let out a rough laugh. "I'm not sure I'd call what we just did exactly *easy*."

Sylas smiles wryly. "Indeed. And on top of that, I meant what I said before about us needing to find a more permanent solution to the curse. Relying on Aerik's tonic gave too many of the Seelie a false sense of security."

Talia clasps her hands in front of her. "But if I can at least spare everyone from the violence and the loss of control while you're looking for a real solution…"

Sylas touches her cheek with a stroke of the backs of his fingers. "I appreciate the devotion you're showing to my people, Talia. Perhaps if we can regain the arch-lords' favor, I could count on them trusting me to preserve such a… resource." He grimaces at the phrasing. "I won't put you in their sights until then."

She sinks back against the seat with a resigned sigh. "Eventually."

"Eventually."

I give her hand a quick squeeze. "You still have so much more freedom now than you did before. No more glamours—we can tell the pack that we hid your injury until you'd gotten to know them a bit because you were self-conscious. No more needing to stay so close to the keep all of the time."

Talia brightens up as I hoped she would. "I know. I'm looking forward to being able to just... *be* without all those worries hanging over me."

Whitt hums to himself and stretches his legs toward the opposite bench. "You know, even the arch-lords aren't half so intimidating when you've found yourself in a position to learn their odd little quirks. A bunch of kooks they all are, I'd say."

Sylas snorts. "Thankfully I know *you* know better than to say that in anyone else's hearing."

As Whitt smirks in response, Talia looks across the carriage at him. Her own smile falters. Abruptly, I'm aware of the separation between us, my oldest brother set apart from the three of us—and based on his reaction the other morning, it's not by our design this time but by his own. I don't like the unexpected division that's formed within our original unit, but if that's what he wants, what can I do about it?

My love appears to have her own ideas. After a moment's hesitation, she eases to her feet and limps over to sit on the bench next to Whitt, gingerly but deliberately. She leaves a foot of space between them, hardly cuddling like she was with Sylas and me, and her stance is cautious, but a twinge of possessiveness quivers through my chest anyway.

I told her it was fine if she wanted him too, that I wished for her to have every happiness—but it turns out that confronted with the reality, a part of me would rather scoop her up and hide her away someplace only for myself.

It's a selfish urge, especially after witnessing the bliss Sylas and I were able to bring her to together. And it feels even more selfish watching the startled expression that crosses Whitt's face now, flickering into something like delight before he recovers to his usual nonchalance.

"I want to hear *all* the crazy arch-lord stories you've got," Talia informs him, leaning back against the side of the carriage. "Laughing at them sounds a lot better than being scared of them."

Whitt relaxes, setting his arm on the edge just an inch from her shoulder so carefully that this time I'm hit with a twinge of brotherly affection rather than jealousy. Whitt and I don't always agree, and I often don't understand his moods, but I've never doubted his loyalty to our family and to the pack. And I can see that same devotion gleaming in his eyes as he prepares to launch into a tale for Talia's benefit.

He fought for her as hard as any of us. If he can offer her things I can't, why shouldn't she have those too?

After everything that's been stolen from her and all the abuse she's had to endure, she deserves every bit of love she'll welcome.

"It's my opinion that Ambrose goes around like he has a stick up his ass," Whitt says in his typical wry tone, "and that might be due to all the cartilage he ingests. I've had it from a member of his household staff that he likes to gnaw on the old bones from the roasts and stews when he's working, as though he's some kind of woe begotten mongrel rather than a regal wolf. Leaves the chewed-up bits all over the floor for the servants to clean up too." He makes a tossing gesture as if flicking a bone across the carriage.

Talia makes a face. "He's the one Tristan is related to, right?"

"Yes. Pricks, the whole lot in that family. Oh, and Celia, our lady arch-lord? I hear she's so terrified of smelly feet that she has her chamber maidens paint her soles with rose petal paste each night before she goes to sleep. Frankly, she'd do better slathering it on that sour face of hers."

Even Sylas guffaws at that. Talia scoots a little closer, so her shoulder rests against Whitt's elbow. "What about the third one?"

Whitt rattles off a story about Donovan's insecurities with being the youngest of the arch-lords, and Talia watches him with rapt attention while I watch the two of them.

No, clever tales aren't my forte. But I have other strengths. If I want to be sure I stay worthy of her, I have to play to them.

My gaze travels past them to the distant horizon now appearing where the trees have fallen away. A kernel of an idea tumbles through my mind. We weren't done out at the border, not by a longshot. I can work on proving myself to Sylas at the same time.

When the carriage comes to a stop at the edge of the forest closest to the keep, we climb off, and Sylas dismisses the materials that made it, a juniper tree springing up in its place. Whitt rolls his shoulders.

"I'll make the rounds, check in with the sentries," he says.

Sylas tips his head in acknowledgment and heads toward the keep with Talia. I hang back a moment, raising my hand to signal to Whitt to hold on.

He raises an enquiring eyebrow at me. "What's on your mind, Auggie?"

There's enough fondness in the teasing nickname that I can let it roll off me. "I just wanted to say, in case it wasn't clear—what Sylas said the other day about Talia and sharing—he was speaking for me too. If you want to pursue something with her, at any point, I won't resent it. I just want her to be happy."

Whitt considers me for a long moment—long enough that the back of my neck starts to prickle with the sense that I might not have been entirely coherent, or at least not to his standards. Then a small smile crosses his lips, more subdued than his usual smirk. "I appreciate the vote in support, little brother."

Without another word, he leaps away, shifting into his wolfish form in mid-spring. As he trots off to survey our domain, I turn toward the keep.

Sylas has stopped on the way there to speak with a couple of our pack-kin, Talia already vanished into the keep. I pause and catch my lord's eye, and when he's finished, he strides over to join me. I wait until we've reached the privacy of the entrance room before I speak.

"I have an idea about how I might be able to advance our cause with the arch-lords at the border."

My lord folds his arms over his chest. "Let's hear it then."

A jab of nerves makes me hesitate, but only for an

instant. He's trusted me with major tasks before, if nothing *quite* this significant.

"I can go back to the border now, alone, and carry out the mission the arch-lords denied. They didn't want to approve of anyone sneaking into winter territory to try to pick off a warrior who could betray their plans, so we won't ask their approval again. If it goes wrong, they can blame our defiance. But if it goes right, I may come up with the information we need to fend off whatever attack they're anticipating."

Sylas studies me with more intensity than Whitt aimed at me. He's watched me train—he's carried out some of that training himself. He knows I'm as capable as any fae warrior out there. *I* know I am. What has all that training been for if I don't put it to use in the field when it matters most?

"You'll keep your distance, only press in if you can catch one alone?" he says. "I don't want you risking yourself against more than one of them, even if I'm sure you could give two or even three a good fight."

I nod adamantly. "Only one, only when I can do it out of sight of any others. I may have to prowl along the border for a while—that's why I think it's best I head out now so I can start tonight."

Sylas's jaw clenches and then releases. "All right. You know your way around those lands now, and you've always known your way around a battle. Do me proud, and make sure you come back hale and whole—for both my and our lady's sake, hmm?"

A grin springs to my lips despite my attempt to remain cool and professional. "You can count on it."

———

Several hours later, as I stalk through the haze that marks the border between the summer and winter realms, I'm starting to think that while I may return to Oakmeet whole, it could be a whole man who's frozen solid.

On the winter side, the wind howls loud enough that I could hear it before I even stepped into the heat haze that's the summery part of the border. Snow whirls through the air, some of it wisping into the narrow strip of the border, bringing currents of frigid air with it. My wolf fur can fend off the worst of it, but the cold is starting to seep through to my skin.

I don't like it. Cold is for leaping into a chilly pond to escape from a heatwave. This constant, icy bluster is pure torture. How can any fae stand to live in it?

I guess that might explain why they're trying to move on our lands, though not why they're doing that *now* after putting up with their wintery weather for so long before.

Thankfully, while I don't know the true name for snow, water was one of my first, and the crisp flakes are nothing but frozen water. With a little coaxing, I've gathered a barrier of snow around my body that both deflects the worst of the wind and hides me from the view of anyone patrolling the edge of Unseelie territory.

I need the camouflage. Even though it's the middle of the night, the light of the near-full moon reflects off all that icy ground starkly enough that my dark fur would be unmissable against it.

I had a close call in the evening when I first slunk out here. I emerged into view of the winter realm just as a squad of five Unseelie warriors were marching past. If my well-honed instincts hadn't sent me recoiling at the first glimpse of them, they'd have charged after me in a matter of seconds and called a whole bunch of their brethren to join the patrol even if they hadn't caught me. I'd have lost my chance and possibly my life before I'd really gotten started, not to mention the disgrace to the pack if the arch-lords found out we defied their orders and failed.

I've passed another, smaller group since then, and spotted a few lone sentries at a distance across the glinting plain, too far for me to risk stalking after them. My paws are starting to ache with the splinters of ice that have collected in the fur around my toes.

I can't stop until I've fulfilled my goal. I didn't say good-bye to Talia for the second time this month for nothing.

Finally, a spindly shape of a sentry ventures closer to the border up ahead. Like all of the Unseelie warriors I've seen, he wears a silvery helm and a similarly pale chest plate with looser plating hanging to his thighs for ease of movement, his padded jacket and trousers an even paler gray to blend into the landscape. He peers into the border haze and then turns to amble toward me.

Perfect.

I prowl a little closer, lacking the patience to simply sit and wait. Anticipation coils through my muscles. This bastard is one of the wretched winter fae who've killed my pack-kin and so many others over the past three decades. For all I know, he slaughtered some of them personally.

I spent too long hanging back waiting for something

to happen when we were staked out here before. It's time to bring a little of the attack back to the ravens.

When he's mere feet away, I pause, letting my form meld into the haze and the gusting snow. The sentry meanders a few steps farther. I gather myself—and pounce.

I'll give him credit: he reacts quickly, squirming to the side the second he's hit the ground, dagger already in hand. But that only gives me the chance to let out more of my bottled aggression. I smack the dagger from his fingers with a swift paw, raking my claws across his palm and wrist as I do, and pummel him harder into the frigid earth. With another swipe, I've sent his helmet spinning into the haze.

His body twitches as if to transform. *Oh no, you don't.* I clamp my jaws tight around his neck, a trickle of his Unseelie blood dribbling over my tongue. A warning that if he tries to shrink into his raven form, I can snap that birdish head from his shoulders before he can so much as squawk in protest.

As the sentry aims an ineffective blow at my chest, I haul him right into the haze where his colleagues won't spot us. Then I shift so quickly I've got a sword at his throat in place of my jaws before he can do more than shudder.

"Why don't you just kill me and get it over with, cur?" the sentry sputters. "Or do wolves like to play with their food now?"

I bare my teeth at him, letting my still-protruding fangs show. "I'd hardly make a meal out of a scrawny feather-brain like you. And you might get to keep your life if you talk quickly. Tell me about the next strike your people are planning against us."

The man manages a choked guffaw. "You think I'd betray my people to save my hide? Go ahead and kill me. I'm not talking."

I should have anticipated he'd reject the opportunity to yield, but I've never taken a prisoner for interrogation before, never battled in circumstances where the future of an entire people could be at stake. I press my blade a tad harder, watching blood well up along the gleaming edge, my mind scrambling for my next move.

If he'd rather die than speak, I can't beat the information out of him. I'm going to have to rely on my wits rather than my brawn. Heart take me if I don't wish Whitt was here to advise me right now.

Well, what would my oldest brother do if faced with a problem like this? I've watched him work his own strategies plenty of times.

He might weave a sort of glamour with his words. Create an illusion that would draw out the answers he needs. Pretend he doesn't need it all that much, so his target has that much less to fight against.

What do I already think I know, that I can simply get this wretch to confirm—and maybe even add a little more as a bonus?

I pick my words carefully, only lying in implication. "You're too loyal for your own good—more loyal than others I've toppled who valued their lives more." Those others were Seelie fae I fought for very different reasons, but he doesn't need to know that. "If you won't tell me anything about the coming assault along this section of the border, you'll lose your life, and I'll simply lose another hour or two finding someone else who will. And then we'll see how many more of your raven necks we get to wring."

"You won't wring any, from what I've heard," the sentry retorts. "When the full moon rises, you're as likely to savage each other as any of us, aren't you?"

The question hits me like a lance of ice straight to my gut. I harden my expression before too much of my shock can show on my face. "That's when your people will attack, is it?" I snarl.

The sentry's flinch as he realizes what he gave away is answer enough. He hasn't denied that they're going to attack *here* either, accepting what I said rather than taunting me about being mistaken. Maybe I can batter a little more out of him while I have the chance…

But he doesn't give me that chance. With a jerk of his body, he starts to contract, his arms slipping from my hold as they fling into wings, his armor rippling away into ebony feathers.

No. If he makes it back to his kind, he'll warn them of what I've discovered, and they'll adjust their plans.

I slam my sword down, and a shrunken head—half-feathered, half-human—rolls to the side, blood gushing from the severed neck.

I push away from the ruined body and wipe my blade on the frosted grass right in the center of the border. His brethren may not find him for days—or if they do, all they'll see is that he ventured too close to our territory and met an expected fate. But that fact gives me no comfort.

Our enemies know. After all this time, the ravens have

discovered our curse. And they mean to use it against us at the first opportunity.

If the Unseelie attack while the border squadrons have lost their minds to the wildness, the blood that drenches the fields next will be all our own.

CHAPTER TWENTY-SIX

Talia

The keep's front door thumps loud enough to startle me out of sleep. I flinch beneath the covers and then go still. It takes a few seconds of straining to listen over the thunder of my pulse before my mind emerges from its dreamy muddle enough for the obvious explanation to occur to me.

August is back.

I throw off the covers and scramble out of the bed so quickly my warped foot jars against the floorboards at an awkward angle. Wincing, I fumble for my brace, not bothering with day clothes or the hairbrush on the bedside table, or anything other than getting to him as quickly as possible.

If he's back, then he's okay. Well, he's okay enough to have made it back. Ralyn made it from the border to the keep so injured he had to spend days recuperating.

By the time I reach the stairs, two hushed voices are

already traveling up from the hall below. Sylas was already awake, maybe even waiting for August. The other man might have sent him some kind of magic-born message to let him know he'd be coming.

I hurry down the stairs, not bothering to try to disguise the tapping of the foot brace's wooden slats, the hem of my nightgown brushing against my knees. When I reach the bottom, August and Sylas have gone silent, watching my arrival.

In that first moment, both their expressions are so grim that my heart plummets. Then a smile breaks across August's face. He strides over and sweeps me up, claiming a kiss I'm happy to return.

After, he nuzzles my hair. "Couldn't wait to see me, huh, Sweetness?"

He definitely doesn't appear to be bleeding profusely or missing any limbs. I beam back at him. "Had to make sure you got here all right. And to find out the news. If you're back so soon, does that mean you managed to question one of the Unseelie warriors?"

August's smile fades. He sets me down gently on my feet and glances at Sylas, who looks as solemn as before.

"What?" I say as the silence begins to stretch uncomfortably. "You can't just *not* tell me."

Sylas's mouth twists as if he'd prefer it if he could take that tactic, but he motions to August.

"Fill her in on the part you've already told me, and then get into the rest."

When August looks at me, his face has fallen so much that I want to kiss him again just to see if that would bring the light back into his golden eyes. My hands clench at my sides, bracing for the obviously bad news.

"I caught one of the ravens' sentries," he says. "And I found out enough to know why the arch-lords are so concerned, if they know even half of it. The Unseelie have learned of our curse. They know that on the night of the full moon, the warriors at the border will be too crazed to properly defend our lands, and they mean to launch an attack then, presumably a large one."

He turns to Sylas. "The sentry essentially confirmed that they'll be targeting that northern section of the borderlands. I'd guess they're still wary of assuming the battle will go easily, so they figure they're better off focusing all the resources they're comfortable assembling into one spot rather than attacking all across the realm."

Sylas nods. "That's what we would do if our situations were reversed. I wonder how they found out after all this time—and how much the arch-lords know. As far as I heard, they hadn't warned anyone specifically about the full moon."

"No, nothing beyond the standard preparations. They didn't say the additional protections they were arguing about were for any specific time or reason." August lets out a huff of breath. "The Unseelie could get enough of a foothold that we'll have trouble kicking them back to their side of the border even once we have our heads again. And that's without considering how many Seelie will fall while we're unable to properly defend ourselves. What can we do? Shoving more forces at the problem will only make the chaos worse."

A chill has collected in the bottom of my stomach.

The Unseelie know the summer fae's greatest weakness, and they're already looking to exploit it. Tomorrow night could become an outright bloodbath. But my horror comes with a twinge of confusion.

I step toward Sylas to catch his attention. "There doesn't have to be any chaos. You've got the cure right here. We make the tonic after all, make sure all the warriors at the border get it—and whoever else the lords can spare. The full moon isn't until tomorrow. There's plenty of time."

I hadn't thought it was possible for Sylas's expression to turn any graver, but I was wrong. He grazes his fingers over my head in a careful caress. "As much as I appreciate your selflessness, Talia, we can't jump straight to that solution. We'd still face all the same problems of keeping you with us and safe once your powers are exposed. If there's any other way—"

"How can there be any other way? You've been trying to figure out other cures for decades. What are the chances you'll come up with something in the next twenty-four hours?"

His whole face tightens, etched with anguish. "We didn't go through all this strife only to throw you to the wolves as some kind of sacrifice now."

The tension radiates off him. I can only imagine how torn he feels. He grappled enough when I first came into his care over keeping me safe despite the benefits he might earn for his pack by offering me to the arch-lords, and that was before he'd made me so many promises. Before not just his pack but his entire society had come under an immediate, dire threat.

He'll have trouble living with himself no matter what he decides.

Fine. Let it be my decision then. *I* can't live with myself if I hide away like a coward when so many lives hang in the balance that I could save so easily.

I raise my chin. "Then don't throw me to them. Put all your thinking toward figuring out your best shot at keeping me safe while offering my blood. It is *mine*, and I don't want anyone dying so that I can hold on to all of it."

Sylas sweeps his arm through the air. "It shouldn't be your problem to solve. We aren't even your people. You were never meant to be here in the first place."

"But I am here. And it *is* my problem, because wherever I came from, you all are my family now. I'm part of this pack. You saved me—let me save you too."

Resistance still shows all through Sylas's stance. Next to him, August looks from his lord to me and back again, clearly hesitant to override Sylas but unwilling to argue in favor of abandoning the border either.

As if there's any real choice here. We could debate all day, and in the end, the only real answer would still be to use me. They just don't want to admit it yet.

I glance toward the wall in the direction of the pack village. Inspiration hits me with a rush of determination. I can end this argument right now, claim the decision so utterly there's no way Sylas will be able to deny it.

I spin away from them toward the kitchen and march to the door at the opposite end, my foot brace clacking in time with my uneven steps. "Talia?" August says, startled. At the sound of him and Sylas following, I pick up my pace as fast as I can without outright running.

They haven't been locking the exits against me anymore. I push past the door and hurry out into the yard by the herb garden and the orchards. At a limping jog, a throbbing pang forming in my foot, I hustle around the side of the keep toward the twisted-off-stump houses where the rest of the pack live.

My lovers' footsteps sound behind me, but they don't know what I'm up to yet, so they're not putting in enough speed to stop me. Soon, they won't be able to.

A few of the fae are up and about in the pale early morning light, puttering around their homes. Not enough to make this tactic really work. As I cross the last short distance around the edge of the keep, I pitch my voice to carry. "Hey! Everyone in the pack! Get up, come out— there's something you need to hear."

Behind me, Sylas's breath hisses between his teeth in dismay. But I've already hurtled onto the field into full view of the houses, the pack-kin who were outside staring my way and others emerging from their doorways or peering from their windows to see what the fuss is about. I plant myself before their puzzled eyes, my heart hammering in my chest, counting on Sylas not wanting to bewilder them even more by charging in and hauling me away but prepared to keep shouting anyway if he does.

I launch straight into the most important part of the matter. "*I* am the main ingredient in the tonic that can cure the full-moon curse. My blood is, I mean. I didn't only just arrive in the faerie world. Another lord keeping me captive and using my blood for the tonic. Sylas—" I trip over my tongue for a second, realizing I probably shouldn't admit to his crime even to his own people. "When I got away, Sylas and his cadre helped me. And now I want to help all of you. As long as I'm around, I don't want any of you to have to go through the full-moon wildness again."

While I've made my announcement, Sylas and August have come to a halt behind me. Sylas clasps my shoulder, but he doesn't haul me away. Too many gazes are fixed on us now, too many gaping fae taking in my proclamation. More slip from their houses—I see Harper outside hers with her parents, her startled eyes even larger than usual.

As the buzz of adrenaline fades, it occurs to me that I must look pretty ridiculous standing here in nothing but my nightgown with my bedhead hair. A blush warms my cheeks, but not enough to stop me from standing tall and taking their scrutiny.

One of the older men starts laughing. "That's absurd. A human's blood, curing our curse?"

"It's true," I say, keeping my voice loud enough for everyone to hear. "If you need proof—someone give me a knife. All I have to do is cut my finger, and you'll be able to smell the—"

As I hold out my arm, Sylas's grip on my shoulder tightens. He steps past me, authority radiating off his pose. "That won't be necessary."

I brace myself for him to try to cover up my story somehow, but I must have played my cards well enough. Too many people heard what I said—too many people who might repeat the story, even if they don't believe it, to fae beyond this pack, who could pass it on to the arch-lords in turn.

"I can confirm that Talia speaks the truth," Sylas says.

"And thanks to her compassion for our pack, we will escape the curse beneath tomorrow's full moon. With that in mind, I expect you to treat her with twice as much kindness and respect as you already have." He glances down at me, his mismatched gaze just shy of a glower. "For now, we have much to prepare."

A pinch of guilt jabs my stomach at the way I've forced his hand, but it was going to be forced one way or another anyway. I think from the way he phrased his confirmation that he's accepted my right to make this call.

Aerik used my blood over and over for his own selfish gain. This time, I can claim it for a cause that matters to me.

Whatever consequences come from that decision, at least they'll be the ones I brought down on myself.

CHAPTER TWENTY-SEVEN

Whitt

"You know," I say, stretching my hands out over the earth, "if we'd really been thinking ahead, we'd have gotten Aerik to throw in his stash of vials when he yielded. He must have a rather large supply he no longer has any use for."

Sylas lets out a low guffaw from where he's standing in the shadows of the parlor doorway, checking on my progress. "Perhaps I'll offer to take them off his hands next month. Your magic appears up to the task today. We should only need a few dozen more."

"On it, oh glorious leader." I shift my concentration away from him to the ground beneath me, sensing with my mind rather than seeing with my eyes in the darkness of the much-too-early morning, and roll the true name for sand off my tongue.

With absolute focus, I will the particles that shiver up

through the soil to meld together into the tiny glass flasks that will each hold one dose of our tonic. The true name's mark, just beneath my left shoulder blade, itches with the amount of power I'm directing through it.

I've certainly summoned *larger* constructs into being, but not quite so many items in a row. The kitchen counters are already packed with vials. Sylas is lucky I even bothered to commune with sand enough to command it. None of the domains we've occupied are exactly beachy, but my fondness for weather magic led me to mastering some of its more obscure forms. I can conjure a mean sandstorm if need be.

Hmm, maybe that would be just the thing to send toward Aerik's domain one day. I'm sure I could manage it without leaving any trace of who guided it there. Let him and his lot find themselves shaking sand out of their drawers and picking it from their teeth for weeks to come.

The minor trauma we got to inflict on them for their yield was definitely not enough.

Sylas wouldn't approve of that plan, though, and I have more urgent concerns at the moment. It's only a couple of hours before dawn, with the full moon approaching at next sundown. Sylas wants to be on his way to bargain with the arch-lords before any sane person has taken breakfast.

As I shape the last few vials, the itch in the mark deepens into a piercing sensation. I restrain a grimace. The vials may be small, but they require quite a bit of precision. With the amount I've created, I've nearly drained my stores of magic, which aren't as bountiful living so far from the Heart of the Mists as they used to be. If we require even more, I may have to sacrifice a bit of my flesh to the process.

Well, it'd be worth it if this gambit takes us back to Hearthshire where I can bask in the deeper thrum of the Heart's energy at my leisure.

I lift the woven basket I've been conjuring the vials into and carry it into the kitchen. A flurry of activity fills the lantern-lit room. Along the islands, pack-kin are sorting the existing vials into groups by squadron according to my written instructions with my best estimates of the numbers at the border. A couple of others are bustling in with supplies Sylas asked for—another bucket of fresh glist-oak sap, another jug of rock-tumbled water. A few more have joined August where he's assembling our tonic in his largest pots, him stirring his current batch and them filling trays of vials with the earlier ones.

Sylas stands off in the corner with Talia, who's perched as so often on one of the stools, although not helping with the preparations in quite the same way as she would with a meal. She's holding out her arm, which Sylas is holding gently while he murmurs over it. A larger vial gleams scarlet with her blood on the shelf beside him.

The few times that Aerik deigned to offer us his tonic in the past, we studied it closely and came up with a pretty clear idea of the main ingredients—ones we didn't realize were simply there to dilute and disguise the only element that mattered. We're replicating that formula as well as we can, since while it may not be essential, we at least know it didn't impair the effects of Talia's blood. But we're not quite sure exactly how *much* we can safely dilute the stuff. It appears my lord has just asked her to contribute a little more of her body's gift.

She doesn't look bothered about it, though. She accepted the initial blood-taking with equal calm, her posture straight and her expression determined. Why she's quite so determined to put her freedom on the line to save a whole host of fae who've mostly been horrible to her, I can't entirely fathom, but perhaps that says more about me than about her.

Our mortal lady is a lovely sight sitting there watching the results of her sacrifice come together, her striking hair cascading over shoulders still slim but no longer spindly, her eyes brightly alert. She knows what she's risking—and she insisted on it anyway.

I hadn't thought I could be more awed by her than in the moment when she summoned her inexplicable magic to bind the men who once caged her, but now the combination of admiration and longing socks me in the gut.

At that exact moment, she glances up and catches my gaze. A small, hopeful smile crosses her face, and I can't bear to do anything except smile back, even though my stomach has just twisted twice as tight.

She wants me. She wants *me*. I told myself she was out of reach, but now that she's shown that's not true, I can't shake the sense that with one touch, one taste, I could destroy everything I care about. How could having her possibly be as simple as August made it sound?

And yet a part of me can't let go of the desire either. No, from the moment she met my eyes in our house by the border and told me she returned the feeling, that hunger has only expanded at a pace too manic to rein in. One kiss on the cheek the other morning, and all I could think about was having her gasping and moaning beneath me.

I shove those memories away and hand over the new set of vials to the pack-kin sorting them. Sylas hands off the container of blood to August and surveys my contribution.

"It looks as though we'll have plenty—including extra doses if we've miscalculated," he says. "If I could get it to every fae who isn't at the border too…"

I wave to the room around us. "Considering we assembled this production line less than a day ago, I think we've accomplished an incredible feat. If anyone complains that we fell short, let them choke on their vial."

Sylas snorts and motions for me to follow him. "I'd like to speak to you for a moment."

Speak to me alone, it appears. We cross the hall to the dining room, where he shuts the door. To my irritation, a nervous prickling runs over my skin.

Given the subjects that have come up between us over the past few days, I may not like the direction this conversation takes. I can't decide whether it'd be worse to have him chide me for refusing Talia's advances or announce that he isn't so keen on allowing me to pursue her after all.

He glances in the direction of the kitchen and then

fixes his gaze on me. "I don't feel it'd be safe for Talia to come with us to the Heart. It'll be harder for me to negotiate her safety with the arch-lords if she's right there for the taking. Since we'll be joining the fighting at the border as soon as we've made our arrangements, I'm going to have August come with me. I ask that you remain here and watch over her."

My eyebrows arch automatically. "So, I'm the babysitter?"

Sylas gives me a baleful look. "I think you know as well as I do that she doesn't need a keeper. But she may very well require protection. We'll keep the sentries watching the edges of our territory, especially to the south —at any indication that the arch-lords have sent forces to claim her, I trust you can ensure that the two of you are nowhere to be found."

Fair enough. I do have extensive knowledge of all the ins and outs of this domain, as loath as I was to see us banished here. I nod. "I won't let them get so much as a glimpse of her."

"Heart willing, it won't come to that in the first place. We'll see what sort of reception I get."

He sighs, and then grasps my shoulder firmly, holding my gaze with both his dark eye and the deadened one that sees more than it should. "I trust *you*, Whitt. As my brother, as my cadre-chosen. I know you will serve her well, in this and in any other ways you choose to attend to her. In case there was any doubt, when I spoke of sharing her affections, it was without reservation. I'd no sooner cage her heart than the rest of her, and I can't think of anyone more worthy of her regard than my own cadre."

I stare at him, speech stunned out of me. Sylas has never been cold—we are summer fae, after all—but I'm not sure I've ever heard him express *his* regard for me that earnestly. It was more the sort of thing taken for granted with the call to the cadre and the responsibilities he's offered me since. And there were times when I wasn't sure his full trust was a certainty at all, rather than a boon I needed to re-earn.

The declaration feels like a peace offering—or perhaps simply forgiveness for things we've never spoken of. Relief sweeps through me, sharp and sweet. Whatever I thought I'd broken here, it either never was or it's mended now.

"I appreciate that, my lord," I say, falling back into formality while I'm unexpectedly fumbling for my words.

Sylas peers at me with deeper attention. "I *am* still your brother as well as your lord. And I wouldn't want to be the sort of lord who holds himself above criticism regardless, as I hope you know. If the way I approached the subject before offended you in some way, I'd want you to tell me. That wasn't my intention."

He's worried… that *he* offended *me*. I can't hold back a sputter of a laugh, but I manage to recover quickly. I set my hand over his briefly in a firm pat. "There was no offense taken. I apologize if it appeared that way. I was taken by surprise—I had some things to sort out in my own thoughts—but my mind is clearer now. Thank you. For your trust and your concern."

Speaking that earnestly myself brings a clenching into my chest, but not enough to offset all that's good about the moment. Sylas offers me one of his subdued but warm smiles, claps my shoulder once more, and turns back toward the kitchen. And I realize there's now nothing standing in my way at all.

After all, if our glorious leader believes in me with all his lordly experience and wisdom, who in the lands am I not to?

CHAPTER TWENTY-EIGHT

Talia

The dawn glow is only just seeping over fields around the keep when Sylas and August load up their carriage. I watch from a short distance beyond the keep's front door, my arms crossed over my chest against the night coolness lingering in the breeze—and against the anxiety twining through my ribs over the mission they're setting out on.

Only the two of them are going, figuring that when —*if*—the arch-lords agree to their terms, there'll be plenty of fae on hand who can help distribute the tonic. They didn't want to leave Oakmeet completely undefended. Sylas assured me that fae law will protect them from any harm from the arch-lords, but I can't help wishing they had a few more allies with them for their own defense.

Of course, it's not just the arch-lords we have to worry about. Even if everything goes well at the Heart, the men I love still plan on joining the warriors in the battle along the border. It'll be *easier* to fight the Unseelie without the curse gripping them, but that doesn't mean it'll be *easy*. Warriors from our pack died in the last skirmish.

To hold the baskets upon baskets of vials, Sylas has summoned a carriage twice as long as the ones that conveyed us before. The magic has left a tang of juniper scent in the air. The thing looks like an immense canoe with a wooden shade arching over the middle portion, albeit an immense canoe that's floating a foot off the ground.

When the baskets are all nestled in their compartments, the two fae men walk back to me. August tugs me into a tight embrace, his heat and musky scent wrapping around me. "We'll be back tomorrow, Sweetness. I always kept my promises before."

Between the lump rising in my throat and the mugginess from lack of sleep that's filled my head, I don't know what to say in return, so I just hug him as hard as I can. He pulls back only far enough to find my mouth, capturing it with a kiss so tender and lingering that I'm tingling down to my toes when he's finished. He smiles, apparently not concerned about our audience—most of the pack has come to see them off too, gathered in a loose cluster at the edge of the village.

Sylas merely tucks a strand of my hair back from my cheek and brushes a kiss to my forehead, but I can feel the affection in that reserved gesture. "Little do the ravens know their downfall will be a single human woman. Get some rest and try not to worry yourself too much."

He glances at Whitt, who's propped in the doorway behind me, and gives his cadre-chosen a confident nod.

Whatever instructions he had for the other man, he's clearly already given them. Then he turns to the assembled pack.

"Thank you all again for your assistance in preparing the tonic. Enjoy this full moon free of the wildness, and let us hope we can ensure we never face it again. I look forward to rejoining you with good news tomorrow."

An eager murmur ripples through the crowd. They bob into bows, with calls of "Thank you, my lord!" and "Safe journeys!" and from Astrid, off to the side, one, "Give those feather-brains plenty to regret!" Sylas raises his hand in farewell, and he and August climb into the carriage.

I stand there watching as it glides away toward the south-eastern horizon. The pack drifts back to their homes, but Harper hesitates. When the carriage has vanished from sight amid the trees and rocky spires, I drag my gaze away, and she wanders over to join me.

"Hey," she says. "How are you doing?" Her attention falls to my arm, where a faint mark shows just above my wrist. Sylas sealed the cut after I gave my blood, but wounds don't disappear in an instant.

Harper and I haven't talked since I made my dramatic announcement to the pack yesterday morning. In the rush of activity that followed, there hasn't really been time to. The wariness in her wide eyes sends a twinge of guilt to my stomach.

"I'm all right. They didn't need to take all that much." I look at the ground and then back at her. "I'm sorry I lied to you about how I came here. We just—we were worried the lord who brought me to the faerie world in the first place would find me, and he… wasn't anywhere near as kind as Sylas is."

Harper blinks, her lips parting with surprise. "I'm not upset, not at all! Of course you'd be careful. You must have been through a lot." She cringes. "I'm sorry I asked you so much about your home beyond the Mists and all that… If they dragged you away against your will and then kept you like a prisoner, it must be painful thinking about what you lost."

"That's not your fault. You didn't know." I take in the houses beyond her, the terrain that stretches out all around the keep, becoming more familiar with every day. "This is my home now. And you helped me feel like I could belong here. And now that Sylas has taken care of the lord who dragged me away, it's safe for me to do more adventuring. You can show me the most interesting places in the domain that are farther out from the keep."

A smile brightens Harper's face. "Perfect. And… People are saying that by giving the tonic to help with this battle, Lord Sylas might be able to reclaim *our* real home in Hearthshire. It's right in the middle of everything instead of out here on the fringes, and if we have the arch-lords' pardon then the other packs will be more friendly again." She throws her arms around me in a hug so quick I barely have time to return it before she's stepped back again, outright beaming now. "If that's true, then you've given us so much more than if you'd just talked up my dress with the lords and ladies."

I grin back at her. "I hope that all works out. But I'll still talk up that dress if anyone asks. It's the most gorgeous thing I've ever worn."

She cocks her head, considering my foot caged in its brace. "The fae who kidnapped you did that to you. No one can heal it?"

"No. August looked at it and said the bones have been set like that for too long." I shrug. "I'm used to it now, though. I can't complain about having to limp when there were years when I couldn't do anything at all. This brace Sylas made for me makes walking a lot easier, so it's not too bad anyway."

Harper taps her lips. "If you could… ask him if he'd make another one that I could examine? I have some ideas —I'd have to work with it to see if I could pull it off."

"I don't see why not." Assuming Sylas makes it back. A shiver runs through my nerves, dampening the good mood the conversation sparked.

Maybe I droop a little, because Whitt stirs in the doorway, where he must have been keeping an eye on me this whole time. "I think this mighty human should get the rest Sylas ordered," he says, ruffling my hair from behind, and yawns. "I certainly need mine."

I can't really argue. My eyelids are getting heavier, the mugginess around my thoughts thicker. Harper bobs her head and ambles off, and I let Whitt usher me into the keep.

Despite my worries, which no lord can order away, I'm so tired that I'm out moments after my head hits the pillow. I wake up to the dazzling sun of what I'd guess is early afternoon, my mind still a bit muddy but too much restlessness winding through my chest for me to think there's any hope of getting more sleep now.

My stomach grumbles, unhappy that the only food it's

had so far today is a hasty sandwich August assembled for me in the wee hours of the morning between batches of tonic. I heave myself out of bed and grimace at the clothes I've been wearing since yesterday, now wrinkled from being slept-in too.

Opening the wardrobe, I'm about to reach for another of my usual jeans and short-sleeved shirts when my eyes snag on the simpler dress hanging next to Harper's gown. The sky-blue one in the style many of the pack women wear that I put on for our dinner with Aerik and his cadre.

I wore it then to make it look as if I was integrated into the pack. Why shouldn't I wear it now that I've proven how much that pack means to me, now that I no longer need to care whether Aerik or any other fae sees me as I really am? It's not a disguise—it's just me. I should leave the trappings of my old human life behind sometime.

This *is* my home now. I already know the people here better than anyone still alive back in the human world. The faerie realm comes with all kinds of dangers, but at least I'm not facing them alone.

I give myself a quick wash in the bathroom and pull the dress over my head. The soft fabric flows over my body, hugging what little curves I have now that my ribs no longer stand out like the rungs of a ladder up my torso. Looking down at myself, I feel like the lady of this keep more solidly than I ever have before.

The kitchen is still a bit of a mess, the pots August used for mixing the tonic stacked beside one of the sinks, shreds of dried reeds from the baskets scattered on the floor. I head to the pantry and emerge with a heel of seed-laced bread that I don't think has been reserved for any upcoming meal.

As I stand there gnawing at it, Whitt saunters into the room, looking shockingly alert for someone who hasn't gotten any more sleep than I have. He takes in my scavenged food and shoots me a broad grin. "I think we can do better than that for our mighty one. Let's see what we can throw together."

He pushes the cuffs of his loose sleeves past his elbows, revealing the true-name tattoos curving all across his muscular forearms, and grabs one of the more modestly sized pots that's still clean. "Stew. Anyone can make a halfway decent stew. At least, that's what I've heard. You must have absorbed some of August's culinary wisdom. Between the two of us, we should be able to produce something absolutely fantastic."

"Aiming high?" I say, unable to hold back a smile.

Whitt clucks his tongue at me. "No other way to live." He adds water to the pot with a hiss from the faucet and thumps it onto the stove. "Let's see what the whelp left us in the cold box."

The cold box is practically a room in itself, a closet-like space full of shelves and air kept chilly through magic, about twice the size of any fridge I remember seeing in my former life. Whitt grabs a papery bundle that I think holds leftover sausage patties, a bowl full of the tiny blue quail eggs, and the few stray vegetables that didn't end up getting used during August's past cooking sessions.

"Pilfer some herbs and spices from the pantry," he tells me. "Whatever catches your fancy."

I enter the dim room cautiously, with no idea what

will be a good match for the assortment of ingredients Whitt has already picked out. But then, that's sort of the point, right? Toss a bunch of stuff in, have fun with it, see what happens. Even if it's a mess, it'll keep me thinking about things other than what Sylas and August are facing right now.

I pull sprigs from a few bundles of herbs I like the scent of and snatch a couple of jars of powdered spices off the shelves. Back by the stove, Whitt has already dumped the meat and the eggs into the pot and is halfway through dicing up the vegetables with one of August's enchanted knives that slides through anything edible like cutting butter. I drag one of the stools over to the other side of the stove and scrape the leaves off the sprigs with my fingernails to sprinkle them in.

"What are you adding?" Whitt asks.

"Spindle-slip, cinnamon, and a bunch of I don't know what they're called but I like them." I sprinkle a dash of the cinnamon and some of the bright orange powder I grabbed after the herbs.

"That's the spirit." Whitt gives me another smile and pours the chopped veggies into the mix. The liquid is already bubbling. He stirs it, peering into the pot. "I feel we're missing something. A stew should be thicker. What've we got for that, mite?"

My mind trips back nearly a decade to my mom grumbling as she attempted to thicken the Thanksgiving gravy. "Flour?" I leap to my feet with a burst of inspiration. "We could try fallowroot." I've only had the stuff in pastries and pancakes before, but the thought of its rich, nutty flavor makes my mouth water.

Whitt nods gleefully. "Everything is better with fallowroot."

I retrieve the small sack of the flour from the pantry and drop spoonfuls in while Whitt keeps stirring until we agree that the base is satisfyingly gooey-looking. Then I toss in a handful of dried berries just because, to his energetic approval. He goes back to the cold box and returns with a chunk of cream—"Because everything is also better with cream"—that absorbs into the simmering mixture in a matter of seconds.

Whitt takes a sip of the broth and frowns, then snaps his fingers. "Pepper." He adds a few unfamiliar syllables that must be a true name with another flick of his hand, and a jar of gray powder flies straight out of the pantry into his grasp. Once he's sprinkled that in and stirred again, he offers me the spoon to taste.

I lick a little off, momentarily concerned, but the flavors that flood my mouth are unusual but tempting enough that I clean the whole spoon. Nutty and savory with a bite of warmth and a zestiness I think is from the egg yolks. "It's *good*."

Whitt snatches the spoon back and waves it at me. "No need to sound so surprised. I think the caulderims need a few more minutes if we don't want to be chewing them for days, and then we'll have a meal."

When he deems the stew ready, I get a couple of bowls and he slops the mixture into them with apparent abandon, although he manages not to spill any. We carry them over to the dining room.

Whitt eyes the regal chair at the head of the table in an unexpected hesitation. Making the decision for both of us,

I limp to the far end where none of us usually sit so there can't be any sense of displacement. Our kitchen experiment managed to distract me from my worries about the men who aren't here. The longer I can hold back those worries, the better.

I drop into the seat right at the foot of the table. With a chuckle, Whitt follows and takes the chair kitty-corner to me. He spoons up a dollop of the stew and pops it into his mouth to chew it with a contemplative expression.

"Well, I probably wouldn't serve it to August, lest he tell me all the things we got wrong, but I'll personally give us top marks."

I laugh and dig in. It's true that the combination of flavors is odd, and maybe a few of them clash in ways that don't entirely work, but our creation is definitely more satisfying than my hunk of bread. And even more satisfying when combined with the memory of freely flinging whatever we felt like into the pot. August might not approve of a technique so haphazard, but it *was* fun.

After another mouthful, Whitt points his spoon at me. "So, mighty one, I gather you're already making plans to leave us."

My heart lurches at the thought of being anywhere but here. I sputter, almost choking on a lump of sausage before I catch the sly glint in his eyes. I make a face at him. "What are you talking about?"

"I was right there when you were discussing future travels with your dress-making faerie friend," he reminds me, smirking.

I'm feeling bold enough with him now to take the smirk as permission to kick him under the table. "I was only talking about checking out other parts of the domain, like a day trip, and I think you know that."

"Ah, but why restrict yourself? The faerie world is full of wonders beyond those you could have dreamed of discovering where you came from. I thought you were such an avid traveler?"

I hadn't really had the chance to do much more than dream about traveling, but remembering that tightens my chest in a way I'd rather avoid. "What should I make sure to see here, then?" I ask instead, raising my eyebrows to encourage one of his spiels. "With all your spying, you must know the best places, right?"

"Hmm, you know me so well already." Whitt's tone is still teasing, but his smirk has softened. He takes another bite of stew and leans back in his chair.

"Let's see… If you're simply interested in breathtaking spectacles, there's the Shimmering Falls not far from the Heart. The water tumbling over that cliff sparkles brighter than the most finely cut diamond, so lush the vegetation around the pool at its base displays foliage and flowers twice as vivid as anywhere else in the land. It's one of August's favorite picnic spots—or was, when we lived closer and the arch-lords didn't object to us passing through their domains at our leisure."

That caveat makes my heart sink, thinking of August and Sylas traveling through those domains now. "You haven't been there in a while, then."

Whitt makes a careless wave of his hand. "Don't look like that. It only means we'll enjoy it nearly as much as you do when we make it there next. Let's see, what else? If you're in the mood for more adventure, I hear the Shifting

Dunes are quite thrilling, although of course you have to watch out for the sand sharks..."

Between bites, he spins pictures of a dozen other fantastical places I can barely imagine being real, answering my awed questions as they come. By the time I'm scraping the bottom of my bowl, my stomach satisfyingly full, I've created a substantial mental scrapbook dedicated to Faerieland. Whitt discusses it all so breezily that a tickling sensation of hope has risen in my chest.

If *he* believes I'll get to see all those places, that Sylas and August will succeed in making their deal with the arch-lords and I'll keep my freedom, then maybe I don't need to worry at all.

Whitt pauses to lick his spoon. "What of your world? What wonders did you plan to seek out there? I have to admit my explorations on that side have been much less extensive."

Still more extensive than mine, I'm sure. I rub my mouth. "There was the series of mountain pools above the jungle, somewhere in... Tanzania? Tunisia? I don't remember for sure. The photos looked so gorgeous. And the pyramids in Egypt—all that desert... The rainforest in Ecuador..."

My stomach tightens unexpectedly. Trying to put those dreams into words makes them feel so flimsy compared to the descriptions Whitt just gave me.

I duck my head. "I used to imagine places like that all the time when Aerik had me. Float away inside my head. Now that I've imagined them so much, I don't know if the reality would actually live up to all those hopes. But—I'm getting a chance to focus on new dreams now."

Whitt's eyes have darkened at the mention of my past imprisonment, but he taps the table with gusto. "Yes. Yes, you are."

He scoops up the last of his own stew and gulps it down. Then he motions toward my bowl. Before I can nudge it toward him, he's already spoken a true word I can recognize from past experience as *clay*. Both his bowl and mine lift from the tabletop and whisk away to the kitchen as if drawn by a homing beacon.

I stare after them and then yank my attention back to Whitt. "You do that so easily." None of the men of the keep have worked magic that casually in front of me before. From the pleased expression that brightens Whitt's face, I suspect he was purposefully showing off.

"Centuries of practice. But I'd better hold off on more than little gestures like that until I completely recover from all my vial-constructing last night." He sets his elbows on the table and leans forward to study me. "How have *your* magical studies been progressing?"

My fingers curl instinctively, recalling the feel of the bronze spoon I was holding just a minute ago. "Well, you've seen what I can do with bronze now. I still need to be upset before it seems to work. But I guess any time it's urgent that I need to use that word, chances are I'll be upset without even trying."

"August has been working on teaching you more true names, hasn't he?"

"We've just focused on light so far. I haven't made as

much headway with that. It doesn't come quite the same way."

Whitt cocks his head. "What do you mean?"

I gesture vaguely. "I can only seem to get the energy right when I'm really happy. And somehow it's harder to *make* myself feel that than it is to bring back fear or anger from my memories."

"Hmm. I don't think that's so odd. There are so many things one can be afraid of or angry about, especially having been through as much as you have. True happiness is harder to find."

My voice comes out quiet. "Yeah." But as I gaze back at him, the rare but no longer unfamiliar glow of joy beams through me.

This has made me happy: goofing around with Whitt, listening to his stories, simply enjoying each other's company. The longing grips me to show him, to make him see that he hasn't ruined anything. On this day that should be agonizing, he's the one who's made it better.

Still meeting his eyes, I raise my hands above the table and channel that emotion into the word. "*Sole-un-straw.*"

Light flares between my palms, dazzling me for the few seconds before it wisps away. When my vision clears, Whitt is staring at me, his expression tensed but otherwise unreadable.

Maybe it was so brief it seemed more like an insult. My cheeks flush. "I—I don't have much control over it yet, even when I *am* feeling happy. I can't manage more than that."

When Whitt speaks, his tone is unusually gentle, with a rough note running through it. "Talia, it was lovely.

There isn't another human in the world who could have conjured even a spark, you know."

A smile stretches across my face, and I find myself saying, before I can second-guess the impulse, "They mustn't have the right inspiration."

His eyes flicker, and he wets his lips. Then he scoots his chair back from the table and beckons to me. "Come here?"

My heart suddenly thumping, I get up and walk the few steps to his side. Whitt reaches out to take my hand, carefully tucking his around mine. He considers our intertwined fingers as if searching for something in the shape they make. His palm rests warmly against mine.

"The more I'm around you," he says, "the more I see how valiant and vibrant and *good* you are. I want you to know I've set aside any fear that you'll ruin anything at all, even unintentionally. But that doesn't mean *I* won't."

I swallow hard. "Whitt—"

He shakes his head against whatever he thinks I'm going to say. "I don't lie, but I'm in the habit of talking around difficult subjects rather than confronting them directly. I stay up to all hours, and I'm irritable if woken for any reason short of the apocalypse. I'm not sure I'll ever fully trust anyone, including myself. I have many stellar qualities, but you'd have trouble finding kindness, patience, or generosity among them."

He rattles those declarations off in a flippant tone, but he's speaking to our hands rather than to my face. When he looks up at me, I raise my eyebrows. "Are you trying to talk me out of wanting to be with you?"

The corner of his mouth twitches, so briefly I can't tell

which direction it was headed in. "Just making sure you know what you're getting into."

Am I "getting into" it? Into *him*? My heart pounds harder. Right here, on the verge, my position feels abruptly precarious. I've already offered so much of myself to the men of this keep.

But I want more. I want everything this unexpected arrangement can bring with all three of them. Maybe it isn't romance the way I might have imagined when I had no reality to judge from, maybe I have no idea where it'll lead, but while I don't belong to them or they to me, I'm more sure than ever that we all belong together. We fit—a lord, a lord's cadre, and their lady—with this one piece that hadn't quite settled into place.

There's so much about the future that I'm frightened of, but I'm not scared of the man in front of me, not even a little. This is my choice as much as giving my blood was, and I'll accept whatever consequences might come from it too.

This is a dream I can already make real.

I squeeze Whitt's hand, grappling for the right words to erase whatever doubt he's still holding onto. "You always find a way to talk that lets me believe everything's okay, no matter how upset I was a second ago. You stay up so you can give your pack-kin something to celebrate, even though none of you really want to be here. You might not always trust me, but when you've realized you saw things wrong, you've fixed your mistake in whatever way you can. And I don't know how you define kindness, patience, or generosity, but I've seen with my own eyes how far you'll go for Sylas and August and the entire pack—and for me.

I couldn't ask for more than that. I wouldn't. I want you exactly like this."

I stop, worried that I've strayed into babbling territory, but Whitt's expression washes away my own doubts. It's as if something has fallen away behind his eyes and through the planes of his stunning face—as if I'm *really* seeing him, without the sly calculation and the affected nonchalance, just a man who never expected to hear anyone speak of him so fondly. Who's disarmed by it with an elation he can't hide or isn't trying to.

Is this the open, joyful version of Whitt I imagined the night of the revel when he talked about how he's always on guard? Maybe not completely; maybe he hasn't lowered all his armor. But it's closer than I've ever gotten before.

Close enough that I can't stop myself from leaning in to kiss him.

CHAPTER TWENTY-NINE

Talia

J ust before my lips brush his, Whitt raises his free hand to catch my cheek—not stopping me but urging me on. Our mouths collide with more force than I was prepared for.

But it's good—so good. His fingers slip from my cheek into my hair, teasing over my scalp. He drops my hand to loop his other arm around my waist, and his mouth slides against mine, hot and firm yet soft, with just a hint of roughness. Each movement of them sends a tingle down through my chest.

He draws out the kiss, coaxing my lips a little apart, tracing the tip of his tongue along the seam, tilting his head to deepen the embrace. It isn't like August's worshipful eagerness or Sylas's commanding passion. The sense rises up with a flutter around my heart that Whitt is *reveling* in me, drawing out every particle of enjoyment he can from our closeness, savoring me as if I'm the most exquisite dessert.

I may as well be made of spun sugar when he's touching me like this. One kiss and I'm already melting into him.

He eases a few inches back with a chuckle that grazes my cheek with the heat of his breath. His voice is raw. "I could get drunk on you."

I trail my fingers over his cheek and into his hair like he did to me. "Then why don't you?"

I'm not sure who closes the last of the distance, but an instant later we're kissing again. Whitt devours me, leaving me aching for more, for things I can't even put words to. With every press of his lips, my breath grows shakier. My knees wobble beneath me, and I find the wherewithal to brace one next to his legs on the seat of the chair and swing the other over to straddle him.

The skirt of my dress rides up on my thighs. Whitt lets out an approving murmur at the increased contact, fitting his mouth against mine even more deeply. His fingers twine in my hair, pulling to the barest edge of pain that somehow provokes an electric pulse of pleasure right down my spine. His other hand strokes up my side to cup my breast.

He seems to know exactly how to touch me to draw out the giddiest waves of bliss. His thumb finds my nipple and raises it to a peak with one swift swivel; his tongue coaxes mine to explore his mouth. All I can do is kiss him back and clutch onto his shirt, holding on for the ride.

He's been with other women before—lots of other women, from how Sylas has talked. He knows what he's doing from practice. But that thought only stirs the faintest twinge of jealousy in me, there and then washed away by the pleasure he's conjuring all through my body.

It's me he's with right now. It's me he *wants* right now. He's taking his time, relishing me, drinking in my reactions and following what makes me whimper with need.

I echo his movements, wanting to spark the same thrill of desire in him as he's lighting in me: tangling my fingers in his rumpled hair, melding my lips to his, running my hand up and down his sculpted chest over his shirt. The groan that escapes him suggests I'm doing something right.

He wrenches his mouth from mine to chart a path of kisses down the side of my neck before burying his face in the crook of my shoulder. His breath scorches my skin as his lips and tongue work over the sensitive span of skin. He skims that spot with the edges of his teeth and then, when I quiver and gasp, nips me with sharper intensity.

It isn't hard enough to break the skin, but the sensation shifts from exhilarating to unnerving so abruptly my whole body stiffens. A memory flickers up of jaws tearing into my flesh, fangs raking through that shoulder—

Whitt jerks back. He holds my face close to his until I relax again with the stroke of his thumbs across my temple.

"I'm sorry," he murmurs. He drops one hand in a caress along my neck to my scarred shoulder, gliding his fingertips over the mottled ridges in the gentlest of caresses. "You taste so good, mighty one. But I will *never* bring my teeth to bear on you where they're not wanted. The ones who savaged you like this deserve to be torn to pieces limb by limb and sent up in flames for good measure."

He follows those words with a delicate kiss to each raised line of scar, until any memory of past pain is lost under the desire trembling through me. I tip my head back instinctively, and he flicks his tongue across my throat before marking a line down to my collarbone with the softest of nibbles.

Slowly, waiting on my encouraging hum, he eases the strap of my dress down my arm. His kisses delve lower, following the fabric until the neckline grazes my nipple to spark a quiver of anticipation.

While Whitt bares more and more of my skin, his is staying frustratingly under wraps. I swallow a needy sound that's almost a whine and focus enough to yank at his high-collared shirt.

"If my clothes are coming off, yours are too," I inform him, a command that would probably be firmer if it hadn't come out breathless.

He grins up at me. "Fair is fair. I do appreciate a woman who knows what she wants."

He loosens the fastenings below the collar and tugs the shirt off over his head, leaving his hair even more rumpled than before. I got a good look at his muscular form in his bed the other morning, but not with quite so much freedom to explore. As I gaze down at him, he merely strokes his fingers along the edge of my dress's straps, not diverting me from my inspection.

Taking him in with my eyes isn't enough. I trail my

hands down from his shoulders to the packed muscle across his abdomen, pausing here and there to trace the whorls and angles of his tattoos. His smooth skin blazes beneath my fingers. I tease them along his sides, finding a spot that draws a rumble from his chest, and then give in to the impulse to taste him as he's tasted me.

I lean in, pressing my lips to a coiled mark on his neck, a jagged pinwheel on his shoulder, a clawed twig-like shape over his sternum. Whitt slides his hand into my hair again, following my progress, a hint of a rasp creeping into his breath. I flick my tongue over one of his taut nipples, delighting at the hitch of his chest, and kiss my way across the powerful expanse to the other.

As I absorb his summery, sun-baked scent, my fingers edge lower. Past his belly button, over the waist of his trousers where my dress is pooled, until the heel of my hand brushes the rigid bulge just below.

Whitt lets out a growl and pulls my mouth back to his. He brands me with a kiss so searing it leaves every nerve in my body quaking with desire.

My touch has awakened something primal in his nature. His tongue tangles with mine with sudden urgency. His hands sweep right beneath the neckline of my dress to caress my breasts skin to skin and then yank the fabric right off them. Hefting me higher against him, he sucks one nipple into the scorching heat of his mouth with a wildness that sends a bolt of sharper pleasure through me.

A cry slips from my lips. I clutch his head, his shoulder, caught in the rush of sensation. Each lap of his tongue and graze of his teeth floods me with a hunger for more. The now-familiar ache is building between my legs. My hips start to rock against him of their own accord, seeking the friction that can bring me to release.

With another growl, Whitt lifts me from the chair and sets me on the edge of the table, standing between my splayed legs. He tugs me tight against him and recaptures my mouth, all but devouring me from his new higher ground. Then he kisses my cheek, the edge of my jaw, with greater restraint. He palms my naked breasts, massaging them until the pulses of pleasure have me gasping again.

As his hands keep fondling me with teasing strokes, he gazes down at me. His voice comes out low and ragged. "Can I ask you one thing, Talia?"

His tone and his use of my name rather than one of his playful nicknames draw me out of my eager haze. I peer up at him, willing myself to focus through the delicious movements of his fingers and palms over my chest. "Anything."

Whitt gives me a crooked smile, heat smoldering in his eyes, the blue more fiery than oceanic now. "What made you talk to Sylas about pursuing me rather than coming to me directly?"

He gives the question a casual lilt, but his gaze holds mine intently. Like when he watched to see my response to his list of his flaws. Does he think I hesitated out of distrust or fear—that something about him put me off?

I kiss him as if the tender pressure of my lips might wipe away whatever worries provoked the question, and then I tuck my head against his neck to hide my sheepishness. "I didn't mean for it to happen like that. I didn't know you were interested, and I—I hadn't even fully realized that *I* was interested that way, and then Sylas checked on me when I was having an... intense dream, and the topic came up like that."

Whitt laughs lightly, his shoulders relaxing, and nuzzles my temple. "A dream, hmm? And what happened in that dream, which I assume featured me? Do tell."

A blush flares in my cheeks, but it's not as if we haven't already gotten more intimate than anything that played out in my subconscious. "You... were kneeling in front of me like when you checked the glamour on my foot brace, and you started kissing my leg. All the way up."

"*All* the way?" Whitt asks, his voice so suggestive I practically burst into flames.

"Well, I woke up before... before it could get that far."

"Hmm. Poor thing. But such an inspired imagination. I'll just make sure not to leave you wanting here in reality."

He's only just finished speaking when he eases back from me to sink to his knees. I stare down at him from my perch on the table, my pulse skittering with a dizzying mix of anticipation and uncertainty. "I wasn't— You don't have to—"

The conspiratorial gleam in his eyes is nothing but eager. "I haven't had anywhere near my fill of you yet."

Whitt undoes the fixtures on my brace and slips it off my foot to set it aside. Then he kisses the warped ridge below my ankle where the bones are fused wrong, so reverently my heart swells with a different sort of ache.

What I said to Harper is true—I can live with a damaged foot—but it's still a handicap to be worked around, a weakness I have to make up for. The veneration in Whitt's lips makes it feel like something special rather than broken. Different but far from wrong.

His mouth travels up to my calf, his thumb gliding gently over the misshapen bump instead. Kiss by tender kiss, he works his way up to my knee, with a teasing swipe of his tongue when he reaches the joint.

As he continues his journey along my inner thigh, the press of his mouth deepens, each kiss lingering a little longer. Partway up, he pauses to slide the skirt of my dress higher and melds his lips to the sensitive skin so passionately my chest hitches. A heady tingling races over my skin to my sex.

I grip the edge of the table for balance, watching his progress, wondering a little dizzily just how far he's going to take this. The ache between my legs has intensified to a throbbing need. His breath spills hot over the tender area just below that juncture, where he has to ease my legs even farther apart to offer his next kiss. My fingers curl tighter—

And, with a sly smirk, he bends back down to nibble the opposite knee.

I hold back a groan, especially because now he's charting a matching path up the inside of my left thigh. The last thing I want to do is divert him even slightly. Hunger knots in my core, threading through my veins. Every muscle has coiled in anticipation, even though I'm not totally sure what I'm readying for. This is already so much more thrilling than my dream managed to portray.

As he edges closer with that skillful mouth, Whitt slides his hands beneath my hiked-up dress and hooks his fingers over the hem of my panties. He raises his head just long enough to tug them down my legs. Then he brushes a kiss to the skin just inches from my sex, and another, and another.

Stroking my hips, he eases me even nearer and inhales with a sound of relish. He must be able to smell the arousal I can feel gathering between my folds. A renewed flush scorches my cheeks, but before my embarrassment can really take hold, he lowers his mouth to taste me there, and all other thoughts fly out of my head with the surge of pleasure.

"Whitt," I mumble, half whimper, half moan, and he hums with delight.

"That's the only way I want to hear you say my name from now on," he murmurs, his breath alone sending all kinds of giddy tremors through me, and leans in to swipe his tongue right over my slit.

He plunders my sex with lips and tongue and here and there a gentle edge of teeth. If I was dessert before, now he's treating me like a full banquet he intends to savor every morsel of.

I sway where I'm balanced on the table and find myself clinging to his hair with one hand, unsure whether I'm urging him on or begging for a reprieve from this exquisite torture. I'm panting, trembling from head to toe. The rush of pleasure keeps swelling through me until it's as vast as the ocean in his eyes.

Whitt suckles my most sensitive spot that can spark the headiest jolt of paradise and then delves his tongue right inside me. I clench around him—sex, thighs, fingers in his sun-kissed locks. The wave of ecstasy tosses me up and over my peak, crashing through me and sweeping me away, leaving me gasping for air.

My body goes limp. Whitt's kisses soften, but he stays where he is, flicking his tongue over the sensitive nub, working his mouth against my folds, until the rush of sensation rises through me again. Then he plunders me wholeheartedly, branding me with bliss as no one else ever has. I bow over him, too overcome to do more than cling on and ride the wave as it careens toward its pinnacle once more, even faster than before.

A shattered cry breaks from my throat—and I'm freefalling over the edge in a blaze that consumes every other sensation.

As I drift down into the afterglow for the second time, Whitt dapples my inner thighs with more kisses. Gradually, my tight grip on his hair releases. I stroke my fingers through the thick strands, and he beams up at me before licking his lips so extravagantly my whole face must turn red. "A perfect meal."

He stands and collects me in his arms. Settling back in his chair, he tucks me against him. Every part of him that touches me feels as feverish as my own skin.

I squirm closer, soaking in his heat, and raise my fingers to his cheek. My other hand skims over his belly again. "I want to— You haven't gotten—"

He catches my hand before I make it to the rigid bulge against my hip and kisses my knuckles instead. His gaze is feverish too, but the embrace he wraps me in is all controlled might.

"We have so much time ahead of us," he says quietly.

"This first interlude—I don't want there to be any chance of you looking back and feeling I took more than I gave."

I don't think there's any chance of that after the heights he just propelled me to, but I can tell how important the principle of it is to him from the resolve in his voice. I settle for slipping my hand along his neck and kissing the crook of his jaw before nestling my head against his shoulder.

The ache of need is gone, but the poignant sensation that wrapped around my heart shines on.

Is it possible to love *three* men at the same time? I never would have thought so, but how can I argue with the emotion unfurling inside me even as I ask the question?

There's enough feeling in my heart to encompass all of them—and I can only hope it's enough to see all three of them back in this keep, whole and happy, beneath tomorrow's sun.

CHAPTER THIRTY

Sylas

I t's said that all of the fae world slants upward to embrace the Heart of the Mists. In most domains, including both Oakmeet and Hearthshire, you wouldn't notice any significant slope to the plains and forests. But at the borders of the arch-lords' domains, the three of them surrounding the summer side of the Heart, the land rises sharply, emerald-green fields arching up to the vast plateau of gold-veined sandstone and winding foliage that holds their castles and our Bastion of the Heart.

No other keep or fortress in the land can hold a candle to the Bastion. It rises from ground as if it grew out of the same rock—which in a sense it did, though coaxed by magic innumerable centuries ago. The currents of gold gleam amid the warm beige of the stone. Having been here at night, I can attest that those veins keep shining even in the dark of a new moon.

Towering over the flower-dotted, grassy terrain around

them, the sturdy walls rise into four craggy peaks like a miniature mountain range—three smaller summits around a taller and broader central one. Birds perch in and soar past the arched windows, while hares nibble clover on the lawn. The thrum of the Heart's energy calls even to those lesser beings.

As August and I trek the last short distance along the path between Donovan's domain and Celia's, the Heart's magic washes over my skin and peals through my body. My chest opens, my pulse singing through my veins in welcome. Despite the vital but perilous mission that brings us here, a smile crosses my lips.

Skies above, it's been far too long since I basked in the full power of our world.

That sensation speaks of the Heart more than anything we can see. Just beyond the Bastion, the shimmering mist of the border condenses into a denser, pulsing glow, one that will fade to the quality of starlight with the descending of the sun. Just a few steps beyond that border, I have to assume the Unseelie arch-lords rule from some gilded fortress of their own.

It's unsettling to imagine our enemies lurking so close at hand, but thousands of years ago, our peoples collaborated in a sort of promise, a spell that flows through the border all the way through the arch-lords' domains and into a few neighboring lands as well. No one has yet come close to shattering their magic, it's so aligned with the principles of harmony and growth that the Heart resonates with.

To cross the border within that stretch, one must swear to do no harm to the fae on the other side—an oath that binds one's will against deceit. A traveler has no such guarantee of good will from the hosts that await them. Unsurprisingly, few choose to make the journey, especially in these recent years while we've found ourselves at war.

August halts for a moment, both to soak in the Heart's energy and to wipe the sweat from his brow. "I forgot what a trek it is," he says with a sheepish smile. "I'll have to add a little more mountain-climbing to my exercise regimen."

I give him a benevolent swat to the shoulder. "If you'd taken the path any faster, I'd have had to rein you in for my own survival. Come on, then. By now, they're undoubtedly waiting for us. Let's not breed impatience and frustration before we've had any chance to make our case."

There are other rules for peace in the domains around the Heart, at least on the summer side of the border. Any fae may travel the routes between the arch-lord's domains unhindered and unquestioned to petition our rulers in the Bastion. However, we're required to make the journey on foot once we reach the steeper slope.

The publicly stated reasoning is that putting in the physical effort shows our dedication and proves us worthy of being heard. I suspect the unstated reasoning is that it gives the arch-lords and their packs plenty of time to observe those who approach and decide how to greet them.

We cross the flowery lawn to the Bastion's entrance, which contains no door, only a couple of stairs up to an immense opening in the stone wall that's arched like the windows. Stepping through it, the twittering of the birds and the rustling of leaves on the nearby trees fades away. The air settles around us still and cool, as if we've walked into a cavern.

But it's a bright cavern, sunlight streaking down across the floor from windows at all angles and the veins of gold glittering across in the inner walls just as they do outside. The flow of the Heart's energy continues pulsing over us, emitting a faint, silvery hum as it courses through the building.

Standing in this place, it isn't that hard to believe a handful of fae with grand hopes for peaceful coexistence could have erected a barrier between the realms that's lasted generations. Magic saturates the atmosphere.

No one lives in the Bastion or within about a mile of it. Linger for too many weeks at a time in this kind of power, and you might go mad with it. They say at least one of the first arch-lords became overzealous and met that fate.

We walk through the airy entrance hall into an even vaster room. The gold-laced, vaulted ceiling gleams several stories high above us. The light that spills through the rows of windows all down the walls forms a shape like a flower with petals spiraling around it on the veined floor. At the edges of that light, lit by it but not caught directly in its beams, stand three golden thrones, spaced evenly around the circular space.

As I expected, the arch-lords already occupy their respective seats. Their cadre-chosen flank their thrones—at least, those of their cadre not occupied elsewhere. They each still have at least one out at the northern end of the border.

You can tell a lot about a lord by the close company they keep and how much of it they keep. Celia, old enough to have seen some of her cadre pass on before her and growing too weary to continue adding to their number, has only one figure by her side. Ambrose, hesitant to trust but even warier of lacking in protection, boasts three. Donovan, either overeager or overcautious in his youth—or perhaps a bit of both—has brought six with him.

Even if I dislike Ambrose's attitudes, I have to admit he has the most ideal outcome. Too large a cadre, and the chances that all of them will be sufficiently dedicated when it counts dwindles. Donovan hasn't been tried enough yet to discover how tenuous some loyalties can be. But then, a smaller group makes it easy to stretch one's authority and resources too thin.

Kellan might have been a bastard, but he did get things done for me. Before our banishment, I had the benefit of Isleen's cadre alongside mine. I don't have near as much authority to extend or tasks to lord over as Celia does, but in the arch-lords' midst, I feel my lack.

Ambrose leans against the arm of his throne with an expression that suggests he's suppressing a grimace. More bulldog than wolf in his appearance as a man, he rubs the jowls of his round face. The new flecks of gray in his sparse beard stand out against his tan skin. Topping his head, his cropped bronze-brown curls with their patina-like greenish sheen hold hints of gray too. He fixes his dark, beady eyes on me.

"You come all the way from the fringes on the day of the full moon, Lord Sylas?" he says flatly. "Shouldn't you be preparing your pack? Or are you so accustomed to savagery out there that you've taken to letting them fend for themselves?"

August bristles but manages to keep his mouth shut. Good man.

I ignore Ambrose's jab, letting my gaze slide from him to Celia to Donovan, acknowledging each with a respectful but not overly deferential bob of my head. "My arch-lords, it's *because* of the full moon that I come before you. My cadre-chosen August has made a crucial discovery about the Unseelie's plans—though one you are perhaps not totally unaware of—and I have brought you the solution to that potential catastrophe as well."

Celia's eyebrows rise to her wispy bangs. A pure ivory-white with a crystalline shimmer, the rest of her hair falls starkly around her narrow, ebony face. If Ambrose could be a bulldog, then she'd be a doe with her steeply sloping nose and heavy-lidded eyes. But her tall frame, though slender, fills out her ankle-length gown with imposingly broad shoulders. No one would mistake her for prey.

"Well, I think we had better hear this, then. But first I'd want to know precisely how your man made this discovery."

August dips his head lower than I did. At my gesture, he speaks. "We were told that it would risk too much for any of you to approve a stealthy foray into Unseelie territory. So my lord gave *his* approval for me to go on my own, so that you couldn't be blamed if our plans went awry. But they didn't. No one saw me except the sentry I captured. I couldn't get much out of the raven, but he cawed enough to confirm what we suspected and to reveal something even worse."

Donovan shifts forward in his throne. Even though the sunlight doesn't hit him directly, the tufts of his hair seem to dance like flames, brilliant reds and oranges mingling together. His mother's had the same effect.

It was her he inherited the throne from, mere months before my disgrace. Her death was brutal and unexpected at the jaws of a pair of chimera she'd gone out to subdue that somehow got the upper hand on her, and the first time I stood before him here, waiting to hear my pack's fate, he was too green to get much of a word in between Ambrose's domineering bluster and Celia's crisp brusqueness. But he caught me on my way down the path to my carriage to apologize and let me know he didn't agree with the sentence, that if he could make a case for me down the line he would, and I haven't forgotten that humility.

Unfortunately, I'm not sure these past several decades have hardened him enough for him to quite hold his own yet. For all his fiery hair and brawny frame, there's a softness to his jaw and stance that shows through. He hasn't been through real fire yet. Heart only knows how he'll be tempered or savaged by the experience when it comes.

"What happened to this sentry after you questioned him?" he asks.

August smiles grimly. "I removed his head from his body right there on the border. If he was found, no one would be able to say it wasn't his own carelessness in coming too close to our side—and he won't have been able to tell anyone what he gave away to me."

Ambrose runs his hand over the plate-mail vest he likes to wear even when he's not on the battlefield, as if to indicate he views every interaction as a potential threat. The faint metallic clink is vaguely ominous. "And what exactly did he give away?"

I take over to spare my younger brother the scrutiny our news will provoke. "The Unseelie have learned of our curse—enough to know that we won't be in any state to defend the border tonight if the wildness takes hold. They mean to attack along the northern stretch where you've each stationed one of your cadre-chosen. From their presence, I assume you had some idea that area was of concern."

Ambrose's mouth tightens into a sour frown. Celia has tensed as well, but her gaze is more searching than accusing. "The sentry told you all of that?"

"I pretended I already knew the location of their next attack, and he didn't deny it," August says. "Then he mocked me for thinking we'd be able defend our lands while we're running wild. There was no mistaking his meaning."

Donovan lets out a short, rough laugh and shakes his head. "So, it was true after all."

They knew our curse had been exposed but doubted it? I turn to him. "How did you come to hear of it?"

Ambrose shoots Donovan a sharp look, but the younger arch-lord has gained at least enough confidence to make his own choice to answer. "The Unseelie last attacked the morning after the full moon. A few days later, we had a letter appear in the grass here just beyond the border, as if the one who delivered it had slipped through only long enough to set it down. It was a warning that our enemies meant to take advantage of our malady, and where."

"It *claimed* to be a warning," Ambrose breaks in. "Why would any of the stinking ravens help us? We had to treat it as a potential trap—possibly not even from their side but from some schemer among the Seelie."

Donovan's hand falls to rest on the golden broach fixed to his padded doublet, ornately carved into the shape of a wolf biting its own tail. It's an heirloom passed on from his mother, and no doubt from her predecessor to her. The tale I've heard is that supposedly the family has some secret to transferring a bit of every fallen relative's spirit into it from their soulstone, keeping all those pieces of their power alive.

I've never encountered any spell by which that effect could be achieved, but I believe the broach has some kind of magic in it. A trusted warrior from my father's pack once reported he'd seen Donovan's mother summon a hail of shooting stars by calling on it. Perhaps her son takes some comfort in the thought of having those ancestors with him. Or perhaps he's dreaming of raining bolts of flame down on his colleague's grizzled head.

As I turn over their words, the pieces of the puzzle click into place. "You sent cadre to that section of border to observe and ramp up protections where they could just in case, but you didn't spread the word—for fear of panic?"

Celia sinks back in her chair, looking weary. "You're

clearly well-versed enough in warfare to understand, Lord Sylas. Even if we felt sure that the note had come from the winter side, and that therefore at least some of the ravens knew of the curse, there's little we could do about that with the loss of Lord Aerik's cure. As to where to bolster our defenses and how, without the ravens potentially catching on and adjusting their plans in response, we have found it difficult to reach a consensus."

"It's good that we know now, though," Donovan says. "For the rest of the day and evening, we can put all of our power into bolstering our magical defenses along the border even more than usual and securing the nearest towns as well as we can. It may not be enough to hold them back completely—"

Ambrose's guffaw is dark. "Those sorry whelps on the front lines will be lucky not to tear *each other* to pieces once the moon rises."

"We'll pull them back as we did last month and limit our self-destruction as well as we can," Celia says firmly. "We have to take every step—"

I clear my throat, interrupting the urgent but unnecessary negotiations so I can begin my own. "You won't need to. None of the squadrons along any part of the border need to succumb to the curse tonight. We've brought the cure."

All three of them stare at me in shocked silence. "Where?" Ambrose demands abruptly.

"In our carriage, in a spot I'll lead your pack-kin to if we reach an agreement I'm satisfied with."

He draws himself up haughtily, his eyes flashing.

"You'd barter over this while the Unseelie forces gather and the full moon is nearly—"

"Let us hear all he has to say first," Celia chides. Her brow has furrowed. "How is this possible? We were given to believe that a crucial resource Lord Aerik brought to bear, the one he's now seeking to obtain more of, could only be found within his domain. We knew he'd expanded his search, but I hadn't thought he'd shared his methods so freely that his efforts could be usurped."

My mouth twists. It's here that I must reveal Talia's existence.

Every sinew in my body balks at the thought. I meant to give her as close to a normal life as I could offer, one free of the demands my kind would place on her after everything she's unwillingly sacrificed for us already. As soon as our rulers know of her existence and the power of her blood, I can't guarantee any of that.

But perhaps I never could. How can I give her anything like *normal* given who she is and how she came to be here? I can still hope to offer freedom and happiness in whatever forms they might take.

And what Talia insisted on was the freedom to make yet another sacrifice on our behalf. If I deny her that right, wouldn't I be caging her in yet another way?

I could speak around the facts of the matter as Aerik did, hold off the discovery, but once it's clear that he obscured the truth, the arch-lords won't rest until they have the full story. I'll only be wasting time better spent ensuring her protection.

I drag in a breath. "Aerik misled you. The only resource necessary to the cure has not been used up but has... relocated itself to reside in my domain, of its own free will. As I feel is for the best, given the treatment it received in Aerik's 'care'."

August stirs beside me, his stance tensing at just that vague mention of Talia's abuse.

Ambrose jerks his hand through the air in an impatient gesture. "By all that is dust, what are you nattering about? Speak plainly, or we can cut right past the speaking part."

To taking the cure by force, he means. My hackles rise, but I keep my voice even. "The only substance necessary to stave off or reverse the wildness is the blood of a specific human woman. From what I've gathered, Aerik kept her existence secret from all but his two cadre-chosen, hiding her away in the most wretched of prisons for all of the years he produced his cure, giving her only enough sustenance to continue that existence. When she came to us, she was near-starved, battered and scarred, and permanently disfigured from the wounds they inflicted on her."

Ambrose sputters, as if the idea that he's been inadvertently drinking human blood to cure his ills disgusts him beyond speech. Celia and Donovan still look bewildered, but Celia is composed enough to speak. "A human woman? And how did you discover this? How did she end up among your pack?"

On the journey here, I thought carefully over how I could present the story within the bounds of truth but without admitting to any crime. The Heart might lash out at me visibly if I attempted to lie in its very presence.

"They must have grown careless," I say. "One day she

was able to unlock her cage to make her escape. We found her not knowing at first what she was capable of, only seeing a being in distress. Once we understood how she'd fit into Aerik's plans—and having seen how he'd treated her—it seemed unwise to return her. He was abusing a valuable resource. We felt it wiser to nurture such a prize."

Speaking of Talia as a thing to be used rather than a person makes my stomach clench, but it's the language the arch-lords will expect in these circumstances. Celia nods, a thin furrow creasing her high forehead. "Have you taken any steps to determine what it is about this human that produces such a powerful effect in her blood?"

"I've made many attempts—tested her skin and hair and her blood itself by the most obvious methods and others besides. I've been unable to detect any factor in her heritage or physical makeup that would create such an effect. I would pursue additional avenues given the chance, but for the moment other matters needed my attention more urgently."

Perhaps when this is over, if we can reach an agreement that keeps Talia out of danger, I'll be able to pursue those answers farther afield with Talia's blessing. Keeping her and my brethren uninjured comes before any of that.

Ambrose clearly found even my practical phrasing in regards to Talia too lenient. He's still stewing over my earlier explanation. "A human who can cure us all—and you've been worrying about her comfort. What of the rest of us?"

It takes even more effort than before to smooth the edge from my voice. "The rest of us can partake of the tonic we've made using her blood as need be. It's only effective if consumed while the blood is relatively fresh. Surely you wouldn't suggest we neglect what we've come to rely on so much, even if it's a human?"

"I'd suggest that the human had best come into our own custody so we can monitor her and her contributions to our people as we see fit," Ambrose replies.

Exactly as I feared, without a moment's grace. My fangs itch in my gums. I've enjoyed the idea of ripping Ambrose's throat out from the moment decades ago when he chuckled as he showed me the tattered flesh that was all that remained of my soul-twined mate when his warriors were done with her. Now I'll add his ribs and his intestines to the list of body parts I'd enjoy seeing violently extracted.

"I haven't stated my conditions." I slide my gaze from him to the more moderate two of the arch-lords. "I have enough vials of the tonic for every warrior along the border and more besides so you can summon additional forces from the nearby domains. Given the dire peril we face tonight, I don't think my terms are particularly extreme.

"My pack has remained in our banishment to the fringes for several decades now while offering nothing but full loyalty to you and to the Heart. Not one of us so banished was ever found to have played a role in the treason we were sanctioned for. Despite our dwindled numbers, we have fought alongside every other pack at the border. My cadre-chosen risked his life and our honor on your behalf to confirm the Unseelie threat, and we uncovered the true nature of the tonic and have revealed it to you."

"More than we can say of Aerik, I'll admit," Donovan says with a quirk of his eyebrows that feels promising.

"Indeed. And he received many rewards for what he did offer. You didn't demand control over his operations when you believed them unmovable." I lift my jaw, my spine stretching to emphasize my height. "I request that I and my pack recover our claim over the domain of Hearthshire. That we be absolved of any continuing suspicion of treachery. And that we be allowed to continue to watch over the human woman as we have seen fit, unless it should conspire that we are no longer able to arrange the cure while she's in our care."

I can't fulfill any promise to Talia without my pack's standing restored. The arch-lords could never justify leaving a being so valuable in the hands of a lord they still officially distrust. Every piece of my demand hinges together.

Ambrose snorts, but Donovan gives a careful nod at the same time. Between them, Celia steeples her hands on her lap, her expression impenetrable.

"You request very much, Lord Sylas," she says. "But you also offer a lot. You would risk our people in insisting on these terms?"

I focus my attention solely on her. I don't need Ambrose's agreement. I've already won Donovan over, and if I have Celia, their votes will outweigh his. But I don't think I've convinced her yet.

"I have faith that the arch-lords will see justice carried out, and I must serve the needs of my pack as well as all my brethren. What kind of lord would I be if I didn't speak for them while I can?"

"Hmm." Her gaze drifts away from me, going distant. Uneasiness winds through my gut. Have I made all the case I can?

A filmy image forms before my deadened eye: a memory of a time long past when I stood before her. The echo of her past self bolts upright from her throne, her hands fisted at her sides, and makes a declaration my mystical vision can't give voice to but that I can read from her lips. *We must respect the Heart and all its tenets!*

The image wisps away, but it leaves a solid sense of certainty in its wake. I do know how to appeal to her sensibilities.

"And if I may add," I say, low and steady, "I ask for nothing more but to see the principles of the Heart carried out. There is no balance in consigning a pack who would serve you well to the fringes. There is no harmony in wrenching a living, feeling being from the one home in years where she's been treated with compassion."

Celia's eyes flick back to me. She sits up straighter. I'm not sure I've swayed her—or that I haven't pushed too far.

"This is too great a matter to put to a vote in an instant," she says. "I say we deliberate—quickly, given the circumstances. Unless my fellow arch-lords object, I ask that you and your cadre-chosen retreat outside until you are summoned."

Neither Ambrose nor Donovan raises an objection, although Ambrose's face has turned even sourer. I bob my head alongside August's deeper bow, and we escort ourselves out of the Bastion.

The brilliant sun beaming over us provides little comfort. August shifts his weight from foot to foot restlessly. "What will we do if they—"

I hold up my hand. "Let the decision come as it will. I'll handle it either way."

It can't be more than a quarter of an hour, but when a man of Donovan's cadre pokes his head from the doorway and calls us back in, I feel as though I've been standing there for days. My heart doesn't lift until we step into the audience room and I catch the trace of a smile lingering on Celia's lips. Ambrose is scowling, but he keeps his mouth shut.

Donovan doesn't restrain his smile at all. "It is my pleasure to speak for all three of us that we accept your terms," he says, and a current of magic ripples into his voice. "Hearthshire will be restored to Lord Sylas and his pack. You will be absolved of any wrongdoing in the treason spearheaded by the Thistlegrove pack. And we will stake no direct claim on the human woman who contributes to the cure as long as you continue to provide all who need it with the tonic."

He's barely finished speaking before Ambrose rises with a sharp clinking of his armored vest. "If you're quite satisfied, let's have that tonic already. No one should have forgotten that we have a terrible battle ahead of us tonight."

I dip my head again in agreement, but even knowing that, my spirits soar. While we have the Unseelie still to contend with, I've won the battle my people have been fighting quietly and without complaint for more decades than I like to count.

All of my pack has gained a sort of freedom today. I'll snap a thousand ravens' necks before I let them steal it away again.

———

Evening has fallen when August and I gather our warriors near the river. I glance from one of them to the other and then to the heads of the other squadrons nearby, who've received their orders—and the word that Lord Sylas has proven his loyalty and can demand the same from them. A few of the warriors offer grim smiles of acknowledgment.

"You've all had your tonic?" I ask my pack-kin, and take in their nods. "Good. If we stick to the strategy discussed, the ravens won't know what hit them before there are feathers strewn across these fields. Let them see easy prey until they lower their guard—and then they'll be the ones pleading for mercy."

Moving among them, I give them each a bolstering cuff to the shoulder or bump of an elbow. Then I step aside and release my wolf.

There's something so perfect about stretching into my beastly form with utter control on a night when so many times before I truly became a beast. The awareness of every muscle and limb prickles through my limber body.

I wheel to confirm that the rest of my pack-kin have transformed at my lead. At my brisk bark, the squadron scatters, August roaming to the south while I wander north.

I weave back and forth on an erratic path, shaking my head, snarling at the grass, snapping at any other wolf I cross paths with. Giving every appearance of being lost in wildness. Let the ravens come. Let them see the chaos they expected.

The sky darkens to black. The round, white face of the moon peers over us. The magical defenses along the border warble, sending increasingly violent shudders through the air. Then they shatter, and hundreds of darkly-feathered bodies swoop through the haze.

Some circle over us, observing. Others soar farther west toward the nearest towns, where other squadrons and dozens of newly gathered warriors from the nearby packs are waiting to dole out the same fate.

So many more of us await the Unseelie forces than they'll have been expecting. But that won't worry them yet, not while they're still caught up in glee over our apparent incoherence.

Anticipation thrums through my veins like the magic of the Heart. Let them come. Let them come and—

The immense birds drop, transforming into armored, winged men brandishing swords and spears as they descend on us. A few of them are *laughing*, reveling in how easily they believe they'll pick us off much as Whitt revels in fairy wine. I allow myself a wolfish grin.

As one being, the wolves of summer spring to attention and lunge at our foes.

We pick those unsuspecting feather-brains out of mid-dive and slam them to the earth, claws already gouging, fangs already chomping. Cries and groans echo across the moonlit plains, too late to give each other warning. They fell on us together thinking to slaughter us in one swift strike, and we've turned the strike back on them.

I tear through one attacker's throat just above the neck of his armor and slash another. There are yelps of wolfish pain in the night, but not as many as the gurgles of our enemies. Everywhere, furred bodies spin and leap and maul, until the grass is splattered scarlet and the earth beneath runs red with raven blood, and the stragglers flee back into the haze.

Watching them, the metallic tang laced through my mouth, I raise my head toward the moon that's haunted us for so many years and let loose a howl of victory. One after another, my pack-kin and my brethren match it, until the very wind shakes with the news of our triumph.

May the ravens hear it all the way in their icy lands and feel a chill of terror in their hearts.

CHAPTER THIRTY-ONE

Talia

As the carriage leaves Oakmeet behind, watching the familiar forestlands, hills, and knobby spires of rock fade into the distance brings a melancholy twinge into my chest.

I found peace in that place. I figured out—maybe not everything—but a whole lot about who I am now and what I want. And I don't think Sylas or his pack have any interest in returning to the domain of their disgrace ever again.

But I can't regret our departure. I might not be fae, but I can feel the shift in the atmosphere the farther we venture from our former home. A softer warmth flows through the air with every mile we travel closer to the Heart. The vegetation around us grows brighter and more fragrant, filling my lungs with floral sweetness and evergreen tang. Hope lights the faces of both my three lovers and the pack grouped on other carriages in a stream behind ours.

We're heading away from the first real home I've had in the fae world but toward the one they've all missed for so long.

I'm sitting tucked next to August on one of the moss-cushioned benches, my head resting against his shoulder as his fingers idly play with my hair. While we're in view of the rest of the pack, I'm still only involved with him. But now and then as Whitt strolls along the length of the carriage, he shoots me sly smiles with a promise of what might come behind closed doors at our destination. Sylas stands at the bow like captain of a ship, but when he returned two mornings ago and announced that the arch-lords had agreed to let him "keep" me, he gathered me in his arms so tightly afterward that the echo of the embrace still tingles through me when I think of it.

We skirt the edge of a valley where a river of lavender-purple water courses, and then weave through ruddy rocks that jut like fingers from grass fine as spider webbing. When another forest looms up ahead, Sylas steps back to sink on the bench across from August and me.

"That's the edge of our domain," he says, tipping his head toward the trees. As we speed toward them, my heart starts to swell with awe. Closer up, it's obvious that they're twice as large as the grandest ordinary trees I've ever seen: trunks as thick as turrets, leaves so broad I could lie on one without an inch of me slipping over the edge.

"Did no one take over your land while you were banished?" I ask. He hasn't mentioned us displacing another pack.

He shakes his head. "It seems neither of the two new lords who set off to form separate packs were bold enough to stake a claim, and none of those who already had their own domains were inclined to relocate to this one." He gives me a rare wide smile. "I like to think they all knew I'd be back before too long."

"If there had been any squatters, the arch-lords would simply have had to find them a new territory," Whitt says. "The summer lands are hardly choked with packs. We do enjoy plenty of room to roam around."

He looks pleased in a more relaxed sort of way than is usual for him too. I snuggle closer to August, anticipation tickling through me. "I can't wait to see it."

Sylas casts his gaze toward the bow again. "Very soon."

The carriages soar between the magnificent trees. They're gliding along too quickly for me to make out many details, but I think I see a flowery vine slithering across one trunk like a snake—or maybe it's a snake that's doing a very good imitation of a vine—and a cliffside that glints like wet copper. Then the trees part to form a sort of avenue toward two of the immense pines, spaced some twenty feet apart with their upper branches reaching out and lacing through one another overhead to form a natural gateway.

Passing through that gateway, I get my first glimpse of Hearthshire's keep. Except it isn't a keep—somehow I assumed it would be, although Sylas has referred to it as a castle at least once.

It looks quite a bit like the building we left behind in Oakmeet: a cluster of polished trunks grown so close together they merged into one being. But the structure stands at least twice as broad and tall as the keep did. A few of the trunks rise higher into actual turrets, and the leafless branches that sprout all across the roof twist into forms that echo the true-name marks tattooed on the fae's bodies.

Patches of moss cling to the smooth wood, and spindly vines crisscross the outer walls, winding in and out of the windows. Wild vegetation has similarly consumed the houses clustered around the sides and back of the castle—more of them than I can easily count. Over fifty, if I had to guess. A pang shoots through my chest at the thought of how much of his former pack Sylas has lost since they called this place home.

When I look at the fae lord, his face is practically glowing, his gaze fixed on his castle. "There it is," he murmurs.

"It's beautiful," I say, awed as much by the joy shining through him as by the building itself.

His gaze jerks to me, and his smile turns slightly sheepish, as if he's embarrassed to have shown his elation so openly. "It'll be spectacular when we've had time to get everything in order. The forest has crept in on the castle grounds. No doubt weeds have swallowed the gardens. But there is plenty of time for that."

August lets out a sigh of relief. "It's good to be home."

Sylas has talked about his family and their pack as if it was separate from his own, but for the first time full understanding sinks in. "You didn't inherit this domain. You built *everything* here from scratch on your own."

"With the help of my pack," Sylas says. "But yes. My father continues to lord over Thundervale. It's not unusual for true-blooded fae to strike out on their own rather than sticking around hoping their elders will meet an early end to give them space to carve their own mark."

I know his feelings about his family are much more complicated than his dry remark would imply. The last thing I want to do in this moment of celebration is push him to think about why he left his very first home. So I don't ask anything more, just drink in the sights and sounds and scents as the carriages come to rest at the foot of the castle.

Sylas climbs out first and swivels to face his pack. I spot Harper nearly falling over the side of her carriage, her eyes wider than ever.

"If you wish to keep your old house, consider it yours," Sylas says. "If you'd rather swap for one now abandoned, by all means. No squabbles, please. We have plenty to go around. Anyone who requires help whipping them back into shape, don't hesitate to call on me or my cadre. We'll have Hearthshire good as ever in no time."

Leaving the carriages holding our luggage behind for now, he strides toward the castle. August helps me out, Whitt right behind me, and the three of us follow the fae lord into his beloved home.

The entrance room reminds me of Oakmeet's too, only the ceiling is a little higher and the room a little longer, and no orbs remain to add light to the space. The leaves on the vines that creep across the walls quiver at Sylas's passing as if even they recognize his authority.

Beyond the entrance room, Sylas turns from the hall into a doorway at his left. We follow, and all at once I see how this domain got its name.

Faded rugs scatter the floor between plump sofas and chairs that have crumpled with the passage of time. They're all arranged to face a stone hearth so massive I could step inside it without fear of bumping my head. I think maybe even Sylas could fit in it comfortably.

Sylas speaks a low word, and flames spring up from the hearth's base. The smell of warmed wood and scorched stone fills the air. We step closer to the warbling fire, drawing together as we do.

Sylas motions me in front of him, placing one hand on my shoulder and teasing the other into my hair before kissing the back of my head. August slips his hand around mine. Whitt hangs back for just a moment before I glance toward him. When he ambles over to join us, I tuck my other hand around his elbow.

We stay there basking in the hearth's heat for several minutes in comfortable silence. I should probably tell them that they can get on with all the cleaning and organizing they obviously need to do—and help them with it—but I'm so content I can't quite bring myself to say the words. My three fae men don't appear to be in any hurry to break the spell of the moment either.

We made it here, all of us together. Standing there between them, not a single part of me doubts that this is where I'm meant to be.

Out of nowhere, a loud knocking reverberates from the entrance room. Sylas makes a vexed sound but eases away from me toward the hall.

"No rest for our glorious leader," Whitt remarks. "Let's see what trouble the pack has managed to get themselves into already."

It isn't our pack, though. Sylas opens the door to reveal an unfamiliar woman in a trim blue jacket and trousers, hemmed with gold. She dips her head, hands a piece of rolled paper to Sylas, and says, "With regards from Arch-Lord Ambrose."

Apparently she hasn't been instructed to wait for a response. She marches back across the lawn to where a graceful white horse is waiting, leaps into its saddle, and has it cantering away before Sylas has even finished unrolling the letter.

Ambrose. He's the arch-lord who's been harshest on Sylas, who blames him for what his mate did, who he was the most worried about objecting to his requests. As I wait for Sylas to read, my body stiffens. At the fae lord's snarl, I flinch.

He shreds the paper into scraps so swiftly I never even see his claws emerge and flings the bits aside. A dark cloud has rolled over the joy that shone in his face. August tenses beside me.

Whitt offers a sickly-looking smile. "I take it he wasn't simply offering happy tidings."

Sylas's hands flex by his thighs. "It may not be anything. But it's probably what I think it is. I should have known better. That mangy prick."

"What did he say?" I venture.

"He 'requests' I call on him in three days' time. Which in arch-lord terms is a demand." Sylas swivels toward us, his unscarred eye so somber the iris has turned nearly black as it settles on me. "And he insists that I bring you with me."

Whitt spits out a scathing curse. "I thought the deal

was settled."

"Perhaps it is. Perhaps I should be more generous in my assumptions, and he only wants to have a look at Talia. But knowing Ambrose, he'll try to weasel around the wording of our agreement and take her into his custody." Sylas's frown deepens. He touches my cheek. "I will not let that happen."

August's arms bulge as if he's preparing to charge all the way to the arch-lord's domain and pummel him, but I can't speak or move at all. Sylas's words resonate through me, stirring up the last question I want to consider.

Ambrose is an arch-lord, the highest authority in the entire fae world. If he intends to take me... how can any of these men possibly stop him?

ABOUT THE AUTHOR

Eva Chase lives in Canada with her family. She loves stories both swoony and supernatural, and strong women and the men who appreciate them. Along with the Bound to the Fae series, she is the author of the Flirting with Monsters series, the Cursed Studies trilogy, the Royals of Villain Academy series, the Moriarty's Men series, the Looking Glass Curse trilogy, the Their Dark Valkyrie series, the Witch's Consorts series, the Dragon Shifter's Mates series, the Demons of Fame Romance series, the Legends Reborn trilogy, and the Alpha Project Psychic Romance series.

Connect with Eva online:
www.evachase.com
eva@evachase.com

Printed in Great Britain
by Amazon